Praise for Lorelei James'
Rough, Raw, and Ready

Rati   orelei
James's   and
better. T   ...but
it's the e   lding
your bre   Ready
needs to   n the
name Lo   your
money's
~ R

Ratir   her
latest off   erotic
and scor   n the
tender lo   the
three love
~ Sh

Blue   )Y is
explosive   n the
open for   his
wife and   issie
complete   rite
and plan   eem
effortless
~ No

Ratir   nce
that lives   gh,
Raw, and   and
readers is   but
sweet, thi
~ Jo

Look for these titles by
Lorelei James

Now Available:

Rough Riders Series
Long Hard Ride
Cowgirl Up and Ride
Tied Up, Tied Down
Rode Hard, Put Up Wet
Rough, Raw, and Ready
Branded As Trouble
Shoulda Been a Cowboy

Wild West Boys Series
Mistress Christmas
Miss Firecracker

Beginnings Anthology: Babe in the Woods
Three's Company Anthology: Wicked Garden
Wild Ride Anthology: Strong, Silent Type

Dirty Deeds
Running With the Devil

Rough, Raw, and Ready

Lorelei James

A Samhain Publishing, Ltd. publication.

Samhain Publishing, Ltd.
577 Mulberry Street, Suite 1520
Macon, GA 31201
www.samhainpublishing.com

Rough, Raw, and Ready
Copyright © 2009 by Lorelei James
Print ISBN: 978-1-60504-404-0
Digital ISBN: 978-1-60504-230-5

Editing by Angela James
Cover by Scott Carpenter

First Samhain Publishing, Ltd. electronic publication: November 2008
First Samhain Publishing, Ltd. print publication: September 2009

Dedication

To every reader, reviewer and fan who contacted me and demanded to know what happened to Trevor and Edgard after *Long Hard Ride*—this book is for you...

And for my editor Angela James (no relation!) who believed in my ability to write this unconventional love story.

Acknowledgements

I would like to give a huge shout out and many, many thanks to my new Brazilian friend, Tarsilla Sampaio Moura, a lovely woman who went above and beyond the call of duty as a fan, to help me with the Portuguese language issues in this book, as well as (retroactively) straightening out those in Long Hard Ride. Obrigada.

Chapter One

Chassie West Glanzer squinted at the lone figure ambling up the snow-covered driveway.

Visitors were few and far between at the remote West homestead, especially on foot in the frigid month of February. The mildly warm day and clear skies could change in a helluva hurry on the high plains of Wyoming and she shivered at an odd sense of foreboding.

Each steady clip brought the man closer, but she couldn't see his face. A long sheepskin coat brushed the thighs of faded Wranglers, drawing attention to the championship belt buckle centered between trim hips. Leather gloves covered fingers curled around the strap of a camouflage duffel bag. This man wasn't one of those young, green city boys looking for "real" ranch work and a wild Western adventure. This guy was one hundred percent cowboy, from the tips of his scuffed Tony Lamas to the brim of his dusty black Resistol.

Chassie probably looked like a rube, or worse that unkempt woman from *American Gothic*, standing in front of their old wooden barn holding a pitchfork. She resisted fussing with her hair and called out, "Something I can help you with?"

When he lifted his head, Chassie's breath caught. Good Lord. He was easily the most dazzling man she'd ever set eyes on. Thick black hair, tawny brown eyes fringed with dark eyelashes, and razor-sharp cheekbones that flared into a blocky jaw. Coppery-colored lips stretched wide and full below a thin blade of a nose. His smooth skin glowed the color of rich coffee liberally laced with cream. At first glance, his body appeared whipcord lean, but she suspected beneath those clothes was a muscular force to be reckoned with.

The duffel bag hit the icy gravel. He pushed his hat back slightly and held out his gloved hand. "Hello. I'm Edgard Mancuso."

When his voice rumbled out tinged with a foreign drawl, she bit back a feminine sigh. "Howdy, Edgard. I'm Chassie Glanzer. And forgive my bluntness, but what the hell are you doin' wanderin' around in the middle of winter? It's a good way to wind up coyote food."

He smiled, all brilliant white teeth, and her knees damn near collapsed. "You're a feisty one, eh? Bet he loves that. I'm looking for Trevor."

"Why? Does he owe you money?" At the man's stark expression, Chassie said, "Kidding. How do you know my husband?"

"We...we're old friends."

Huh. If that were true, why wasn't the man's name familiar?

Edgard carefully removed his gloves. "I guess he didn't tell you about me. We used to be ropin' partners on the Mountains and Plains Circuit."

"Really? He might've mentioned it in passing, but he hasn't been rodeoin' professionally for a couple of years. Where are you from?"

"Brazil. This is the first time I've been in the U.S. since my run of luck with Trevor ended a few years back."

Chassie gave him another once-over. "If you were on that circuit, did you know my brother, Dag West?"

"Uh-huh. I roped with him several times. Talented heeler and a good guy. I heard what happened. I'm sorry."

"Thanks." Chassie wrapped her fingers around the pitchfork handle and hefted it out of the straw. "You wanna come up to the house?"

"That'd be great."

"Is Trevor expecting you?"

Edgard released a strangled laugh. "Ah. No."

"Thought you'd surprise him?"

"Something like that."

"Come on then. I'm about due for a break anyway."

The crunch of boots on the ground was the only sound as she and Edgard trekked the long driveway to the old farmhouse.

Was this old friend of Trevor's comparing the humble West homeplace to the Glanzer showplace she'd heard about but had never seen?

Didn't matter. The house she'd grown up in looked better now than it had in fifteen years. After Chassie's mother died, her father wouldn't "waste" money fixing the problems, preferring to let the place fall into ruin. He hadn't had the knowledge or the drive to do the basic home maintenance himself. Yet he was too proud to hire his nephews, Chet and Remy West—owners of a construction company—even after they'd offered to do the work at cost.

Between running the ranch and doing all the household chores, Chassie's exhaustion at the end of the day hadn't allowed for worries about peeling paint or figuring out what'd caused the leak in the living room ceiling. Or to discover why the front porch sagged in the right corner.

Chassie had refused to squabble with her father about household issues or anything else. She'd suffered enough traumas listening to Dad and Dag snapping and snarling at each other like rabid dogs over the dumbest things. To what end? Bitterness, regret, stupidity, and pride had killed both father and son.

But as soon as Trevor Glanzer hired on for shit wages, things'd begun to change. He'd cajoled Harland into springing for new paint and spruced up the crappy siding. He'd harassed the old man into buying shingles so Trevor could put on a new roof. Trevor resealed windows, fixed the furnace and installed a new water heater. Chassie helped him restore the house and often wondered if that's why she'd fallen for him.

Right. His work ethic coupled with his smokin' hot physique...she hadn't stood a chance. Her immediate lust upon seeing golden-haired, golden-skinned Trevor whip off his shirt and climb on the roof half-naked had been an epiphany of sorts. Watching his tanned muscles straining, his buff body dripping with sweat as he hammered shingles, Chassie fantasized about having Trevor hammering into her.

Because of Trevor's reputation with the ladies and purported outrageous sexual appetites, she'd figured he wouldn't look at her twice—a petite, flat-chested, poor ethnic cowgirl was not the type of woman bad boy rodeo stud Trevor Glanzer pursued. Even if he'd overlooked those details, she was

11

his friend's little sister and sort of his boss.

But Trevor *had* noticed her. Even...wooed her, country style with every ounce of his cowboy charm. Accompanying her on horseback as they'd checked cattle. Picking wildflowers and winding the colorful blossoms through her braided hair. Taking her dancing at local honky-tonks. Stealing kisses while washing dishes after supper.

Eventually sneaking into her room and loving her in the creaky, antique iron-framed bed. Rolling around with her in the warm sunshine in the hayloft for a steamy bout of fun sex. Staking his claim by fucking her mindless over a sawhorse in the machine shed. His secret sweetness was as much a part of him as his unmistakable sexual fire. Lust bloomed into love for both of them pretty damn fast.

Trevor stayed rock solid through the unexpected deaths of her brother and father. Their mutual love of the land, the Western lifestyle and determination to rebuild the ranch, despite the odds, strengthened their bond. The day Trevor climbed up on the roof, shouted his love for her and asked her to marry him, she'd never been so sure of anything in her life.

So a year after they'd repeated those solemn vows in front of a judge, Chassie's heart still skipped a beat when she saw her hunky husband. Trevor was crouched over a makeshift plywood table in front of the porch, wrenching on the motor for the backup generator. He muttered to himself and swore, so he hadn't heard their approach.

"Trev, there's—"

"Hang on." Metal grinding on metal screeched in the cold air. Then, "Motherfuckin' piece of shit."

Chassie glanced at Edgard who'd gone completely still.

"That's not the way to talk in front of company, hon."

"Who's here?" Trevor spun around and froze.

A beat passed. Then Edgard said softly, "Hello, Trevor."

No one spoke; no one moved.

Trevor roared, "You motherfuckin' piece of shit." He threw the wrench and bulled toward Edgard.

Crap. Maybe they weren't friends after all.

Instead of tackling the man and pounding him into the ground, Trevor slapped Edgard on the back. Clasping him in a bear hug, lifting him in the air, practically swinging him in a circle.

Whoa. She'd never seen her husband so...exuberant. From seeing an old friend she'd never even heard of? Chassie's eyes met Trevor's in confusion and he hastily set Edgard down.

"Ah. Sorry, man. It's just..." Trevor turned away.

As he composed himself, Chassie fired a sardonic look at Edgard. "Well, I reckon he's happy to see you after all."

For Christsake, Edgard was here. Standing in his goddamn front yard.

Next to his wife.

How was he supposed to deal with this situation? At least he'd stopped himself from laying a big, wet kiss on him.

Kissing another man. In front of his wife.

Fuck.

Chassie wasn't aware of his relationship with Edgard. Hell, he'd barely mentioned the years they'd team roped and traveled together because he didn't know if he could keep the truth about that intimate relationship hidden from her—the woman had an uncanny emotional sense. So Chassie must be wondering about the male stranger her husband hugged like a long lost love.

Not a long lost love. Just a former rodeo pal. Keep it light. Friendly.

Trevor spun back around and grinned. "Shocked the shit out of me, Ed, to see you on American soil again. What're you doin' here?"

The tensed lines around Edgard's mouth diminished. "Just passing through."

"Where's your vehicle?" Chassie asked.

"It broke down outside of Sundance. The mechanic said it'd be a week before they can get the parts to fix it."

"Which repair shop?"

"Ah...D&F?"

"They'll treat you right. My dad used to work there. I'll warn ya. They are slow as molasses in February. If they say a week it'll be at least two."

Edgard groaned.

"Meantime, where are you stayin'?"

"I haven't decided."

Chassie was so selfless Trevor wasn't surprised when she offered, "Any friend of Trev's is a friend of mine. You're welcome to stay here as long as you want. We have plenty of room."

Say no, Edgard. For both our sakes say no.

"That's very generous, Chassie. I'd like that."

Shit.

"No problem. You wanna come in and get settled? Have a cup of coffee to warm up?"

"That'd be great."

Chassie brushed past Trevor and started up the porch steps.

He could handle his former lover under his roof for a couple of days. No sweat, right?

But when Trevor's eyes caught Edgard's, the punch of lust whomped him as sharply as a hoof to the belly, making him just as breathless.

Dammit, don't look at me that way, Ed. Please.

Edgard banked the hunger in those topaz-colored eyes and Trevor silently breathed a sigh of relief.

The blank stare was a reaction they'd both mastered during the years they'd spent together on the road. If sponsors, promoters or fans caught wind of his and Edgard's nocturnal proclivities they would've been blackballed. Or would've been beat to shit on a regular basis if the other rodeo cowboys suspected he and Edgard weren't merely traveling partners. There'd been no choice but to become discreet.

Nothing discreet about the way Edgard had eyeballed him.

"Trev, hon, you comin'?"

"Go on. I'll be right in after I take care of this motor." He retreated to the barn, needing to find his balance after being knocked sideways.

Edgard was here. Trevor's gut clenched remembering the last time he'd seen the man. Remembering the misery on Edgard's face, knowing his face reflected the same desolation when they'd said goodbye three and a half years ago.

Crippled by pain, fear, and loss, Trevor hadn't had the balls to wrap Edgard in his arms one last time. He'd snapped off some dumbass comment and done nothing but sit on his ass in the horse trailer like a lump of moldy shit and watched him go.

No. *Let* him go.

He'd gotten drunk that night. And every night after for damn near six months. He'd fucked every woman who'd crossed his path. Sex and booze did nothing to chase away the sense he'd made a huge mistake. Or on the really bad nights, his all-too smug relief that he'd never really felt "that way" about Edgard and he was glad the too-tempting bastard was gone for good.

Yes, not only had Trevor mastered the outward lie, he was a master at lying to himself.

Watching his friends pair up, marry, and start families only emphasized Trevor's unhappiness. Every part of his life seemed meaningless. Chasing that elusive gold buckle. For what? To instill a sense of family pride, even when Trevor knew nothing he accomplished would be good enough for his father, former world champion Tater Glanzer?

The final straw occurred after the threesome with his buddy Cash Big Crow and Cash's then-girlfriend, Gemma Jansen. It wasn't an odd thing for Cash to call him and ask for help in giving Gemma an experience she'd never forget: fucking two men at the same time. Trevor'd always held a secret attraction to the bawdy Gemma, so he'd shown up, more than willing to oblige.

But during the course of that sexual encounter, what'd started out a fun, sexy and raunchy romp became awkward— and very apparent three was a crowd.

It'd never bothered Trevor to be considered the sweet-talking bad boy of the rodeo circuit. But the cavalier attitude toward sex came home to roost that summer night, when he realized that's all he was to his so-called friends. Good time Trevor; he'll fuck your women, drink your booze and back you in a bar fight. But don't call him for anything important because he's just another horny, drunken cowboy who'll be gone chasing eight and the gate at dawn.

The next day, Trevor swore off women, sex, booze and rodeo.

That summer also marked the breaking point with his family. For years he'd suffered infighting with his siblings about who'd take over the sizeable Glanzer ranch. Trevor hated how his dad played his kids against each other, especially when everyone in five counties snickered that Tater Glanzer had no intention of passing on the ranch until he was dead. Not only was his old man too mean to die, at age sixty-one it'd be a helluva long time before they'd need to build a pine box for the ornery SOB.

So two years ago, Trevor loaded up his horse, his measly belongings and cut himself off from his entire family. He hadn't regretted it. Next to marrying Chassie West, it was the best thing he'd ever done.

Chassie.

Just the whisper of her name in his head brought a smile to his face and calmness to his soul. She'd made him feel like a real man, a worthy man, for the first time in his thirty-year existence. Treating him like a rancher, not another good-for-nothin' washed-up rodeo cowboy. Listening to him when no one else would. Understanding him when he scarcely understood himself.

His sweet, loving, funny and stubborn wife embodied everything beautiful, good, honest and true in the world. She was every damn thing he'd ever wanted in a life partner and never thought he'd find or that he deserved. Trevor hadn't believed in love at first sight until he'd met Chassie West.

You believed in it with Edgard.

Had he?

Yes. No. Maybe.

Shit. Trevor scrubbed his hands over his face. No, it wasn't love right off the bat with Edgard, even when he'd suspected that was what it'd become, even when he'd refused to admit those feelings to Edgard or to himself. He'd fought his damn attraction to Ed, mostly because it pissed him off to be attracted to a man.

It'd been hard as hell to comprehend. He'd never so much looked at another guy the way he looked at Edgard. Not once, in all his sexual escapades starting when he was a green lad of fifteen, had Trevor fantasized about fucking another man...until he'd hooked up with the quiet, intense, sloe-eyed Brazilian.

No one besides their traveling partner, Colby McKay, ever knew the true nature of their relationship. As additional cover, Edgard participated in the wild sexual exploits on the road to rodeo glory. With a bevy of buckle bunnies following the three of them, the other male rodeo contestants lumped Edgard in with Trevor and Colby as players in musical bed partners.

Edgard's preference for men wasn't obvious to anyone.

Except Trevor. Edgard never touched him suggestively. Nor did he come right out and state his desire to throw Trevor in his bed and fuck him like an animal.

After months of hot looks and evocative comments getting him nowhere, Trevor figured he'd have to make the first move. It'd taken him a pint of Jim Beam to act on the attraction and even then he'd made a clumsy pass at Edgard. Kissing him sloppily. Groping him between the legs.

But Edgard refused his advances, saying he wouldn't let alcohol be an excuse for them becoming lovers. Trevor would either come to Edgard completely sober or not at all.

So Trevor swallowed his pride, his fear, and practically begged. Edgard remained leery. Until that first explosive touch. In the two and a half years they were together, the heat between them never cooled, yet Trevor wondered if the urgency and secrecy contributed to the appeal.

Is that why Edgard was here? To rekindle that flame? To tempt Trevor away from Chassie? Or had Edgard found a new love and needed to prove there was nothing left between them but molten memories and deep regret?

Only one way to find out.

Trevor trudged from the barn and headed for the house.

Chapter Two

By the time Trevor finished scrubbing the machine oil from his hands, Chassie and Edgard had returned to the kitchen.

Chassie said, "Who wants coffee?"

"Sounds great, Chass."

"There's cookies, unless Trev ate them all. The man has a serious sweet tooth."

"Then I oughta munch on you, darlin', since you're so durn sweet." Trevor nibbled the side of her jaw and Chassie squealed. He reached above her head for the coffee cups on the pegs.

Trevor turned and saw Edgard staring at them. Not with jealousy, but with longing. Simple affectionate moments had been rare between them and Trevor remembered it was one of the things Edgard had needed that Trevor hadn't been able to offer him. Why did he feel just as guilty about that shortcoming now as he had back then?

Chassie poured the coffee. Trevor automatically grabbed the milk jug from the fridge and set it next to Edgard. He snagged a spoon from the dish rack, passing it and the sugar canister to Edgard, ignoring Chassie's questioning stare.

Didn't mean a damn thing he remembered exactly how Edgard liked his coffee. Not a damn thing.

"So, Edgard, what are you doin' in our neck of the woods?"

"Reliving some old memories. I drove past my grandparents' place yesterday. With the shabby way it's looking I'm wishing I would've bought it when I had the chance." He smiled wryly. "I'm kicking myself for letting another thing slip through my fingers."

"Grandparents?" Chassie repeated, not noticing Trevor's rigid posture after Edgard's comment. "You from around here?"

"Yes. And no." Edgard relayed the story about his mother. Getting pregnant as a foreign exchange student, giving birth to Edgard before his biological father, a young cowboy, died in an accident. She'd returned home to Brazil and married Edgard's stepfather.

"Whoa. That's kind of soap-operaish, isn't it?"

"Mmm-hmm." Edgard blew across his coffee. "But it does make me an American citizen so I can come and go as I please in the good ol' U.S. of A."

Trevor listened as Chassie asked a million questions about Edgard's life and Brazil. They finished off the pot of coffee and the time passed pleasantly. He even managed to meet Edgard's gaze a couple of times.

The phone rang and Chassie excused herself to answer it.

Silence hung between them as heavy as snow clouds in a winter sky.

Eventually, Edgard said, "She doesn't know anything about me. Not even that we were roping partners. Not that we were..." He looked at Trevor expectantly.

"No." Trevor quickly glanced at the living room where Chassie was chattering away. "You surprised?"

"Maybe that she isn't aware of our official association as roping partners. There was no shame in that. We were damn good together, Trev."

The word *shame* echoed like a slap. As good as they were together, it'd never been enough, in an official capacity or behind closed doors. "What are you really doin' here?"

Edgard didn't answer right away. "I don't know. Feeling restless. Had the urge to travel."

"Wyoming ain't exactly an exotic port of call."

"You think I don't realize that? You think I wouldn't rather be someplace else? But something..." Edgard lowered his voice. "Ah, fuck it."

"What?"

"Want the truth? Or would you rather I lie?"

"The truth."

"Truth between us? That's refreshing." Edgard's gaze trapped his. "I'm here because of you."

Trevor's heart alternately stopped and soared, even when his answer was an indiscernible growl. "For Christsake, Ed.

What the hell am I supposed to say to that? With my wife in the next room?"

"You're making a big deal out of this. She thinks we're friends, which ain't a lie. We were partners before we were..." Edgard gestured distractedly. "If she gets the wrong idea, it won't be from me."

"Maybe *I'm* gettin' the wrong idea. The last thing you said to me when you fuckin' *left* me was that you weren't ever comin' back. And you made it goddamn clear you didn't want to be my friend. So why are you here?"

Pause. He traced the rim of his coffee cup with a shaking fingertip. "I heard about you gettin' married."

"That happened over a year ago and you came all the way from Brazil to congratulate me in person? Now?"

"No." Edgard didn't seem to know what to do with his hands. He raked his fingers through his hair. His voice was barely audible. "Will it piss you off if I admit I was curious about whether you're really happy, *meu amor*?"

My love. My ass. Trevor snapped, "Yes."

"Yes, you're pissed off? Or yes, you're happy?"

"Both."

"Then this is gonna piss you off even more."

"What?"

"Years and miles haven't changed anything between us and you goddamn well know it."

Trevor looked up; Edgard's golden eyes were laser beams slicing him open. "It don't matter. If you can't be my *friend* while you're in my house, walk out the fuckin' door. I will not allow either one of us to hurt my wife. Got it?"

"Yeah."

"Good. And I'm done talkin' about this shit so don't bring it up again. Ever."

Chassie bounded back into the kitchen. If she sensed the tension she didn't remark on it. "My coffee break is over. Gotta get back to the grind. What're you guys gonna do?"

Trevor gathered the cups and dumped them in the sink. "I'll help you finish up outside."

"No, that's okay. You stay and catch up with Edgard."

"Darlin', it ain't every day I offer to let you boss me around," Trevor pointed out with a teasing smile.

Edgard stood. "If it's all right, I might stretch out. I'm bushed. Been a long morning and a long walk this afternoon."

Trevor stared at him. Edgard had walked the twenty-five miles from town? In the cold?

"If you're hungry later, help yourself to whatever you can find. I already showed you where the towels and stuff are in the bathroom so make yourself at home."

"Thank you, Chassie, you are very kind." Edgard headed for the stairs.

When he was gone, Chassie hooked her fingers in Trevor's belt loop. "Come on, you're my slave for the next couple hours."

"Mmm. I like the sound of that." He lowered his head, teasing her lips before plunging his tongue inside her sweet, warm mouth. Kissing her until her heart raced beneath his palm and her body swayed closer. Trevor pulled back so they were a breath apart. "But I get my shot at bein' the master to your slave later, right?"

Her soft moan smacked of sexual need and instantly stiffened his cock. "No ropes this time."

"That ain't no fun."

"Neither is disinfecting the birthing equipment in the barn."

Trevor groaned. *That's* what we're doin' today?"

"Yep. Has to be done when it's not sub-zero outside and you volunteered, bucko."

"Lead on, master."

She grinned. After she turned around, Trevor whacked her on the ass hard enough to elicit a yelp and she ran away from him, laughing.

Damn. He loved being married to this woman. He'd be wise to remember that.

Two hours later Chassie peeled the sodden clothes from her body. Her T-shirt was halfway over her head when the bedroom door creaked open.

Before she unstuck the wet cotton from her arms, Trevor's big hands landed on her bare hips. She jumped and lost her balance, allowing Trevor to pick her up and lay her across the bed on her back.

"Well, well, who do we have here?" He crawled up her body,

keeping her arms tangled up in the shirt so she couldn't see. He squeezed her legs together with his powerful thighs. "A half-naked woman. Is it *my* half-naked woman? Can't tell by lookin' since your face is covered, so I'll have to find another way to figure it out."

The first flicker of Trevor's warm tongue over her cold nipple had her bowing off the bed. Chassie's arms and legs were immobilized—not that she tried to scramble away when Trevor started suckling the puckered tip.

"Sure tastes like my woman."

"Funny."

He grazed her nipple with his teeth and she gasped.

"I recognize that gasp. You *are* my woman." Trevor swamped her with the sensual attack of his mouth. Lapping. Licking. Nibbling. His hands came into play, the callused pad of this thumb sweeping the underswell of her breast, then his fingertips drawing ever-smaller circles around her beaded flesh. Plucking and twisting one nipple while his mouth suckled its twin.

Chassie's face heated, her breathing escalated and the wet shirt molded to her face, making it difficult to draw a lungful of air. "Trevor. Get this shirt off me. I'm suffocating."

One fast yank and the shirt hit the carpet. She opened her eyes. Trevor's face was flushed. His pupils were dilated so no color remained. Need pulsed off him and thickened the air.

"Want you, Chass. Want you bad."

"Luckily you have me." She reached for him.

"Uh-uh. Keep your hands above your head or I'll get the ropes out."

"Bossy."

"Yep."

"What if I don't wanna be bossed around today?"

"Tough. You'll take whatever I dish out."

Lord. He was in a mood.

He pushed off the bed, whipped his wet Wranglers and his pearl-snap shirt in a pile. His beautiful naked body was back on top before she'd taken two breaths. His mouth crushed hers in a drugging kiss. He skimmed his rough-skinned hand across her belly and between her legs. Upon finding the inside of her thighs soaked, he dragged his lips free, growling, "You're always so wet for me. That's one of the things I love about you, Chass. I'm absolutely fuckin' lovesick with everything you give to me, everything you are to me. In bed and out."

His sweet, but reluctant confession surprised her.

Trevor wiggled two fingers into her pussy and swirled them in her slick cream. He withdrew and plunged deeper, grinding the bony heel of his hand on her clit as he dove back in for another thorough taste of her mouth.

As Chassie rocked her pelvis, Trevor's cock left a slick trail on her hip. She wanted to circle her fist around that velvety male hardness, stroking until his ejaculate exploded on her stomach. She wanted to clamp her hands on his ass and force his cock to replace his fingers.

Trevor wasn't swayed by her pleading whimpers. He maintained complete control, building her to the pinnacle.

Every pulse point hummed on a different frequency. Chassie squeezed his fingers with her internal muscles.

He feathered openmouthed kisses to the base of her neck. "Come on, baby. You're close."

"Then use your mouth. Suck on me."

"Later. You're gonna come like this now." Trevor rotated his hand, added a third finger and circled his thumb over her swollen clit, stroking and rubbing the spots in tandem.

The change from random to deliberate concentration sent her careening into a double-whammy orgasm. Her pussy throbbed around his fingers, sucking them deeper with each spasm, while her clit pulsed beneath his thumb. When Trevor bit down on her right nipple, Chassie flat-out screamed.

Trevor scattered kisses across her breasts. Followed by a lazy sweep of his tongue up her neck. His rapid exhalations stirred the hair by her ear when he murmured, "Better?"

"Mmm. Always better when you touch me."

"Good. Roll over. I want your ass."

His words sent dark excitement zipping through her again. He'd warned her from the start he was sexually demanding. If they became lovers, no part of her body was off limits to him. Ever. He'd fuck her pussy, her mouth, her tits and her ass, whenever, wherever and as often as he pleased.

Chassie's limited sexual experiences had in no way prepared her for Trevor Glanzer ruling her in bed. His concession to easing her into anal sex consisted of fucking her first with his fingers, then with a rubber dildo. Finally in a hard, fast, primitive manner that proved his complete possession.

It was heady stuff to be the focus of total sexual energy from a man such as Trevor; wickedly gorgeous, wickedly experienced and wickedly virile. Trevor pushed her boundaries and she trusted he'd never hurt her in his quest to bring her complete sexual satisfaction. Sometimes Chassie wondered what Trevor considered kinky.

"Come on, baby, roll over. Keep them arms above your head."

As soon as Chassie was on her belly, Trevor hiked her hips into the air and kneed her stance wider. Then all that burning, brawny male flesh brushed the inside of her thighs.

His thumb swept across her hole, over and over, bringing those sensitive nerve endings alive. Making her want. Tingles shot up her spine until she trembled.

"You're so sexy. This ain't gonna be gentle."

"I'm used to that by now."

He flattened his tongue on her tailbone and licked straight up to the hairline. "Complainin'?"

"Hell no."

His chuckle pealed in her ear, danced like electricity across her skin. Trevor spread cool, wet lubrication over the pucker, easing one finger in. The sound of his rapid breathing as his free hand slicked more lube on his cock was beyond sexy.

Trevor's finger slipped out. His plump cockhead circled her anus before he pushed it past the tight ring of muscle and all the way into her ass on a single glide. He hissed. He withdrew slowly, even when she sensed his entire body vibrating with the need to pound into her. "Never get used to how hot and tight you are. Never." With her ass cheeks in his hands, spreading her completely open to his cock and his hungry gaze, he rammed her with enough force the headboard smacked into the wall.

Chassie's world boiled down to the basics. Male heat surrounding her and the burning friction from his powerful thrusts. The scent of his sweat and the underlying hint of her own musk. The continual *bang bang bang* of the headboard. The loud slap of skin on skin. Trevor's rhythmic squeezing on her butt cheeks. Her fingers curled into the cotton sheets as he fucked her into oblivion.

His heavy breathing turned into grunts. "So fuckin' close. Bear down. That's it. So goddamn good." He shouted her name as he started to come, his pelvis slamming into her backside. Every thrust was punctuated with a loud groan, more animal than human. Liquid heat burst inside her.

She loved every second of making this man lose control. Her hand slid between her legs. She stroked her swollen clit as her ass muscles milked his cock and it wasn't long before she was coming again. Trevor knew when her orgasm hit. When she cried out so did he. One last hoarse shout, and he quit moving.

She collapsed to the mattress with a sigh.

He layered his damp chest over her back and kissed the slope of her shoulder.

"I didn't know being my cleaning slave turned you on so much."

Trevor nipped her ear. "You turn me on. In every way imaginable."

Time spent outside in the cold air always made her husband extra frisky. But it'd been different today. A sharper edge to his lust. A more desperate need. "Something definitely got into you today."

"Something?" He rolled his hips and his semi-soft dick twitched inside her. "Who's in who right now?"

"Get off me, you brute." She sucked in a quick breath, even when he eased out with painstaking care. "I think you broke the headboard."

"Was worth it. You oughta be talkin'. One of them shrieks rattled the damn light fixtures. If Edgard was sleepin', he wasn't after that."

Damn. She'd completely forgotten about their houseguest. Chassie wondered if Trevor had forgotten too.

Or was that the reason for his overly amorous behavior? To prove to his buddy that marriage hadn't tamed him? He was still a wild man between the sheets?

A ripple of anxiety surfaced again and it wasn't as easy for her to shrug off this time.

After Trevor returned from the bathroom he flipped her on her back. "*Now* I'm ready to taste that sweet spot."

Definitely in a mood.

Chapter Three

Thump thump thump.

Edgard sprawled on the bed in the guestroom next to Trevor and Chassie's bedroom, staring at the ceiling fan, listening to them having sex.

For the second time.

Which was pure torture.

No doubt in Edgard's mind that Trevor was fucking his hot little wife just to prove a point: Trevor didn't want him. Trevor didn't need him. Trevor knew full well that Edgard heard every squeak of the bedsprings, every deep male groan, every feminine plea, every collective gasp and pleasured scream through the paper-thin walls. Every telltale bang of the headboard.

Thump thump thump.

How fucked up would it be if Edgard unzipped his jeans and started whacking off to the sounds of their passion?

Seriously fucked up. Pathetically fucked up. Perverted.

"What you do with other men is perverted and wrong. You disgust me. You disgust all of us. You should be ashamed."

Yeah. Great timing for that ugly memory to pop up.

With the life altering events he'd suffered recently, Edgard wondered if he'd ever be happy again. Through his haze of melancholy his mother's lilting voice reminded him, "You find happiness where you least expect it. When in doubt, go back to the beginning."

Thump thump thump.

Was it sheer idiocy that Edgard considered Trevor a beginning? When Edgard was the one who'd ended things between them? Yet here he was, wishing for things he couldn't have. Creating more miserable memories to drown in.

Thump thump thump.

Then silence. No squeaking. No groaning.

Was Trevor indulging in his softer side with his wife? Kissing her sweetly and cuddling her to that amazingly hard, sweat-covered body? Giving Chassie the intimate connection in the aftermath of loving that Edgard used to revel in? That rare affection he'd been so desperate to have?

Feminine giggles followed by male laughter echoed against the wall and put an ache in Edgard's soul.

Enough.

Edgard pushed to his feet, adjusted his throbbing cock and headed downstairs. The burning need to tuck tail and run was riding him hard as he slipped outside, but once again he was reminded he had nowhere else to go.

Later, when they'd sat down to supper, Chassie said, "So, Edgard, you feelin' up to a little honky-tonkin' tonight? There's a great band playin' at the Rusty Spur."

Startled, Edgard peered up from his bowl of stew. "Is there a special occasion for going out dancing?"

"No. Why would you ask that?"

Edgard shrugged. "Because if I remember correctly, Trevor wasn't all that crazy about dancing."

"He isn't." Chassie grinned at him. "But he convinced me he loved two-steppin' when we were dating. So I figure him tryin' to skip out on it now that we're married is cheatin' at best, false advertising at worst."

Trevor snorted.

"Besides, I refuse to let us turn into one of those married couples who are old before their time. Don't do anything fun, don't try anything new, just work or become homebodies watchin' the boob tube as entertainment."

"Right. You just wanna flaunt your hot little ass at all those horny ranch hands who didn't pay attention to you when you were single," Trevor said dryly.

"Can you blame me? It's such sweet revenge to see them trippin' over their boots and tongues when they see me shakin' my groove thang." Chassie snagged a dinner roll. "Please make my whole night, Ed. Tell me you love to dance and you were Brazilian national tango champion or something."

He smiled back, absolutely charmed by Trevor's wife. "I can't claim champion status, but I know my way around a dance floor."

"Yay! I take it you and Trevor went dancin' once or twice when you were traveling together?"

Chassie didn't mean he and Trevor danced together as partners, but it did remind Edgard of the few times he'd convinced Trevor to dance with him when they'd been alone. It'd been disastrous. The man had two left feet. "Ah. Yeah. We went out to the rodeo or community dances sometimes."

"Come on, dish the details on my husband's bad behavior on the circuit."

Another loaded question. Edgard countered, "You trying to get me in trouble, Miz Chassie?"

"No, but I'd like to hear an insider's point of view since Colby won't tell me nothin' either."

"That's because your cousin is a smart man."

"Pooh. It's not fair. You guys all stick together and keep your dirty little secrets. That stuff happened a long time ago. What's the harm in telling me now?"

Trevor and Edgard made a point of not looking at each other.

"Just one little teeny-tiny thing?" Chassie pleaded, "Please?"

He glanced at Trevor who shrugged indifferently.

"Okay. Must've been five years ago, at a rodeo dance down south someplace, this pesky woman wouldn't leave Trev alone. Just to get rid of her, Trev agrees to dance with her and she leads him out on the floor. Trev spins them around, stops, and acts like he's gonna barf. She freaks out and dumps him off with her friend, who Trevor had the hots for in the first place. So Trev's pulling this, 'I'm so woozy' line of crap, convinces the little bunny he needs to lay down—"

Chassie rolled her eyes.

"—and being the good Samaritan, the woman escorts him back to the living quarters in the horse trailer, where Trevor had a miraculous recovery. They ended up dancing after all."

Edgard shook his head and sent Chassie a sly look. "'Cept it was mattress dancing."

"Trev, you dog," Chassie said, slapping his arm.

Trevor howled, "*Ow ow ow*," and they all laughed.

"This is gonna be fun tonight with you two wild boys. Finally I'm gonna have some sort of reputation to rival my cousin Keely's."

Edgard wasn't convinced the three of them together out on the town was the best idea. "You sure you want me to come along, Chassie? I don't wanna be a third wheel."

"Trev is relieved to be off the dancin' hook, aren't you, hon?"

"Yep. I'll be more'n happy to hold down a barstool and guard the beer while you're two-steppin'." Trevor gave Edgard a genuine grin. "You don't know what you're in for, Ed. Chassie can go all night."

"I'm the lucky man to test your stamina? All night?" He grinned. "I'm all over that."

"I'll bet a guy like you has plenty of stayin' power," Chassie shot back with a sexy growl. "I'm lucky, showin' up with the two hottest guys in the county. That uppity Brandy Martinson is *so* gonna eat her heart out."

"I'm sure she's used to no one noticing her when you're in the room, sweetheart," Edgard drawled.

"Ed, stop flirtin' with my wife." Trevor pointed at Chassie. "And you better behave, missy. I ain't opposed to puttin' you over my knee and paddlin' that badonkadonk if the situation warrants it."

She stood and started stacking plates. "You threaten to spank me but you never follow through." She paused, looking thoughtfully at Edgard. "Since I'm not Trevor's usual type—a big boobed blonde—I wondered if Trevor's claim is true or if he's feedin' me a cowboy line."

"What line would that be?"

"That he's always had a thing for asses and it's the first body part he notices."

Right. How could he answer that? Edgard's eyes darted to the clock on the microwave. "Wow, look at the time. Need help cleaning up?"

"Chicken," Chassie taunted. "I will get to the bottom of all these secrets you two have."

Trevor's face read, *I hope not.*

"Let me finish them supper dishes, sassy woman." Trevor snapped the air by her butt with a dishtowel. "Get yourself gussied up and remember, we ain't got all night."

The bowls crashed in the sink. "Trevor Glanzer. Are you implying I'd need all night to make myself presentable?"

Edgard grabbed the spatula in Chassie's hand and stepped between them, effortlessly herding her toward the stairs. "No, he's reminding you to hurry up because he's anxious to show you off. I imagine Trev gets a kick at seeing those poor suckers drooling over you, knowing you're gonna be mattress dancing with him at the end of the night."

"Such sweet bullshit, but I'll take every bit of flattery fallin' from those sugar lips, sugar." Chassie left a loud, smacking kiss on Edgard's cheek.

Edgard experienced a beat of utter pleasure, even when a sound resembling a jealous growl drifted from the sink.

"I like him, Trev. He can stay as long as he wants." She darted an arch look over her shoulder at her husband. "However, you might be sleepin' in the barn."

The band started off the first set with a cover of Dierks Bentley's "Lot of Leavin' Left to Do" and the dance floor filled.

Chassie parked herself between Trevor and Edgard and thoroughly enjoyed the questioning glances sent their way. With his swarthy good looks, it was pretty obvious Edgard wasn't from around here.

"I wanna dance."

"Chass, can you wait until I finish my beer?"

"But I love this song." When the chorus kicked in, she joined in, "*Before you go and turn me on...make sure that you can turn me loose.*"

Both men stiffened.

"What? You don't like my singing?"

No answer from either one.

"Well too bad," and she sang along a little louder.

"Christ. You're in a feisty mood," Trevor grumbled.

"Yeah? Guess that counters the bad mood you're in."

"No need to bicker." Edgard set down his bottle. "Come on, I'll dance with you until your feet blister and the cows come home."

The bass line started for Jason Aldean's "Hicktown" and Edgard swung her into position.

Oh he was smooth. He glided them from one edge of the dance floor to the other, never missing a beat, never stepping on her toes, never once checking out any of the other female dancers. His focus was solely on her.

When the song segued into Kenny Chesney's "Don't Blink" Edgard smiled down at her. "Go again? Or would you like to stop?"

"Again."

"Somehow I knew you'd say that." He pulled her body closer to his and they swayed to the slower tempo.

While Chassie was squeezed against Edgard, she couldn't help but notice how good he smelled, a subtle scent that intensified when her nose brushed the gap between his shirt collar and his skin. She inhaled several times and wondered if the dizziness was just from the spinning.

"You okay?"

She tilted her head back. "Yeah. Why?"

"You were sniffling."

"Not sniffling, sniffing. I hope you don't think it sounds dorky, but man, you smell great. Really great."

Edgard actually blushed. "Ah. Thank you."

"I didn't mean to embarrass you."

"I'm not used to such genuine compliments."

"Really? I'd think you'd be immune, considering the way you look, because you probably get them all the time."

"Not so much lately."

Chassie peered into his face. "I might be totally off base, but you seem kinda unhappy. On guard. Like you're waiting for the other shoe to drop."

"Is that so? How can you tell?"

"At times your pretty smile doesn't quite reach your pretty eyes."

"You are a flirt, Missus Glanzer." He smiled softly. "But you are a perceptive little thing."

She bumped him with her hip. "Hey. Who you callin' little?"

"You. What are you, about five foot nothin'?"

"Hah! I'm five foot two and a quarter. Bein' small in stature doesn't mean I haven't been filled to the brim with my share of sadness, that's for damn sure."

"So that's why you're so good at recognizing it in others?"

"Yeah. I wish I wasn't. I wish I could just be a happy-go-lucky bubblehead with nothin' on my mind. It'd be easier."

"It'd be easier for me too, sweetheart." Edgard urged her to move a bit faster as his polite way of ending the discussion.

When the song finished, Chassie latched onto his shirt as she stood on the tips of her boots. "Any time you need to talk, track me down. I may be a lousy singer, but I'm a good listener."

His warm lips brushed her forehead. Twice. Then he pressed a kiss to her mouth. Twice. "You are beyond sweet. Thank you. I'll keep that in mind."

Back at the table, she released his hand and grabbed her purse, booking it to the ladies room. Didn't it just figure the next woman to walk in the bathroom was none other than Brandy Martinson? Chassie plastered on a fake smile when Brandy sidled up to her.

"Chassie! I was just looking for you. Who is that good-lookin' guy you were dancin' with?" Brandy applied a coat of shiny orange lipstick, and smacked her lips together in a self-kiss before smiling cagily at Chassie in the mirror. "Because you were awful familiar with him."

Chassie jerked a paper towel from the dispenser. "So?"

"So, you two look so much alike with your darker skin tones and dark hair I figured he had to be a relative."

A relative? Chassie patted Brandy's shoulder in a false show of comfort. "Aw, honey, you oughta wear your glasses all the time so you don't get so confused."

Brandy retorted, "You tellin' me the gorgeous guy you were cozied up to ain't your kin?"

"Nope."

"Good Lord." Brandy's smooth white hand stopped mid hair fluff. "And Trevor didn't mind you slow dancin' so suggestively with another man?"

"Trevor encouraged it actually."

"Did he encourage that man to kiss you too?"

Damn. Chassie didn't have near the experience with the female game of cat and mouse as the catty Brandy did. She tried a breezy laugh. "Oh that? It didn't bother Trevor in the least."

"How very...interesting." Brandy leaned into the mirror to check the concealer under her eyes. "So who is this mystery man who's allowed to kiss you in public?"

"A friend of Trevor's. They used to be ropin' partners on the circuit a few years back."

Done with her hair and face, Brandy spritzed on perfume. "He's just visiting?"

"For now. But I don't mind tellin' you I hope he sticks around. He's really good with his hands." When Brandy froze mid-thirty-ninth spritz, Chassie bit her cheek to keep from laughing. She amended, "I mean, he's a good hand."

"Oh." A malicious spark flared in Brandy's eyes. "I'm not surprised he's the wayward type. You seem to have a thing for picking up, ah, stray former rodeo cowboys."

Brandy might as well have sneered *washed-up* rodeo cowboys. Chassie allowed another smug grin. "Yeah, it's a terrible chore watchin' all those big muscles bulging as my *strays* are workin' up a sweat. I especially hate the way they strut around in old, tight-fittin', faded Wranglers as they're loadin' haybales or bent over machinery. It does get tiresome, them constantly tryin' to take care of me."

"Yes, I can see how the orphaned country girl scenario might be appealing to men like that—for a while. But we both know how easily cowboys get bored and move on."

Chassie nodded. "That is the sad truth. Which reminds me, didn't your boyfriend Stevo go back to his pregnant wife?"

"Ex-wife," she spit. "And for your information, *I* ended it before he crawled back to that low-class breeder bitch."

"Good for you. Nice chattin', Brandy. See ya around." Chassie made a beeline for the door before things deteriorated.

Chassie didn't hate many people, but snotty Brandy Martinson topped the list. From the first day they'd wound up in the same first grade class, Brandy had turned her pert, freckled nose up at Chassie. Brandy was a pampered town girl; Chassie a poor rural girl. Brandy's natural blonde hair and big blue eyes were the ideal, whereas Chassie's mixed ethnicity meant looks of pity rather than jealousy. As she matured,

Chassie accepted her heritage both as an Indian and a rancher, while Brandy maintained her air of superiority for being born pretty, white, and privileged. Years later Brandy still relished putting Chassie in her place, since she considered Chassie far beneath her social status.

A mental snort sounded in Chassie's head. As if Wyoming was the pinnacle of high society. As if being a "nail technician specialist" meant something besides Brandy filed fake claws and gossiped all day while drinking Diet Coke.

But she *hated* Brandy still had the power to make her feel like a dirty little rez reject.

Chassie wasn't paying attention as she shuffled down the darkened hallway. She glanced up from her seen-better-days turquoise ropers into her husband's smiling face.

"You all right, darlin'? You been gone a long time. I was gettin' worried."

She wrapped her arms around Trevor's waist, melting into him. "I'm better now that you're here. God, Trevor, I love you. Thank you for marrying me."

Trevor tipped her head back so he could look in her eyes. "Baby? What's really goin' on?"

Crisis of faith. Sometimes when faced with the type of woman Trevor used to date and could've married, she wondered why he'd chosen her. "Nothin' that dancin' with you won't cure."

"Be a pleasure to put a smile back on this pretty face I love so much." He guided her to the dance floor and held her closely through four songs. After the last note of the steel slide twanged, she stepped back. "Thanks, handsome."

He kissed her square on the mouth. "You're welcome. But you're gonna hafta block my lower half until we get to the table, 'cause dirty dancin' with you like that always gives me a hard-on."

"I noticed. That's sweet, Trev."

"Sweet?" he growled. "I ain't feelin' sweet. Not. At. All."

"You can show me your not-so-sweet side when we get home. But I am feelin' guilty for abandoning Edgard."

"He's a big boy. He can take care of himself."

Once the crowd parted, she caught a glimpse of Edgard. He wasn't alone, but he didn't appear too pleased about his visitor.

Chassie's eyes narrowed at a puffy blonde head atop a

narrow set of shoulders.

Brandy.

She didn't understand the sudden burst of jealousy nor her need to act on it. She spun around right into Trevor. "Do you trust me?"

"Well, yeah, but—"

"Good."

Chassie skirted the table and snuck in behind Edgard, sliding her hands down his chest until their faces were side-by-side. "Hey, sugar pie. Didja miss me?" She feathered her lips over his neck and flattened her palms against that rock-hard abdomen.

Edgard sucked in a quick breath. "I, ah, yeah, I did."

"I thought so. Hope you weren't too bored."

"Baby, keep it PG in public, okay?" Trevor jerked the stool next to Edgard and parked himself, as if he didn't mind his wife openly touching another man.

Thank you for playing along, Trev.

Trevor said, "Brandy." No hello, how are you, or inane small talk.

In a fit of dating confessions, Chassie spilled her guts to him about how poorly Brandy treated her over the years. In a show of camaraderie, Trevor gave Brandy the cold shoulder whenever they crossed paths.

Edgard picked up on the vibe. He plucked her hand from his stomach and kissed her knuckles one at a time, tossing off Portuguese phrases.

The display was for show, but Chassie's knees went weak anyway. Edgard might've been reciting a damn grocery list in that sexy-assed accent, but frankly, she didn't care. She could listen to those honeyed masculine tones all damn night.

Brandy stood abruptly and snapped, "I have to go," before she flounced off.

Trevor and Edgard exchanged a devilish look.

When Chassie tried to snag a barstool, Trevor tugged her onto his lap. "Least you can do is show *me* a little affection after actin' so shameless with my best buddy, you brazen hussy." He nipped her earlobe and chills raced down her neck.

"I take it she wasn't a friend of yours?" Edgard asked.

"No. I know it was petty and third-gradish, but I'm so sick

of her smarmy little comments that I wanted to prove..." Her gaze zoomed to Edgard and guilt punched a hole in her bubble of one-upsmanship. "Crap. I'm sorry. Were you seriously tryin' to hook up with her?"

A horrified expression distorted Edgard's face. "No!"

"She's not your type?"

Another strange look passed between her husband and his friend. "Not my type at all."

"Good. Because she's a total bitch. Do you know what she asked me in the bathroom? If Edgard and I were related because we looked so much alike."

Trevor choked on his beer.

She angled her head to look at him. "What?"

"Ah. Nothin'."

"Do you think we look alike?"

"Besides the fact you're a foot shorter than Ed, your hair is reddish brown where his is black? Not to mention your eyes are hazel, Edgard's are gold? You're part Indian, he's Brazilian, you have tits and he has a big cock? Yeah. You two are so much alike you could almost be goddamn twins."

Chassie laughed. "See? Brandy refused to believe that a man as hot lookin' as Edgard could possibly be with me voluntarily. So I don't care if she thinks we're havin' a threesome every damn night, it serves her nosy ass right."

A sputtering sound came from Edgard, then from Trevor.

Her gaze flicked between the two men. "What is *up* with you guys?"

"Darlin', didja ever think that Brandy is gonna take great pleasure in tellin' everyone in the county that you're bangin' your husband and his friend? And it won't be disputed because half the damn county is in this bar right now, watchin' you feelin' him up. Watchin' me *let* you feel him up." Trevor took another drink of his beer.

"I'm not lyin' when I say I don't care. Let 'em think what they want."

"But, Chass, baby—"

"God, Trevor, what is wrong with you? They'll think what they want anyway, especially if we start denying it, claiming it was all a joke. Screw 'em. We might as well have fun with it." Chassie upended Trevor's beer. "What say you, Edgard?"

"I say I think it's time to hit the road."

"Good idea." Trevor removed Chassie from his lap and stood.

"You guys are no fun, I swear." Her eyes twinkled. "Maybe the three of us should hold hands on the way to the truck."

"Definitely time to go." Trevor dragged her out of the bar.

Chapter Four

A few days later, the three amigos, as Chassie secretly called them, stood outside, drinking mugs of coffee. The morning started out typically chilly for February but Chassie knew the forecast for afternoon predicted a balmy fifty degrees.

Edgard hung back while Trevor and Chassie discussed the day's schedule. Checking cattle was their priority, twice every day, rain, snow, sleet, or heat. Chassie took the early morning shift while Trevor tended the herd in the evening. Rarely did they do the check together; it was a waste of manpower in their small operation.

Before he retreated to the barn, Trevor discouraged Edgard from helping with chores again—a reaction Chassie didn't understand. Every damn day there was more work to be done around the ranch than time to do it. The fact Edgard had volunteered filled Chassie with relief. The fact Trevor discounted it filled Chassie with resentment.

She frowned as she backed the truck underneath the feed hopper. Something was up with Trevor. But whenever she asked him what was wrong, he wouldn't talk. Rationally, she knew most men were like that, especially cowboys, keeping concerns to themselves. But she'd believed Trevor was different. No, he had been different, which was why his about-face bugged her so much. Her husband was keeping secrets and she had a pretty decent idea what about.

Money.

The end of last summer they'd crunched numbers and figured out pretty quickly in order to stay competitive in the cattle market, they'd have to increase the size of their herd. Which they did. But it left them at absolute capacity for grazing areas. Land leases from the state or individual ranchers were few and far between. Bottom line: they needed more land.

As luck would have it, their neighbor to the south, Gus Dutton, was kicking around the idea of selling his acreage. Gus gave them a heads-up—it was an unwritten rancher's creed to offer neighbors with bordering ranches a shot at purchasing the land before offering it to strangers. Not only had Gus approved of Chassie and Trevor's improvements to the West homeplace, he understood the struggle of trying to get ahead when developers and "hobby" ranchers were swallowing up land all around you.

So, giddy at their apparent good fortune, Trevor and Chassie had scheduled an appointment with the family banker to discuss their options. But the banker's news wasn't good. Although Chassie owned the West ranch land outright, she had no credit history. Same went for Trevor because he'd spent years living hand-to-mouth on the rodeo circuit.

The banker did present an option. Because they were otherwise debt free, if they could come up with ten percent of the purchase price as a cash down payment, the bank would be willing to lend them the remainder.

Not the answer they'd hoped for, but one which showed the banker's faith in their ability to procure the funds. A totally misplaced faith since the couple was strapped for cash and living on next to nothing as it was.

If they didn't assure Gus Dutton they could meet his price, Gus would offer the parcel to the other neighbors whose land bordered his on his south end—the McKays.

Her cousins already owned most of four Wyoming counties. For the first time in her life she understood her father's resentment toward the ranching family. If the McKays got their hands on Dutton's land it'd feel like encroachment, whereas if she and Trevor bought Dutton's land, it would feel like progress, despite either way they ended up with the McKays as neighbors.

Neither she nor Trevor owned anything worth anything. No antiques, or jewelry or heirlooms. Their pickups were running on baling twine and prayers. The farm equipment was ancient. They could sell off a couple bulls, a couple horses and it still wouldn't put a dent in the kind of cash they needed to come up with.

The financial situation weighed on Trevor, making him feel like he couldn't provide for her. He'd considered asking his dad to loan them money, but Chassie would rather lose out on the land than have Trevor beholden in any way to his father.

Which put them back at square one; dreams without the resources to realize them. So when that pensive look settled on her husband's handsome face, she didn't push.

The passenger's door slammed and Edgard climbed in, startling Chassie out of her brooding, as "cake"—feed pellets for the cattle—filled the metal bin in the truck bed. "Hey, aren't you supposed to be checkin' on the repair status of your truck?"

"Yep. It's not done."

"I'm not surprised. Does Trevor know you aren't in the house twiddling your thumbs?"

"No. I beat feet past the machine shed where he's wrenching on some piece of metal and cussing like a truck driver. I'm here, I might as well help out. I like helping out. Actually, I miss doin' the work."

"Consider yourself the official gate-opener again," Chassie said, shifting the truck into first gear. "It'll be nice to have your company." As Trevor had all but ignored Edgard in the last few days, Edgard had taken to riding along with her in the morning and hanging out with her in the house in the afternoons. They'd had some damn interesting conversations.

After they'd passed through the first gate and pasture, she said, "Tell me more about your ranch in Brazil. Is it a family operation?"

Edgard pushed his hat back with a gloved hand. "No. I bought it with my rodeo earnings. It was close to my mother and stepfather's place."

"Was?"

"Is. Translation error."

The truth? Or just a way to cover up the slip?

"Anyway, it's small compared to the wide open spaces in Wyoming, only about two hundred acres."

"How many cattle can you run on a spread that size?"

"I had three hundred head."

Again with the past tense. "That's a lot of cattle on not a huge acreage."

"There's a lot of rain, which means a lot of vegetation, so

there's plenty of feed. I'll admit our cows are smaller and leaner than the ones I see here."

The herd swarmed the truck, recognizing the sound of food. Chassie pulled the cord on the hopper and the cake dropped to the ground beneath them as they putzed along.

"I know it's crass to ask, but how many head are you and Trevor running?"

"Four hundred. We got an eighty percent pregnancy rate with breeding in early summer, so we're crossing our fingers for the birth survival rate to be around that same percentage. Even counting the heifers."

"Universal truth that they're notoriously paranoid first time mothers, eh?"

She smiled. "Must be. So bein' so far south, do you calve around the same time of year?"

"Yep."

"And you aren't there to help out?"

He angled his head toward the window. "This place is beautiful. So different from the jungle."

Chassie let the blatant subject change pass as they bumped over the rutted tracks. Her gaze caught on a moving object three hundred feet down the fence line. She snagged the binoculars from the middle of the seat and focused on the sagebrush. Not more than thirty seconds passed and she saw it move again.

"Shit!"

"What do you see?"

"A goddamn coyote." She eased the truck into a half circle for a better view. She shoved the stick into neutral and pushed the emergency brake to the floor. Carefully, she reached for her "varmint rifle" on the gun rack behind her. No need to dig for ammo because it was already fully loaded.

"You gonna shoot it?"

"Yep." Chassie didn't bother to look at Edgard when she said, "Got a problem with that?"

"No. We have our share of predators in Brazil."

"The Wiley Coyote, Bambi lovin', PETA members don't understand why I'd wanna kill a cute, fluffy little animal who's only actin' on instinct. After livin' on this land my entire life, I know those beasts are licking their chops for a cow to fall behind so they can attack it. Gets worse when we start calvin'. If it comes down to my livelihood or a coyote's, it's my instinct to remind those scavengers I'm at the top of the food chain for a reason."

"Can't argue with that logic."

With the window rolled down, she poked the barrel out the window and trained her sight on the bushes. "Come on out," she taunted. "It'll only hurt a little bit."

Edgard chuckled.

A reddish-gold face broke through the underbrush and Chassie fired. The animal jerked and ran. She ignored the slight ringing in her ears and fired again. The coyote dropped beyond the rise. "Hah!"

"Didja get it?"

"Probably."

"You're a good shot."

"Comes from lots of practice, on all sorts of guns, with all sorts of prey."

Edgard muttered, "Remind me not to piss you off."

Holding the rifle across her lap, she popped the emergency brake and slammed the truck into gear.

"What do you do with it if it's dead?"

"Nothin'. Leave it as crow bait."

"You don't skin it?"

She shook her head.

"Why not? Isn't there money in skins?"

"The hide and tail should be worth cash, but you'll see why the majority of coyotes around here are worthless."

After Chassie crested the rise, she slowed, seeing the form lying on the grayish-white snow. Once they were within ten feet of the carcass, she stopped the truck.

They both hopped out and met at the hood.

"Holy shit that's nasty," Edgard said.

The male coyote was scrawny, emaciated to the point each rib showed. The front and back legs were stick-thin and covered in oozing sores. The animal's fur was matted in places; bald spots dotted the rest of the skeletal body. Only four teeth were visible from the slackened jaw.

"What is it?"

"Scabies. It's an epidemic. It doesn't matter, young, old,

male, female, the disease thrives in the dens. Lucky thing this one is out of the gene pool before mating season starts."

"Yeah. He looks like he's had some good luck all right."

Chassie couldn't resist teasing, "Hey, there's a hacksaw under the seat. We could chop off the paws and convince folks that coyote feet are much luckier than rabbit feet. Bet we could make a pile of cash."

"You have a seriously sick sense of humor."

She smacked a kiss on his baby smooth cheek. "You're so sweet. You ready for lunch?"

Edgard gave a mock shudder. "I take it back. You are plain evil."

Since they were already out and about, Chassie took Edgard on an extended tour of the ranch. She pointed out the river valley and the summer grazing lands beyond it.

"You really love this chunk of earth, don't you?"

Chassie's cheeks flamed. "Sorry. I'm a little enthusiastic even after twenty-five years."

"You've never lived anywhere else?"

"Never wanted to."

He seemed to consider that. "So are you just content to stay here carrying on the family tradition, living on land, doing the same types of agricultural things that haven't changed for three generations?"

"I didn't say that. There's been a few changes since Trevor and I took over. Things my dad wouldn't consider but were necessary. There are lots of new avenues I'd like to try."

"For instance?"

"I'd like to raise goats."

Edgard laughed.

"No. I'm serious."

"Does Trevor know?"

"Nope. I'd never convince him it's an animal we need. So it's pointless to ask him for a llama too." She smiled. "I miss the old dairy cow we had before my mom got sick, so it'd be fun to have goats to milk. Heck, I'd even try my hand at makin' goat cheese."

He chuckled again. "Chassie the goat-herder. There's a fantasy worth visiting. I'm getting an image of you wearing a skimpy X-rated Little Bo-Peep type costume with black vinyl fuck-me boots and a leather whip instead of a staff."

"Kinky. You sound exactly like Trevor." And why did the idea that Edgard found her fantasy material please her so much?

They chatted easily, as if they'd been friends for years, which was odd, considering Edgard and Trevor were the ones who supposedly had the long-term friendship. Odder yet was the fact Chassie hadn't seen any sign of that close friendship.

By the time they returned to the ranch, a couple of hours had passed, during which they'd discovered a mutual love of horror flicks, card games, and 1970s soul music.

But if Trevor's angry expression was any indication of his mood, she doubted he'd be thrilled to learn of the interests she and Edgard shared. The second she'd parked the truck, he stalked over and threw open the door. "Where the hell have you guys been?"

"Feedin' cattle."

"It doesn't take three fuckin' hours to feed the cows."

"We had extra time so I took Ed on a tour of the ranch."

"Durin' this private tour with Ed, did it occur to you that you hadn't taken your goddamn cell phone along? And maybe I worried that you'd gotten stuck or something?"

Stung by his sharp tone, she retorted, "If you were so worried you could've tracked me down on one of the four-wheelers."

Trevor growled.

Sugar worked better than vinegar with her grumpy—jealous?—husband. Chassie jumped into his arms and he staggered backward. Before he started another diatribe, she peppered his scowling face with kisses. "I'm sorry. I'm so sorry. I didn't mean to give you more gray hairs, darlin'. Let me make it up to you. However you want."

"I like the sound of that." Trevor whacked her ass twice before setting her down.

Edgard stopped in front of the truck. Trevor took a step back from Chassie and from Edgard and they didn't so much as look at each other.

Weird. "You guys hungry?"

"It's at least an hour until lunchtime," Trevor pointed out.

"We on a shed-jewel now?"

Her snooty pronunciation of *schedule* always amused him. He gave her his dazzling cowboy grin and her stomach flipped. Lord, she loved being married to this man.

Trevor bent down and kissed her. "Lunch later. I wancha to look at something in the barn first."

Edgard said, "I'll leave you to it. I'm going up to the house for a bit."

Chassie followed Trevor into the metal barn. Stalls covered half of one side. Tractor parts littered the walking space on the other side. She stepped over the makeshift partition and saw Trevor stopping in front of the farthest stall.

She sidled up beside him, needing to stand on the lowest rung of the gate to see over the top. Meridian, the beautiful quarter horse they'd purchased the first month they'd married, stared back. "Is it time already?" Chassie asked Trevor.

"Either that or there's a big storm comin' 'cause she is mighty restless. She don't wanna eat, neither."

"Hey, girl." Chassie held out her hand. "It's okay. Come on. Come over here."

Meridian didn't move.

Normally whenever Chassie showed up, Meridian pranced right up to her. Not so today. "Is she okay?"

"For now. We'll have to see. That's why I brought her in. I didn't trust that she wouldn't run off to that grove of trees she's so partial to."

No amount of coaxing would bring Meridian any closer.

"Forget her. I have something else I wanna show you." Trevor snagged her hand and half-dragged her to the tack room. "Ta-da."

A big mound of tangled ropes and reins were piled in the middle of the room. "What's all this?"

"I finally cleaned out the horse trailer. Lookit what I found. Hell, I forgot I even had half this stuff."

Lined up alongside the snake-like pile were saddles, spurs, spurs and more spurs. Saddle blankets. Flank straps. Bits. Bridles. Brushes. Halters. Lead ropes. It looked like they'd opened a Western tack store.

"What're you gonna do with all this?"

"Separate it out. See what's worth keepin', what's worth sellin' and what needs hauled to the burnin' barrel."

Chassie glanced over at him. "Is this a project that requires my help?"

"Nah. Just tryin' to tie up a few loose ends. Been a pigsty and I needed to reorganize it because I won't get a chance when calvin' starts." Then Trevor stepped in front of her, forcing her to look up at him. "I found something else you'll like."

"Is it a candy bar? 'Cause, I'm jonesin' for a big chunk of chocolate."

"Nope." He snatched a braided purple rope from the slats. "Feel this. Isn't it soft? You'll appreciate that, trust me."

"Why's that?"

"Because it won't mark your skin." Trevor eliminated the short distance between them. "Now's the time for you to make it up to me for playin' hooky with another man. Put your hands behind your back."

"But—"

"I can use one of the scratchier ropes to tie you up if you'd prefer?" She shook her head. "Good. Wrists together, behind your back."

Chassie complied. Might not be politically correct, but she was secretly thrilled when he demanded her sexual obedience.

Trevor moved behind her and wound the rope tight—but not too tight. "Let's go out in the main room, where there's a little more hay."

"Hay for what?"

"As a cushion for your knees."

Chapter Five

Trevor hooked a finger in Chassie's front belt loop and led her to two rectangular haybales stacked together. He tossed his Carhartt jacket on the ground and faced her with a devilish smile. "Whatcha waitin' for, darlin'?"

"I'm gonna suck you off right here?"

"Yep." His fingers went to his belt and he slid the leather strap from the belt loop, yanking the buckle away.

She seemed mesmerized by the jerky, impatient action.

"Chassie," he said sharply.

Obediently she dropped to her knees right in front of him with her back to the door.

"Good girl."

The heavy silver buckle dangled on one side, the finished end of the buffalo skin on the other side. He popped the button on the waistband, watching her face as he worked the zipper. With the fabric sides separated, Trevor tugged the jeans down past his hips, groin and thighs to his knees, leaving him in navy blue boxer briefs.

The patches of shadow in the building made her hazel eyes appear enormously large. Trevor ran his right index finger over her strong jawline. "So obedient." He rotated his right hand and cupped her jaw. His left hand positioned his cock in front of her mouth.

Those pale lips opened. Chassie looked up at him for direction.

"Suck the head." The shock of that warm, wet heat enclosing the sensitive skin caused his dick to jerk against her top teeth. He hissed.

Chassie kissed the small nick before she licked the thick rim. First with just the tip of her tongue, barely there whips of heated velvet intensified by her shallow breaths drifting over the wetness.

Chills raced from the nape of his neck to his tight balls. Trevor heard a noise and looked away from the sexy sight of his wife sucking his cock. It'd be easy to miss the outline of a man in the darkened corner by the door, but Trevor was attuned to him.

Edgard shifted to the side and stared straight into Trevor's eyes.

There it was, that challenge. *Show me.*

It'd always driven Edgard crazy to see a woman blowing Trevor. Sometimes Edgard demanded Trevor bring one of the buckle bunnies into their sex games, just to watch Trevor's body move as he fucked the woman. Edgard participated on occasion, but normally he'd whack off while Trevor had his cock in the woman's throat. Or in her pussy. Then as soon as the woman left, Trevor was either on his knees servicing his demanding male lover, or spread-eagled on the bed while Edgard reamed his ass.

Golden eyes glowed feral as a cat's in the darkness as Edgard slid his hand down his own chest, to the crotch of his jeans. His palm drew circles over the bulge beneath the zipper and his breath puffed out in clouds of steam.

Don't let him in this moment between you and your wife.

But the reality of Edgard watching them had Trevor's cock rivaling concrete for hardness. He glanced down at Chassie. Shoulders thrown back, eyes closed, lips stretched around his prick. So beautiful. So willing. He wrapped her thick braid around his palm and pulled. "Faster."

Chassie increased the rhythm without hesitation.

Trevor clutched her head and snapped his hips, driving his cock all the way in her saliva-slick mouth. Her lips tightened as he pulled out. She increased the suction, knowing exactly how he liked it—tight and wet. "Oh yeah." Trevor's heart thundered, droplets of sweat forming on his forehead, even in the cold.

The harder he pumped into Chassie's mouth, the faster Edgard's hand stroked.

A tingle began in his spine and zoomed to his balls like a zip line. He loved this part. The buildup. When every muscle in his body went rigid with anticipation.

Trevor didn't bother to hide the thoughts as he returned Edgard's stare. *Don't you wish it was you on your knees in front of me? Pulling these guttural moans from my throat? Sucking down the taste of me?*

A soft, affirmative noise echoed back to him.

He refocused on his wife's face. "Chass. Oh, baby, that's it." He seized her bobbing head, ceasing movement as the base of his spine heated. His cock swelled, lifting off her tongue before he exploded, come jetting out fast like a rocket booster. "Uh. Uh. Uh. Yeah!"

She swallowed steadily as every part of his body throbbed.

Trevor floated back to reality from that white space where nothing existed but physical awareness. He looked at the desire burning in Chassie's eyes as his cock slipped free from her mouth. He helped her to her feet and crushed her against his chest. "You... Damn, woman, I can't even think straight."

Chassie trailed kisses up his neck. "Please, my turn now. I'm dyin'. Touch me. Untie my hands."

"Don't need your hands for me to touch you, darlin'." He curled his fingers around her shoulders, holding her steady for his hungry kiss.

A little squeaking moan burst in his mouth at the dueling play of tongues, the quick nip of teeth, the soft, wet slide of lips on lips and he smiled. He loved that noise, like his kiss was a welcome surprise.

Chassie broke away. "Fuck me, like this, right now. Keep my hands tied, I don't care."

"Hang on, I'll take care of you." He made short work of her belt. Unbuttoned and unzipped her jeans, loving the way her warm skin felt so soft beneath his rough fingertips as he shimmied the stiff fabric and her silky underwear below her knees. Trevor leaned over and picked up his coat. He tossed it over the haybale and whispered, "Spin around and bend over."

Chassie's whole body shook. Partially because she was so turned on, partially from the shock of having her ass hanging out in the cold winter air.

Trevor pressed behind her; his thighs cool, his thick sex still hot as it brushed over her bound wrists. Meaty hands squeezed her hips, then one slid between her hipbones and the coarse texture of his palm caused her belly to flutter. The fingers followed the cleft of her sex, straight through the curls to where she was sticky and aching.

He growled, "Baby, you're already wet."

She pumped her pelvis. "More."

Trevor dipped his middle finger into the wetness and stroked her clit lightly, creating a slippery, tingly sensation. "Like this?"

"Faster." He started a rub/swirl combo and Chassie knew she wouldn't last long. "Oh. That's it."

Without missing a stroke, he placed his mouth on her ear and sucked the air clean out.

It sent her over the brink, as he knew it would. A dizzy, whirling sensation fogged her brain; a continual pulsing cinched her pussy muscles, her ass cheeks, her nipples into one synchronized throb. She bowed back into the curve of Trevor's neck and gasped at every delicious pulsation.

"Put your feet on my boots."

Neither could adjust much, constricted by jeans shoved to their knees, but Chassie managed it.

Trevor swore. "Looks like I'm gonna hafta untie your hands after all. Brace yourself on that haybale, darlin', 'cause I could fuck you right through it."

The second the ropes were off, he maneuvered her over his coat, tilting her ass higher. Chassie placed her palms on the haybale and Trevor thrust hard and deep.

With her legs tightly trapped between his, he couldn't pull all the way out. Trevor's fingers found their way between her legs again. "One more."

"I can't, even when it feels—GOD, what was that?"

"Something new." Trevor tapped her puffed up clit during a longer stroke. "I call it Trevor's tantalizin' tantric trick." Two shallow thrusts, then a deep stroke as he tapped her clit.

She gasped. "You've never done this before."

"Been savin' this secret love technique for a special occasion."

"What's the occasion?"

"It's Tuesday."

Thrust, thrust, stroke—tap. Thrust, thrust, stroke—tap. Thrust, thrust, stroke—tap.

"Trevor!"

Thrust, thrust, stroke—tap. Thrust, thrust, stroke—tap. Thrust, thrust, stroke—tap.

"It's called circle of threes," he panted.

Thrust, thrust, stroke—tap. Thrust, thrust, stroke—tap. Thrust, thrust, stroke—tap.

Chassie's heart and blood began to follow the rhythm.

Thrust, thrust, stroke—tap. Thrust, thrust, stroke—tap. Thrust, thrust, stroke—tap.

"You're gonna come like this, Chass, and you're gonna come hard. Just feel, baby. Let go of everything."

Thrust, thrust, stroke—tap. Thrust, thrust, stroke—tap. Thrust, thrust, stroke—tap.

Something shifted in the corner of the barn, stealing her attention from the tribal tattoo drumming throughout her body. She squinted at the dimness and saw him.

Edgard.

Heat suffused her face. How long had Edgard been there? Since she'd given Trevor a blowjob? Had it embarrassed him so he didn't want to call attention to his presence?

Or had it turned him on so much that he didn't want to leave?

Thrust, thrust, stroke—tap. Thrust, thrust, stroke—tap. Thrust, thrust, stroke—tap.

Or maybe Edgard hoped to join in? Chassie knew her husband was no stranger to threesomes. She'd never experienced that type of kink, never been curious about trying it...until now. What would it feel like to have both men touching her body? Two sets of hands, two mouths, two cocks competing to make her scream with pleasure?

Thrust, thrust, stroke—tap. Thrust, thrust, stroke—tap. Thrust, thrust, stroke—tap.

Her gaze dropped to Edgard's midsection. Even in the muted light she saw his silver belt buckle hanging by his thigh and his jeans were undone. His right arm moved.

Thrust, thrust, stroke—tap. Thrust, thrust, stroke—tap. Thrust, thrust, stoke—tap.

Holy shit. Edgard was jerking off. Jerking off right in front of her. Jerking off to the rhythm Trevor had set.

Chassie couldn't see Edgard's face, just the lower half of

his body. She realized he had a perfect view of Trevor's hand between her legs and Trevor's ass pumping as he fucked her. A shiver rolled from her neck to her belly.

Thrust, thrust, stroke—tap. Thrust, thrust, stroke—tap. Thrust, thrust, stroke—tap.

Trevor growled, "I wanna take your ass like this. Pumpin' into that tight little hole, drivin' you crazy, bringin' you off with my hand as I come deep inside you, feelin' your muscles squeezin' every drop from my cock."

Chassie's eyes wandered to the shadow in the corner when she heard a soft half gasp/half groan. Edgard's fist made a *slap slap slap* sound and then stilled as ropes of come jetted out of the end of his cock and splatted to the dirt floor.

Trevor abandoned the tantric trick and pushed her at a deeper angle over the haybale as he fucked her like an animal and came with a roar.

The altered pace unleashed vibrations in her clit, her pussy, her nipples, and her anus. She literally sobbed, unable to breathe, to think, to move, wanting the sensations to stop. Wanting them never to stop.

Trevor murmured sweet words in her hair. He pulled out of her body and semen trickling down the inside of her leg brought her back to sanity.

When Chassie opened her eyes and looked to the shadows, Edgard was gone.

But he was far from forgotten.

Chapter Six

Trevor was standing by the fence, untangling a pile of ropes he'd unearthed in the horse trailer, when he heard the gate to the corral squeak open. He didn't bother to turn around because he sensed who'd tracked him down.

Edgard.

Big surprise. How he'd managed not to be alone with the man for the last two weeks was a minor miracle. He automatically tensed when the plodding footsteps stopped behind him. "Something wrong with Meridian?"

"No. She's fine."

"Then whatcha need?"

"What the fuck is this?"

Trevor didn't rise to the bait, as he hadn't for the last several days. Calmly, he asked, "What?"

"This." Edgard threw the pristine, custom-made saddle on the ground within Trevor's peripheral view.

Shit. How had Edgard found it? And why in the hell had that bastard gone snooping around instead of figuring out what was wrong with Meridian like he'd promised?

"Trev? I asked you a question."

"You know damn good and well what it is, Ed."

"I figured you would've gotten rid of it by now."

"Well, I didn't."

Edgard practically growled, "That don't tell me why you still have it. That don't tell me nothin'."

Trevor turned his face toward the opposite fence to gaze across to the mountains. His reasons for keeping the saddle seemed sentimental, sloppy and stupid now, but he'd be damned if he'd share those reasons with anyone, least of all Edgard, the man responsible for those feelings.

Bootsteps made a sucking sound in the muck of the corral as Edgard closed the short distance between them. "I ain't gonna drop it. Answer me."

"Fine. You said I could do whatever I wanted with it. So I kept it."

"You didn't use it at all, did you?"

Trevor shook his head, keeping his eyes averted.

"Why not?"

"I have plenty of other saddles, saddles I like better."

"That's a piss-poor excuse. Try again."

He stayed mum, wishing the damn mud would open up and swallow him like a sinkhole.

"Were you hoping if you kept it I'd come back?"

Trevor's heart said *yes* but his mouth stayed tight as a rusty hinge.

"Answer the fucking question, Trevor."

Edgard's arrogant streak snapped Trevor's forced patience. "What do you want me to say? It's obvious I saved the goddamn saddle."

"Why?"

"Because it reminded me of you, all right?" He kicked a chunk of mud and stalked away. "Fuck this and fuck you."

Edgard rattled off something in Portuguese, something Trevor vaguely remembered as being a plea. Or was it a threat?

Dammit. His feet stopped. Trevor's gaze zeroed in on Edgard, who'd circled him until they were standing less than a foot apart.

"Tell me why."

Be cruel, that'll nip this in the bud once and for all.

"I didn't keep the fuckin' thing because I had some girlish goddamn hope you'd come back lookin' for it like Cinderella's lost glass slipper, and we'd pick up where we left off after you left me." He locked his eyes to the liquid heat in Edgard's, not allowing the man to look away. "Especially after you made it crystal clear you weren't ever comin' back."

Angry puffs of breath distorted the air between them.

Several beats passed before Edgard retorted, "But I am here now, aren't I?"

"What? Am I supposed to be flippin' cartwheels about that fact? I don't know what you want from me, Ed. Take the saddle back if that'll make you happy. I've got no use for it. I never did." Angry, disgusted with himself, Edgard, and the whole uncomfortable situation, Trevor spun and walked toward the barn.

Edgard laughed—the taunting, soft laughter that was guaranteed to raise Trevor's hackles and his ire. "It's that easy for you? To get pissed off and walk away?"

"Yep. You've got no right to act so goddamned surprised since it's a trick I learned from you, *meu amigo.*"

Not two seconds later, the air left Trevor's lungs as Edgard tackled him to the ground. Trevor rolled to dislodge the man from his back; Edgard countered, took a swing and missed. Trevor bucked and twisted his shoulders, but Edgard anticipated the move and used the momentum against Trevor to try and shove Trevor's face against the fence.

Before Edgard cornered him and held him down completely to land a punch, Trevor rolled again and pushed to his feet. A noise echoed behind him, but he ignored it as he fisted his hands in Edgard's shearling coat, dragging him upright until they were nose to nose.

"What the hell has gotten into you?"

Edgard attempted to jerk back. Trevor held tight.

"This is why you came here?" he yelled in Edgard's face. "To sucker punch me and knock me in the fuckin' dirt?"

"No."

"Then what?"

Edgard didn't move. He just breathed hard and stared hard at Trevor without flinching.

Trevor's rapid breaths sliced the cold air but couldn't cut through the icy tension. "Answer me, goddammit."

"I came here for this," Edgard said angrily, wrapping a hand around Trevor's neck and smashing their mouths together.

The shock of Edgard's insistent lips caused Trevor to open his mouth in protest, which played perfectly into Edgard's plans as he jammed his tongue right into Trevor's mouth.

Damn damn damn. His token resistance was just that—a momentary struggle with guilt as his body reminded him it'd been an eternity, a fucking *lifetime*, since he'd lost himself in Edgard's hungry kiss. Trevor's willpower vanished as the velvety smoothness of Edgard's lips slid against his, coaxing, teasing, demanding a reaction.

Trevor gave him one; a hot, deep, wet mating of lips, teeth and tongue as he thoroughly devoured what he'd been denied, what he'd secretly craved these last three years.

When Edgard groaned in Trevor's mouth, the vibration traveled down Trevor's throat straight to his cock. His immediate hard-on was the invitation Edgard sought and Edgard ratcheted the kiss up another level.

Trevor instinctively matched his exhalations to Edgard's broken breaths, countered the bold strokes of Edgard's tongue with soft suction, found that familiar old lover's rhythm until even the beats of their hearts seemed synchronized. The sensual assault filled something in Trevor that he hated to admit had been empty.

Warning signs went unheeded as the ferocious kisses continued, kicking Trevor's need into high gear. But the unfamiliar prickle of Edgard's beard on his cheek began to rouse him from that dark desire. Coupled with the low-pitched masculine moans—not Chassie's feminine sighs—and Trevor broke away, knocking Edgard's hands free.

"Stop. No."

"Yes," Edgard grabbed Trevor's shirt. "*This* is why I'm here. Because it's still there, Trevor. This need didn't go away just because I did."

"It don't matter."

"It should. God. Please let it matter."

"Ed—"

"Don't. Just...don't." Edgard gently rested his forehead against Trevor's and retreated into silence.

The heat of their bodies, the cold air, the confusion, the passion, the anger, the guilt, all swirled in Trevor's head until he didn't know which way was up. Unable to squirm either closer or away, damn near unable to breathe, Trevor squeezed his eyes shut and gave in, leaning against Edgard, just for a moment.

Finally he dredged up a semblance of sanity. "I love her, Ed. I'm not with her because she was my second choice."

"I know. Why do you think it hurts me so bad, *meu amor*?"

My love. That single, familiar endearment could prove to be his undoing. Another pause lingered before Trevor said, "I can't do this. I swear to fucking God I cannot do this again."

"We'll figure something out this time."

"No."

"Look at me."

Trevor shook his head.

"Goddammit. Look. At. Me."

Heart thumping crazily, Trevor pulled back and caught the golden gaze that'd haunted his dreams since the day they'd gone from friends to something more.

Edgard curled one hand around Trevor's face, keeping the other fisted in his shirt. "Tell me how to fix this."

"We can't and talkin' about it ain't gonna change nothin'."

"We were always better at fucking away our problems rather than talking them out, eh?"

No hint of a smile graced either of their faces.

"Neither one of those is an option now." Trevor angled his head and impulsively kissed Edgard's rough palm before stepping back. But he'd forgotten Edgard's sheer strength as the man halted his retreat.

"You don't remember how good we were together? Our pricks rubbing together as we rolled on the bed until we exploded? You don't remember how wet and eager my mouth felt sucking every drop of spunk from your cock? You don't think about how deep I reamed that tight asshole of yours as you bucked and begged me for more?"

Flashes of their past encounters made it impossible for Trevor to move away.

"The bondage games, your ass, cock, and balls spread for my taking. Jacking each other off in the silence of the horse trailer because we couldn't wait another second to be together. That burning need for a fuck or a suck or a handjob from a man who knows exactly how you like it—is any of that ringing a bell? Or is it making you hard as a fencepost, Trev? Because I remember how hot you burned when I talked dirty as I was fucking you."

"Stop."

"You don't want me to stop, you stupid, stubborn bastard." Edgard snarled and devoured Trevor's mouth in another possessive, bruising kiss.

Before Trevor could break free from the temptation, a distressed gasp somewhere to the left speeded up the process. Trevor shoved Edgard away. He spun so fast he lost his balance. But the damage had been done.

Chassie stood in the shadows in absolute shock.

Chapter Seven

Not happening. Not happening. Not happening.

Her body, her will, her consciousness appeared to be floating in another dimension, as this one shifted and twisted into the surreal. She couldn't believe her eyes.

Not happening. Not happening. Not happening.

She had not witnessed her husband in the arms of another man. She had not seen him kissing another man like he was everything in his world. She had not heard the details of how they'd been together, what they'd been together. She had not imagined how badly they wanted to be together now.

Not happening. Not happening. Not happening.

The mantra she'd used during her childhood to vanquish nightmares wasn't working this time.

It was happening and she'd been a party to it all. From the corner of the chute where she'd been an unwilling voyeur in the details of her husband's past life. She'd watched Edgard approach and accuse. She'd heard the angry longing and denial in Trevor's words and posture. She'd observed the mating ritual—the banter, the fight, the manifestation of desire resulting in pure physical passion.

Chassie couldn't process it. Not even when Trevor said, "Chassie, baby, let me explain."

She couldn't speak. Not even when she wanted to scream.

But when Trevor started toward her, she found the will to move. And so she did. She turned and ran.

"No! Chassie, wait! Don't go."

Tears blurred her vision. Instead of running into the barn, she raced for the open field beyond the fence. Before she'd reached the gate and her freedom, two strong arms banded her upper body, lifting her off the ground.

Her flight instinct fled and her fight instinct was in full gear. She kicked and thrashed and when she had enough air in her lungs, she began to holler. "Don't you touch me!"

Trevor flinched.

"I mean it. Let me go! Let go of me right now, you cheating goddamn bastard!"

"Chass. Calm down."

"*Calm down*? Fuck that and fuck you." Chassie jerked her body sideways.

"I don't want to hurt you, so stop fightin' me."

"Stop touching me when I said to get your goddamn hands off me."

"You really don't want that, sweetheart."

A frustrated scream tore from her throat. "Yes I do. Let me go right fucking now."

"No."

"You're a lying son of a bitch and I want you to let...me...go!" she shrieked, hating the way he'd immobilized her. Chassie drummed her bootheels into his shins, trying to bruise his body as badly as he'd bruised her heart. She'd twisted so violently against his iron hold that her hair had come loose from her ponytail and swirled around her head. A few strands stuck to her tear-stained face.

"Fuck, that hurts, you little hellcat."

"Good!" Anger renewed her determination to inflict pain on him. As she screamed and cried and kicked she knew she was completely out of control. But fighting back was her only option. Her mind and body relived the absolute desolation she'd felt upon seeing the man she loved with another, seeing the longing and apparently long-denied need as Trevor had kissed Edgard like he was everything Trevor had ever wanted, everything he'd ever needed, and she was just a second-rate substitute.

"Chassie. Please. Stop. I'm beggin' you, baby, seein' you like this is breakin' me into a million fuckin' pieces and I..." He paused. "Please. I need you to understand."

The raw pain in his voice gave her pause. She quit struggling. After a minute or so, Trevor sighed and gentled his hold, even as it seemed to strengthen him.

Neither one said a word.

Her rapid exhalations stirred her hair. Her blood pulsed angrily and her skin actually hurt. Her eyes smarted from hot tears. Her skull pounded like she'd taken a 2X4 to the head. But that was nothing, nothing compared to the ache spreading inside her, leaving her both heavy-limbed and strangely hollow.

"Thank you," Trevor whispered against her crown.

"Let me go."

"If I do will you talk to me? Give me a chance to explain?"

Chassie managed a pitiful laugh. "What's to explain? You married me when you were in love with someone else."

"Baby, it's not what you think."

"I don't have to think. I know what I saw."

The silence was broken by Edgard's approach. Trevor's whole body tensed.

But Chassie wasn't about to back down. She wasn't in the wrong. She blew the hair out of her eyes and met Edgard's baleful stare dead on.

Edgard said, "I'm sorry. This wasn't supposed to happen."

"It did happen and if you want him so goddamn bad, you can have him. I'm done with him. For good."

Rather than snap off a nasty comment, Edgard did the unexpected: he cupped Chassie's face in his hands and wiped her tears. "You don't mean that, Chassie. You're angry. You should be. But you need to listen to Trevor."

"I've heard enough."

"No, you haven't heard the important part."

"And what part would that be, Edgard?"

"The part that concerns you."

Her scathing comeback dried up.

"Don't throw away everything because of a stupid mistake. Or your pride." Edgard smoothed his cold thumbs over her hot cheeks. "Nothin' happened between Trev and me besides some angry words and some frustrated kisses."

"You wanted something to happen."

Edgard nodded. "But it didn't."

Chassie searched his eyes for a sign of regret or smugness but all she saw was pain.

"Talk to him, Chassie. Don't walk away."

"Why shouldn't I?" she half-whispered.

"Because if you do, you'll give me exactly what I want."

"Which is what?"

"Him."

Without waiting for Trevor to dispute the statement, Edgard hefted the saddle on his shoulder and disappeared into the barn.

And without asking, Trevor released her.

It took every ounce of Chassie's nerve not to crumple into a pile and weep. She started toward the house, not caring if Trevor followed, even when she knew he would. Her fingers fumbled as she removed her boots, coat and gloves, numb in body, soul and spirit.

In the kitchen she went straight for the liquor cabinet. After downing two shots of whiskey and nursing a third, she faced her husband.

A ghostly pallor replaced Trevor's usual rosy glow. He snagged the decanter, swigging the alcohol directly from the bottle. One. Two. Three solid mouthfuls.

A million questions tumbled in Chassie's head but one pushed front and center. "Are you gay?"

"No."

"Did I not just see you in a lip lock with your former male ropin' partner?"

"Yes. Before you ask, I ain't bi either. It's just…" He gestured helplessly. "It's just Edgard."

Chassie couldn't look at him, his mouth swollen from Edgard's kisses, his cheeks reddened from razor stubble, the agony burning in his eyes. She needed to remain in control and keep the gut-wrenching emotions in check. She spun back to the window, but focused on the amber liquid in her shot glass.

"Don't tune me out, Chass. Please."

"I'm not. I'm just tryin' to figure out a way to ask if you ever had sex with Dag."

He sucked in a harsh, surprised breath. "God, no."

Once again Chassie had that overwhelming sense of betrayal. "Does everybody suspect the truth about you and Edgard? Am I a laughingstock in the whole rodeo community? Everyone knew you took pity on poor Chassie West and married her because she was naïve and no one else wanted her?"

"No, baby, it ain't like that. Not at all." Trevor made a rough sound, a cross between a frustrated sigh and a snort. "You know how goddamned hard it is to keep a secret in that community. So if there'd have been rumors about me'n Ed, you'd've heard 'em."

True. There'd been whispers about Dag's sexual preferences for years, but she'd suspected her brother's proclivities before she'd heard the gossip. "How long were you and Edgard...?"

"For two and a half years."

"And during that time no one suspected?"

"Why would they? Edgard and I were together because we were travelin' and ropin' partners. And it wasn't like all of a sudden I stopped chasin' women. There were always plenty of women around."

"That's just another great visual I needed."

"You knew a lot stuff about me before we got married."

"Not this."

"You think I wanna talk about this, Chass? You think I wanna relive all that past shit with my wife? You can't believe I get off hurtin' you. And I know this big mess is hurtin' you bad." She heard the slosh of alcohol as Trevor tipped the bottle and drank again. His voice was whiskey rough. "Hurtin' you, when I love you so goddamn much is killin' me."

That much wasn't a lie. Which was probably why this situation tore her guts out. Even now she didn't doubt Trevor's feelings for her. From the moment they'd slipped on their wedding rings and repeated their vows, Chassie hadn't worried he'd cheat on her with another woman.

The idea of him cheating on her with another man had never crossed her mind.

Trevor interrupted her thoughts by saying, "I take that back. One person did know."

"Who?"

"Colby. Only because he was our other travelin' partner and he ah...came in at a bad time one night. He didn't understand, but me'n him have been friends forever. Colby is of the 'don't ask, don't tell' mindset and Channing found out when she followed the circuit with us. Then Colby got injured and Ed went back to Brazil."

A burst of anger ripped through Chassie. Her cousin Colby

hadn't warned her about marrying a man who was in love with another man? "Why did Edgard go back to Brazil?"

"Problems with his ranch down there. Problems with me because I couldn't give him what he wanted."

"Which was?"

"A monogamous relationship. I couldn't be..." Trevor paced behind her. "Edgard is the only man I'd ever felt like that about and it freaked me out. Christ. I didn't want to want him that way, but I did. Even after we started havin' sex, I never quit bein' with women. It wasn't because I was in denial of bein' gay or bi or any such shit. Edgard knew I wouldn't give them up and he didn't ask me to. That wasn't fair to him. Hell, even if women had stopped appealin' to me and I woulda been free to be only with him, I still wouldn't have done it."

"Why not?"

"I woulda lost everything. I know them kinda relationships are acceptable in a big city, but we both know that ain't so out here."

Chassie thought of her brother and the years he'd fought to hide what he was. That struggle led Dag to douse his bitterness with alcohol, causing him to make bad decisions and the combination had eventually killed him. "Was your time with Edgard just some kind of man-lust experiment?"

"I don't know."

"Then who am I supposed to ask, huh?" The smartass response tumbled out before she could stop it.

"I deserved that." Clothing shifted. Liquor slopped against the bottle. "All I know, all I've ever known, all I ever wanted to be was a Wyoming rancher. Yeah, I chased the gold buckle due to family pressure, with my pa bein' world champ and all. I fooled myself tryin' to buy his pride by followin' in his footsteps. Truth was, I hid on the circuit. I didn't wanna go home and ranch with him because the thought of spendin' every day of the rest of my life at my pa's beck and call was the worst kinda punishment. Can you imagine how cruel my family—and everyone in the community—would've treated me if they'd known how I felt about Edgard?"

She froze. "How did you feel about him?"

"Chassie—"

"Did you love him?" *Do you still love him?*

"C'mere." Trevor urged Chassie to face him. "It's been three and a half years since I've seen or talked to Edgard, Chassie. I'm in love with you. You're my wife. You're everything I ever wanted. You're the one I chose."

"How can I believe that you didn't settle for me because you didn't have the balls to choose Edgard? Now he's here. You've broken with your family. This could be your chance to finally be with him. You don't have to settle for your second choice."

Trevor trapped Chassie's face in his hands. "Listen to me. You weren't sloppy seconds or the goddamned consolation prize. From the moment we met, you were it for me, you understand? I fell madly, crazily in love with you. Just you."

She didn't want to cry, but dammit, the tears started falling again.

"Chassie, baby, you weren't my last choice; you were my first choice. My only choice. I wanted to give you everything that I'd never given another human being: my loyalty, my faithfulness, my love, and my name. I cannot imagine my life without you." His fingers tightened on her scalp. "I'll send Edgard away. He never should've come here and I shouldn't have let him stay."

"That's not the issue."

"Then what is?"

"You should've told me about him—who he was to you—from the start. I knew you weren't a saint when I married you, Trevor. I could give a shit who you'd bedded before we met. Dammit, we've talked about some of the women you fucked, the women I know personally, and your preference for threesomes. Honestly, those didn't bother me. But you not tellin' me about your relationship with Edgard? That bothers me. You've assigned significance to him by keepin' your past relationship with him hidden." She scrutinized his too-blank face and felt as if a brick wall had sprouted between them. "He was very important to you, wasn't he?"

Finally Trevor nodded.

Her stomach sank as if she'd swallowed a spur. "I can't handle you keepin' things like this from me. I lived in that world of half-truths and secrets for years, and I won't ever again."

"So did I. Which is why I didn't tell you about him."

They stared at each other for several excruciating minutes, at an absolute stalemate.

"So what now?" Trevor asked.

"I don't know. I need some time to sort it out. And you and Edgard need to talk. Not only about what happened in the corral today, but about your unresolved issues from the past and why he tracked you down now." Chassie removed Trevor's hands from her face. "I can't be with you until that's settled."

"But—"

"No buts. I'm goin' to Wheatland to Zoey's bridal shower. I'll clear out for a day or so, just like I'd planned."

A stark look darkened his blue eyes. "No. Baby, don't leave me. We can work on it here, together—"

Chassie placed her fingers over his lips. "Trevor, I love you, but I'd be lyin' to both of us if I didn't admit I hate you a little bit right now."

His whole posture slumped and his eyes were shiny with unshed tears.

She steeled herself against her need to soothe him. "Give me some space. Stay here, take care of the ranch, and talk to Edgard. I'll be back."

Trevor frowned. He paced to the door. He returned and got right in her face. "Okay. But if you don't come home to me within two days, I'm comin' after you, Chassie. You're mine. And I ain't ever lettin' you go."

Might make her a pathetic fool, but Chassie needed to be held by the only man who'd ever held her heart. She wrapped her arms around his waist, pressing her face into his chest, listening to the rapid thump of his heartbeat. "Promise me one thing."

"Anything, baby, anything for you."

"Please don't turn to Edgard when I'm gone. Don't touch him, don't kiss him and don't fuck him. Please, promise me."

"I promise."

She backed away without looking at him. "I have to finish packing."

"You sure about this, Chass? Sure that leavin' is the best way to handle it?"

No. "I'll have my cell with me, but please don't call. I need some time to think. I deserve that much."

She'd started for the stairs when Trevor called out, "I love you. I've never said that to anyone else in my life. Think on that." The outer door slammed.

Chassie loaded her lone suitcase in the truck and climbed in. As she headed down the driveway, she glanced in her rearview and saw Trevor standing alone in the middle of the road, his hands jammed in his pockets, watching her leave.

Hit the brakes. Don't go.

It was almost as if she heard Trevor's thoughts.

With a renewed burst of determination, she hit the gas and the open road.

Chapter Eight

Edgard stayed in the barn and closed his eyes, wondering why'd he'd given in to his masochistic tendencies. Was he that much of a prick he'd hoped to come to Wyoming and find Trevor miserable? Married to a shrew? Longing for him? Filled with regret? Did Edgard expect Trevor would secretly beg Edgard to take him back?

Hell, Edgard didn't know what he'd do even if that warped fantasy came true, especially after meeting Chassie.

Trevor's wife was nothing like Edgard expected. In the years Edgard traveled with Trevor, Trevor's taste in women could be described as trashy, trashier and trashiest. Easy girly-girls with a "do me, cowboy" gleam in their eyes and notches in their fancy rhinestone belts. Buckle bunnies with dyed hair, fake boobs, fake tans, fake nails, sporting expensive high-heeled fashion boots, low-cut shirts and low intellect. Real live cowgirls need not apply for a spot in Trevor's stable.

Those loose women—young and old—knew the score. One night as a no-holds-barred sexual plaything, not only for Trevor, but for whichever cowboy buddy Trevor invited along. Usually Colby volunteered as the third player. Occasionally Edgard bucked up for the fun and games. Adventurous women took on all three men at once. Their reputations as bad boys of the circuit were well earned. Partners and the positions might've changed, but the rules never did: get off, get out, and get moving to the next town.

Even back then Edgard realized Trevor chose only horny, shallow women who didn't allow him emotional attachment, because every sexual encounter was temporary until Trevor found the woman who shared his longtime dream for home, hearth and a family of his own.

Chassie West fit the bill.

She was one hundred percent Wyoming cowgirl. Inquisitive, stubborn, knowledgeable about everything from livestock to environmental issues to up-to-date technology. Upon first glance, her pint-sized frame made her appear far younger than her twenty-five years. Up close she carried herself like a gunslinger, shoulders back, chin out, venom in her eye, ready to take on anything or anyone that crossed her in any way.

Chassie's sunny personality and genuinely helpful nature were completely guileless, yet those shrewd brown eyes missed nothing. From the first time he'd looked into those soulful depths, he'd seen her sadness and knew she recognized the same in him. Even when Edgard doubted her sorrow could be attributed to her feelings for Trevor, like part of his unhappiness was. Yet, her unspoken sense of failure, disappointments and guilt had been a bond of sorts between them, as much as the way they both felt about Trevor was an odd connection.

But was it the hidden glimpses of her waif-like stature that had drawn Trevor in? Chassie wasn't beautiful in the traditional sense. No artfully applied makeup masked the ethnicity of her sharp facial features. Her long mane was stick straight, usually braided, not teased and shellacked into a perfect helmet. Her work-roughened hands hadn't ever seen the inside of a manicure studio. Her curves were in her hips and in her smile, not on her chest.

All in all, Chassie West Glanzer was something very special.

And that sucked because she deserved better than the treatment she'd received this morning. When Edgard realized she'd witnessed the encounter between him and Trevor, he experienced guilt on a level he'd never imagined. Upon seeing the horror and pain on her sweet face, Edgard had the overwhelming desire to race to Chassie and wipe her tears, hold her close and murmur platitudes, which was damn stupid, since his damn stupid actions and words caused her distress in the first place.

What a fucked up mess.

How could he make this right? For Chassie? For Trevor? And for himself?

Leaving wasn't an option. Much as he liked Chassie, if the

woman was foolish enough to walk away from Trevor for good, so be it. He'd be around to pick up the pieces. Besides, it wasn't as if Edgard hadn't warned her of his intentions.

So why did he still feel guilty?

Because he was. He'd done a stupid thing, which wasn't really new when it came to his dealings with anything or anyone involving Trevor.

The far barn door slid open and Edgard tensed. Chassie's truck had roared up the driveway not ten minutes ago. Knowing Trevor, he'd fly in, spewing accusations at him, tossing off hurtful remarks, doing his level best to goad Edgard into a physical confrontation.

Isn't that what you did today? Pushed Trevor to see how far he'd go with you?

Yes.

Fuck, he was a selfish bastard. He and Trevor were used to each other's antagonistic behavior, poor Chassie wasn't privy to how they'd normally settled their differences. Nor was she aware that Edgard and Trevor had ended up in dozens of knockdown, drag-out fistfights in their years together.

The last time they'd fought, Trevor's need to win had been particularly vicious. Edgard's surrender consisted of allowing himself to be tied naked to the slats in the horse trailer, standing, his ass level with Trevor's erect cock. Trevor had fucked him hard; hard enough bruises striped Edgard's thighs. Trevor fucked him twice like that, not letting Edgard come, making him beg. Then Trevor released the ropes and sucked Edgard off to the most explosive orgasm he'd ever had.

Thinking about Trevor sucking you off isn't helping you stay neutral about this situation.

Edgard willed his dick to quit pulsing, determined not to give into Trevor's need to provoke him.

Sex would be off-the-charts fantastic, a little voice prodded him.

No. The aftermath would suck. Not only would Trevor blame him for them fucking like dogs, but the person it'd hurt the most was Chassie. And they'd both hurt her enough already.

But Trevor didn't swagger in, full of fire. He merely walked to the far side of the stall, several feet away from Edgard and draped his arms over the top of the wooden partition.

Meridian was restless. She ignored her owner and flicked her tail in annoyance at nothing.

They didn't talk; they didn't fight. They didn't fill the void with chatter; they didn't hurl accusations back and forth. They just stared at the hay-strewn stall and skittish horse in hellish silence.

A solid twenty minutes passed. Edgard timed it in fifteen-second intervals so it stretched out like twenty hours.

When Trevor ran the back of his hand across his cheek where Edgard's beard had abraded the skin, another punch of guilt tightened Edgard's gut. "I'm sorry."

"I know."

Edgard let the moment linger. "So what now?"

"I dunno. Chassie left for a day or two. Said she needs time. Can't say as I blame her. This whole thing is majorly fucked up."

"But she is comin' back?"

"Says she is."

"Good."

Trevor finally looked at him. "Don't fuck with me, Ed. I ain't gotta lotta patience left today."

"I'm not." Edgard shoved a hand through his hair. "Look, honest to God, Trev, I didn't plan for that to happen. I just..." This was one of those times when translation was a bitch. He knew what he wanted to say, but couldn't find the words for it. "Given all the shitty things we used to do to each other, I'm sure you don't believe me."

Trevor spit tobacco juice on the ground. "Know the strange thing? I do believe you. Besides, we both knew it was gonna happen sooner or later."

Edgard was shocked Trevor had admitted that much.

"But see, I don't know how to handle this stuff between us any better now than I did three and a half years ago."

"You and me both."

More uneasy silence.

Finally Trevor sighed. "I can tell you got something else on your mind."

"How?"

Trevor gestured to the hand Edgard jammed in his hair. "That hair thing. You still do it when you're agitated. I remember you used to do it a lot around me."

Jesus. It killed him that Trevor hadn't been as aloof as he'd pretended. Or maybe Edgard had been so self-centered that he'd been aloof to Trevor's perceptiveness.

"So spill it since we're already hip deep in shit."

Edgard caught himself touching his hair and dropped his hand. "I want you like fucking crazy, Trev. That hasn't changed."

"I know."

"But do you know that I'm not gonna do anything about it?"

Trevor's suspicious gaze snared his.

"I won't be making moves on you while Chassie's gone."

That blue-eyed stare narrowed further.

"Betcha think that's contrary to my behavior today?"

"Maybe a touch."

Edgard laughed. "It's true."

"Lemme see if this washed-up rodeo cowboy has this right. You want me. You came all the way to Wyoming from Brazil so you could have me. Now that my wife knows what we used to be to each other, and she's gone...you're sittin' on your hands?"

"Uh. Yeah."

"I can't believe I'm gonna ask why, but why?"

"I'd actually hoped to feel nothin' when I saw you again. You are everything I remembered you to be, better actually, probably as a result of marrying Chassie. She is..."

"Is what?" Trevor asked sharply.

"Sweet. She doesn't deserve this. I never want to see that horrified look on her face again."

That comment sent Trevor back into full retreat.

Great.

After a while, Trevor said, "Know something funny? Chassie wants us to talk. She thinks it'll help if we get everything out in the open."

"So she doesn't realize that was our issue? That we couldn't be open?"

Trevor frowned. "First time you've said 'we' in that old argument, Ed. You always blamed me for us not holdin' hands and shit."

"I've learned the hard way maybe you were right about the

kinda baggage other people hide when they're showing a different face to the world."

When Edgard didn't elaborate, Trevor demanded, "You gonna explain that comment? Or you gonna sit there with that smug-ass look and make me guess?"

"Trying to explain it when you're in a piss-poor mood would be a waste of breath." Edgard gave Trevor a cool once-over. "And for the record, I'm not acting smug. I'm just as screwed up about all this with Chassie as you are."

"Right. I'm sure you're happy as shit."

Seething, Edgard snapped, "You never had the balls to tell me how you felt when we were together every goddamn day, so don't you *ever* fucking presume to tell me anything about the way I feel now when you haven't seen me for three and a half fucking years."

"I didn't mean—"

"Yeah, you did, so just drop it. Jesus."

"Fine."

"Fine," he retorted.

Meridian grunted and her tail slapped the wall again.

Time dragged on, yet there was no place Edgard would rather be than right there, even if they both were angry, frustrated and not speaking. Hell, it was practically normal for them.

Casually, Trevor remarked, "You're playin' with your hair again."

Edgard lowered his hand. "Sorry."

"Don't be. Long as we're bein' honest and chattin', all friendly like, I wanna know if you stabled a corral full of young studs durin' the last few years? Or did you just pick one stallion to ride?"

For claiming to be a plainspoken man, sometimes Trevor's verbiage confounded him. "A few one-nighters here and there. Guy named Reynaldo stuck around longer than most."

"How long?"

Edgard shrugged. "Less than a year. I wasn't sorry it ended, just the way it did." Rey's outburst, "*I won't spend my life in the middle of a fuckin' jungle with a dirt-covered rancher*", and Edgard had been glad to see the ass end of him.

"Bad break up with Reynaldo send you scurryin' back to

the States?"

Trevor's tone smacked of conceit and Edgard sought to shatter his cool. "No. Rey was a great fuck. Nothin' that boy wouldn't do in bed. He wanted a sugar daddy, a citified *papai* with deep pockets. When Rey realized it wasn't gonna be a free ride, he bailed to richer pastures. He never was worth a shit with the livestock."

"But I'll bet he was a pretty boy, huh?"

"Yep. Thought I'd try since that type ain't ever been my taste."

Trevor grimaced. "And yet, somehow I'm offended by that statement when I got no right to be."

"Sorry to burst your bubble, Trev, but you ain't been pretty a day in your life. You're hot as shit in that, don't-fuck-with-me-I'm-totally-hetero way, but definitely not pretty."

"This conversation is deteriorating."

"You brought it up."

"Yeah, I did."

"Turnabout is fair play. How many bunnies hopped on you in that same time frame?"

"Way too many. I could lie and say I was such a fucktard because I'd been drinkin', but mostly I was stone cold sober after the first six months after you left." Trevor picked at a chunk of wood in the gate top. "I was miserable drunk and miserable sober."

Edgard lived that existence too. "Damn good thing I barged my way back into your life and livened things up, eh?"

Trevor laughed. "Asshole. You always could make me laugh. Especially at shit that ain't funny."

How pathetic did it make him that Edgard lived for those moments of Trevor's unrestrained laughter?

"We had some good times, Ed. Easy to forget we were friends first. Even when we were nailin' each other at every chance, we were still friends."

"Sometimes I miss that constant companionship more than the sex."

Trevor appeared to be weighing his response—probably disbelief.

"What?"

"Speakin' of missin' companionship...she ain't been gone

an hour and I already miss her. We haven't spent a single night apart since I moved in."

Be petty to point out after Trevor and Edgard became lovers they hadn't spent many nights apart either.

"Think that's sappy? Think I'm pussy-whipped?"

"No. I'm jealous as hell. But if you get too lonely, remember, you can always crawl in bed with me. I'll warm the *cock*-les of your heart."

"Goddammit, you're offerin' to polish my pole after all that 'I ain't touchin' you' line of bullshit..." Trevor's voice trailed off when he noticed Edgard's big grin. "Real funny. You're a fuckin' riot, Mancuso."

"Just trying to lighten things up. I know this is serious stuff, but I'm tired of standing around doing nothin'. Don't you have fence post holes to dig or some menial, backbreaking, punishing shit work?"

Trevor rolled his eyes. "What part of livin' in the tundra is confusin' to you, jungle boy? The ground is frozen solid."

"There's gotta be other chores that need done."

"Trust me, there's plenty to do around here, especially with Chass gone."

Meridian neighed loudly and flopped to the ground.

"Shit." Trevor opened the door to the stall. "This's been goin' on for days. I have no idea what's wrong."

"Do you want me to call the vet?"

Trevor tossed off, "Can't afford it. You're way better with horses. You wanna give me a hand? Maybe between the two of us we can figure something out."

For the next few hours they worked side by side. Without sexual tension. Without covert looks. Without accidental touches. Just two ranchers doing a job that'd been a normal part of their lives, separately, but never together.

And for Edgard, it was enough. For now.

Chapter Nine

Chassie was such a basket case that she drove around for over an hour without remembering her destination.

Wheatland. For her friend Zoey's bridal shower.

Right. Like Chassie had any business passing out marital advice.

But she couldn't go home, not after she'd made such a point about needing time to sort things out. She could check into a motel. Hole up in misery and anonymity. Or she could drive to Denver and pour her heart out to her cousin Keely.

Damn humbling to realize she didn't have any place to go and few people in her life she could really talk to. Even if she claimed a dozen close girlfriends, the my-husband-is-in-love-with-another-man scenario smacked of an episode of *Jerry Springer* and wasn't a topic she felt comfortable discussing with anyone. She suspected whoever she told would tell someone else—in complete confidence of course—and that person would tell another person, and so on. The gossip, which Trevor and Edgard had managed to avoid for years, would run rampant.

Not to mention people would gape at her with pity. She'd grown up being the brunt of those soft-eyed expressions. First because she was mixed race, unclaimed by her mother's tribe and shunned by most of her father's relatives. Didn't help that Chassie's family history included her father, who'd built a reputation as a real asshole, her mother's status as a doormat, and the rumors about Dag before and after his tragic death. Chassie was the little half-breed with the weird name who'd worked herself damn near to death to keep a ranch her lazy father had never wanted.

Yeah, this situation would be the real kicker.

Gossip had run amok when Trevor Glanzer married her. Now that Chassie really thought about it, why had Trevor pursued her with such zeal? Because he couldn't be with Edgard? So he'd settled for her? Or because Trevor broke ties with his family and wanted a ranch to call his own? What would be an easier way to get quick land ownership than to charm the plain, simple daughter of a drunken fool? A lonely young woman who was set to inherit a ranch? A rundown ranch, to be sure, but it'd be a perfect place to start.

That possibility filled her with such nausea that she pulled along the side of the road and dry heaved. Chassie left the truck running and pressed her forehead into the steering wheel. Wouldn't solve anything to bang her head against the molded plastic as she repeated *dumb, dumb, dumb* to the empty cab but she wanted to do it anyway.

"I love you. I've never said that to another person. Think on that."

Maybe that's what hurt the most. Chassie believed Trevor really did love her. She'd hoped for once in her life she alone would be enough to make someone happy.

But even on the best days, didn't you sense that pocket of emptiness inside Trevor?

Chassie had chalked up those niggling doubts to them living in an isolated location away from his friends and Trevor's estrangement from his family. She'd never imagined he'd be pining for a lover. A lover he'd convinced himself he could not have.

A semi whizzed past, rocking her truck with a whoosh of cold air. She lifted her head and stared at the snow lining the ditches. Dread sat in her chest like a lump of coal as the drive to Wheatland loomed. She felt too raw to face party games, shiny new pans and the shiny new hope in Zoey's eyes.

Chassie dialed Zoey's number, apologizing about missing the bridal shower as she spontaneously concocted a lie about Trevor being sick. It put her back to square one. Nowhere to go and still wanting to talk to someone she could trust.

It hit her. Trevor said Colby knew the truth. She could talk to him. Dammit, he owed her after keeping this secret.

The line rang several times before Colby's wife Channing picked up with a breathless, "Hello?"

"Channing, it's Chassie."

"Hey. No, honey, I'm not going anywhere. Dang it, hang on a second." A cry, then the scratchy noise of a receiver being shifted. "Sorry. Gib is cranky and insists I hold him all the time. So what's up?"

"Is Colby around?"

"No. He won't be back until later tonight. He went to an equipment auction with Cord and Colt and his dad. What did you need?"

"Just to talk to him."

"You could try him on his cell."

Chassie fought the urge to cry. "No, that's okay."

"Chassie? Is something wrong?"

A sob was all she could get out through the tight feeling in her throat.

"Did something happen to Trevor?"

"Yes."

"Oh dear Lord, what?"

Don't cry. Be strong.

She cleared her throat. "Edgard came back."

Silence.

"Why didn't you tell me about them?"

Gib started to cry. Channing said, "Why don't you come over and we'll talk about it?"

"I'll be there in thirty minutes."

Not nearly enough time to formulate all the questions she had, but it was a start.

Channing and Colby McKay's log house was as enchanting and homey and perfect as a cabin from a fairy tale. A fire burned in the slate fireplace. The scent of sugar cookies and coffee wafted from the kitchen. Toys—trucks and horses mostly—littered the living room.

Chassie sank into the oversized chenille loveseat. Western art decorated the log walls, as well as a few pieces she recognized as her cousin Carter McKay's artwork. Hand knitted blankets in earth tones hung off the arms of the couch and the antique rocking chair. Children's books were stacked on the sturdy pine coffee table next to a box of crayons, a pad of paper, a plate of smashed up animal crackers and a half-eaten banana.

Channing came around the corner and paused. "More coffee?"

"No. I'm fine."

"Be right back." A minute later Channing plopped on the couch directly across from Chassie and adjusted her shirt over her pregnant belly. She propped her feet up on the coffee table with a big sigh. "Much better."

Chassie had spent time around Channing at various family events over the last few years. Her cousin's wife was sweet, thoughtful and almost too nice to be true. Colby worshipped her. So Chassie was struggling with how this woman would view the situation between her, Trevor and Edgard.

"Let's get right to it. Tell me what happened after Edgard showed up."

While Chassie talked, and talked some more, Channing refilled her coffee cup. Twice. Chassie realized Channing's up and down movement wasn't because the subject matter bothered her; rather it was as close as she could get to pacing without actually pacing.

After Chassie finished speaking, Channing handed her a tissue. "Thanks. I didn't mean to cry."

"I'd think it was odd if you weren't crying."

Chassie looked up. "Why didn't anyone warn me about Trevor's past with Edgard?"

"Anyone meaning Colby or I?"

She nodded.

"Because, sweetie, and this may be hard to hear, but the details about that past relationship isn't our right to share with you."

"How did you find out?" Chassie demanded.

Channing met her angry glare head on. "I'll tell you everything you want to know on two conditions."

"Which are?"

"You promise that what we discuss is never repeated outside this room. And you keep an open mind about what you hear and don't pass judgment on anyone involved until you've had time to think about it. Thoroughly."

Chassie figured that'd be the most difficult promise to keep. But she wanted to know so badly...no, she wanted to *understand* so badly that she agreed.

"You asked how I found out about Trevor and Edgard? I walked in on them having sex." Channing appeared to wait for Chassie's gasp of outrage, and when she didn't hear it she continued. "Long story short: Four years ago this summer, I wanted a wild Western adventure with a real cowboy. Colby said I could travel the circuit with them for ten days if I agreed to be their personal buckle bunny for all three men. Sometimes at the same time."

Chassie's jaw dropped. "You...and...Trevor...did it?"

"Yep. And me and Trevor and Colby. And me and Trevor and Edgard. And me and Trevor alone. And me and Colby alone. Obviously I clicked with Colby from the start." She smiled. "No regrets because it was about experiencing all the sexual situations I'd fantasized about."

Chassie reached for her coffee cup on the table and took a big drink to wet her dry mouth.

"Shocked?"

"Uh. Yeah." The true jolt of it would probably sink in later. Or would it be absorbed by the first, more brutal shock she'd had earlier?

"You are aware of Trevor's past sexcapades?"

"Yes. I honestly didn't care about who he was with before me." Chassie paused. "I'm not upset Trevor was with you, Channing. But I am shocked he wasn't only with women but also with men."

"Man," Channing gently chided. "Trevor hasn't been with any other man besides Edgard."

"You're sure?" Chassie gently chided right back. "Been damn near four years. How do you know Trevor hasn't been with another guy?"

"I looked in his eyes when he told me about falling for Edgard and I've never seen such confusion and raw anguish. What he felt for Edgard went against everything he'd ever known. Trevor couldn't give Edgard what Edgard needed, even when Edgard filled something in Trevor that Trevor needed. And Edgard couldn't stomach not being enough for Trevor, so Edgard returned to Brazil. Trevor wandered for a year or so. Made some tough decisions that'd been weighing on him for years."

"The situation with his family," Chassie said.

"Yes. Then he met you." Channing leaned forward but Chassie didn't have the guts to look her in the eye. "Trevor loves you, Chassie, don't doubt that."

"How can't I?" Chassie wiped her tears. "God. This is so fucked up."

"Yeah, sweetie, it is." Channing stood and returned to the kitchen.

Grateful that Channing had given her time to collect her thoughts, Chassie straightened her slumped shoulders, letting her head fall back onto the puffy couch cushion. She heard Channing return and settle across from her.

"Channing, can I ask you something that might sound a little stupid and paranoid?"

"Sure."

"Do you think Trevor married me because he felt sorry for me after my family died? Or do you think he married me because I inherited the ranch?"

"Neither. Did back-to-back funerals spur Trevor to pop the question faster? Probably. Not out of pity, but because he loved you, he wanted to be with you and he didn't want you to be alone."

"Do you really believe that?"

"Don't you?"

Chassie lifted her head and looked at Channing for the first time since they'd begun this conversation. "I don't know what to believe."

Channing didn't offer an opinion, she just waited.

"I love him. He's everything to me. So how can I go home knowin' he's always been pining for someone he can't have? Someone he didn't even have the balls to tell me he wanted? Now that he's broken with his family, there is a much better chance he'd consider it, right?"

"No. I'll repeat it. Trevor loves you. He's chosen to make a life and a home with you."

Doubts plagued her—was it really a choice he'd freely made? Even now as a do-the-right-thing cowboy, Trevor would stick with her out of guilt or out of loyalty.

Did Chassie want that? Would she take Trevor any way she could get him? Even if it meant Trevor was miserable?

She blurted, "What did you do when you walked in on

Trevor and Edgard havin' sex?"

"With both those glorious men naked? As I was gorging myself on all sorts of sexual experiences I watched them finish what they'd started. It was beautiful. Powerful. The hard bodies. The harder kisses. Strong and fast and a little mean." She frowned. "It surprised me that Edgard was dominant."

"No," Chassie breathed. "But Trevor is so...forceful."

Channing rubbed circles on her baby bump. "I'm not gonna lie. Seeing them together, lost in passion, was hot as hell. But it broke my damn heart to see how much affection they had for each other afterward. How they only dared express it when they were alone. I couldn't imagine not being able to touch or kiss or tease Colby whenever I wanted. I realized not everyone gets a happily ever after and it made me more determined to get one for myself."

Quiet pervaded as each woman was lost in her own thoughts.

Chassie drained her cold coffee. "I was half-afraid to leave them alone together today. Even after Trevor promised me he wouldn't touch Edgard while I was gone."

"Do you believe him?"

"Strangely enough, yes. But I have a sneakin' suspicion Edgard can be pretty damn persuasive."

"True, but I don't think Trevor will cheat on you."

She shot Channing a dark look. "He cheated on Edgard all the time."

Channing wagged a finger at her. "Ah-ah. Not true. Trevor was always up front with Edgard about wanting to be with women."

"Was Edgard with women too?"

"Yes. Not like Trevor and Colby, but Edgard played his share of bedroom games with the women who took all three of them on."

Maybe she hadn't imagined Edgard flirting with her. Or was his attention just a ploy to make Trevor jealous?

"One time he told me..." Channing shook her head. "Never mind."

"We're beyond *never mind*."

Channing's eyes were clouded with thought. "Once Edgard told me he wasn't bisexual. Insisted on it, actually. But I think if he was truly one hundred percent gay, he never would've been with women, no matter what Trevor wanted."

"But don't men think about sex differently than women? A hole is a hole and any old hole to put their dicks in will do at the time?"

A snorting laugh. "I suppose. I've known a few gay men who get all pissy when talk turns to bi men. It's the norm for them to diss 'switch hitters' wanting to have it both ways. But I'm more inclined to believe there are few pure gays out there. I believe you fall in love with the person, not their sexual organs. And sometimes it's not what is expected."

Channing's pause burned through Chassie's patience. "What?"

"What do you think about Edgard?"

"The first thing that pops into my mind?" Chassie paused and admitted, "I'm jealous."

"Of their past?"

"Sort of. Mostly it's because Edgard has a part of Trevor I'll never have. A part that was so special to Trevor he couldn't even tell me about it. And the flipside of that paranoid feeling is smugness, because I know if I demand Trevor send Edgard away, Trevor would do it. He probably wouldn't be happy. He'd secretly resent the hell out of me, but Trevor would do it." Frustrated, Chassie smacked the pillow. "Dammit. I wish I could just hate Edgard. It'd be easier."

"Why?"

"Besides the fact he wants to fuck my husband?"

"Chassie."

"Fine. The man is flat-out beautiful. That sexy Portuguese accent is hot enough to melt the polar ice caps. He's sweet. Lord, he's so damn sweet."

"I always liked that about him," Channing murmured.

"He's a damn hard worker. He's quiet, but it's a quiet strength, which is something neither Trev nor I have. He's refereed a couple of arguments between me and Trev, so he's got a diplomatic streak we're lacking."

"Edgard used to get pissed off if he thought Colby was being mean, or if either Trevor or Colby were putting me in a traditional role as cook, cleaner, and laundress."

Chassie drummed her fingers on the cushion. "You know,

that reminds me...Edgard was the one who calmed me down after I saw them kissing today. He's the one who urged me to stay and listen to Trevor when I tried to bolt."

Channing's eyebrows rose. "He was?"

"Yeah. Hell, he even apologized. Said he wouldn't do anything to hurt me." Chassie fell silent as all the questions without answers spun around in her head. "And it might sound stupid as shit, because it's in complete opposition to everything I've just said, but how can I ignore the fact that Edgard loved Trevor so much? And Edgard walked away from Trevor—even when it wasn't what Edgard wanted?"

"You can't. You shouldn't."

"Edgard loved Trevor enough to let him go." That idea sank in, low, seeping into the marrow of her bones and she shivered with raw fear. "God, Channing, I don't know if I could do that. I don't know what I'll do if Trevor decides he made a mistake marryin' me and wants to..."

"Wants to what? Leave you and run off with Edgard?"

Chassie nodded and wiped her cheeks.

"I won't try and convince you that's an irrational fear. But I will ask what you'd be willing to do to keep that from happening?"

"Anything." She repeated vehemently, "I'd do anything."

"Be more specific. What would you do?"

"You mean like go to counseling or something?"

Channing shook her head. "I mean would you really do *whatever* it takes to keep Trevor happy and with you? Even if the option he chooses isn't the easiest one for you? Or Edgard? Even if the solution is the best one for Trevor? Even if it's an unconventional solution?"

Chassie frowned, not following Channing's train of thought.

"Think of it in the terms of that old saying 'my friend's enemies are my enemies', not that you and Edgard are enemies."

"You're suggestin' something like...my lover's lover is my lover?"

"Exactly."

Her gaze flicked to Channing. "Whoa. All three of us? Living together in a...ménage?"

Channing nodded. "The French word *ménage a trois*

originally meant household of three, and it didn't just refer to sex as a threesome, but three people living together under one roof, so that...lifestyle choice has been around for a long time. It's nothing new."

"It's new to me! I'm supposed to consider welcoming my husband's former male lover into our life? And into our home? And into our bed? Sharing Trevor with Edgard? Just to make Trevor happy?"

"Stranger things have happened in the name of love, Chass. And you already told me you'd do *anything*. If you are serious then you'd better not discount the possibility because that is a reasonable, fair and possible solution."

"But...I can't fathom how much more complicated that'd make...well, everything." Wouldn't it? Wouldn't that be harder?

Not harder than losing Trevor for good.

A cry sounded from the baby monitor, startling Chassie.

"There's my boy. Think about it."

"I doubt I'll be able to think of anything else."

"Good. Be right back." Channing disappeared down the hallway.

Chapter Ten

Crazy thoughts spun in Chassie's head. How would a three-way relationship succeed for the long term? Dealing with sexual situations? And jealousy? Sleeping arrangements? Financial responsibilities? Raising a family with one mother and two fathers in a part of the country that shunned anything out of the norm?

From the monitor came, "Mama, Mama," and bouncing squeaks Chassie imagined were from Gib jumping in his crib at the joy of seeing his mother. Channing murmured and the boy giggled.

That sweet sound made her smile. Chassie definitely wanted children someday and she knew Trevor did too. Did Edgard? Or did he have that sneering "breeder" mindset so many same-sex couples had?

Thump thump thump. A little ball of energy barreled around the corner and ran straight at Chassie. Gib hit the soft couch cushion belly first, grabbed hold of the fabric in his fists and hoisted himself up. The boy didn't sit; he bounced. One, two, three times and the last bounce he landed on his diapered butt.

Chassie gasped and he giggled.

"Gib. No bouncing. I mean it."

He blinked innocently at his mother. "Daddy?"

Channing sighed. "Daddy's gone, so you're out of luck with his 'boys will be boys' parenting philosophy."

"This darlin' face is impossible to resist, Channing."

"Tell me about it." Channing straightened Gib's shirt. "Can you say hi to Chassie?"

Gib stared. No doubt the kid was all McKay. No doubt he'd be hell on wheels, a serious heartbreaker with those deep dimples, mass of unruly black curls and enormous blue eyes. When Gib said, "Hi," and crawled in her lap, Chassie melted...for the thirty seconds the kid actually sat still. He heaved himself to the floor and was off again.

"How old is he now?"

"Fifteen months. And yes, he's always like this. Busy from sunup to sundown."

Chassie glanced at Channing's belly.

"I'm five months along. When Gib was nine months old, I thought how much harder can one more kid be?" She smiled ruefully. "Then he started walking and getting into everything under the sun. I'm afraid he'll learn how to climb out of his crib next because it's the only place I can keep him corralled."

Gib ripped around the corner of the couch and stopped in front of Channing. He patted her stomach with both hands. "Baby."

"Yes, honey, that's the baby."

"Mine baby."

Her smile softened and she lovingly brushed the curls from his face. "Yep, he's your baby."

"You already know the sex of that one?"

"Even if the ultrasound hadn't confirmed it, I'd be pretty safe in planning for another boy. Kade's the only one who's produced a girl so far."

"Mama, Mama!"

"What, sweetie?"

Gib looked over at Chassie, challenging, "Mine mama," and threw himself at his mother.

Channing laughed with delight and hugged him close, kissing his rosy cheeks until that sweet, innocent, boyish giggle burst free again.

"He's a little territorial, isn't he?"

"Comes by it naturally. He gets it from his father." She stood and planted Gib on her hip. "Let's have a snack, hmm?"

For the remainder of the afternoon and early evening, Chassie was glad for the distraction of the rambunctious boy.

Chassie could tell Channing was tired and she felt guilty the pregnant mother elected to stay up with her after Gib finally conked out.

"Colby should be home any minute."

"Then you should go to bed. I'll be fine waiting up alone. Really."

"I know you will. But I'd like to see my husband while I'm still conscious." Channing closed her eyes and leaned her head back. "Did you call Trevor?"

"No."

"Does he know where you are?"

"He thinks I'm in Wheatland at a bridal shower." Chassie braced herself for Channing to gently suggest she call him, but Channing didn't say a word.

Chassie stared at the fire, trying not to think about how much her life had changed in one short day.

Tick. Tick. Tick. The minute hand on the clock clicked and the bell dinged. Yippee. She'd managed to kill thirty minutes.

She was sure Channing had fallen asleep, so she was surprised when Channing murmured, "You really should watch them together. When they're naked in body and soul. It's as heartbreaking as it is beautiful. Then you'll understand. Then you'll do the right thing."

Watch who? Understand what?

The front door opened. Boots hit the tile and Colby strolled into the living room.

Channing's eyes blinked open. She appeared sleep-dazed for a second until she saw Colby. Then she smiled widely and pushed to her feet.

"Hey, shug, no need to get up. But since you are..." Colby leaned down and kissed her. Thoroughly. "Mmm. Missed you today, darlin'. How you feelin'?" He placed his big hands on her belly.

"Tired. This baby's been twisting like he's on a bull."

"Poor Mama, cookin' up another wild cowboy." Colby rubbed circles on the baby bump. "Gib in bed?"

"He wasn't happy you weren't here to tuck him in and play horsy. But he settled for Chassie reading to him."

Colby finally looked at her. "Hey, Chass."

"Hi."

"I'm off to bed so you two can talk." Channing gave Chassie a wan smile. "Try to get some sleep tonight, okay?"

"I'll try. Thanks for lettin' me just barge in and cry on your shoulder."

"No problem. That's what family is for."

Family. Maybe for the first time she really thought of Channing as her family too.

Colby said to Chassie, "Hang tight. I could use a beer, you?"

"Yeah."

"Why don't you get them while I tuck my wife in. I'll be back in a bit."

Ten minutes later Colby returned. He tossed another log on the fire before he flopped across from her. He knocked back a drink of beer and sighed.

"Long day?" Chassie noticed Colby looked unusually exhausted.

"I hate bein' away from Channing because I know she's doin' stuff she ain't supposed to when I ain't keepin' an eye on her."

"Is everything okay with the pregnancy?"

Colby swigged his beer. "She's already had some contractions. Some spotting. She's not even supposed to be liftin' Gib, and that's the hardest thing for her not to do. She says it's normal, but I worry."

Shame swamped Chassie for busting in on Channing without warning and monopolizing her time. "I didn't know. I wouldn't have—"

"I'm glad you were here. Havin' company is a treat for her. Chan's been housebound with this pregnancy and Gib can be a real pistol."

"He definitely has energy to spare."

"That's my boy." Colby's grin was there and gone.

The logs in the fireplace crackled.

"I'm whupped, so let's get to it. When did Edgard show up?"

"Two weeks ago." Chassie purposely droned on so this retelling had less tears, figuring Colby wouldn't appreciate them. Truth be told, she hated to cry. It was so damn pointless, it changed nothing.

After she finished, Colby grabbed two more beers. He appeared to be in a mental tug of war as he slowly peeled the label from the bottle.

"Why didn't you tell me?"

"I'm sure Channing already explained, since she and I are on the same page. But I'll say it again." Colby looked at her. "It's not my secret to share. I imagine you feel a little betrayed by me too."

Chassie nodded.

"Trevor and I've been best friends since kindiegarten. We weathered some rough shit together. I have four brothers, and they're great, but Trevor's like the brother...I chose. And it's the same for him, bein's that everyone in his family is a complete dickhead."

"I've heard about his family but I haven't met them."

"Consider yourself lucky," he said derisively. "If it threw me for a goddamn loop when I figured out him and Edgard were more than ropin' partners, I can't imagine how them assholes in his family woulda reacted. I didn't pass judgment, mostly because I didn't understand. That said, I still covered for them on the circuit and no one ever found out."

It pained Chassie to ask, but she did anyway. "Do you think Trevor and Edgard were in love?"

"Ah hell, Chass, how am I supposed to answer that?" Colby downed half his beer.

"I'm dyin' here. I found out the man I love, the man I married for Christsake, had a long time love affair with another man that I knew nothin' about."

Colby brooded for a bit. "Lemme ask you something. Would it've been better or worse if a woman showed up knockin' on your door?"

"Worse," she said automatically.

"Why?"

"With Edgard, I suspect it isn't the same type of love Trevor has given me. It's completely different. Separate. It doesn't have anything to do with the way Trevor loves me."

The truth of that statement hit her hard as a hammer to the head. Was it possible she wasn't jealous about Edgard, just hurt because she hadn't known about him? Chassie met Colby's stare.

"Think on that statement very carefully before you make any rash decisions."

She opened her mouth. Closed it. She couldn't argue with

that.

"How long's Ed here for?"

"I don't know. He's been evasive whenever I've asked."

"That's weird." The beer stopped midair. "He and Trev haven't talked at all about Ed's place in Brazil?"

"No. I thought it was kinda strange that Trev was avoidin' bein' alone with him and avoidin' personal conversation. Now I know why."

"How are things goin' with you and Trev at your homeplace?"

"Good, I guess. Takin' it day by day."

He picked at the beer label. "You heard anything about Gus Dutton sellin' his place south of yours?"

Chassie was a horrible liar. She settled for hedging. "What've you heard?"

"That his kids and grandkids never visit and he's tired of bein' alone since his wife died. He ain't run any cattle for a few years." Colby pinned her with a shrewd look. "You leasin' his grazin' land?"

"We did this past summer. Why?"

Colby shrugged. "Curious. Sweet piece of dirt with all that creek frontage. Me'n Cord have been eyein' it the last coupla years, and Dad for a while before that. We'd be mighty interested in givin' old Gus a little better than fair market value for it."

I'll bet you would.

She stood and studied the orange flames reflected in the glass fireplace panes. "Thanks for talkin' to me. I don't have anyone to talk to about this. I'd never hurt Trevor. Even as I'm standing here practically bleeding inside, I would protect him at all costs."

"I know you would. I know he feels the same way, even though it probably don't seem like it." Colby reached for her hand and squeezed. "Good night, little cuz."

"'Night."

Chassie crawled between the flannel sheets. Channing's rambling, *"You really should watch them together when they're naked in body and soul. Then you'll understand, then you'll do the right thing,"* ricocheted in her head, mixing with the other gut-wrenching images she couldn't erase.

The desperation in their kiss. The anguished longing as they'd stood pressed forehead to forehead in the corral. The murmured words. Their guilt. Their sadness.

As Chassie drifted into the realm between asleep and awake, she knew what she'd have to do. She just hoped she'd have the courage to ask and the guts to survive it.

Colby was dead tired. He'd spent all day worrying about leaving Channing alone as he faced another McKay family situation. Lying to his wife didn't sit well with him. She'd been mighty upset regarding Edgard's surprise reappearance in Wyoming and Chassie's not-so-surprising impromptu visit. He had an aversion to upsetting Channing with more bad news.

All that coupled with ten hours spent with his brothers, staring at each other like a bunch of idiots as they waited for word. Compared to stressful days like this, it'd been easy getting thrown off the back of a bronc or a bull.

Stay out of it. It ain't your concern.

Like hell. He'd always felt guilty about Chassie. She was a sweet, hardworking woman who'd lived with family drama and disappointment. The gossip of her brother's not-so-secret preferences was partially what'd justified Colby to keep the truth about Trevor and Edgard under his hat. He'd seen what a few missteps and rumors had done to Dag's career. When Dag started losing, then Dag started drinking. It'd spiraled from there.

Dag's fatal accident sent Uncle Harland to an early grave. But had the crises sent Chassie into the arms of the first man who noticed her?

No, Trevor hadn't taken advantage of Chassie. Trevor was a decent, honest, hardworking guy. A good guy.

A good guy who's been mooning for another man for years.

Fuck. Colby couldn't let it slide. Not this time.

He propped his feet on the coffee table and hit speed dial number four on his cell phone. It rang once.

"What the hell are you doin' callin' me at eleven at night, McKay?"

"I got some stuff to say to you. Stuff that can't wait."

"What kinda stuff?"

"It has to do with your wife."

Chapter Eleven

Trevor's grip increased on his phone. "What are you talkin' about?"

"Where's your wife, Trev?"

I don't know.

When he hadn't heard from Chassie, he'd panicked and looked up her friend Zoey's number in Wheatland. She'd informed Trevor that Chassie had called with her regrets earlier in the day. So Trevor looked like a fool for not knowing the whereabouts of his own wife.

Trevor admitted he and Chassie had a tiff before she'd left and she wasn't answering her cell. He'd jokingly offered the soon-to-be newlywed advice: never drive away mad. It seemed to allay Zoey's concerns.

But not Trevor's.

He'd paced all damn afternoon, troubled something might've happened to her. Edgard suggested they check her favorite local haunts and the silent drive through the snow-covered county roads proved fruitless, as did the scan of the diner, the feed store, all three of the town's honky-tonks. Trevor was half-afraid Chassie'd hit the interstate for Denver and the comfort of her cousin Keely McKay.

As much as Trevor liked Keely, she was the dead last person he trusted with the secret of his past with Edgard. He suspected hotheaded Keely would suggest Chassie dump Trevor and move on. Then Trevor realized if Chassie hadn't gone to Keely, his phone call would tip Keely off something was up between them.

So he did nothing. Worried sick about his wife, he'd tried not to punch holes in the wall to mark his hourly frustration.

"Trevor? You still there?"

"Yeah." He stalked to the window and glared into the inky darkness. "To be honest I don't know where the hell Chassie is. I'm goin' fuckin' crazy, man."

"Take a deep breath, buddy. She's here."

Trevor's heart rate doubled. "Chass is there?"

"Yep. Channing said she'd been here most of the day, talkin' to her and playin' with my son."

"Jesus, that's good news." He pressed his forehead to the cold glass and closed his eyes. "Thank God she's okay." His stomach pitched. "She is okay, isn't she?"

"Not really. She's seriously fucked up about you and Edgard."

His sick feeling intensified. "She told you?"

"Who else was she gonna go to? Chassie's hurtin' big time. Why the fuck didn't you come clean with her when Ed first showed up?"

"I don't know." *Liar. You didn't tell her because you were afraid this'd happen; she'd leave you.* "I thought maybe..."

Colby snarled, "Maybe? I'm pretty goddamn sure you knew exactly what'd happen with you and Ed, no *maybe* about it. It sucks that Channing and I had to fill in the blanks about personal shit that should've come from you. Should've come from you a helluva long time before now."

"You think I don't fuckin' know that?"

"No. I think you don't know which way is up when you get within a foot of that Brazilian, not to mention not havin' a fuckin' clue as to what to do about this situation with your wife."

"Why don't you tell me what I should do?"

"Man up."

Trevor snorted. "*Man up?* For Christsake, what kind of bullshit advice is that, McKay?"

"I'll make it plain as day. Forget about livin' up to anyone's expectations or ideals but your own. Do the right thing for the first time in your life."

"Are you suggestin' I...let her go?"

"I'm just sayin' it's an option if you ain't got the balls to admit what you really want to her or to Ed. I'd rather see her heartbroken and able to move on, than miserable, livin' a fuckin' lie. *Your* lie, not hers."

"But—"

"But nothin'. I'm done talkin'. She's comin' home tomorrow. You'd better be ready to deal with this, 'cause we both know it's been hangin' over your head for years." Colby hung up.

With deliberate care Trevor closed the phone. He didn't move, just watched his hot breath leave jagged patches of steam on the cold windowpane. He sensed Edgard behind him, even when Edgard didn't utter a sound.

Finally Trevor turned around.

Edgard retreated, keeping a healthy space between them, his gaze somber. "She's okay?"

He nodded and saw Edgard's posture relax.

"Thank God."

"Guess she asked Channing a buncha questions. Played with Gib all day." He smiled faintly. "Chass does love babies."

"She mentioned wanting a brood of her own."

"When did she tell you that?"

Edgard shrugged. "Before you get bent out of shape, I'll remind you I've hung out with Chassie a lot in the last two weeks. Way more than I have with you." His gaze searched Trevor's face. "What else did Colby say about...?"

Trevor narrowed his eyes. "About us?"

"No, about the situation, because it hasn't been about 'us' since you met Chassie, regardless if I was here or not."

"But you are here now. And I hope you ain't suggestin' that your showin' up out of the blue had nothin' to do with Chassie takin' off today."

"Is that what you want, Trevor? For me to admit fault?"

Dammit all to hell, he'd gotten trapped by the pain in Edgard's eyes once again. He shook his head.

Edgard sighed. "If I would've stayed in Brazil this wouldn't have happened. But you cannot stand there and tell me that this situation is one-sided."

"You kissed me, remember?"

"Distinctly."

Trevor's cheeks heated. "What was I supposed to do?"

"Push me back with disgust. Knock me on my ass. Scream that I'm a perverted fucker." Edgard threw up his hands. "Jesus. You should've threatened me. Become enraged by the insult that I imagined even for the slightest moment you might like fucking me. Demanded I get the hell away from you and never come back. But you didn't do any of those things."

I couldn't. God help me, I didn't want to.

"Would you have acted angry and offended if you'd known your wife was watching us?"

I don't know.

"Are you sorry I'm here?"

I don't know.

Edgard rubbed the heel of his hand on his forehead. "Don't answer. I don't know if I could stand it if the answer was yes."

"Didn't you tell me you were prepared for my rejection from the minute you showed up?"

"Yes."

Trevor wanted to shake the answers out of him. "Why?"

"I'd already lost everything in my life that mattered to me, so I stupidly thought I had nothin' else to lose by coming here." Those golden eyes flickered. "I was wrong. So very, very wrong. Pointless to discuss now. I'm goin' to bed though I doubt I'll get a lick of sleep."

"Jesus, Ed. You can't drop that on me and walk away."

"Yeah, I can. I'll see you in the morning." Edgard ducked through the kitchen doorway. The stairs creaked without pause and his bedroom door locked with a click of finality.

The house was silent. Trevor had never felt more confused or alone.

The sun's pinkish rays lit the horizon, ending Trevor's night of tossing and turning. No need to dress since he'd slept in his clothes. Half a pot of coffee later, he headed out to do chores.

When he returned to the house, Edgard sat at the kitchen table. The man always looked damn fine in the morning, freshly showered, wearing clean, crisply ironed clothes, his cheeks and jaw shaved smooth as a baby's butt, a spring in his step and a sparkle in his eye. Annoying, really.

But today Edgard looked a little worse for the wear. Dark circles emphasized his tired eyes, stubble coated his angular face, and he wore the same clothes as yesterday. He mumbled into his coffee cup. Edgard's usual chipper self must've slept in.

"How's Meridian?"

"The same."

"What do you need done this morning?" Edgard blasted Trevor with a warning look. "And don't say nothin'. It'd be an insult to Chassie because I know she works her ass off before noon."

What the hell? Ed was being protective of *his* wife? "I already fed the cattle."

Edgard lifted a brow. "This early?"

"Yeah. I couldn't sleep."

"Chassie didn't call?"

Trevor shook his head. "Thought I'd get all my shit done early so we'd have time to talk when she comes home."

"Sounds like a plan. Where were you off to?"

To pine over another thing I can't have in my life.

Jesus. That sounded pathetic. Trevor twisted a version of the truth. "Our neighbor to the south is thinkin' about sellin' his place. He's given us first shot at it. Still hush-hush."

"I take it there are other folks who'd want that piece of land?"

"A few. Kind of an Old West code, if you like your neighbors, you offer it to them first. But it ain't like we'd get it cut rate. Gus's usin' the money to live off for the rest of his life, so I got no interest in screwin' him out of a fair deal."

"But?"

"But I don't know if Chass and I can afford the down payment, say nothin' of the buyout price." Embarrassed, Trevor scowled. "Thought I'd head over and see how he's doin'."

"You want company?"

"Yeah, I'd like that."

Edgard smiled. "See? That wasn't so hard."

Rather than step in another nest of snakes, Trevor snagged his coat and headed outside.

Once they were in the truck, Edgard asked, "Who're the other neighbors who could meet the asking price?"

Trevor threw it in reverse and gunned the engine. "That's what sucks. Gus's neighbors on his south end are the McKays."

"Colby?"

"McKay is McKay around here. Their massive ranch crosses the borders of several counties and employs the sons and cousins and a half dozen or so ranch hands. Buyin' that acreage is a fart in a windstorm for them. But for Chass and me, it'd be a way to guarantee we can make a go of it."

Silence.

He could feel Edgard's gaze burning into him. "What?"

"How soon does Gus need a guarantee you have the funds?"

"That's what I'm aimin' to find out today."

Edgard nodded and went silent again.

Gus Dutton's place had gone to seed in the years since his wife passed on and his offspring decided they were too good to ranch in Wyoming. Still, Trevor couldn't imagine why Gus'd move to the desert to be with those ingrates.

Gus ambled onto the sagging porch and hobbled down the steps. "Mornin', Trevor. Where's the missus?"

"Weddin' shower in Wheatland."

"Pity. She's a mite easier on the eyes than you are." He jerked a thumb to Edgard. "Who's that?"

"This is my old ropin' partner, Ed Mancuso. Ed, this is the orneriest coot in the county. Which was why he and Harland West were such good buds."

Edgard thrust out his hand. "Nice to meetcha, Gus."

"A roper, eh? You any good?"

"Used to be. I ain't competing any more. But them rope skills do come in handy on the range."

"I hear ya," Gus said. "So what brings ya by, Trevor?" He rubbed his gnarled hands together in exaggerated glee. "Got earnest money for me?"

Trevor grinned even when his face felt encased in plastic. "Come on, Gus. You were married for a helluva lot longer than me. Chassie's the one with the checkbook."

Gus grinned at him. "Always knew that pretty little gal was the smartest of the West lot." Gus focused his rheumy eyes on Edgard. "You a rancher around these parts too, now that you ain't travelin' the circuit no more?"

"Not exactly."

Gus squinted suspiciously at Edgard. "Where'd you say you was from again?"

"He didn't say, but Ed's been livin' on his ranch in Brazil."

"Brazil, as in South America?"

Edgard scowled. "Well, more specifically—"

"—specifically he was born right here in Wyoming," Trevor interjected and relayed the sad tale of Edgard's mother and father and his family connection.

Gus was appropriately wide-eyed. "Hell, boy, why didn't you say you was related to the Bordens out by Cloud Peak? I knew your grandpa and your grandma. Good people. Your last name ain't Borden?"

"No, sir. My stepfather adopted me when he and my mother had their first child, so I'd have the same name as my siblings. My middle name is Borden."

"Good enough. Now you fellas wanna take a look around?"

"If it wouldn't be too much trouble."

"No trouble a'tall. We'll take your rig, Trevor, that way I can point out the interestin' stuff to Ed."

The tension mounted in Trevor's truck when Edgard slid into the middle of the cab, right next to him, with Gus on the outside. To make matters worse, the stick shift was centered on the floor so Edgard had to straddle it, putting one foot on Trevor's side and one on the passenger's side.

Edgard scooted in, leaving about a foot between them.

"Move in," Gus instructed. "I need a little extra room to stretch my bum leg out."

The truck bounced as Gus hoisted himself in and Edgard's left thigh pressed Trevor's right leg.

"Ah. Much better, huh?"

Trevor turned his head the same time Edgard did. His eyes locked on those full lips. Dammit. Edgard's mouth was so close he could smell his sweet-coffee breath. His gaze traveled up the line of Edgard's nose and connected with yellow-brown eyes.

There it was. That jolt of something deeper than lust.

"We goin' or what?" Gus demanded.

"Yeah, we're goin'," Trevor said, breaking the moment. Putting the stick shift in gear, right between Edgard's legs, Trevor's fingers brushed close enough to feel the heat drifting from the crotch of Edgard's jeans.

They were going all right. Straight into the mouth of temptation. And just Trevor's luck; this time he was in the driver's seat.

Don't get a hard-on. Don't get a hard-on.

But with Trevor's muscular thigh rubbing against his, and the almost constant necessity for Trevor to shift, Edgard fought a losing battle. His cock was so sensitive he feared Trevor's palm on his crotch would send him over the edge.

"See that?" Gus said. "Used to be a stock dam. So dry the whole damn thing dried up." He chuckled at his own joke.

"Where else do you have water?" Edgard asked.

"Miller's Creek. Snakes through the canyon, but there's a couple flat places the cattle can get to."

"Does the same creek run through Chassie's and your place?"

Trevor shook his head. "Our stock dams are about in the same sad shape. We do have a natural spring, which means we don't hafta haul as much water, but no creek frontage."

An additional water source would be worth the price of the land. Edgard knew out in the high plains desert, access to fresh water was a higher commodity than gold. No wonder the McKays were so hot to have it.

"Hey, swing by the old homeplace, would ya?"

"Where is it again?"

"Down that embankment. Whoa. Right. Hard right."

"Shit. Hang on." Trevor cranked the wheel, which sent Edgard crashing into him with enough force he had to brace his hand on Trevor's thigh.

Gus was too busy laughing to notice Trevor's surprised gasp.

Don't squeeze that firm thigh. Don't do it.

Edgard briefly let his fingers trace the inside crease of Trevor's jeans as he pushed off to return to his own space.

The simple move seemed to rattle Trevor.

But Gus was running off at the mouth again so the moment was short lived.

For the next two hours the trio bumped across the frozen ground. Each directional shift sent them careening into each other, and if Edgard could believe his eyes, the zipper on Trevor's jeans bulged more than normal.

As much as Edgard would love to pretend the feel of half of Trevor's body rubbing against his, whether accidental or on purpose, was foreplay, it wasn't. And he'd do his part to keep

Trevor's promise to Chassie even if it damn near killed him.

"So whatcha think of my place, Ed?"

"If I say I don't know why you'd wanna live anywhere else, Trevor and Chassie would both shoot me."

"That ain't an answer," Gus pointed out.

"I know." Edgard grinned. "But it's the best you're gonna get outta me, Gus."

Back at the ranch, while Trevor used the bathroom, Edgard finagled the answers he needed from Gus on a couple of things.

Then they were off, on their way home.

Finally Trevor said, "Gus is old school. But I'm surprised he didn't ask you more questions about your operation in Brazil. He lives for shit like that."

"It ain't as interesting as it sounds. Ranching is pretty much the same world over."

"What were you two talkin' about when I came back outside?"

Edgard shrugged, not willing to divulge anything yet. "Just shooting the breeze. He has an opinion on everything and needed to share it with me. I figure he's pretty lonely."

"I reckon. He and Agnes were married for sixty years, so I can't fathom why he'd leave this place and never look back."

"It seems his decision will work out good for you."

Trevor snorted. "If we can convince the banker we're a good risk."

Edgard drummed his fingers on his knee. "Would you consider asking your family for the money?"

"Fuck no. I ain't gonna be beholden to my pa for nothin'."

"Even if it means letting the McKays have the land?"

Trevor brooded. Fiddled with the radio station. Messed with the heating system vents. Finally he sighed. "I don't know. Askin' Tater would be a last resort. It sucks ass."

It wouldn't be a last resort for me. I'd love to suck your ass.

Great. He'd finally managed to get rid of his hard-on only to stir it up again with that debauched visual. He shifted uncomfortably. "Who's helping run your dad's place?"

"My brother Brent. Such a kiss up. I never liked him. Pa knew it, which was why he put Brent in charge when I threatened to leave."

"Threatened?"

"Old bastard didn't think I'd do it. When he pulled that 'I'm cuttin' you out of the co-op' threat, I called his bluff. Told him to do whatever he wanted. Brent took over, so I left." The corners of his mouth twitched. "But not before I knocked that pussy on his fat ass."

Edgard laughed.

"I ain't been back since."

"No contact with anyone at all?"

"Minimal. My other brother is on the circuit. Brent will do whatever Dad tells him to do. My sisters and their freeloadin' husbands are just as bad. So I figure I ain't out much."

"They know Chassie?"

"About her? Yeah. Met her yet? Hell no."

"You know I ain't a big fan of your family, but that seems...odd."

The muscle in Trevor's jaw bulged. "My asshole father called me, drunk as shit, and announced I'd dropped to the bottom of the peckin' order, except he called it the 'totem pole', when I married a red-skinned...shit, I can't even repeat it." His hands curled around the steering wheel. "Chassie heard."

Edgard's stomach dropped. "Oh, Jesus."

"Tater Glanzer can be a dickhead to me all he wants, 'cause I'm used to his meanness. But when he brought my sweet wife into it? He went too far. Even if he was drunk off his ass and probably don't remember nothin'."

"I can understand why you'd stay away from them."

"Can you? I thought your family was all rainbows and butterflies and I'm-okay-you're-okay happy shit."

Trevor turned off the main road and they started up the long driveway.

"Maybe at one time. Things change." Sadness, anger and grief spun in Edgard's head. Here was his chance to come clean with Trevor about what'd gone down in his life in the last year. "Sometimes things change one helluva lot. Sometimes leaving is the only option."

He braced himself for Trevor's questions, but the man kept his eyes forward and he knew why Trevor hadn't responded. Chassie's truck was parked in front of the house.

Trevor barely put it in park before he jumped out of the truck and barreled up the steps into the house.

Edgard stared at the aluminum screen door and listened to the engine clicking as the motor cooled. "Sometimes leaving is the only option," he repeated, knowing saying it out loud didn't make it any easier to do.

Chapter Twelve

The door banged open. Chassie turned just in time to see Trevor running—*running*—toward her.

He swept her into his arms, peppered her face with kisses, muttering, "Thank God you're home. I missed you. Baby, I missed you so damn much. Don't ever leave me again."

She wrapped herself around him and held on. Breathing him in. Listening to his heart thundering beneath her ear. Renewing her vow to do whatever it took to keep this man she loved in her life forever.

Trevor said not one word; his actions spoke volumes. His palms smoothed over her hair and down her neck. Hands followed the contours of her shoulders, her spine, the curve of her hips and the globes of her ass, then his fingers trailed back up, starting the process all over again. Feelings of love, reverence, hope, possession, apology, passion, fear, need...all there solely in his touch.

A shuddering wiggle of her body caused Trevor to drop his arms as if he feared he'd been crowding her.

Chassie rose up on her tiptoes and brushed kisses on the sexy cleft in his chin. Once. Twice. Three times. Her lips meandered up to his mouth, where she whispered, "I missed you too," and she devoured him in a bruising kiss.

Trevor let her lead for a change and it felt damn good. She dragged hot, openmouthed kisses down the strong column of his throat, loving the way he tasted there, loving the scent of his sweat and really loving his soft, helpless groan when her tongue touched a sweet spot at the base of his neck.

"Chassie, we need to—ouch!"

Her lips curved into a smile after she'd bitten him.

"What was that for?"

She blinked at him innocently. "What? That little love bite?"

"Little? Christ, woman, I think you drew blood."

"Poor baby." Chassie kissed the red mark. "That's what'll happen every time you try to talk. I don't want to talk."

The front door opened. She half-expected Trevor to jump back (with guilt?) but he didn't move. She pressed her lips to the other mark before she spun around.

Edgard paused on the rug.

What was he waiting for?

For you to prove you don't have a gun aimed at his head for being in love with your husband. Make the first move.

"Hey, Edgard."

His smile was warm, lighting up his entire face. When the glow reached his eyes, the hazel tones were transformed into a mellow gold. "Hey, Chass."

She couldn't help but return that beautiful smile.

"I'm glad you're back."

"Are you?"

Trevor didn't speak. He appeared to have quit breathing.

"Yes, I am." Edgard looked at Trevor. "Might I borrow the truck for a little while?"

"Where you goin'?" Chassie asked as Trevor tossed the keys over.

"I want to check on my pickup in person and light a fire under them to get going on repairs." He shifted his stance. "There are a couple other things I need to do before I leave town."

"Leave?"

Edgard's gaze zipped to Trevor, but Trevor kept his focus on Chassie. "Yes. Why?"

"Because we need to sit down and talk tonight. All three of us, before there's any serious talk of leavin'."

After a long pause, Edgard nodded. The door shut with a soft click.

Without another word, Chassie hooked her finger in Trevor's belt loop and towed him upstairs to their bedroom. She locked the door and leaned against it.

Her take-charge husband stood in the middle of the room like he was facing a firing squad.Trevor's pale blue eyes were wary, his normally full lips flattened in a thin line. Jaw clenched, neck muscles tight, even Trevor's broad shoulders were hunched almost to his ears. He jammed his hands in the front pockets of the dirty jeans he wore. "What now?"

"Strip."

Trevor opened his mouth, reconsidered and snapped it shut. He doffed his clothes quickly.

"Lie on the bed. On your back. Close your eyes."

He rolled down her grandmother's star quilt. The bed creaked and a buck-ass nekkid Trevor stretched out on the sheets without complaint.

Chassie undressed and crawled on top of Trevor so they were skin-to-skin. Back to basics, nothing between them but breath and bones. Shuddering heat rolled off him, not solely from desire, but from relief. She rested her head on his chest, situating herself so the sharper planes of her body wouldn't injure any of his vital parts.

After a minute, he circled his arms around her. She didn't chide him for his presumption; she took comfort in the feel of his body against hers from head to toe.

Despite their combined body heat, her skin cooled quickly. When she shivered, Trevor shifted and pulled the quilt up over both of them. Even beneath the covers his fingers lightly stroked her back. Like he couldn't touch her enough.

Chassie's eyes drifted shut. She floated into sleep; his muted whispers in her hair a sweet lullaby.

She awoke disoriented. The shadows and light in her bedroom indicated afternoon, not morning. Had she overslept?

Callused fingertips skated up her arm.

Chassie lifted her head and stared into Trevor's sleepy blue eyes. "Whoa. Time warp. How long was I asleep?"

"I don't know. I drifted off right after you did."

"How long have you been awake?"

He smiled. "Long enough to come up with a plan to seduce my very sexy wife."

"You know what they say about the best laid plans..."

"*Laid* bein' the word I can work with, bein's we're both nekkid."

She trapped his hips between her knees and dangled on all

fours above him. "Maybe I don't want your seduction."

The pulse in his neck jumped. "Ah. Okay. I'm willin' to wait until you're ready...to talk or whatever."

"Really?"

"Uh-huh."

"Good. Because you were startin' to piss me off, Trev."

"Sorry."

Chassie lowered her face until their lips were a hair apart. "Maybe there ain't any seduction involved. Maybe I just wanna be a little mean. Maybe I want sex on my terms."

Trevor's loud groan disappeared as she thrust her tongue into his warm mouth, licking at every inch until that's all she could taste—Trevor on her lips, rolling over her tongue, flowing down the back of her throat, filling her up.

When his arms moved, she expected he'd latch onto her shoulders and flip her to her back. She anticipated fighting him. Being forceful and more than a little harsh appealed immensely, but those strong hands gently cradled her face and Chassie was lost in his tenderness.

Yet, Trevor wasn't completely passive. His cock bumped against her belly, leaving a slick, intimate kiss. The muscles on his body's lower half were tensed, primed and ready for action. She did the unexpected and rubbed her toes down the outside of his calves.

His upper body bowed off the bed. Trevor's breathing was decidedly ragged as his lust-filled blue gaze caught hers.

Chassie pressed a moist kiss to the vulnerable spot below his ear. When goose bumps broke out across his flesh, she did it again. And again. Breathing on the spot until Trevor could scarcely lay still. She zigzagged her tongue over the curve and hollows, stopping to nibble on corded tendons.

Still hanging above him, she shimmied backward and kissed the dark blond trail arrowing the way to her destination. She didn't detour to tease his nipples. She didn't plunge the tip of her tongue into his belly button. Or nip the tender skin between his hipbones; she kept a southward progression.

"Chassie. Baby. You don't have—"

She angled her head, placed her teeth on the inside of his left thigh, and bit. Hard.

"Fuck!"

"I can do a matching one on the other side if you wanna keep talkin'?"

He shook his head.

"Good. Watch me."

Chassie licked up the length of his shaft.

He hissed.

She poised her lips at the weeping tip. Her tongue darted out and circled the plump head. She felt the slick pre-come on her tongue, but didn't taste it. Just let the wetness build—hers, his—until her mouth was watering. Then she swallowed his cock in one smooth, deep gulp.

Trevor's hands fisted into the sheets and he bit his lip to stop from crying out. Or from swearing like a sailor, as she sucked and deep throated him exactly as he liked it.

Having his cock in her mouth always made her wet and ready. Although this foreplay was minimal, she didn't want to wait. Chassie scooted up, aligned her sex to his and sheathed his cock to the root.

"Uh, ah," burst from his mouth instead of words.

Her palms were flat on the mattress by his head and his hands were still clenched in the sheets. She put her lips on his ear. "Trevor. Touch me."

Immediately those working-man hands she loved were on her shoulders and sliding down her back.

A shiver of desire prompted her to move on him, a gradual push until that stiff organ was buried deep. A side-to-side grind teased her clit perfectly, a slow slide as that male hardness eased out.

He said gruffly, "Kiss me while you're lovin' on me, Chass. Please."

She rocked on him slow and easy; the kiss was languid and sweet. They were adrift in the pleasure of the friction of damp bodies, the gentle creaking of the old bed, the familiar scent of skin and sex and body-warmed cotton sheets.

When Trevor's body tightened beneath hers, he broke the kiss. She gloried in hearing her name repeated on his lips as his pelvis arched, bathing her insides with heat. As she bore down, prolonging his orgasm, prolonging the moment when he belonged only to her, her own release tumbled her straight into the abyss with him.

Keeping their intimate connection, she nestled against him and closed her eyes.

They might've dozed. They might've fallen into the blank space where lover's time is static.

Trevor kissed the top of her head. "You warmed up now?"

"Mmm."

He whispered huskily, "I love you."

"I know."

"You do?"

Chassie lifted her head from the warm haven of Trevor's chest. "Yes, I do. You loving *me* is not the issue."

"I figured." Trevor tugged on her braid, wrapping the thickness around his palm. "I didn't sleep much last night. I wandered up here and went right back downstairs to crash on the couch." He smooched her wrinkled brow. "Alone. I couldn't stand that you weren't here. It was like part of me was gone. I've never been so goddamn happy to see your piece of shit truck as I was when we pulled up."

"Sweet talker. Where were you guys?"

"We headed over to Gus's to take another look. Don't know why the hell I torture myself."

"You told Edgard about us wanting to expand?"

"Yeah. Asked his opinion. Come to find out Gus knew Ed's grandparents."

Chassie kept her expression neutral. The bit about Wyoming being rife with coincidence and everyone knowing everyone else wasn't as unusual as closed-mouthed Trevor discussing their private business with Edgard. "What was Edgard's take on the land?"

"Find any way to buy it. Even if it means borrowin' from my pa." Trevor scowled. "I doubt the old man would consider a short-term loan, even when I know damn good and well he's lent my siblings money to build their places. I'm almost scared if I tell Pa what the money is for, he'll suck up to Gus and buy it right out from under me, just so he can fuck up my life."

That statement wasn't Trevor being paranoid. From what he'd told her, Chassie wouldn't put any dirty, nasty trick past Tater Glanzer when it came to getting the upper hand on his offspring.

"But, it don't matter none, 'cause unless you've hidden a

winnin' lottery ticket someplace, we're fucked. Ain't no way we can come up with the down payment."

"Trev. It's okay."

"No, it ain't." A bitter snort stirred her hair. "I'm some great catch, ain't I? Never made enough from rodeoin' to buy more'n a lousy horse trailer. I'm livin' on your ranch. I can't find the money to buy Gus's acreage. And my former partner—no less than a male lover—shows up and you realize I've kept a pretty goddamn big secret from you. Hell, Chass, maybe Colby was right. Maybe you are better off without me."

"Colby said that?"

"Not in so many words."

Chassie placed her hand over his mouth. "This ranch isn't mine; it's ours. You've cared more in the last two years than either Dag or Dad did in the last twenty years. This is our home, where we get to make the rules. Yeah, I'd like to have Gus's land, but if we don't get it, then we weren't meant to have it. All things happen for a reason."

He gave her a considering look. "Do you really believe that?"

"I do. Just think, if you hadn't filled in on the circuit as Dag's partner, we wouldn't have met. I wouldn't have been able to keep the ranch by myself after Dag and Dad both died. So after we got married this place became ours. And havin' you in my life is worth way more than any piece of land."

Trevor kissed her. "And you wonder why I love you so damn much." His eyes flickered to the window. "And what about Edgard showin' up? You think that happened for a reason? You haven't changed your mind about my worth?"

"I ain't gonna lie, it knocked me for a loop." She managed a small smile. "Might sound stupid, but yeah, there is some cosmic reason Ed showed up now. I'm workin' on understandin', Trev. I really am."

"That's all I can ask." He kissed her again, and gently separated their bodies. He sat on the edge of the bed and looked over his shoulder. "Why don't you laze in bed a bit longer? Get some shut-eye and I'll finish a couple things." He dressed and slipped out of the room.

Chassie snuggled beneath the covers and was glad to be home, even if everything in her life, all her perceptions and misconceptions about love were about to change dramatically, whether she was ready for it or not.

Chapter Thirteen

A spicy aroma greeted her as she entered the kitchen. "That smells great."

Edgard turned. "Hope you don't mind me taking over your kitchen."

"Mind? I hope you don't mind if I lay a big, wet, sloppy kiss on you for fixin' supper."

A strangely hopeful look flickered in his eyes. "I wouldn't mind that at all."

Before she lost her nerve, she walked over to him and kissed his cheek. "Thank you. Trevor has a lot of great qualities, but cookin' ain't one of them."

"Did he wow you with his chili? Or his recipe for cowboy beans, which actually is—"

"Chili," they said in unison, and then laughed in unison.

"Needless to say I do all the cookin'."

"Does that bother you?"

"Not at all. Why?"

Edgard shrugged. "Because in this day and age lots of men cook. I like to cook."

"Have you always cooked?"

"My mother made sure I knew the basics and I took it from there. I lived by myself and it was either learn to cook, or I'd be eating spaghetti, chili and frozen burritos forever." He shot her a considering look. "It's no longer the norm around here? Sticking to those old gender roles?"

"Not at all. See, it's not that Trev and I are stickin' to traditional roles in this marriage, but I'm better in the kitchen than he is. I don't mind, since I can't fix machinery worth a damn." Chassie peered at the pan on the stove. "But if you tell me that's a pot of chili, I'm gonna brain you with the lid."

He grinned. "It's not. It's Brazilian style stew."

"Whatever it is, it smells damn good. Thanks."

"You're welcome."

"Where's Trevor?"

"Had to help Gus with something."

"Oh." Chassie glanced at the clock. Her nap had lasted longer than she'd expected because it was almost five o'clock. "Would you like a beer?"

"If you're having one."

"Yep." Chassie planned on having a whole lotta beer. She definitely needed alcohol to get the conversation started and probably an entire case to follow through with her plan. She took two bottles of Bud Light from the door and passed one to him. *Snick, hiss, pop* echoed, as the lids were untwisted.

Edgard's backside rested against one counter; hers on the one across from him. She gulped her beer, cautioning herself to be tactful and calm, but what burst forth from her mouth was, "Are you in love with my husband?"

He visibly paled. And knocked back an equally big swallow of Budweiser in lieu of answering.

"I've heard Trevor's side. I talked to Channing and to Colby. So that leaves you."

"And if I say yes, Chassie? What then?"

"I'm totally thinkin' we have a gunfight in the street to determine who's tough enough to win Trevor's affections," she said lightly.

That brought a slight smile. "You are a smartass."

"And you are avoidin' the question, *meu amigo*."

"Jesus, do you know how hard it is to look at you and answer that question?"

"No harder than it is to look you in the eye and ask it."

"Touché." Edgard picked at the label. "Do I love him? That's what I came here to figure out. Or if I'd given so much importance to the memory of him—to the memory of us—that I wasn't able to move on."

"Like you'd somehow...glorified your past?"

Edgard nodded. "I seemed to remember only the good times. And because we weren't public about our relationship, there were plenty of bad times."

Chassie inhaled a slow breath. "This ain't me bein' cruel, but I hafta ask. Did you honestly believe he'd take you home to meet his folks and you'd settle down on a little ranch, just the two of you?"

"No." Edgard let the bottle dangle between his fingers and repeated, "No. Never. That's one of the reasons I left. I realized Trevor could never be for me what I needed."

"Is that another reason why you're here? To see if I'm enough for him??"

Those honey-brown eyes met hers. "Yes."

"Have you come to a conclusion?"

"Not even fucking close. I'm more confused than ever."

"That makes two of us."

Silence stretched as they pretended to drink their beer.

Finally Chassie broke. "I told Channing it'd be easier if I hated you."

Edgard studied her. "You did?"

"Yeah."

"You really don't hate me?"

"No. Are you shocked?"

"Completely."

"I actually like you." She swigged from the bottle. "Ain't that a kick in the ass?"

"I guess we're even on that account, because there's something mighty likeable about you, little Chassie."

She snorted. "Little." Then she drained her beer and slammed the empty on the table, avoiding his gaze. "Jesus, it sounds stupid in my head, and it'll sound even dumber when I say it out loud. But I can see why Trevor was drawn to you."

Edgard stiffened up.

His defensive posture made her blurt out, "It ain't only that GQ cover model face and smokin' hot body you've got goin' on. You are like him in so many ways. Yet so different. You complement him. Not in the same way I do. And that doesn't seem like such a bad thing. And I can't believe I even think that, let alone said it."

The air crackled with tension.

"That isn't helping clear up my confusion, Chassie."

"I don't give a flying fig if it is or not. It needed to be said."

"Got anything else that needs to be said?"

"Yeah."

"Then spit it out."

She didn't answer. She didn't know if she could.

The dryer buzzed in the cellar.

"Look at me."

Chassie shook her head, hating how the demand wrapped within his silken command caused her heart to pound faster.

Then Edgard was in her space. His hand cupped her jaw, forcing her head up. "You do not get to drop that bomb and then pretend you didn't light the fuse as you're standing there holding the match."

"That fits, because I feel like I'm walking through a goddamn minefield when it comes to this. None of this makes sense. You're in love with my husband and despite those warning signs I could actually lose him, I'm..."

"What? Tell me."

"I'm not sorry you came."

Edgard's gentle grip increased. "Are you messing with my head to get back at me because of my past with Trevor?"

"No."

"I'm supposed to believe that all of a sudden you just accept..." His eyes burned with suspicion. "I see the lie in your eyes."

"Not a lie."

"Bullshit."

"What you see is insecurity and determination to see this conversation through, but not a goddamn lie because I'm bein' completely honest with you. And myself."

"And with Trevor? Does he know you intended to start this conversation?"

"No."

"Why not? Didn't it come up during pillow talk after you spent all afternoon fucking?"

"Jealous?" she taunted softly.

"Like you wouldn't fucking believe."

Tears welled in her eyes. "Stop. You're hurting me," she whispered.

Edgard's hand dropped like it'd become dead weight.

Chassie wilted against the counter. Blood pulsing. Vision

115

blurring. Confusion screaming in her head.

Several brutal seconds passed.

His eyes focused on where her fingers rubbed on her jawline. "Let me see."

"It's fine."

"Then let me see it."

She lowered her hand.

He winced. "Shit. I'm sorry."

"Don't worry about it."

"I do. Jesus. Looks like Trevor ain't the only one with a mean streak. You've been nothin' but sweet and thoughtful to me since the minute I arrived. And how do I repay you when you have the *coragem* to confront me about all this confusing shit?" His rough finger traced the hot, sore spot. "By manhandling you."

Her stomach flipped at his gentle touch.

Edgard murmured, "I'm sorry, *querida*, so very, very sorry. Sometimes I can be a total ass. I'd say I learned it from Trevor, but I think he learned it from me." His warm lips skated over her jawbone in a teasing, soft kiss meant to soothe, meant as a sweet apology.

If it was just an apologetic kiss, why did her skin tingle? Why did her pulse beat like a trapped bird's? Why did she consider angling her throat, urging him to explore every ridge and hollow with those beautifully full lips?

Why in the hell didn't he stop?

And then he did. Edgard practically jumped backward.

They stared at each other in absolute uncertainty without speaking.

That's when Trevor walked in.

Chapter Fourteen

"What the hell is goin' on?"

Chassie snatched the empty beer bottle from the table and took it to the garbage can. "Nothin's goin' on."

Trevor turned to Edgard...who blinked at him innocently.

It'd looked like the two of them had been about to come to blows. Over what? Him?

Maybe you're imagining it.

No. There was tension crackling between Chassie and Edgard. But if neither one would come clean, then he wasn't about to push the issue. Enough issues lingered between them.

"What's for supper?"

"Edgard cooked." She paused. "Chili, I think."

Chassie and Edgard exchanged a look, then burst out laughing.

Weird.

Edgard said, "It's Brazilian stew."

Trevor frowned at Ed. "What the hell is in that?"

"Whatever is leftover in the fridge and a can of stewed tomatoes."

"Sounds good. You guys ready to eat?"

Chassie pointed at the sink. "Soon as you wash up. You want a beer?"

"No. Water's fine."

"Ed?"

"Water is fine for me too."

Once the food had been dished up, they gathered around the table and ate in silence. Trevor peeked at Chassie out of the corner of his eye. She was on her third beer, which was damn strange since she rarely drank more than one.

Edgard shoved his empty bowl to the middle of the table. "I talked to the mechanic this afternoon."

Trevor paused mid-bite. "And?"

"And I'll be good to go day after tomorrow," Edgard said, fiddling with his napkin.

Trevor almost demanded, "Already?" but he cautioned himself to stay cool. "They say how much the repairs'll run ya?"

"Five hundred."

"That ain't bad."

They talked specifics on the repairs, delving into the minute details neither of them gave a shit about, just to keep the conversation going. Just to avoid discussing what Edgard's leaving really meant.

After five or so minutes of senseless car chatter, Chassie slapped her hands on the table, startling both men. "Enough. There's been enough goddamn secrets, lies, and skirting the goddamn truth. No more. We're gonna talk this through, startin' right now."

"Chass, I don't think—"

"Do you want Edgard to go?" she demanded.

Trevor's gut clenched at the thought of Ed leaving again. But how could he admit that? Out loud? To his wife? He studied the checkered tablecloth.

"Fine. If you can't be honest, maybe he can." Chassie focused on Edgard. "Do you want to leave here? And I'm not talkin' about Wyoming. I'm talkin' about our home."

Edgard's gaze zipped from Chassie to Trevor and back to Chassie before he shook his head.

The tightness in Trevor's body faded.

"I'm pretty sure Trevor doesn't want you to go. But this conversation is over if he doesn't have the balls to admit it to you or to me."

Their gazes burned through him, incinerating his damn pride. He looked up, right into Edgard's eyes. "I don't want you to go."

If Trevor thought his admission would loosen the tension in the room, he was sorely mistaken. The sticky silence went on.

The furnace kicked on, breaking the still, heated air.

"Bizarre as it might sound, it was what I wanted to hear."

Chassie finished her beer in one greedy gulp and reached for another. "Let's get to it."

"Get to what?"

"You know. *It*."

"Baby, you've been hittin' the Bud a little hard—"

"So? I needed the liquid courage."

Trevor frowned. "Liquid courage for what?"

A determined glint shone in Chassie's eyes. "To tell you that I want to see you and Edgard together."

"See us together...how?"

"See you together sexually."

His eyes threatened to pop out of his fool head. "Jesus, Chassie, you can't just—"

"Yes, I can and you'll damn well let me finish. I wanna watch you two touchin' each other. Bein' together like you used to be. As lovers."

"Why?" burst from Trevor's mouth before he curbed it.

"Channing told me how beautiful it was watchin' you guys. I need to see it for myself. Maybe then I'll understand."

Trevor swallowed his disbelief as he reached for Chassie's hand. He didn't speak for a bit.

A disgruntled, "What?" tumbled from her pursed lips.

"You were ready to kick me out yesterday after just seein' Ed kissin' me."

"Ah yeah. I know."

"It made you jealous. So you think you can handle seein' what we are when we're really together? Sexually? As lovers?"

Chassie looked straight at him. "I want to try."

He considered her.

"What? You don't believe me, do you?"

Trevor shrugged. "Hell, if you remember, you offered me to Ed at one point yesterday, sayin' you were done with me."

Edgard snorted softly.

A feeble smile appeared on Chassie's face.

"Then you asked me *not* to be with Ed while you were gone. Which I respected." His eyes cut to Edgard. "Which we both respected."

"I know that too, Trev."

"So how am I supposed to believe you want me to be with

him now? How can I believe you ain't gonna change your mind?"

"I said things out of anger because I was hurt. Because it was such a shock that I didn't know anything about him or how you felt then or now." She tried to dislodge his hand but he held tight. "It didn't have to be a shock. You could've told me."

"You're wrong, Chassie. Telling you would've served no purpose," Edgard said.

After Edgard spoke, her gaze zoomed to him. "Why?"

"If Trevor couldn't admit how he felt about me to *me*, or even to himself, what chance did he have of explaining it to you so you understood? Especially when he knew how much that declaration would hurt you?"

"It would've hurt no matter what. With all the confusing thoughts runnin' through my mind, one thing stuck out, one thing haunted me."

"Which was what, baby?" Trevor asked.

"Longing. I saw it on your face. I saw it on Ed's face. I didn't understand it. But I had seen it before. Off and on since the first time we met." She squeezed her eyes shut. "Made me think of my brother because I'd seen it on his face too goddamn many times to mention. I never knew what it meant when he'd get that far off look. Now I think I do. If Dag would've trusted me, if he would've trusted one person in his life, one person that he didn't have to lie to, one person who would try to understand, one person who loved him no matter what he did, or who he loved, would it have made a difference?"

"I don't know, but you can't beat yourself up about that, Chass."

"Too late, even when I can't go back and change the past. Not Dag's past, not the past you two shared, but I can go forward. We all can go forward. Start fresh."

Chassie opened her eyes. "Neither of you used my absence last night as an excuse to be together like you both longed to." Her laugh was soft and sob-like. "It sounds crazy, but I know neither of you want to hurt me, you'd rather hurt yourselves again and I can't live with that either. So seeing you two together is what I've come up with to start. If either of you has a better idea, I'm all ears."

Edgard snatched her free hand. "So if Trevor and I are together tonight, what does that mean for tomorrow night? And the nights after that?"

"I don't know. I wish I could guarantee I won't have a screaming, hissy jealous fit at seein' your hands on him, Ed. But the only thing I can promise is that for tonight, it's not about me. It's about you two. What you bring to each other. I won't stand in your way, I won't pass judgment. I won't participate, I'll try like hell not to interrupt. I'll just be there watching."

Edgard's eye caught Trevor's and the pure heat caused his desire to escalate and his cock to harden.

Still, Trevor held that split-second of doubt. Was Chassie doing something that'd hurt her in the long run just because she knew it was what he wanted now?

The greedy part of his brain screamed, *Why are you questioning her motives when she's given you a goddamn green light—go go go!*

"You understand if I start touchin' him tonight, I won't be able to stop."

Chassie nodded.

"Good." Edgard softly kissed Chassie's hand and set it on the table. He stood. Before he even turned toward Trevor, Trevor was out of his chair and on him.

Their mouths met in a furious kiss. Trevor trapped Edgard's face in his hands. He inhaled Ed's whole mouth like a sumptuous feast, making up for the mere crumbs he'd tasted the day before.

For the longest time they remained plastered body-to-body in a deep lip lock. Reacquainting themselves with the urgency of long denied desire and endless, unstoppable kisses.

Edgard pulled away with a gasp, resting his forehead to Trevor's. His entire body shook. He clutched Trevor's arms as the breath sawed in and out of his lungs.

Trevor smoothed his hands over Edgard's silken hair, repeating, "It's okay."

"I wanted...I needed..."

"I know."

"I never thought..."

"Me neither."

"I'm...I can't believe..."

"Same goes." He traced the shell of Edgard's ear with his

thumb. "I'm here. We're both here."

Edgard seemed to regain control. He lifted his head and pressed his mouth to Trevor's. "Let me have you first."

Trevor's belly muscles tensed with anticipation and his cock jerked against his zipper.

"Now." Clasping their hands together, Edgard led them out of the kitchen and into the living room.

The fluorescent bulb in the ceiling bathed the room in bright white, making Trevor feel as if he'd stepped from the darkness into another reality.

They stopped in the center of the room in front of the couch. Trevor heard the springs squeak a second later, but when he turned to see if Chassie had followed them, Edgard's fingers on his jaw kept him facing forward, facing only Edgard.

His gut clenched. It was impossible to look away from Edgard's triumphant eyes.

"Do you know how many times I jacked off to this fantasy? Trying to decide what I'd do to you first if I ever had the chance again?"

Trevor shook his head.

"Sometimes I rip your shirt open, sucking your nipples while I give you a handjob." Edgard placed his lips on the side of Trevor's neck. "Sometimes I get your jeans down around your knees, then rub our cocks together until we both shoot on your belly. But the one I wanna fulfill now? Having your cock in my mouth." Edgard's breath drifted hot and damp over the collar of Trevor's shirt before he stepped back. "Clothes off."

The plain white T-shirt sailed over Trevor's head. He managed to unbuckle his belt. His knit boxers hit the floor the same time as his jeans and he kicked them away. Last thing to go were his socks. Then Trevor stood naked in front of Edgard, his cock erect, his face flushed, waiting and wanting.

"Ranch work agrees with you." Edgard flattened his palms on Trevor's pecs and held them there for a second before slowly sliding his hands to Trevor's ribs, landing solidly on his hips. Amidst openmouthed kisses Edgard murmured, "I wanna keep kissing you. I wanna keep touching you."

"I'm good with that." Trevor felt rough-tipped fingers roving down the outside of his leg and his cock twitched when Edgard dropped to his knees in front of him.

Firm male lips tickled the coarse hair on his thighs, back

and forth in an erotic arc until Trevor trembled. "You like that."

"You know I do." Trevor grabbed his cock with his right hand and Edgard's hair with his left, forcing Edgard to look up. Brushing the sticky cockhead over Edgard's parted lips, he said, "You wanna suck it, you're gonna suck all of it." He cupped Edgard's jaw, pushing his chin down and slid his shaft in halfway.

A moan reverberated up the length of his dick. While Edgard sucked, he slipped one hand between Trevor's legs.

Trevor withdrew, warning, "No ass play. No strokin' my balls. Mouth on my cock, hands on my thighs."

"Whatever you want."

"Open wide." His hips snapped and he was buried balls deep in that blistering wet heat. Trevor didn't move, he gave himself permission to feel. Edgard's lips stretched around the base of his cock and his tongue stroked the underside of his shaft. The warmth of Edgard's body radiating from beneath his clothes. The need to create that explosive friction had Trevor pulling back with the intention of slamming deep.

But Edgard wasn't ready to release him. He sank his teeth into the hard flesh just enough to keep Trevor's cock in place, digging his fingers into the tops of Trevor's thighs.

Trevor growled. He absorbed the sensations, the liquid heat surrounding his cock increased as Edgard's mouth filled with saliva.

Finally Edgard swallowed. The movement constricted the muscles around the head of his cock at the back of Edgard's throat and sent a shockwave to his balls.

"Christ. Like that. Again." Trevor held perfectly still, allowing for that mouthwatering buildup as his cock throbbed.

This time Edgard swallowed with more gusto.

Trevor groaned, sliding his hand down Edgard's face, sweeping his thumb across the hollowed section of Edgard's cheek. "No more teasin' me." When Edgard's eyes glittered with that same overriding need, Trevor whispered, "Not a power thing. Because I'm dyin' for my turn." He pulled out slowly, prolonging the light scrape of teeth on the underside of his shaft.

"Hard. Hard and fast," Edgard panted. "Like you used to, like you want to."

Curling his hands around Edgard's head, he yielded to lust.

Every rapid, wet stroke brought him to the point of detonation. When his legs wobbled, Edgard steadied him even as that clever mouth destroyed him. His balls nearly disappeared they drew up so high and tight.

"Close. Jesus. Ed. Please. God. Now." Trevor realized he had a death grip on Edgard's head and let his left hand fall to his side.

Edgard never missed a beat as he reached for Trevor's hand and threaded their fingers together, resting their joined hands on Trevor's thigh.

It wasn't the raw suctioning power of Ed's eager mouth, or the wickedly accurate tongue that sent Trevor over the edge, but the understanding, the acknowledgment, the simple touch of Edgard's rough-skinned hand in his.

Trevor came in hot spurts, the sensations so intense he could only verbalize his enjoyment in a series of grunts. Edgard sucked in time to every pulse of his cock, prolonging the pleasure until Trevor's entire body quaked.

"Stop," he said hoarsely. "Jesus, Ed. Stop." His spent cock slipped free from Edgard's mouth, shiny, damp and red. Sated.

Edgard nuzzled the crease between Trevor's crotch and thigh, trying to catch his breath.

With the fingers of his free hand twisted in Ed's silky, dark hair, Trevor allowed the quiet moment to soothe him.

"Trev."

He glanced down and Edgard clasped his forearm and rolled to his feet. Edgard's compact, powerful body was right in front of him, their hands still clasped together.

The gold disappeared from Edgard's eyes and they darkened to black. His lips, always temptingly full, were ripe and lush and trembling. Trevor softly said, "Hey," and angled forward. He nibbled and teased Edgard's mouth before diving in for a full-out, tongue-tangling kiss.

Trevor tasted himself on Edgard's tongue. It was a darker flavor than Chassie's mouth after she sucked him off.

Chassie. Guilt swamped him. First time he'd thought of his wife since he'd touched Edgard.

He broke the kiss in small increments. "Your turn. Strip."

Chapter Fifteen

As Edgard yanked off his T-shirt and pants, he wondered how far he could push Trevor in front of Chassie. In the past Trevor had been content to let Edgard lead, especially at the beginning of their sexual relationship. He'd watched Trevor fuck enough women to know Trevor preferred to be dominant. After what he'd seen in the barn between Trevor and Chassie, that preference still held true.

Part of Edgard's dominance had been an attempt to win Trevor over. To convince the stubborn man what they had inside and outside the bedroom was worth keeping. Now with Trevor married to Chassie, had his need for control changed?

Dismissing his brooding as pointless, Edgard glanced over at Trevor. Those pale blue eyes filled with appreciation and heat. Those strong, callused hands were clenched in fists by his naked flanks. When Trevor allowed his gaze to travel the full length of Edgard's body, Edgard forced himself to stay still, even as he willed Trevor to make the first move.

Trevor did. He ran a single blunt fingertip from the middle of Edgard's throat in a line straight down to the tip of his cock and back up. Slowly. Then he slid his palm down to Edgard's sternum and spread his fingers out like a starfish. "I forgot how your chest hair felt against my skin," he murmured, almost to himself.

I didn't. Touch me. Put your goddamn hands all over me.

Edgard might've voiced those demands in the past. Not now. Now he needed Trevor to show him the pace he could handle. So as Edgard's breathing grew more labored and his cock grew harder, he waited.

And Trevor sensed Edgard's restraint. He sidled forward.

"So in your dirty fantasies, Ed, what'm I doin' first? Fallin' to my knees?" Trevor's hand skimmed Edgard's torso as he spoke. "Or am I jackin' you off?" Then that strong hand closed around Edgard's cock and tugged. "Or do you just bend me over the couch from the get-go?"

"Are those my options?"

Trevor chuckled against Edgard's shoulder. "Maybe we oughta start out with option number two and work our way around the wish list?"

"Uh. That'd be—" Edgard gasped when Trevor's work-roughened fingers stroked his balls, while firm lips traced the arc of his collarbone. "Whatever you want."

"Why you handin' me the reins, partner?"

Edgard angled his head as Trevor's lips traveled up the slope of his neck, letting the feel, the scent, the nearness of Trevor consume him.

"You afraid Chassie can't handle seein' me takin' what you love to dish out?"

"It crossed my mind, *sweet Jesus*, I like having your mouth on me."

"I know." Trevor nipped Edgard's earlobe hard and growled, "I ain't hidin' anything of what we do from my wife. Like you said, we've come this far, ain't no sense in turnin' back now and pretendin' it ain't what it is. Tell me what you want."

Just like that, domineering Edgard reappeared. "Suck my nipples while you're jacking me off." Edgard fisted his hand in Trevor's hair and pushed Trevor's face to where he wanted that eager mouth on his chest.

A thick growl escaped as Trevor licked the flat disk.

Edgard couldn't tear his eyes away from the contrast of Trevor's pink tongue against the darker tones of his nipple. The sound of Trevor's contentment when he rubbed his cheek on the furred mat covering Edgard's chest burned into Edgard's ears like his favorite song.

Then Trevor stopped worrying the nipple with his teeth and switched to the other side.

"I want your mouth," Edgard said.

"Where?" Trevor lifted his head.

"On mine." He and Trevor were nearly the same height, which made the change easy as Trevor continued the handjob.

The kiss wasn't as frantic as earlier. But it was long and slow and deep. Edgard hungrily ran his hands over every section of Trevor's skin he could reach. Edgard had dreamed of this day so many times he didn't expect he could stop himself from coming fast. And it boggled his mind how quickly they'd picked up that old rhythm—as if they hadn't been apart. That idea spiraled Edgard's need higher.

But it was Trevor who dissolved the kiss. "You're close, Ed. Come on. Give it to me. Let go. I've got you."

"I'll give it to you." Without warning, Edgard removed Trevor's hand from his cock and shoved Trevor to his knees.

Trevor grabbed Edgard's hips. He swallowed Edgard's cock an inch at a time, letting the wetness work him clear to the root.

It was pure, sweet heaven seeing his prick buried in Trevor's mouth. The fringe of dark lashes fluttering as he closed his eyes. The high color on those high cheekbones. His nostrils flaring as he attempted to regulate his breathing.

No, Trevor hadn't forgotten how to make Edgard lose his mind. Edgard sampled other men who had the cock sucking technique down to an art, but Trevor's raw enthusiasm turned him inside out.

"More," Edgard said. "I need more."

Trevor's head bobbed faster in shallow strokes. His tongue and lips worked Edgard's cock while Trevor's hand worked his balls. His saliva-slick middle finger rubbed the sensitive ridge of skin leading to Edgard's hole.

A tingle rocketed down Edgard's spine, gathering steam between his legs and shot straight out the end of his cock like supercharged jet fuel. He pumped his pelvis, wanting to feel the entire length of his cock enclosed by that wet heat.

But Trevor clamped his hands on Edgard's hipbones, keeping him in place. He wrapped his lips halfway up his shaft, sucking every spurt, then tonguing the tip of Edgard's twitching cock.

Blood rushed to Edgard's head; his vision dimmed as black and white spots danced beneath his lids. His limbs felt heavy, his body woozy. In the back of his mind, he wondered if Chassie would think him less-than-manly if he passed out in the face of such pleasure.

Pleasure provided to him by her husband.

Edgard opened his eyes and noticed his fingers were gripping Trevor's hair. The soft strands were a dozen diverse shades of blond, giving Trevor an angelic look. Coupled with Trevor's devilish grin...and Edgard had been a goner from the first smile.

A smile Edgard saw immediately after his cock slipped free from that smirking mouth. "Good, eh?"

"Very good, *meu amor*."

The sound of Chassie shifting restlessly on the couch behind them brought Edgard out of his orgasmic stupor. He slid his fingertips down the outside of Trevor's face. His thumbs tenderly stroked Trevor's strong jawline.

Trevor pushed to his feet. Edgard expected him to back away, so it shocked the hell out of him when Trevor circled his arms around him and buried his damp face in Edgard's neck. His admission, "Jesus, I missed you," was nearly inaudible.

But it was loud enough to lodge in Edgard's heart and his soul.

As much as he craved the affectionate side of this man, Edgard lifted Trevor's face and pecked him on the mouth. "Same goes. But Chassie needs you. Go to her now."

Another quick kiss and Edgard retreated, snatching up his clothes and heading upstairs without looking back.

Chapter Sixteen

"Where's he goin'?" Chassie said just to break the awkward silence.

"He's givin' us some time." Trevor crouched in front of her. His eyes searched hers, the pale blue irises clouded with concern. "Talk to me, baby."

When Chassie didn't respond, Trevor curled his hands around her hips, jerking her forward. His quick movement surprised her so much she flinched. Dammit. She hadn't meant to do that.

The muscle in Trevor's jaw rippled, a sign he'd clenched his teeth together.

She reached for him, the need to soothe automatic. She took time to glide her hand up his arm, wanting the contact of his skin on hers. "Trevor, you startled me, that was all. I wasn't recoiling from your touch."

"You sure?" Trevor's scrutiny was the most intense he'd ever given her. "I don't want no secrets between us."

"I'm sure. It was..." Were there words to describe how she'd felt at seeing her husband's unadulterated joy at being with another man?

"Was what?"

"Not what I expected."

Trevor's face inched closer. "Explain that right now."

"I thought I'd hate it. Before, in the kitchen? When we were just talkin'? I figured I'd probably jump in and put a stop to it if it was more than I could handle."

"You didn't stop us."

"No. Part of me was relieved."

"Why?"

"Because now I know it isn't me."

He squinted at her. "What wasn't you?"

Chassie focused on the continual stroke of her thumb over the cut of muscle in Trevor's biceps. "You have a voracious sexual appetite, Trev. I understood that when we hooked up. And I...well, I told you I wasn't overly sexually experienced."

"That never bothered me, just like it didn't bother you that I'd been with more'n my fair share of women. Even some women you're good friends with."

"I know. It's just sometimes, right after we'd made love or had sex or whatever, you'd get this far off look in your eye. You didn't realize you even did it. Bein' paranoid, I had it in my mind that I hadn't measured up and you were disappointed in me in bed and didn't want to say anything."

"Chassie, baby, you know that's not—"

"Let me finish." Chassie mustered the courage to look in Trevor's eyes. "Today, after seein' this, I realize that was wrong. You weren't critiquing my performance. You weren't even thinkin' about me, were you?"

He briefly squeezed his eyes shut and blinked them open. "Fuck. I'm sorry."

"Don't be. Like I said, I'm more relieved than anything."

"Relieved? That I was thinkin' about another...man?"

"Crazy female logic, right? It hurts, yeah, but it probably makes no sense when I admit I'd be even more freaked out if it were a woman lodged so deeply in your thoughts."

A scowl distorted his face. "But now?"

"But after seein' you and Edgard together, I understand you get something from bein' with him, something I can't give you, even if I become the perfect lover. You do the same for him. There's a need. There's a connection. I saw it and it felt a lot more like love than experimental man-lust from your past." When Trevor's eyes darted away, she demanded, "I'm right, aren't I?"

"You askin' me if I love him?"

Chassie shook her head. "I'm tellin' you I'd understand if you did."

A heavy pause lingered before Trevor met her eyes.

Her stomach lurched at the raw emotion he didn't bother to

hide. "Jesus, Chass. What did I ever do to deserve you?"

They'd suffered enough emotional turmoil with no clear solution, so she strove to lighten things up. "Maybe the question oughta be what should you do to keep me? I need reassurance you find me as enthralling as the Brazilian. Because, darlin', he is one smokin' hot specimen of man flesh."

Trevor frowned.

Chassie wasn't finished. "You've got that All-American boy next door look, tall, built and handsome, with your tousled blond hair, blazin' blue eyes and shit-eatin' grin. Then there's this jaw that seems made of granite and the sexy dimple in your chin." She let her fingers trace the delineated lines of his triceps, biceps and forearms. "You're all hard muscled shoulders, chest and pecs, ripped abs. This set of pipes are highly lickable." She bent her head, her tongue following the path her hand forged. "And don't get me started on your lower half."

"Am I sensin' another 'but' here, wife?"

"Yep. But I'd totally be lyin' if I didn't admit feelin' a bit lightheaded when faced with Edgard's dark good looks, slumberous eyes, killer smile and sexy accent. All those yummy extras wrapped up in a lean athletic body that knows its way around ropin', ridin' and ranchin'? Mmm. He fills out a pair of Wranglers like nobody's business. But when Ed stripped to nothin'? And I caught my first look at his big, long—"

Trevor smashed his mouth to hers. When their tongues twined, she was slightly shocked at Trevor's altered taste—she detected a hint of Edgard's mouth as well as a hint of semen. This close, she could smell Edgard's scent on Trevor's skin. Just then Trevor seemed to remember Edgard had come in his mouth not ten minutes past and he stiffened.

"It's okay. I don't mind," Chassie said against his lips and took the kiss to the hungry, needy pace she craved.

Before too long Trevor's hands started to wander. Thumbing her nipples through her shirt, squeezing her breasts. Impatiently unsnapping the buttons on her blouse and releasing the front clasp on her bra.

She loved the way his callused fingers rasped against her hot skin and gooseflesh broke out across her chest and arms as a result of his touch.

His hand spanned her belly and eased over her waistband.

He tapped her knees, a signal for her to spread herself open. When he stroked the seam of her jeans and found them damp, he abruptly ended the kiss. "Christ. You're ready. From watchin' me and Ed together?"

"Umm—"

Trevor made a snarling noise, pushing Chassie until her shoulders bounced on the cushions. Then his face was inches from hers. "It drives me fuckin' crazy that you're turned on. Take off the pants. Now."

No surprise her demanding husband reappeared and hadn't been permanently cowed by Edgard's aggressiveness. She smiled slyly and shimmied out of her jeans.

"Why're you still wearin' panties?"

"Because you said to take my pants off. Which I did."

"Fine. We'll do it my way." Trevor clamped his hands on her hips, scooting her down until her lower half hung off the couch as he rolled her plain white panties to her ankles. Once he had them off her body, he slingshotted them across the room.

"Hey—"

"Spread 'em. I wanna see every inch of that sweet pink pussy."

Chassie stretched her legs wide and Trevor's hands flexed on her butt as he lifted her to his mouth.

He inhaled before he did anything else and a shudder rolled through him. "Goddamn I love the way you smell. I like tastin' you even better." He deftly licked at the slick spots dotting the inside of her thighs.

Every time he repositioned his head, either his prickly beard brushed across her hot tissues, or the soft strands of his hair teased her clit. Then the middle of her thigh. The curve of her knee.

Chassie shouldn't be embarrassed by how fast she heated up, but at times she wondered if it were normal.

You went beyond normal when you demanded your husband and his male lover perform for you live like some gay burlesque show.

Yet, her voyeurism hadn't bothered either Edgard or Trevor. So maybe the only shame in their exhibition was in the feeling there should've been shame when there was none.

Then Trevor's mouth was sucking on her sex, returning her

focus to how much he loved giving her pleasure and she thought of nothing else.

Lapping at the syrup that coated her folds, he said, "Mmm. Mmm. Mmm." That humming noise sounded again right before Trevor jammed his tongue deep into her channel. He flicked faster inside her walls, tasting her from the inside out.

Her hands landed on his head and she tried to direct him to where she wanted his mouth.

Trevor lifted his face and looked at her. "I'm inclined to make you wait."

"Easy for you to say. You already got yours, gave Edgard his and I had to sit there and do nothin' but watch."

Trevor's expression didn't change. "You didn't touch yourself at all when Ed and I...?"

"No, and it was hard not to because, God, it was really something to see. Trevor, I ache."

His gaze dropped to the bit of flesh poking out from between her pussy lips. He murmured, "Can't have that." Then Trevor fastened his mouth to her clit and began sucking. The impact caused her to arch into his mouth hard enough she felt the bite of his teeth on her pubic bone.

Between his concentrated attention and the live porn as foreplay, her blood pooled in that nerve-rich tissue and coiled like a hot snake hissing to be unleashed. The licking, throbbing sensations coalesced and the climax ripped through her so quickly she couldn't moan, she couldn't speak and she was fairly sure she stopped breathing. Chassie clutched handfuls of Trevor's hair as she rode out the orgasm on his face.

Trevor continued to nuzzle and kiss her mound, as she came down from such sharp, sweet pleasure. After she peeled her eyes open, she smoothed his wild hairdo back into place and sighed. "Better?"

His smile lit up her world, reminding her he was her world. And she'd do anything in the world to keep him. "Yeah. That was—"

"Not enough." Trevor grabbed her, flipped her on her back on the floor and levered his body over hers. "Never enough when it comes to you." His hand shook as he pushed a section of hair behind her ear. "Chassie, I love you. You know that, right?"

"Yes." She turned her head and kissed his palm. "Forget

everything else and show me."

The unhurried pace, a dreamy reconnection of bodies and hearts and souls was exactly what they both needed. Yet even after they climbed into their marriage bed, curled around each other, offering lovers' words of reassurance and devotion in the darkness of the night, Chassie knew everything had changed, and she wasn't sure if either of them were fully ready to deal with the emotional backlash.

Chapter Seventeen

There was no time the next morning for awkward moments or uncomfortable lags in the conversation. Edgard knocked on their door at five a.m. after he'd found a problem when checking on Meridian.

Trevor dressed and raced out with Edgard while Chassie started a pot of coffee. It was damn cold out—the thermometer read a frigid twelve degrees—and they'd need to warm up after they dealt with whatever ailed the horse. She pulled her hoodie more tightly around her head as she buttoned her coat.

As she crossed the yard, her breath puffed out in a white cloud, freezing her nose. She slid the barn door open and snuck inside.

No grunting animal sounds or encouraging human voices. By the time she saw the grayish light of the stall door open to the outside corral, she knew it was too late.

Wordlessly, Edgard and Trevor backed away so Chassie could climb up and peer over the slats.

She didn't want to look. But she did.

"Baby, I'm sorry. I know how much she meant to you."

Tears welled as she stared at the beautiful dead mare outside in the small pen. Her foal was dead, half in/half out of the birth canal. "How'd Meridian get outside?"

Edgard said, "She was restless when I first got here. I opened the door, thinking she might calm down if she could move better. She wouldn't let me near her, it was dark and I didn't realize where the foal was until it was too late."

She'd seen her share of livestock deaths and animal stillbirths, but this one hit her hard. "Oh, damn, girl. I'm so sorry."

Strong hands squeezed her shoulders.

Chassie found her voice. "If I would've checked on her in the middle of the night like I was supposed to—"

"Don't matter. Nothin' even the vet could've done."

"That don't make me feel better."

"Don't change the facts, Chass, regardless of how it makes you feel."

"No kiddin'." She hated this cold, tough side of Trevor that reminded her of her father. She hopped down and faced her husband. "What happens now? We can't afford—"

"You think I don't know we just lost three grand overnight, not includin' what that foal woulda brung? You think I don't know we can't afford to replace her?" Trevor spun around as if to punch the wooden slat. "Jesus, Chassie, I'm not stupid."

She slapped her hand over her mouth to keep from berating him for his jerkish behavior.

"That's not helping," Edgard snapped.

"Know what will help, Ed? Find me a goddamn place to put Meridian's carcass that ain't by the herd and where the ground ain't frozen solid. Least that stubborn mare had the good sense to die outside so I can get to her with the farmhand and I don't have to use the machine to tear apart the damn barn."

Chassie's tears fell on the cold hay-strewn floor as Trevor fumed and paced and muttered.

"Know what else'd help, Trev?" Edgard's tone was measured. "If you'd shut the hell up and walk it off."

"Fine."

Harsh, cold silence lingered.

Edgard's gentle hands boosted Chassie's chin and wiped the wetness from her face. "I'm sorry about Meridian."

She blinked. Some hard-as-spurs ranch wife she'd become. While her husband and his best friend sniped at each other, trying to find a solution to the problem of disposing of the dead horse, all she could do was stand like a statue and weep in silence.

Her father's voice boomed in her head, *"You're too emotional, Chassie. Too easily swayed by people and animals. That's why it takes a man to run a ranch. A man don't let emotions get in the way."*

"I'm sorry I'm such a crybaby."

"Don't be."

She couldn't speak around the lump in her throat. Beneath his reserved manner Edgard was calming and compassionate. She was half-tempted to throw herself into his arms for comfort since her husband was being such a jackass.

"Chass, sweetheart, why don't you let me deal with this?"

By the look in Edgard's eyes she knew "this" meant the disposal of the animal and Trevor's mood. She swallowed hard. "Why? Because I'm a weepy woman?"

"No. Because the same thing happened to me on my ranch last year." As he paused, appearing to weigh the rest of his answer, his thumb kept feathering over her jawline. Softly. Sweetly. A light touch that aroused rather than reassured. "I wished to heaven I'd had someone to take care of it, or help me, or hell even to cry with, but I ended up doing everything all by myself and it sucked big time."

His constant caress sent goose bumps cascading down her neck. She shivered, wondering how she could possibly feel anything but sorrow. Wondering how she could possibly be contemplating the press of Edgard's full, soft-looking lips against hers in the ultimate show of comfort.

Edgard's eyes narrowed. Again, she feared he knew the direction her thoughts had taken. Her face heated. But he didn't stop touching her. And she didn't mind.

Trevor barked, "Chassie. You goin' back to the house? Or doin' the mornin' feedin'? 'Cause it's too goddamn cold out here to be standin' around cryin' about a dead horse while lettin' the cattle starve." He stomped to the tack room and slammed the door.

"I see he's still a total asshole when he's upset, huh?" Edgard muttered.

"Yeah."

"He's always been that way when something happens that he can't control."

"I figured. He was probably an asshole to you a lot, huh?"

Edgard shrugged. "I got used to it."

"Well, that makes one of us 'cause I sure as hell wouldn't put up with it." She sniffed. "Luckily it doesn't happen often."

"Good. I'd hate to have to kick his sorry ass for being mean to you."

"You'd do that for me?"

"In a heartbeat, darlin'," he drawled, mimicking Trevor.

Chassie smiled. Edgard smiled back.

"Get your chores done, Chass, and I might have a surprise for you later."

"Why?"

"Just because." Then he leaned forward and placed his warm, damp lips on her cold forehead, letting the less-than-platonic kiss linger before he entered the stall.

Three hours later Trevor and Edgard disposed of the horse, a nasty, depressing job every rancher hated doing but was a natural part of life on a ranch. Stock deaths never got easier—Edgard knew that held true not only for him, but for all folks who made their living from the land and were entrusted with the care of animals.

They rode in the truck after fixing the heat pump that'd frozen overnight in the stock tank in the north pasture and Trevor was brooding.

Edgard preferred moody Trevor to standoffish Trevor. He'd been involved with Trevor long enough to know the events of last night were not a topic for discussion. He knew better than to offer Trevor a show of physical comfort.

That'd been another issue between them, Edgard's need for casual affection and Trevor's refusal to give it to him outside the bedroom. Edgard hadn't been looking for deep kisses, or walking arm in arm as they'd sauntered down the sidewalk, just an occasional touch when they were alone.

It'd taken him a year to realize the only time they'd truly been alone were those nights on the road after they'd checked into a motel. Colby, while not necessarily homophobic, only agreed to stay on—after he'd literally caught them with their pants down—if they kept their relationship strictly professional in front of him. At all times.

Edgard also knew Trevor's reluctance to even simply hold Edgard's hand was practical: if they became accustomed to touching in semi-private spaces such as the truck, or the horse trailer when they were getting ready to compete, it'd be easy to slip up and touch in public.

So rather than strike a balance, Trevor instituted a strict "hands off" policy. A policy Edgard hated and mocked at every opportunity, but it was a policy Trevor didn't bend on. Trevor's private affection had been worth it.

For a while anyway.

Dwight Yoakam droning in the background didn't mask the edgy stillness hanging in the air. Edgard took a sip of his coffee as Trevor hit a bump and warm liquid sloshed everywhere. He muttered and stripped off his leather glove with his teeth, mopping up the spot on his jeans.

"Shit. Sorry. Didn't mean to do that."

"It's okay." He drained the rest and shoved the cup in the cup holder. "Been drinking coffee since the crack of nothin' anyway. Probably had enough."

Trevor shot him a look. "Why'd you get up so early?"

"Couldn't sleep." Edgard didn't elaborate.

It surprised him when Trevor admitted, "I wasn't sleepin' either. I heard you."

"You did?"

"Yeah. Now I'm thinkin' if I would've gotten up when you did maybe we coulda saved that damn horse."

Edgard frowned. "But you told Chassie—"

"I told Chassie what she needed to hear so she didn't feel guilty," Trevor said irritably. "If anyone's gonna be takin' on the brunt of the guilt around here, it's gonna be me, not her."

"Which is noble, Trev, but you didn't have to be so cruel to her."

"You tellin' me how to handle my wife, Ed?"

"No. I'm telling you after what she's been through in the last couple of days you should've expected she'd be an emotional train wreck. You should've been more sympathetic to her losing the horse, not less." Edgard mentally braced himself for Trevor's temper to explode.

But it didn't, he just nodded. "I know. Even as that mean shit was runnin' out of my mouth like I'd developed a case of scour, I couldn't stop it." Trevor hit the brakes and threw the truck in park. His hands gripped the steering wheel below where he'd placed his forehead. "Ah fuck. I can't believe what a prick I am sometimes."

Trevor's shoulders rose and fell quickly. Was Trevor crying?

Or hyperventilating? Either way, Trevor wouldn't accept his comfort, so Edgard stayed immobile, aching for the chance to pacify the man in mind or body. To ease him in some way, because seeing Trevor hurting was still like a knife in his gut.

Finally, Trevor sighed. "I never wanna be like him. Never."

"Be like who?" Edgard asked, even when he knew.

"Like my father."

Edgard didn't offer him any false words of comfort.

"It scares the hell out of me. Chassie don't know what a bastard my dad was. Still is. I didn't tell her about some of the shit he'd pulled because I...goddammit, I worried she wouldn't marry me because she'd be afraid I'd turn out like him.

"Now I can't tell her because I'm afraid with all the other stuff that's happened, she'll kick me to the fence. Seems I can't tell her nothin' without fear of losin' her." His short bark of laughter rivaled the cold for bitterness. "I suck at this spillin' my guts stuff. I always have. You know that probably better'n anyone."

"Yeah, well, it's a lousy excuse. It always has been."

Trevor slowly lifted his head and gave Edgard an incredulous look. "How is that smartass answer supposed to help me?"

"Oh, so *now* you want my help?"

"Well yeah, since it's obvious I fucked up and it's obvious you think *you* know how to fix it."

"Fine." Edgard pointed to the cell phone clipped on the dash. "Call her. Say, 'Baby, I'm sorry I was an asshole. I love you', but for Christsake don't qualify it."

"Qualify it, meanin' what?"

"Don't tack on, 'I was an asshole because I'm under stress', just apologize. Period."

They stared at each other.

"That's it?"

"Sometimes the smallest gestures have the biggest impact."

"Can't be that easy," Trevor muttered, snatching the phone. He faced out the driver's side window but didn't lower his voice.

"Hey, Chass. No. Nothin's wrong. I just wanted to say...I'm sorry. You know, for earlier today. In the barn. I was a jerk." When Trevor started to tack on, "Because..." Edgard reached over and smacked him on the arm. Trevor whirled back around.

"Jesus, Mancuso. What the fuck?"

Edgard shook his head and mouthed, "No excuses."

Still glaring at Edgard, Trevor said, "No, nothin' happened. Ed spilled his coffee all over himself. Yeah. He's fine, even when he's graceful as a bear." Trevor mouthed, "Asshole," at Edgard. Pause. "Sure. Sounds good. We'll be home for lunch in a bit. Love you too, baby."

After he snapped the phone shut, he stabbed the antennae at Edgard and warned, "You ain't allowed to gloat, *meu amigo*."

"I promise not to start humming the Mexican hat dance and clacking my castanets in victory," he said wryly.

"You're hilarious." Trevor put the truck in drive and they were bumping across the uneven terrain.

Edgard squinted at the unfamiliar stark scenery outside his window. Dirt-covered snow stretched across miles of flat prairie; dead clumps of brownish grass poked through the thin layer of white. Wind stripped the moisture away from the ground in places, leaving patches of red dirt. Skeletal trees, rocks, tumbleweeds scattered along the fenceline added to the vastness and the loneliness of the scene.

Isolation. Desperation. It fit Edgard's mood, not only today, but for the last year.

Gruffly, Trevor said, "Thanks."

"You're welcome."

Silence filled the truck cab. So many things had been left unsaid. Again. Maybe they were doomed to be stuck at that impasse. Unable to go back; unwilling to move forward. The events of last night seemed so far away, in that surreal state where Edgard questioned whether it'd really happened.

A few minutes later, out of the blue, Trevor spoke again. "You've changed, Ed. You always were quiet, that strong silent type of guy, especially in public, but you're even more so these days. What gives?"

"So glad you noticed," Edgard muttered.

"I've noticed lots of things."

Edgard's head whipped around at the silky resonance in Trevor's tone. "Yeah?"

"Yeah. But mostly I notice how you get a little prissy when I bring up something you don't wanna discuss."

His mouth dropped open. "Prissy? For Christsake, I've

never been prissy a day in my life."

Trevor grinned. "See? That right there was prissy."

"Fuck off."

"Just sayin'..."

Trevor's you-know-you-love-me grin had always been Edgard's downfall. He smiled back. "Asshole."

"So, you gonna tell me why you don't wanna talk about what happened to you in the last few years?"

Edgard didn't respond. Didn't know where or how to start, actually. He focused his attention out the window, absentmindedly pinching the tips of his wet leather glove between his fingers and thumb. "It doesn't matter."

A warm, dry hand covered his, stopping his restless fingers, and damn near stopping his heart. Edgard didn't move. He was frozen in that place between hope and fear.

"It matters to me," Trevor said.

Edgard waited for Trevor to realize they were still touching and jerk his hand back. But he didn't, he kept holding on. And yeah, maybe it did make Edgard prissy, but the urge to weep overwhelmed him. He cleared his throat. "What happened is my mother died."

"Oh, shit, buddy, I'm sorry." Trevor squeezed Edgard's hand. "When?"

"About a year and a half ago. Car accident. A shitload of bad stuff happened afterward."

"Family stuff?"

"Yeah. It sucked. Big time. I still can't talk about it."

A moment of silence. Of acceptance. "Lemme know if you change your mind."

Edgard nodded and Trevor didn't pester him further.

But Trevor continued holding Edgard's hand in silence until they returned to the house, proving the smallest gestures did have the biggest impact.

Chapter Eighteen

Trevor spent the hours after lunch in the office catching up on paperwork. Maybe he'd find a way to come up with the money to pay Gus.

Right. Might as well wish for a pot of gold.

Country music played in the background while Chassie did laundry and scurried around the house cleaning. A peppery aroma wafted in and he sniffed with appreciation. Swiss steak. One of his favorites.

Edgard had borrowed his truck, but hadn't been forthcoming about his destination. Truthfully, Trevor needed the break from both his wife and his former roping partner.

His life was one fucked up, confusing mess. Being with Edgard last night hadn't cleared up his inner turmoil, just added more fuel to the fire. Trevor loved his wife with an all-consuming passion. But if it was all consuming, what the hell was he doing thinking about...doing Edgard again?

He shoved his office chair to the wall and propped his feet up on the small desk. It was more than sex. He and Edgard had been good friends before becoming lovers, sharing everything, from their love of playing practical jokes, to ways to stave off boredom on the range. Although their life stories were vastly different, they'd clicked. After spending eight years on the circuit surrounded by men, Trevor admitted to himself that he needed male companionship. Chassie was great, but he missed that macho bullshit and competitiveness he'd gotten from his rodeo buddies.

After he'd moved on, from both his family and the circuit, he'd been so busy scrambling to make a living he hadn't thought much about friendship. Colby had been his best friend for years, both on and off the circuit. Naturally things'd changed after Colby's injury and Colby settled down with Channing.

But before that, their friendship changed when Colby discovered Trevor and Edgard were together, because Trevor confided in Colby less and Edgard more. They'd still participated in threesomes, foursomes with whatever chicks tripped their triggers, but when the romp ended, more often than not, Trevor crawled in bed with Edgard. Which left Colby alone most nights.

The last year on the circuit tempers were short, even after Colby started winning consistently. Being a selfish bastard, Trevor hadn't noticed Colby's loneliness until Channing joined them on the road.

After Colby's injury, Edgard left and Trevor hadn't gotten close to anyone again until Chassie. Much as he loved everything about her, moving onto her homeplace meant he hadn't met many of the locals besides Gus and Chassie's assorted West and McKay relatives. Chassie wasn't overly social, but she'd grown up outside of Sundance and, whenever they went to town, it was obvious she knew everyone.

He'd liked having Edgard to tool around with in the truck. Fixing equipment, doing shit work that Chassie shouldn't have to deal with—though she'd pop him upside the head for hinting she had less guts than any man. Lord. He'd really missed that "buddy" part of his relationship with Edgard and it'd be worse once Edgard left.

So where did that leave them? Despite the comment his truck was ready, Edgard hadn't indicated he'd be moving on soon. Chassie hadn't been chomping at the bit to kick him out either—even after last night. It boggled Trevor's mind that not only had Edgard sought out Chassie to soothe her after the business with Meridian, he'd exerted a calming influence on her that day she'd caught them together, an easy solace that Trevor hadn't managed after being married to the woman for a year.

In reality, Chassie had spent more time with Edgard in the last two weeks than he had. Edgard had accompanied Chassie on the morning cattle checks. She'd taken him to town for supplies. They cooked supper together. Hell, that flirtatious Brazilian had been teaching Chassie Portuguese and how to tango.

If Edgard stuck around would Trevor be jealous if Chassie and Edgard became close in a way that had nothing to do with him? Even when Trevor didn't have a right to be? Would Chassie be jealous? Or would she roll with it like she'd rolled with everything else?

She knocked on the door and poked her head in. "Hey, hon. Edgard's back. There's something he wants to show me in the barn."

Trevor grinned. "Chass, baby, a country girl like you oughten be fallin' for that tired old line. For shame."

"It's only a tired line if it don't work. Obviously it's worked on me, since I'll be in the barn with him."

"Can I come? Or is this a private showin'?"

"Please." She rolled her eyes. "After what I was shown last night, I think that 'privacy' ship has sailed for all three of us, don't you?"

No coy bullshit. "I'm damn glad you're always so straightforward. It's one of my very favorite things about you."

Chassie blushed. "Thank you. But your sweet-talkin' ain't keepin' me away from my present."

Trevor lifted both brows. "Edgard bought you a gift?"

"So he says."

"This I gotta see." He slipped on his coat as Chassie nearly skipped ahead of him to the barn.

Inside the dark space, she yelled, "Ed? Where are you?"

"Back here, sweetheart."

Sweetheart?

Chassie raced to the corner stall and stopped at the open door. "Omigod. Are you serious? Is that really for me?"

"Yep. She's all yours. Nothin' to be scared of. She's friendly. Really friendly. See?"

"Edgard, you sweetie-pie, I could just kiss you!"

Talk about being friendly.

"That's a mighty big temptation."

"Look at her. She's darling."

"Oh for fuck's sake," Trevor muttered. He'd kill Edgard if he'd bought Chassie a horse. Kill him.

The stall had been cleaned since this morning and a fresh layer of straw spread out. Chassie was on her knees. Edgard was right beside her. Close beside her. Practically on top of her.

The next sound he heard wasn't a whinny, but a *baaa-baaa*. Chassie laughed and leaned against Edgard, allowing Trevor to see the animal.

"Why in the hell did you buy her...Jesus, is that a *goat*?"

"Yep."

He blinked. Nope. The furry creature was still right there. "Why did you buy my wife a goat?"

"Because she wanted one."

"Right. Since when have you wanted a goat, Chass?"

"Since always," Chassie retorted. She returned her focus to Edgard. "Do you think she'll be lonely?"

"Not for long," Edgard said with a big smile.

"Always?" Trevor repeated. "Why didn't I know that?"

"Because you don't know everything about me, Trevor. A girl's gotta have some secrets."

"Yeah? If it's such a great big secret then how did Edgard hear about it?"

"Chassie told me one of the first days we were out doing chores."

"I'm surprised you remembered. We've talked about a lot of stuff."

"And some stuff, not so much, eh, *querida*?"

Trevor ground his teeth together. "What kind of stuff?"

But Chassie ignored him as she was too busy rubbing her fingers on the top of the goat's head. "Ooh, feel right here. She's so soft." She placed Edgard's hand under hers and they stroked the grayish-white coat together.

A goat. Chassie wanted a goat? What else didn't he know about his wife?

Probably nothing as earth shattering as your love affair with a man.

"I can't fuckin' believe this."

"Why not? Is Edgard buyin' me a goat what *gets your goat*, Trev?" Chassie teased.

Edgard busted out in deep belly laughter and he high-fived Chassie.

"Very funny, Chass."

"I thought so." She cooed, "Isn't she sweet?" at the animal.

Edgard kept grinning at Chassie with a very pleased look on his face. "Not as sweet as you."

Chassie bumped him with her hip. "Do I need to get a bucket to catch the honey drippin' from your mouth today?"

A low-pitched chuckle. "Maybe."

Trevor stood there dumbfounded, feeling as if he'd materialized in another dimension.

"So tell me about my new pet. What's her name?"

"Greta. Marlin said this little gal has a great disposition and she didn't have any problems giving birth."

"She's pregnant?" Chassie squealed.

"At least her name ain't Billy." Trevor trip-trapped into the stall. He dropped to his knees to get a closer look at the creature, which was trying to eat a balled up piece of leather. Familiar leather. His eyes narrowed. "Hey. Is that my glove?"

"Oopsie." Chassie gently tugged it out of Greta's mouth, chastising, "Bad girl, Greta."

The nanny goat lowered her head in apparent shame and let out a mournful *baaa-baaa*.

Edgard and Chassie both laughed.

"Did you feed her?"

"Not yet."

"She probably needs a drink first. I'll get a bucket of water." Chassie was off like a bullet.

Greta butted Edgard in the chest until he scratched behind her ear. She butted him again and he shifted sideways until he and Trevor were hip-to-hip.

Just as Trevor was about to open his mouth, Edgard said, "Before you chew me out, Chassie needed something to cheer her up today."

"Agreed. How'd you find a goat seller when you've only been here two weeks?"

"I asked Gus. He told me about Marlin Jones who lives out by Devil's Tower. I'd planned to wait and take Chassie with me so she could pick one herself, but like I said, after losing Meridian this morning, she needed a pick-me-up."

As they petted Greta, Trevor grumbled, "At least you didn't buy her a damn horse."

"Well, now that you brought it up, there's something else I need to tell you."

Trevor's head swiveled toward that silky voice. "You didn't—"

"No, I didn't." Edgard's brilliant smile and mischievous eyes caused Trevor's stomach to flip. Talk about pure sexual power. "You are so easy, Trev."

"Ha ha. Asshole. Buyin' my wife gifts. I oughta kick your butt."

"You're just pissed you didn't think of it first. Besides, if I wasn't allowed to gloat earlier, then you ain't allowed to pout now."

"I ain't poutin'. Why would you think that?"

"Because that lower lip of yours is sticking out. Then again it always has." Edgard's slumberous gaze dropped to Trevor's mouth.

That seesaw sensation jumped in his gut again.

"Damn, your mouth is tempting, way too tempting." Edgard lowered his head.

Trevor remained motionless, one hand buried in the goat's pelt. The sweet, soft tease of Edgard's firm lips, the sharp scrape of teeth and a bristly beard, the erratic bursts of warm breath morphed into a gentle kiss. Trevor didn't pull back; he just closed his eyes and let it happen.

Their bodies didn't touch, but the palpable heat between them expanded. The subtle movements and wet glide of mouth on mouth was calming and tender and unexpectedly erotic. But necessary. Lord. As his heart rate picked up and Edgard's taste danced on his tongue, Trevor realized just how necessary this kiss was.

An hour—a day—a week later, Chassie cleared her throat behind them.

Neither man jerked away guiltily. But knowing his lips were shiny and wet from Edgard's, it was hard for Trevor to meet his wife's curious gaze.

But oddly enough, her eyes were on the slyly grinning Brazilian. She set the water bucket down. "So, Edgard, was that kiss Trevor's way of thankin' you for buyin' me a goat?"

"Yes. Although...it's got me wondering how he might've thanked me if I'd've bought you a horse."

Chassie laughed. Not a forced polite chuckle, her real, honest laughter. "You know, I was wondering the same thing."

"Yeah? You could tell me your idea. Whisper it in my ear, soft and low, like this," Edgard's voice dropped to a sexy bass rumble. "Then we could compare ideas to see whose is the best."

"You're so bad, Edgard, usin' that sexy Portuguese drawl against me," she taunted. "No wonder Trevor can't resist you. You tryin' to put us both under your spell?"

Good Lord. They were flirting. Right in front of him. Trevor couldn't look away. Especially not after his cock had taken notice of their sexy, playful banter.

"Is it workin'?"

"Mmm. Depends."

"On?"

"On whether I'll be watchin' again or participating in your magic act tonight."

"Definitely participating. Would that sweeten the offer?"

"How about if we find out just how sweet it can be after supper?"

"Deal." Edgard jumped to his feet. "Let's eat. Right now."

"I'm starved," Trevor added.

Chassie laughed. "You guys are insatiable."

As the implications of this next step and the possibilities stretched before them, Trevor figured this'd be the shortest meal ever.

But he hoped it'd be the longest night of his life.

Chapter Nineteen

They'd made an effort to keep the conversation low-key while they ate, discussing normal, everyday ranch issues. Upcoming calving, Greta. The sad situation with Meridian. The weather report.

An electric hum crackled in the air and Chassie was going to jump out of her skin. She cleared the plates and stored the leftovers in Tupperware. Wiped down the counters and ran water in the sink with a hefty squirt of soap.

A warm body moved in behind her. Hot breath tickled her ear. "Leave 'em, Chass. Come upstairs. I want you."

"But—"

"No buts, baby. This was your idea." Trevor spun her into his arms. He kissed the top of her head, then tilted her chin up to look into her eyes. "You were flirtin' with Edgard. I don't know whether I oughta punish you or reward you."

"You're not mad?"

"Turned on beyond belief. And..." Trevor aimed his gaze out the window.

"And what?" Chassie flicked the deep dimple in his chin, trying to get him to look at her.

"Truthfully, I'm a little nervous."

She'd expected him to say jealous. "Why nervous? Isn't a threesome old news for you and Edgard?"

"This isn't the same old threesome."

"Why not?"

"Because you're involved and it makes me psycho to imagine any man besides me touchin' you. Ed and I haven't ever been together...as lovers, in a threesome. Before it was me with the woman and him watchin' or both of us with her, but not he and I together...ah hell, it's just different, okay?"

Oddly enough, Trevor's nerves calmed Chassie's. "I'm glad. I'm glad I'm gettin' a part of each of you that no other woman has had."

"No other woman has ever had my heart."

As true as she believed that statement to be, Chassie knew Edgard owned a piece of Trevor's heart long before Trevor had given the rest to her. For the first time since she'd found out about them, since she'd seen them together as lovers, she didn't feel threatened. "Where is Edgard?"

"Upstairs in our room. Let's not keep him waitin'." Trevor clasped her hand and kept hold of it until they reached their bedroom.

In their large bedroom, Chassie shifted from foot to foot, antsy, scared and unsure if she should strip or what. "Maybe we—" Then Trevor started kissing her in that sweet, sure way of his. Kisses so slow and hot and deep she melted inside. Her body became as pliant as silly putty.

He unbuttoned her blouse, taking his time sliding it off. Next he unfastened her jeans, his mouth scattered kisses across her belly and he tugged the denim free from her legs. She was down to her bra and panties, enjoying more of those drugging kisses when unfamiliar hands landed on her hips.

She gasped, whipping around to look at Edgard.

A stark naked Edgard. A fully aroused, stark naked Edgard.

"Whoa. You're umm...you're all..." Why? Trevor still was fully clothed.

"I thought you were all right with this?" Edgard asked.

"I-I." *Stop babbling.* "I guess. I just..."

Edgard caressed her cheek, like he had earlier in the barn. And like earlier, her pulse took off like a runaway horse. "You just what, Chass?"

"I didn't think you liked—"

"Women?"

Chassie nodded.

"I like you. You're a woman."

She blurted, "Why? Because I'm flat-chested and I look like a guy?"

He smiled, not gently but with utter male heat. "Oh, there ain't a guy-like thing about you, sweetheart, and trust me, that ain't a bad thing."

"Oh." In for a penny; in for a pound. "So you aren't here for Trevor's sake? Takin' one for the team?"

Trevor snickered.

"I'm in Wyoming because of Trevor. I'm in this bedroom because of you and Trevor."

"Me?" Her gaze dropped to his hard cock.

"Yes."

She managed to drag her eyes away from the rosy, uncircumcised length of maleness. "Why?"

"Don't you think it stands to reason that if you're attracted to Trevor, and I'm attracted to Trevor, and he's attracted to both of us, that you and I might be attracted to each other a little?"

Of all the crazy thoughts ricocheting in her head, that one, the most logical one, hadn't occurred to her.

But hadn't she and Edgard been flirting and testing the boundaries since the moment the sexy Brazilian sauntered down the driveway? Slow dancing? Doing chores? Cooking together? Hadn't it turned her on knowing Edgard had whacked off as he watched and listened to her and Trevor fucking in the barn?

She'd assumed they'd both gone out of their way to forge a relationship because of a need to please Trevor. But maybe they'd tried for a relationship out of a need to please themselves. And wouldn't it make sense that the relationship that was an offshoot of their individual relationships with Trevor would be sexual in nature too?

It made perfect sense and no sense at all.

Chassie scrutinized Edgard's gorgeous face and didn't see confusion. Just desire. He wasn't eyeballing Trevor; he was looking straight at her. So that molten desire was for her.

Impatiently, Trevor said, "We gonna stand here all night and talk? Or what?"

"No." Chassie angled her head and gently bit the fleshy outer part of Edgard's thumb.

Edgard's eyes flashed fire.

Chassie smiled gleefully and spun toward her—whoa—now totally naked husband.

"I don't know what I'm doing here, guys."

"Luckily we do. Relax and let it happen," Trevor said. "Keep kissin' me as we're both touchin' you."

At first it felt unnerving with Trevor's hands caressing her face and another set skimming her bare shoulders. Edgard unhooked her bra and took it off, allowing her breasts to brush Trevor's hot, muscled chest.

The situation changed from unsettling to promising when Edgard's tongue traced her spine down to the waistband of her panties. His warm hands slipped beneath the fabric and her underwear slithered to the floor. Then those same slow-moving hands smoothed up her calves, the backs of her knees, her thighs to the curve of her ass.

Between Edgard's constant feathery strokes and Trevor's endless hungry kisses Chassie was dizzy with want.

Trevor growled, "Bed. Now."

The quilt had been stripped back to the sheets. She hopped into the middle of the mattress and awaited further instructions from her large-and-in-charge husband.

But Edgard eased in behind Trevor, resting his chin on Trevor's shoulder as they both stared at her. Curiously. Eagerly.

Chassie watched the men, fascinated by the physical and emotional contrasts. Trevor's fair hair and chiseled Nordic features against Edgard's caramelly skin and exotic, dark good looks. Their body language spoke volumes, one stoic and one persistent. Edgard bulled his way into Trevor's space entirely, silently demanding—and receiving—Trevor's attention.

Almost on cue, Trevor relaxed, nuzzling the side of his face into Edgard's—a surprisingly shy move. Part of her ached for him and how much he must've missed Edgard's affection, even when he'd only had it in private.

"Your call, Trev. What do you want to do?"

Trevor's chest rose and fell rapidly. "I want to make her come with my mouth. Then I want to fuck her. And while I'm fucking her, I want you to fuck me."

Chassie's sex clenched with want.

"You sure?"

"It's been so long, Ed. It's been…since you…since that last time in Cheyenne." He closed his eyes. "And I need…Jesus, do I need—"

A noise, growl-like in ferocity, ripped from Edgard; he took Trevor's mouth in a short, brutal kiss.

Their unrestrained behavior unleashed hers and she moaned.

Instantly Trevor was swarming her, all predatory male. "I recognize that sound."

"I-I, please—"

"I'll please you, all right. Spread 'em wide, Chass, you know how I like it."

Her thighs parted and she arched her pelvis, letting him see the glistening wetness there.

"And me?" Edgard asked, somewhere off to the right.

Trevor's hot gaze never strayed from Chassie's. "You get to watch me lickin' the sweetest pussy in the world." He bent his head. One long lick. Followed by another. And another. Each lap of his tongue became shorter. More precise.

She teetered so close to the edge of orgasm that Chassie clutched Trevor's hair in her fists, desperate for that headlong rush into pleasure.

He looked up. "No hands. Ed make sure her hands stay outta my way."

"If you insist." Edgard circled both her wrists in one strong hand, pinning them above her head. His face was inches from hers. "Leave them so I can touch you. There will be consequences if you disobey."

"What kind of consequences?"

Edgard didn't respond. His exhalations ruffled the damp skin of her neck as he placed his lips in the hollow of her throat.

Right then Trevor sucked on her clit.

"Oh God." Her pelvis pushed forward to force additional contact with that sucking mouth.

But Edgard's hand slid down her belly and the activity on her clit stopped.

She lifted her head and saw silent communication pass between them. Trevor fluttered just his tongue over that throbbing bit of flesh.

A wet lash on the very tip of her nipple made her cry out. It happened again. And again. Delicate licks interspersed with gentle, fleeting sucks. It was heaven. It was hell.

The dual tongue flicks on separate needy areas were like nothing she'd ever experienced. Wet heat swirled from her chest to her crotch until the pulses synchronized, and she came, gasping, writhing, and damn near screaming. Her whole body throbbed. *Throbbed.* Not just her pussy, not just her nipples, every single inch of her skin buzzed. As she struggled for air, soft lips brushed her mouth in a passing kiss. Once. Twice. Three times.

Chassie blinked her eyes and Edgard kept his gaze on hers. He murmured in Portuguese and nuzzled her jawline before straightening up.

Trevor rested on his knees and kept a grip on the top of each of her thighs. He grinned and licked his lips with great gusto. "Mmm. Mmm."

"I want a taste."

Both Trevor and Chassie looked at Edgard as he angled forward and kissed Trevor.

Edgard broke free and challenged, "Maybe next time I can get it directly from the source."

An odd sensation unfurled in her belly when Edgard came closer. He did that seductive nuzzle again, all warm breath and teasing caress of hot skin. He pressed his mouth to her ear and whispered, "Sweet Chassie. I want to fuck your husband. And then I want to fuck you."

Chapter Twenty

Edgard wanted to pounce on Trevor. Bend him over the mattress and pound into that tight little ass so hard Trevor would be walking bowlegged for days.

"Chass," he whispered loud enough for Trevor to hear, "do you have a strap-on dildo?"

"No. Oh *God*, I like your lips right there, Ed."

Edgard smiled and sucked a little harder on the tendon straining in her neck. "So you don't have any sex toys?"

"Well yeah. A couple of different vibrators. Flavored lube. Handcuffs. Rope. A velvet mask. Why?"

"Just curious."

"Why're you so curious?" Trevor asked.

He straightened up. "Honestly?"

Trevor's cheekbones were flushed with color, his pale blue eyes intent as he nodded.

Want want want kept echoing in Edgard's head whenever he was near the man. Edgard inhaled and exhaled slowly before answering. "I wondered if Chassie ever used a strap-on on you."

Something dark and unidentifiable quickened in Trevor's eyes. "No. Not interested."

"Why not?"

"Because the only thing I've ever wanted, or ever had up my ass, is your cock, Ed. It was you or nothin'."

Edgard couldn't stop from reaching for him. Touching those strong arms and that vulnerable face. "Next time I wanna look in your eyes while I'm fucking you."

"Or when it's my turn to fuck you."

A heated pause filled the air. Edgard nodded. "Right now I

believe hands and knees will be best for everyone."

Chassie lifted halfway and reclined on her elbows. "Do you want me just to watch this time?"

"No," Edgard and Trevor said simultaneously.

"Good. Although, I'm probably gonna wish we were in front of a mirror so I can see the looks on both your faces as you're together again." Another one of those mysterious expressions crossed her pretty face before her gaze skittered away.

Trevor was highly intuitive when it came to his wife, because he immediately crawled across the bed until he hung over Chassie's prone body. "Baby? What's goin' on? Tell me. No more secrets, remember?"

"Will you still want to be with me? After you're with Edgard? After he gives you what you really want?"

"Hey now. I've had what I wanted the minute you agreed to become my wife."

Edgard tried not to intrude. He didn't want to be hurt by Trevor's declaration, even when it was the truth, but it sliced clear to the bone.

"This is all so confusing," Chassie whispered. "I love you, Trevor. I don't wanna lose you. I'll do anything to make you happy. Anything. I can't expect you not to feel something for him when you so obviously do. And I don't think what I'm feelin' is jealousy at seein' you with him."

"Then what is it?"

"Just plain old fear I'll come up lacking again when he and I are compared."

Damn. Damn. Damn. "We'll stop. I'll go," Edgard said softly. "This isn't working for you, Chassie, and I won't hurt you again. Not ever. Not for anything. Not even for a shot at"—the only man I've loved—"being with Trevor."

Chassie shook her head and grabbed Edgard's hand. "See? This isn't what I wanted either. I won't cast you out like some soap opera diva, even though I'm feelin' like one, laying here dissecting this situation when I should just go with it."

He studied Chassie, flat-out amazed by her. By her generosity, by her caring and concern not for herself, but for Trevor. For him. For what they'd lost.

Trevor hadn't moved. He hadn't taken his eyes off his wife. "Ed is right. We can stop."

"No!" She squeezed Edgard's hand. "I won't do that to any of us. God, I'm thrilled you're wantin' me to be a part of it and not sneakin' off to the barn when I've got my back turned."

"Chassie, darlin', we'd never do that."

"Don't you think I know that? Don't you think I know how damn...*noble* you both are? Don't you think that makes me feel like shit for stopping this before you even get started? When I know it's killin' both of you?"

Edgard attempted a different approach. "While noble is hardly the word I'd use to describe anything happening in a barn...I will ask if you were having fun with both of us before, when we were both touching you?"

"Well, yeah."

"So don't think beyond that right now." Edgard brushed his mouth across her knuckles. "That's what I do. Live in the moment."

"Does that work?"

"Ask me after I've gotten what I've been dreaming of for the last three and a half years. Ask me when I walk down that hallway and go to bed alone and he's in your arms all night."

Another weighty pause hung; no one budged, no one seemed to breathe.

Chassie's lips curled into a watery smile as she touched Edgard's face. "Sounds like we oughta be pissed off at Trevor for makin' both of us love him. The jerk is gettin' the best of both worlds."

"He is a bit of a bastard," Edgard said with mock sternness.

"Hey, I can't help that I'm such a damn loveable bastard." Trevor kissed Chassie's forehead and rubbed his cheek against Edgard's. "I have an idea. If you still wanna do this."

Edgard made himself nod rather than shout out, *Fuck yeah we're still doing this.*

"Flat on your back, Chass. Let's prop your hips under a bunch of pillows. So I'm fuckin' her like this and you're behind me. That way she can see my face and yours, Ed." He refocused on Chassie. "Will that work, baby? So it ain't like we're pullin' train on you and you're in the lead car with no idea what's goin' on in the caboose? So you can look in my eyes and I can look in yours while we're all lovin' each other?"

Again, Edgard realized Trevor's instincts were dead on

when it came to his wife. What had Trevor understood about him that he'd never bothered to share? What else had he assumed about this man but had never taken the time to verify? Edgard's tendency to blame everything on Trevor had been part of the problem, a problem he hadn't acknowledged until right now.

"That sounds way better than a mirror," she murmured.

"I'll grab the pillows from my room." Edgard needed a second to clear his head. He paced, letting his conflicting emotions wash through him before he had to don the mask of casualness.

He returned to see Trevor's face buried between Chassie's thighs again, but he was on his knees, not flat on his belly. Edgard clutched the pillows to his chest until Chassie quit giggling and they both noticed him.

Talk about awkward. "Maybe I should..."

"Grab the stuff outta the nightstand while I finish proppin' up this pretty pussy." Trevor snatched the pillows.

Edgard's anticipation was waning. Until he saw the brand of lubricant he and Trevor had always used. Strange, that a squeeze bottle of lube would bolster his spirits, but it did. He turned around and Trevor was right in his face.

Trevor spread his hands over Edgard's chest, digging his fingertips into the springy hair. "We seemed to have lost our momentum. Maybe this'll get it back." Trevor's mouth ate at his as he rubbed their cocks together.

The swollen heads were bumping and sliding, mixing the slick beads of pre-come on bare bellies until Edgard couldn't stand it. He wanted to bury his cock in Trevor's heat. Feel Trevor's body clamping around him. Hear the surprised moans rumbling from Trevor's chest every time he nailed that gland as he rode him.

When Edgard began to grind with more force, Trevor broke away. His eyes said everything his mouth couldn't.

"I'll be gentle, *meu amor.*" Edgard brushed his lips over the shell of Trevor's ear and whispered, "At least until you beg me not to be."

Trevor shuddered.

Edgard wouldn't be denied this bit of foreplay. He tugged on Trevor's earlobe with his teeth, not bothering to hide his ragged breathing. "Get in position so I can touch you."

Trevor levered his body over Chassie. He stole a kiss and her slender fingers curled into his shoulders as he pushed inside her.

While Chassie and Trevor rocked together, Edgard knelt in the space between Trevor's calves and rolled on a condom. He squirted lube on his fingers and coated his cock.

Trevor's beautiful, strong back, ridged with muscles, was stretched out before him like a feast. Edgard rubbed his stubbled cheek and chin over the arched section of Trevor's lower spine, reacquainting himself with the feel and the scent of Trevor's skin. He slowly ran his tongue up Trevor's backbone, refreshing his memory of the taste of Trevor's sweat. In the years they were together, he always wanted to fuck Trevor before Trevor washed off the grime of rodeo, loving that distinctive dusty, salty, leathery tang.

Ignoring his own pounding heart, Edgard nipped the tips of Chassie's fingers, still clutching Trevor's shoulders. He traced the path of Trevor's spine down, not stopping at the cleft of his ass, but zeroing in on that puckered hole.

Even as Trevor automatically clenched, he tipped his hips up, wanting more. Edgard swept his finger over the most sensitive portion of the outer ring of muscle. When he felt that pucker relax, he slipped just one finger in.

Trevor lifted his head from Chassie's neck and groaned.

Didn't take long before one finger became two. It also didn't long for Trevor to start thrusting back instead of forward.

He removed his fingers and kissed the scars on Trevor's back. The one from Tulsa. The one from Cheyenne. When Edgard reached the one he'd given Trevor in Denver, courtesy of a broken beer bottle and his temper, he dragged his mouth over it several times. Edgard pushed back to his knees and, without warning, grabbed a butt cheek in each hand, pulled them apart and fit himself into Trevor's ass in a single smooth glide.

They both hissed.

When Edgard began to thrust, he followed the rhythm Trevor had set with Chassie, long and slow. Too slow.

Chassie gasped, "Trevor, move faster."

That's when Edgard knew to cut loose. His strokes grew deeper. He curled his hand on Trevor's hips for leverage. Needing a deeper angle, he slid his left palm up to Trevor's shoulders only to encounter another hand. Chassie's.

Their passion-fueled gazes clashed and she laced their fingers together and they held on to the man they loved. Edgard's head spun at the eroticism of fucking Trevor while holding Chassie's hand and looking into her eyes.

"Shit. More. Ed. Come on. I'm fuckin' close."

Edgard pulled all the way out of that clenching channel and slammed in. Once. Twice. Thrice. Four deep strokes. Trevor's anal muscles became vise-like, clamping down on Edgard's cock as he pumped into Chassie.

Chassie arched beneath Trevor, grinding her sex side-to-side until she came with a surprised gasp.

The visual and physical stimulation was too much and Edgard came in a long groan of satisfaction, his cock motionless inside Trevor as those tight muscles did all the work, milking every hot spurt. Edgard rested his head in the space below Trevor's neck, rubbing his cheek over the damp skin, letting that salty scent coat his face. When his breathing leveled out, he licked Trevor's hairline, placing a kiss below his ear. "Still good as ever," he murmured and slowly pulled out of that molten heat.

Trevor tossed all the pillows to the floor and stretched out on top of Chassie, burying his face in her neck.

"Mmm." Chassie didn't appear to mind Trevor's full weight on her.

It didn't appear either noticed when he left them and snuck back to his room alone.

Chassie didn't know how she'd fare facing Edgard, if things would be awkward or what. She took care of Greta early the next morning. She made a list of supplies and sat down at the kitchen table with her first cup of coffee when Edgard entered the kitchen.

Good Lord was the man magnificent. He rarely sported a scruffy morning beard, preferring to be freshly shaven and cleaned up, but not in a fussy, prissy way. She smiled. "Mornin'. Would you like coffee?"

"That'd be great." When she started to get up, he waved her back. "No need to wait on me. I'm used to fending for myself." Edgard took a cup off the dishrack, filled it and grabbed the milk from the fridge before he sat across from her.

"You hungry?"

"I'll let you know after I'm fully awake." Once he'd doctored his coffee to his liking, he drank half in one gulp. "Ah. Better." His golden eyes focused on her. "How is Greta?"

"Funny. She is the oddest little thing."

"How so?"

"She's curious as a kitten. Gets remorseful when your tone is stern. She's playful and affectionate."

Edgard grinned. "I did good in picking her?"

"Very good. I can't believe I actually have a goat."

"Have you checked cattle yet?"

Chassie shook her head and stood.

"I'd be happy to help since I don't have anything else to do."

She reached for the coffee pot, refilling both their cups. She stopped behind him and studied the sweep of his dark hair. Edgard's words from last night had haunted her after she'd woken up in Trevor's arms and found Edgard gone. On impulse, she set her chin on his head, wrapping her arms around his neck. Damn he smelled good. Felt good too. "Last night was great. Thank you for..."

Shoot. Were there words to explain? Thank you for offering reassurance you weren't trying to steal my man? Thank you for fucking my husband right in front of me and not behind my back? Thank you for making me feel sexy and like you really wanted me there and I wasn't an annoying byproduct of getting it on with Trevor?

"Thank you for what, Chassie?" he asked hoarsely.

"Thank you for everything. Especially when you were so sweet when I was worried, you know, me having a personal crisis, freaking out last night..." *Take a deep breath.* "Dammit. I'm so bad at this."

"It's okay. I oughta be thanking you."

"Maybe we oughta talk about something else." Chassie kissed his crown and squeezed his body one last time before she returned to her own seat. "So you goin' into town to see if your truck is done?"

His coffee cup stopped midair. When Edgard looked at her she realized he'd misunderstood. She covered his hand on the table with hers, which had clenched into a fist at her thoughtless blathering. "I'm not tryin' to get rid of you, Ed."

"You're not?"

"No, in fact, I'd like it if you stuck around for a while. Trevor never wants to admit we need help, but with calvin' startin' in the next couple weeks, and we can't afford to hire a hand, even temporarily...well, we'd—*I'd*—like it if you stayed." It clicked he had a ranch of his own to run half a world away and she amended, "Unless of course you can't and you need to get back to Brazil."

Edgard drained his coffee. "No place I need to be, so if you want me to stick around, I will." He scrambled to his feet, giving her his back. "Does Trevor know you asked me to stay?"

"No. But do you really think he's gonna complain after last night?"

He spun and gave her a smug smile. "Nope."

After they'd let the ritual of pouring coffee settle the unease between them, Chassie said, "I'm sorry you slept alone."

Edgard shrugged. "I'm used to it."

"Even when you were traveling with Trevor?"

He expelled an exasperated sigh. "Chassie, is this something you really wanna hear?"

"It's something I need to hear if you're in our life."

Our life seemed to jar him. "You are just as damn curious as Greta, aren't you?"

"Worse. And I'll warn you I'm stubborn as a mule and tenacious as a bulldog. I'll keep pesterin' you until your answers suit me."

"Why?"

"Because I've got nothin' to lose if I ask these questions and everything to lose if I don't."

A considering look crossed Edgard's face. "You are wise beyond your years, aren't you?"

"I feel much older than twenty-five, that's for damn sure."

"Yet, you don't look a day over eighteen," he murmured.

Chassie rolled her eyes. "You don't need extra sugar in your coffee this mornin', your mouth is already so damn sweet, so start spillin' your guts."

He smiled. "Most nights on the road, after Trevor and I hooked up, Trevor and I slept in the same bed. Unless he and Colby were out or if they were entertaining buckle bunnies in our motel room. Then I crashed in the horse trailer."

"Were you jealous? When he was with women?"

"Sometimes." Edgard dumped another spoonful of sugar in his coffee. "Mostly I was accustomed to it."

"Did you ever, oh, go fuck another guy and rub it in his face afterward?"

He didn't seem surprised by the question. "Once."

When Edgard didn't elaborate, Chassie waved her hand in front of his face to snag his attention. "Come on, Ed. This is juicy stuff. You can't stop now."

"We were at the Denver Stock Show. Somehow I ended up going to dinner with Trevor and his family. His brother Brent started talking shit about a hired hand who'd recently come out. Brent spewed all these dumb gay jokes. Normally, I ignore that kinda behavior, consider the source and all that. But Trevor drank too much—like he always does when he's forced to deal with his family—and he joined in, acting like a homophobic prick because that's what his family expected."

"What'd you do?"

"What could I do? I was beyond pissed off. Trevor not telling anyone about us was always a big issue between us. I understood his reasons and never pushed it. But when he made fun of guys who had the balls to come out of the closet? That was a line he shouldn't've crossed. I hated he'd done it in front of me." Edgard shoved a hand through his hair. "After dinner, the whole family loaded up and went to the big rodeo dance. I declined.

"I burned my bootheels getting to the gay cowboy bar in Denver and hooked up with a dentist who was in town for the rodeo. I spent the night in his hotel room and didn't see Trevor until the following afternoon when we had to compete."

Chassie figured she wouldn't much care for Trevor's jealous reaction, but she wouldn't be surprised by it.

"We sucked in the arena. Lost our chance for points or purse. Soon as we were alone he lit into me. We fought. Not with words. With our fists. We beat the shit out of each other, Chass. It was ugly."

"Where'd it happen? Since you were always so discreet?"

"In the living quarters of the horse trailer. Trev said something. I said something back. He took the first punch. I landed the last. Christ, we were rolling around on the floor, bleeding—"

"Whoa—bleeding?"

Edgard closed his eyes. "When we were shoving each other some beer bottles got broken and we just kept going, stomping all over them. Trevor slipped and fell and I didn't help him up, I just kept beating on him. So he has a cut on his back and I have a gash on my arm as a memento."

She didn't comment since she couldn't imagine the frustration they'd been dealing with *before* Edgard stepped out on Trevor.

"Colby damn near had to break down the door. He threatened to find new traveling partners if we didn't get a handle on the situation. Somehow we reassured him we'd deal with it, but that was the beginning of the end for us."

"What do you mean?"

"Trevor wanted to be with me only on his terms. I was tired of the secret life and the lies it took to maintain it. At the time...I couldn't see past my self-righteous streak that I wasn't gonna hide who I was from anyone any more."

At the time? Strange way to phrase it. "The dentist reminded you of that?"

"He reminded me lots of men live together openly. Did I engage in a one-night stand to hurt Trevor? Probably. But it ended up hurting me too because it gave me a taste of what I could never have. At least not with Trevor. I'd never been into the multiple partner, circle jerk, meaningless fast encounters in the clubs or bathrooms. I've always been..."

"What?"

"Choosy."

"And that's bad?"

"No, that's just not the norm."

"Dag was so far in the closet he suffocated in there," Chassie said. "I don't know what normal is. I'd rather be hurt by upfront honesty than hurt by a long-standing lie."

"I used to think that too." Edgard picked at the plastic seam in the tablecloth.

Finally Chassie's nerves couldn't stand whatever he was hiding. She covered his hand with hers. "Tell me."

"I saw Dag that night I was in the gay bar in Denver."

Her stomach swirled her coffee into a frothy latte. "Who was he with? Shit. No, don't tell me." She inhaled. "Yes. Tell me. Please."

"A skinny, young Goth looking kid. No one I knew. No one from the circuit. No one I'd ever seen, which wasn't surprising. They were dancing...and dammit, Chassie. I don't wanna—"

"Tell me. He's dead and I realized too late that I barely knew him or his life outside of here."

Edgard locked his gaze to hers. "Dag looked happier than I'd ever seen him. Comfortable in his own skin. After seeing him smiling and relaxed with that twinkie, I knew why he'd been so damn combative on the circuit."

Hot tears sparked in her eyes. "The last year he was so angry. And drunk. God. He was always drunk and when he was home he and Daddy were always at each other's throats. I'd've given anything to see him happy just one time. Did he recognize you?"

"No. Dag didn't see me. And I was used to dealing with Trevor and his secrecy and denial so I never let on I saw him." He sighed. "Hell. I never even told Trevor I saw Dag, Chass. But it stuck in my head and eight months later I returned to Brazil."

"So there's been no one since Trevor?"

"I didn't say that," Edgard hedged. "I tried a couple random encounters in Sao Paulo and I felt...worse than when I was obsessed with getting laid. I met a guy, Reynaldo, who did some remodeling for me. We hooked up, we were out, but it was casual. Six months into it I took Rey home to meet my mother and the rest of my family. He knew my heart wasn't in it, even when I never mentioned Trevor to him."

Chassie frowned. "Never?"

Edgard shook his head.

"What happened when you took him home?"

"My mother didn't like him." His humor vanished. "Then she died and everything went to hell. Reynaldo..." He scrubbed his hands on his scalp. "Chassie, can we stop talking about this now? Please?"

"I think that's probably smart," Trevor said as he sidled into the kitchen. "I'm sorry about your ma, Ed. I know how close you were to her."

"Thanks."

Trevor poured the last of the coffee in his mug and shut off the pot. "Cattle been fed yet?"

"No. But Greta has."

He scowled, but it was playful, not mean. "Damn goat's probably eatin' better than us." Trevor put his hand on Edgard's shoulder; more loverly than friendly. "I'll take care of the cattle. You comin' along to help me?"

Edgard beamed from Trevor's simple affectionate gesture. "Absolutely."

They belong together. You can't come between them.

Chassie's inner vixen offered her jealous side a seductive dare, *Oh yeah? Stick around and watch me because I plan on being between them a lot.*

Yes, it was shaping up to be a very promising day.

Chapter Twenty-one

True to her mental promise, a couple hours after supper, as the three of them were watching TV, Chassie said casually, "Anyone hungry?"

She paused, waiting for them to look at her. When they did, she vamped, "For a Chassie sandwich?"

Silence.

Trevor said, "I'm famished. How about you, Ed?"

"I could eat again."

The next thing Chassie knew, Trevor whooped, plucked her up and raced upstairs to the bedroom with Edgard hot on their heels.

"This ain't gonna be a leisurely meal," Trevor said as he set her down.

Edgard added, "More like fast food." He whipped off his shirt, then went to work on his buckle.

Chassie noticed Trevor's socks balled up and his jeans undone.

"Whatcha waitin' for, darlin'? Strip."

Her fine motor skills suffered when faced with the reality of these two hot, naked men. Her face heated. Her heart pounded. She just...froze. Yeah. Big talker. Taunting them and acting like petrified wood as she realized both those big cocks would be buried inside her.

"Lemme help." Edgard unbuttoned her blouse, kissing each inch of skin he bared. When he reached the last button, he fell to his knees and worked on her jeans.

Trevor moved in behind her and slid her shirt off. His lips trailed across the slope of her shoulder as he unhooked her bra, dragging the straps down her arms. Edgard tugged until the denim pooled around her ankles.

Then three of them were buck-ass nekkid. Chassie was feeling unsure when Trevor spun her around.

"I'll get the condiments," Edgard said, causing Trevor's sharp bark of laugher.

"Sexy as it is to see you bitin' your lip, I know it's a sign of nerves. You changin' your mind?"

"No. Thinking about it is one thing; doing it is another."

"This'll give you something else to think about." Trevor's mouth came down on hers.

The fiery kiss and Trevor's hands on her breasts spiked her desire, chasing away her anxiety. She arched closer and almost forgot about Edgard until she felt his hands caressing her ass and his moist breath on the back of her neck.

They were relentless in building her need quickly. She couldn't think beyond roving hands and hot mouths and the sudden gush of wetness between her thighs.

"Baby, let us have you, just like this."

"Standing up?"

"Mmm-hmm. Put your foot up on the bed so Ed can getcha as ready in the back as you are in the front."

Slippery coolness brushed across her rectum as Edgard inserted a finger. With his left hand gripping her left hip, he methodically swept his thumb across the dimple above her butt causing goose bumps to tingle up and down her spine.

And Trevor kissed her in that single-minded manner that made it seem he was kissing her entire body, not just her mouth.

"One more, Chassie, don't tighten up," Edgard spoke near her ear and added another finger to her ass.

With four fingers stretching her, Chassie nipped Trevor's bottom lip as she retreated from the kiss. "Then I'm ready for my drive-thru special."

Both men chuckled against her, making her whole body vibrate anew.

"Ed? You suited up?" Trevor asked without breaking eye contact with Chassie.

"Yep."

Trevor scooped her up and placed her legs around his

waist. "For this first time we'll go in separately. Next time, I wanna see your face as we ram into you together."

She didn't doubt there'd be a next time and she couldn't wait to experience every bit of pleasure these two men could offer her. She lowered onto Trevor's cock and tipped her head back with a heartfelt moan. "Damn. That's always so good."

Trevor pulled her butt cheeks apart so Edgard could line his cock up. "Rock your hips back a little, baby. Good. Like that." Just the cockhead popped in through the tight ring of muscles and she tensed.

"Relax, naughty girl. Ain't no shame in admitting you like taking it up the ass." Edgard sank his teeth into her nape and pushed past her resistance until he was completely in.

Chassie gasped at the full, hot sensation. She squeezed her muscles and both men groaned.

"Baby, is it okay for us to move?"

She nodded, even when she wanted the time to wallow in every pulse and throb of their cocks filling her. She needed hours to writhe between the two sweaty, hard male chests.

Trevor pulled out. When he thrust back in to the halfway point, Edgard withdrew. Slowly. And Chassie knew they could feel the head of each other's cocks between the thin walls of tissue as they thrust into her body oh-so-slowly.

She wrapped one arm around Trevor's neck as the pace quickened. He kissed her, swallowing her surprised humming moans. When Trevor's lips slid to the side of her throat and Edgard's mouth was there too, they closed the gap so their mouths could connect. The kiss was pacifying, not what she'd expected. A primal, powerful feeling overtook her at seeing these two strong, controlled men, together with such abandon. Fucking her with abandon.

"Like that. Don't stop."

A teasing side-to-side grind had Trevor's pubic hair rasping over her distended clit. Chassie couldn't hold off. The small orgasm expanded into a breath-stealing, blood-throbbing climax when Edgard yanked her hair, fully exposing the sweet spot of her throat for Trevor to suck on as Edgard nipped at the curve where her shoulder met her neck. They plunged in tandem. Hard. Deep. Perfectly timed.

Her world boiled down to gripping hands and hungry mouths and the push/pull of all that male hardness stretching her as every inch between her hips and her thighs pulsed.

The rapid clenching of her interior muscles brought impatient masculine growls and pistoning hips. No words were spoken as they came simultaneously. Trevor's seed bathed her insides. Edgard's movements stilled; his cock twitched against the snug channel of her ass. She wished he wasn't wearing a condom so she feel that same molten heat coating the walls of her anal passage.

Edgard's sweaty forehead landed on her nape and Trevor buried his nose in her neck. Their labored breathing drifted across her skin, creating a fresh set of goose bumps through the warmth radiating from their bodies.

Trevor followed the line of her throat up to her mouth and kissed her. "Didja like your sandwich, baby?"

"Mmm. It appears my bread is gettin' wilty."

"Who you callin' wilty?" Trevor mock-growled and thrust his hips a couple times.

Shoot, her head was muzzy. She'd meant to say lettuce was getting wilty, meaning her.

"I think she's too polite to tell us she really wants a double-stacker," Edgard said silkily as he snapped his pelvis. "We're more than happy to oblige your appetites, Chass."

That's when Chassie noticed neither cock inside her had softened completely. "Did you guys take Viagra or something?"

Ignoring her, Trevor said, "You're on the bottom this time, buddy." He captured Chassie's gasp in his mouth as Edgard pulled out.

Still keeping her wrapped around his torso, still kissing her, still touching her with tender reverence, Trevor backed them toward the bed. The sound of running water echoed from the bathroom and a minute later Edgard emerged.

He reached for another condom. But Trevor snatched it and set Chassie on her feet. "I wanna see her puttin' that on you." Trevor flashed her a wicked grin. "With her mouth."

Gently pressing on Chassie's shoulder, Trevor watched her drop to her knees. After she was between them, he said, "Suck on him, baby. I wanna see what you can do to Ed's cock."

She eyed the foreskin.

"Just pull it back and hold it at the base to get to the

head."

"Maybe you should give me an up close and personal demonstration," Chassie challenged.

Trevor crouched beside her. He circled his fingers around the tip of Edgard's cock and pushed the skin back, exposing the plump purple head. "See? Like that."

Chassie tickled the slit with the very tip of her pink tongue. When Trevor tried to stand, Chassie clamped her hand on his wrist. "Maybe you should help me."

Oh yeah. Two hot, wet tongues on his prick would drive Edgard wild. Trevor loved to get the upper hand with the domineering man, and getting to kiss his wife at the same time they teased their lover? What a bonus. He whispered, "Watch," and sucked Edgard to the root.

Edgard's entire body twitched.

Right after Trevor released every glorious inch of that uncut cock, Chassie took her turn, drawing Edgard's length to the back of the throat. She swallowed and retreated. They alternated twice more, but when Trevor's lips opened to receive the head again, Chassie placed her mouth on the other side and tangled her tongue with Trevor's in an openmouthed kiss.

Kissing each other and the tip of Edgard's cock at the same time was one of the most erotic things Trevor had ever done.

"Sweet mother of God," Edgard groaned.

So they tortured him with wet tongue flicks, soft sucking and nips from two sets of teeth. All the while looking in each other's eyes, competing to see who could wring a louder moan from the Brazilian. Working his cock and balls together, sneaking kisses until Edgard clutched their hair in his hands and jerked them away.

"Enough," he croaked. "Put the goddamn condom on."

Ripping open the package, Trevor held the circle of latex in front of Chassie's lips and she rolled it down Edgard's dick with her mouth. Trevor couldn't fathom getting any harder than he was right at that moment.

With a sound akin to a growl, Edgard latched onto Chassie's hips and they fell back on the bed with him on the bottom and his legs dangling on the side of the mattress.

She spun and pinned Edgard's hands above his head. "Leave 'em there."

"Oh. So you think you get to be the boss now?"

"Yep." Chassie impaled herself and pressed her tits to his chest, rubbing on him like a cat. "I love the way your chest hair feels on my nipples."

Trevor watched the muscles in Edgard's throat tighten as he arched his neck, lost in the nipple play he loved. Coating himself with lubrication, Trevor stopped Chassie's rocking motion. He aligned his slicked-up cock to her sweet little rosebud, gritting his teeth at the pleasure as he breached the resistance and slid into her tight passage to the hilt.

Savor it, warred with, *she's loose and ready, fuck her like there's no tomorrow.* Trevor held his breath, not sure which action would win out.

But she was too busy tormenting Edgard to give him a cue, so he waited, watched and ground his molars into dust.

"Can I move now, Trev?" Chassie asked.

"Yeah. However you want, baby. You're in charge. I'm just along for the ride."

Edgard said, "Don't tell her that. She'll torture us both."

"The best way to torture you, Mr. Dirty Talk, is to not let you be in charge," Chassie retorted.

"She's already got your number, Ed."

"Is it sixty-nine?"

Chassie laughed. "Just for that smartass answer. I'm gonna go slow. Real slow. Not-let-you-come-for-a-long-time kind of slow."

True to her word, his wife kept the pace slow enough Trevor had ample time to lube up his fingers. He reached down and slipped both into Edgard's ass.

Edgard's eyes flew open. Trevor's heart melted at the blatant love he saw in those tawny depths. This was so perfect, so right, the three of them loving on each other. And for once Trevor didn't hide his face or his emotions from Edgard either. He let them shine through.

That's all it took. Edgard whispered his name, bucked his hips, bore down on Trevor's fingers and came with a hissing moan. Trevor and Chassie weren't far behind.

Edgard took his time using the small master bathroom after Trevor and Chassie finished their turns. He tossed the condom, washed his hands and face, and managed to avoid looking at himself in the mirror.

When he returned to the bedroom, the lights were off, save for the low wattage lamp glowing on the far nightstand. Trevor and Chassie were already in bed. Dammit. How was he supposed to find his clothes in the dark?

He'd tried being quiet as he searched for his briefs, but Chassie heard him rummaging around and sat up. He whispered, "Sorry."

"It's okay. Can you turn off the light before you come to bed?"

Come to bed? Surely she didn't mean...?

Edgard didn't budge until Chassie held out her hand to him. "Yes, with us. Might be a tight fit." Her smile lit up the room even in the near darkness and sparked something deep inside him he was half-afraid might actually be hope.

"I don't mind."

"I didn't think you would. Before you ask, the invite is for all nights, not just tonight. Don't think for a second this is asked out of pity." She looked over at her snoring husband. "We both want you here. Some of us are just better at putting it into words."

"I know."

"He's workin' on it," she said quietly. "He'll get there."

"I know that too, *querida*. And I'm also aware I have you to thank for getting him this far."

After clicking off the light, Edgard climbed in beside Trevor. He closed his eyes at the familiar feel of Trevor's warm body and the unfamiliar feel of Chassie's hand enclosed in his.

"Good night, Edgard."

He choked out, "'Night," over the lump in his throat and wondered if they'd notice the tear stains on his pillowcase come morning.

A raging hard-on and Trevor's lips brushing his nipples woke Edgard from a deep sleep. He cracked his eyes open, expecting it to be another damn dream.

Nope. Trevor looked down at him and said huskily, "Want you. Want you bad."

Edgard's gaze landed on Chassie curled up on Trevor's other side. "Is she...?"

"Sleepin'? Yep."

"Would she be okay with this?"

"Let's ask." Trevor ran his hand down the outside line of her naked body. "Chass? Baby, you awake?"

"Mmmff."

"Do you mind if Edgard and I screw around a little bit this mornin'?"

She mumbled, "No. Just don't bounce me off the bed."

Trevor rolled on top of Edgard so they touched from head to toe and everywhere in between.

The everywhere in between caused the contraction in Edgard's groin. He traced the bend in Trevor's waist and canted his hips, his hands clutching Trevor's ass as Trevor began to move slowly.

"Just like this," Trevor growled, rubbing their cocks together in a sweet glide. "Like the first time. You made me do all the work."

Edgard pressed his mouth against Trevor's throat, licking at the throbbing pulse. "I needed to be sure you wanted me so you couldn't claim afterward it was something *I* did to *you*."

Trevor's response was a soft snarl and he tipped his head to reach Edgard's mouth.

The hungry kiss belied the slow, methodical slide and grind of Trevor's cock against his. Edgard let the reality wash over him. He was really here with Trevor, skin-to-skin, making love in the predawn hours.

With Trevor's wife asleep in bed next to them.

Before his sleep-addled brain wrapped around that bizarre statement, the rubbing strokes became faster. Shaft-to-shaft, the friction of cockhead over cockhead, the intense kisses, the welcome weight of Trevor gyrating on top of him and Edgard groaned, shuddering at the punch of need he always felt for Trevor. Of rightness whenever they touched. As close as he was to orgasm, he didn't want this encounter to end.

Trevor trilled his lips over Edgard's jaw to his ear. "Come for me. Come on me. Show me you like what I'm doin' to you."

"I like everything you do to me. I always have. Since that first time."

"Then look at me. See what you do to me."

Edgard watched Trevor's eyes go opaque and his mouth

slacken as he climaxed, leaving a blast of wet heat on Edgard's stomach.

Trevor kept rocking through the slickness, through his own orgasm, and buried his face in his favorite spot on Edgard's neck with a soft sigh.

Only then did Edgard let go, every heated pulse poignant as he wondered how he'd ever walk away from this man again.

Three nights later, nestled between two hard male bodies, Chassie groaned. "I swear to God I oughta be hearin' circus music we've done it so many different ways."

Both Trevor and Edgard laughed.

"Don't get me wrong, I am not complaining." She turned and kissed each man on the shoulder. "This has been hot and sexy and fun as hell. I never imagined the many, many, *many* positions we've tried even existed."

"But?" Edgard prompted.

Chassie propped her chin on Trevor's damp chest, making room for Edgard to scoot in and tangle his legs with theirs. "But can we crash now? I'm tired. We have to run errands in town tomorrow and I'd rather not be walkin' funny and covered in love bites."

"Mmm. I believe Ed and I are both sportin' your love bites, darlin'." Trevor dragged his finger between Edgard's hipbones, stopping at the big red mark she'd gifted Edgard with during a particularly frantic moment last night. "In fact, I think we both owe you a coupla love bites to even things up."

She muttered, "I had to go and open my big mouth."

Edgard leaned over and bit her earlobe. "What a great idea."

"You're insatiable. Both of you."

"Darlin', you don't know the half of it. Now why don't you lay back and close your eyes? This won't hurt."

"Much," Edgard said and each sank their mouths into a different part of her body.

She screamed, but it wasn't in pain.

Chapter Twenty-two

"Medium rare, basted, wheat toast, extra hash browns." Trevor closed the menu, handing it to the waitress with a smile.

Edgard said, "Give me the same."

Chassie had already ordered and was scrutinizing the newspaper.

"She's new," Trevor said after the waitress disappeared. "Wonder where she's from?"

"With that accent I'd guess some place in the Ukraine."

"She's unusually pretty with them icy white-blue eyes and dark skin. Think she's a natural blonde?" Trevor asked.

"You're a pervert," Chassie said without looking up.

"Just tryin' to get your attention, darlin'."

"You both gave me plenty of attention last night." Chassie harrumphed and flipped the page.

Trevor grinned, knew it looked cocky and didn't care.

"This is a cool place," Edgard commented as he checked out the restaurant.

Dewey's Delish Dish definitely embodied the diner atmosphere. Vinyl covered stools surrounded the curved counter, booths lined the walls, and an old-fashioned glass pie case packed with sweets rotated by the cash register. The colors weren't traditional black, red and chrome; instead Macie McKay redecorated in shades of brown, green with a splash of bronze. It was a classy joint while retaining the hometown feel. Trevor figured business must be booming if it was half-full at ten in the morning on a weekday.

"Tired?" Edgard asked.

"Not bad. You?"

"Nope. I'm rarin' to go." Ed reached for another packet of sugar on Trevor's side of the table, his voice dropped. "You sore?"

Their eyes met. Trevor smirked at the sexy Brazilian. "Nope. I'm rarin' to go."

"Sex maniacs. Neither of you asked me if I'm tired. Or if I'm sore," Chassie grumbled with good humor.

Edgard leaned into her direct line of vision. "Chassie, sweetheart, are you tired?"

Trevor followed suit and scooted closer. "Chassie, baby, are you sore?"

Her mouth twitched. "If I admit I am who's gonna kiss it and make it all better?"

"Me," they said simultaneously.

"Maybe I should draw straws to see who goes first."

"Maybe you should let us take turns," Edgard offered.

"Or maybe you should take both of us on at once and see if this go around we can both make you sore and tired?"

"Very tired."

"Exhausted."

"Sore in all the right spots."

"Hell, she won't be able to get out of bed for days," Trevor said.

Chassie's gaze went from Edgard's face to Trevor's. "You guys bet on how fast you can heat me up? Knowin' I'll shovel in my breakfast in record time because I'm dyin' for you to create a Chassie sandwich when we get home?"

Trevor's cock went from interested to fully erect in about ten seconds. "Screw eatin', I'd rather screw you."

"Screw that, I'm starved." She sipped her coffee. "Besides, anticipation is good for you—Mr. Harder-Faster-Now. Don't you agree, Ed?"

His shoulder hitch was noncommittal.

"Maybe Ed and I oughta give you a front row seat on exactly how sore *Ed* can make me."

"Dammit, Chass, knock it off."

"You guys started it." She aimed a challenging smile at Edgard and dropped her voice so they strained to hear her. "Don't think you're off the hook. So, Mr. Dirty Talk, which way you wanna take me first? I'm gonna take a wild guess and say that an ass man such as yourself—"

Edgard hissed, "Stop."

"You wanna pound into my ass while suckin' his cock?"

"Don't taunt him 'cause he will make you pay for it," Trevor warned.

Chassie ignored him. "Or do you want me suckin' your cock as Trev's givin' you the high hard one? Can't you feel it? Can't you see shootin' your load on my chest as Trevor's pumping his into you?"

Just like that, Chassie pushed Edgard over the edge.

"Big talk. You just earned yourself double trouble. Be prepared to face the consequences, *querida*."

"Good. Bring it. Serves you both right. Thinkin' you can tease me any time you want and I can't turn the tables even once? Besides, we've planned too much running around today to be screwin' around so we'll save my 'consequences' for after supper."

Edgard's response was silk encased in steel. "Wrong. You no longer get to make those decisions."

"Like I ever did."

A deep voice said, "Chassie?"

Three sets of eyes zoomed to the edge of the booth. A man dressed in a black Carhartt coat held a baby girl wearing a bright pink cap and a tiny purple coat trimmed with pink fur.

"Kade!" Chassie hopped up and hugged him, then cooed, "And Princess Eliza. Lookit you, girlie, you're gettin' so big." Chassie pointed to the open booth space beside Edgard. "Can you join us?"

"Just for a minute." Kade sat. Immediately Eliza clenched both hands in the newspaper and jerked it toward her as she squealed with glee. Kade distracted her by yanking off her hat and shoving the crumpled paper back at Chassie. "Watch out for Little Miss Grabby Hands."

"Gotcha." Cups, silverware and napkins were relocated against the back wall.

Kade seemed to notice the others at the table. "Shit—I mean shoot, Trevor, didn't see you there. How you doin'?"

"Good. I don't hafta ask how you're doin', seein' the smile on your face is a mile wide whenever you look at this sweet thing."

Eliza whapped Kade in the face with the tassel on her hat. He patiently lowered the furry pink cap. "True. I've never been better." Kade's gaze zeroed in on Edgard.

"This is my old ropin' partner, Edgard."

Kade gave Edgard a quick nod. "Nice to meetcha. I'm Kade McKay. Forgive me if I don't shake your hand, I don't have enough hands these days."

"Not a problem," Edgard said, smiling at Eliza, who'd whipped the hat in his direction, batting her long eyelashes at him with a soft *goo*. "She's beautiful. How old is she?"

"She's nine months and luckily she takes after her mama in the looks department."

Trevor bit back a laugh. He'd been around the McKay family his whole life and that little doll was all McKay.

"Where you from?" Kade asked.

"Brazil."

"That's quite a trek. What're you doin' here?"

"Catching up, goofing off. Visiting old rodeo pals. Trevor and I team roped on the M&P circuit. I went back to my ranch right after Colby's accident in Cheyenne and figured out me'n Trev weren't going anywhere." Edgard added hastily, "I meant, not making any progress in the standings. Been a few years since I'd hit the States and since I had downtime I thought I'd do a little sightseeing."

"That's where I recognized your name, you traveled with Colby. So you must've known Dag while you were on the circuit?"

Edgard nodded. "I roped with him once or twice. Sad situation."

"Yeah, but it's worked out in some ways." He looked from Trevor to Chassie. "So, when you two gonna add to the family cradle rolls?"

"Not for a while. Is she walkin' yet?" Chassie asked, changing the subject.

Kade shuddered. "No, thank God. Although, she crawls as fast as a June bug and she's hard enough to keep track of."

Eliza bounced on his leg. "Dah! Dah, dah, dah!"

"Whatcha need, sugar?" Kade kissed the top of Eliza's dark head and slid the hat back to her. "This?"

Happy gurgling baby sounds followed.

Despite Chassie's deflection about the baby comment, Trevor noticed Chassie's expression soften at seeing her cousin so enamored with his child.

"I haven't seen you in Sundance for ages. You're still livin' outside of Moorcroft, right?"

"Yep. Normally I'm on the ranch this time of day, but we're Mama's errand runners this mornin' so we hadta come inta town. Droppin' off stuff at the store next door for Aunt Indy before we head back home, ain't we, baby girl?"

"Mamamamamamamama!"

"We're seein' your mama soon." Kade smiled at his daughter's outburst and smooched Eliza's forehead again.

A surge of jealousy hit Trevor at Kade's casual, easy affection with Eliza. He wanted a baby—boy, girl, didn't matter. He wanted to see that soft, sweet expression on Chassie's face as she looked upon their child.

"So Skylar isn't with you?"

"No. Sky's slavin' at the factory, gearin' up for the launch of the herbal ointment line. She'll be sorry she missed seein' you, Chass. So you'd better fill me in on what you've been up to lately, 'cause you know she's gonna grill me."

"Not much. Workin'. More workin'. What about you? Besides hangin' out with two gorgeous girls day and night?"

"'Bout the same. Hit a slow patch." He caught the hat before Eliza flung it off the table. She shrieked her displeasure.

"Waitin' on calvin' ain't fun."

Kade's gaze flipped to Trevor. "Ain't that the way it goes? Hurry up and wait. Then it seems like you never have enough time or help. I ain't lookin' forward to a month of no sleep." He glanced down at Eliza, who was happily smacking her hands on the table. "Though I'll probably be more prepared this year after spendin' most nights up with Little Miss Insomnia here."

"We're hopin' Ed will stick around and help out," Chassie said.

Edgard looked up. "Like I said earlier, I got nothin' else going on. I'll stay as long as you want me." His meaning was clear, if only to Trevor.

"Hey, Chass, have you heard from Keely lately?"

"No, why?"

Kade shrugged. "You been keepin' in touch with anyone

else from that side of the family?"

"Not really." She said, "I take that back. I stayed overnight with Colby and Channing a couple days ago."

"And everything seemed fine?"

"Besides Channing bein' pregnant and housebound with a rambunctious fifteen month old?"

"Was Colby around?"

"Not during the day. When he came home late, he was worried about leaving Channing alone because she's doin' too much."

"Did Colby say where he'd been?"

"Equipment auction with Cord and Colt and Uncle Carson. Why?"

"It's the damndest thing. Normally I keep in touch with Cord and Colt regularly, but in the last few days? Nothin'. It's like they're all on vacation together. Carter and Macie are in Eagle River and she's due to pop any day so I doubt Carter knows what's goin' on back here. Dad even tried goin' over to see Carson when Ma freaked out because Aunt Carolyn wasn't returnin' any of her calls."

Chassie frowned. "Any? Aunt Kimi and Aunt Carolyn are on the phone like twice a day."

"I know, that's why Ma was concerned 'cause it'd been three days since they'd spoken. Uncle C met Dad at the door and wouldn't let him in the house, tellin' him Aunt C was feelin' poorly and might be contagious."

"That'd explain it, wouldn't it?"

Kade paused when Eliza fussed and squirmed. He turned her around, tucking his forearm under her butt as she snuggled her face against his chest. Eliza's big blue eyes were losing focus as Kade rubbed her back. It surprised Trevor how fast the baby girl ran out of steam.

As he waited for Kade to answer, Trevor wondered if he'd be a good father. A natural like Colby and Kade. God knew his kids would suffer if he reverted to Tater and Starla Glanzer's lousy childrearing skills.

Wrong. He'd never pit his kids against each other. Never belittle them in public or private. Never give them impossible standards to live up to. Never make his children feel they needed to earn his love. He'd give his love freely. Frequently.

Just like he'd learned with Chassie.

Like you're beginning to do with Edgard?

Before his thoughts wandered down that slippery slope, Kade started talking again, more softly this time.

"You'd think if Aunt C were so contagious then Colby, Cord, and Colt's trucks wouldn't have been parked out front, would you?"

Chassie's eyes narrowed on Kade. "What day was this?"

"Five, six days ago."

"That could've been one of the days I was at Colby's."

"So if Aunt C is contagious, then no way would Colby take a chance on draggin' a flu bug or whatever back to his pregnant wife," Kade pointed out.

"Dammit. He lied to me. Why?"

"Don't know. If Aunt C is sick, with something like cancer, wouldn't she want family around?"

"Kade, much as I love my McKay cousins, we both know Carson and Carolyn deal with their immediate family stuff in private. They always have. They always will. It's one of the reasons my dad was so upset when both his sisters married into the McKays. They take care of their own to the exclusion of everyone else."

Kade sighed. "I know. My ma claims she ain't like that, but really, ain't we all that way? Closin' ranks? Makin' sure we're protectin' what's important to us in our own house even if we've gotta shut everybody else out of it?"

Trevor, Chassie and Edgard exchanged a quick look. Could they keep everyone out of their business? Immediately Trevor quashed that hope. Nothing was ever that simple.

Was it?

"What about your brother? Don't he and Colt still live together?" Chassie demanded.

"Yeah. But accordin' to Buck, Colt bailed around that same time. Given Colt's past, we weren't too sure he hadn't gone off on a bender, as much as it pains me to think it, let alone say it. So me'n Buck were mighty relieved to hear Colt was accounted for."

"What do you think is goin' on?"

"Don't have a clue. That's why I asked you. I'd appreciate you givin' me a call if you hear anything."

"Same goes."

The food arrived. The waitress said, "Anything else?"

Kade said, "Would you mind packagin' up a couple of them pierogi Sky likes so much?"

"No problem." The waitress smiled at a sleepy Eliza. "I'll put in a slice of chocolate cake and toss in one of those soft sugar cookies for sweet baby too."

"What's a pierogi?" Edgard asked.

"Meaty, potatoey goodness wrapped up in chewy crust. Domini here, makes the best pierogis this side of Budapest."

Domini blushed prettily. "Mr. McKay. You flatter me."

"How many times have I told you to stop callin' me that?" He gestured to the trio in the booth. "Have you met my cousin and her husband? Domini, this is Chassie and Trevor Glanzer. They live on Chassie's family's homeplace out west of town. This is their friend Edgard...didn't catch your last name."

"Mancuso." Edgard reached for Domini's hand. "Pleasure to meet you, Domini. Forgive me for being so blunt, but where are you from?"

Domini blushed harder.

"Never mind. Why don't you wrap us up about half a dozen of the pierogis?" Edgard winked at Chassie. "Be all right if I cook tonight, sweetheart? I'm looking forward to an easy, fast supper because we've got some issues to deal with afterward."

"Then I'll come up with something warm, sticky and sweet for dessert," Chassie cooed.

Trevor choked on his hash browns. The cheeky bastard was flirting with his wife. And she was flirting back? In front of her cousin?

Domini blurted, "I'll throw in a couple of sugar cookies for you too," and practically sprinted away.

"You rodeo guys are horn dogs. I swear to God Eliza ain't ever datin' a cowboy." His hold tightened on the sleeping baby.

"What goes around comes around, cuz." Chassie chomped a bite of toast and her eyes twinkled at the Brazilian. "So tell me about Domini, Kade. She new around here? I think Edgard's interested."

Edgard's fork froze halfway to his mouth and Trevor hid his smile behind his napkin. Lord, that woman was just plain ornery. But the joke was on her because Edgard had such...inventive ways to discipline ornery.

"You know Macie's friend Kat?" Chassie nodded. "Kat brought Domini here from Denver last fall."

"I've never seen her."

"She's a helluva cook, always in the kitchen, which is too bad 'cause she's mighty easy on the eyes, ain't she?"

Edgard didn't answer, even when Kade addressed the last part of the question to him.

Kade brushed his lips over Eliza's head. "Anyway, Kat is in Eagle River while Macie is on maternity leave and Velma is wintering in Phoenix. Kat put Domini in charge."

"Domini doesn't act like she wants to be in charge."

"She's shy. But I think that's more from her circumstances than her personality."

"How so?"

"She's a refugee, immigrated four years ago and has only been speakin' English that long."

"And how is it you know so much about the beautiful, mysterious, shy Domini?" Trevor teased. "Does Skylar approve of you tastin' her *pu*...rogue-ees?"

"You're fuckin' hilarious, Glanzer. I know her because she and Nadia, another Bosnian woman who works for Sky, are sharin' a house since Nadia's divorce. And my nosy sister-in-law has taken a special interest in Domini. Which means the potential for Domini turnin' into a mouthy, tattooed pain in the ass has skyrocketed."

Kade hadn't noticed India enter the restaurant, nor that she stood right behind him.

Chassie and Trevor kept a straight face when India said, "You're sliding, Kade. You didn't mention I've corrupted sweet, innocent Domini into getting pierced in some interestingly intimate places."

"Jesus Christ, India. Why the fuck are you always sneakin' up on me like that?"

"Because I can. And I'm telling my sister you're still swearing in front of the baby." India stepped forward and propped her hand on her hip. "Or maybe I won't tattle because I'd totally pay to see the look on Sky's face when Eliza's first word is cocksucker. And by pay, I mean see *you* pay. For years, McKay."

185

"Ha ha, you wish. Eliza's already said her first word." He beamed at Chassie. "It was Daddy."

"Figures," Chassie muttered.

"It was *doo doo* and you extrapolated from there, daddy-o," India inserted.

Trevor grinned. India was as funny and rude as he'd heard. Lord, he'd be afraid to be in a room with her and Keely McKay.

Kade stood and shifted sleeping Eliza, turning his shoulder when India tried to sneak in and steal the baby from him. "Huh-uh, this girl is all mine today. We'll go before India ruins your meal."

"Hey!"

"Great seein' you guys. Keep in touch." Kade managed to slip Eliza's hat on with one hand without waking her. "Indy, would you go up to the register and grab the to-go package for Sky?"

"Did you pay for it?"

"Nope." He winked and strode out.

"Cheap bastard," she shot at his back.

"Are they always like that?" Edgard asked.

"Yep. Don't let their sniping fool you. They're crazy about each other. Kade has always wanted an annoying little sister and India is more'n happy to oblige." A wistful look crossed her face. "I'm jealous actually. Trev's fallin' out with his family means I've lost my chance for any sisters-in-law."

"That ain't such a great loss," Trevor mumbled.

After they'd finished and requested another coffee refill, Chassie grabbed the newspaper. "Guess what? There's a rodeo in Gillette this weekend."

"So? There's a rodeo every weekend."

"But this one has a guaranteed purse of ten grand. Plus, the entry fee is like next to nothin'." Her gaze flicked between him and Edgard. "You guys bein' former ropin' pros could win it."

Edgard laughed.

"Seriously. You guys could walk away with a pocketful of cash and we'd be closer to the down payment we need."

"We'd still be short and it'd just piss me off." Goddamn, it rankled he couldn't get a handle on that situation. Time was running out, too.

"Think about it." Chassie scooted out of the booth. "I'm hittin' the ladies room. I'll meetcha out front."

He and Edgard were lost in their own thoughts. Trevor studied the people in the diner going about their daily business. Running errands, waiting for calving season to start, worried about money, dealing with relationship issues. His gaze landed on a pair of older ranchers, heads bent together, deep in discussion. He wouldn't assume they were anything but good friends. So who was to say those old gents hadn't been fucking each other silly at every opportunity for the last forty years?

And who really cares?

It was arrogant to assume people would gawk at him and Edgard sitting together sipping coffee and judge them to be longtime lovers.

Besides, lots of guys maintained close friendships and shared a place to hang their hats. Buck, Colt and Kade McKay had bunked together for half a dozen years before Kade got married. Hell, Chassie's cousins Remy and Chet West even built a house together. No one thought it odd.

A doubtful voice reminded him those examples were family. If Edgard moved in with him and Chassie permanently it'd be a topic of gossip all over the county.

Wouldn't it? Especially if Edgard ignored the come-ons from local women who'd believe he was unattached? Or would the backlash come down on Chassie?

"Trev?" Edgard prompted. "I've been thinking about something."

"What?" Trevor watched Edgard's scarred fingers smoothing the folds in his paper napkin. He tried not to imagine those same fingers smoothing the zipper marks on Trevor's cock, which was getting harder by the second.

"Chass has gone out of her way to push our buttons all morning, hasn't she?"

Trevor glanced up and a warning pinged in his head. "Yeah, but I'll admit that look in your eye scares me a little."

"It should."

"What're you gonna do?"

Edgard's confident smile glinted as dark and dangerous as a shark's. "Push back."

Chapter Twenty-three

Edgard waited until they'd loaded up at the grocery store and the feed store before he broached the issue of Little Misbehavin'.

Chassie chattered between them in the truck, oblivious to the wicked looks Trevor and Edgard were exchanging behind her back. When she realized no one had spoken, she stopped talking. "What's going on?"

Trevor removed his hand from Chassie's thigh and placed it on the steering wheel. "Do you remember me warnin' you about teasin' us in public?"

"And me telling you there'd be consequences in private?" Edgard added. "Time for your first disciplinary lesson."

"What? No way. I thought you were kidding."

"Darlin', Edgard never jokes about that."

"But—"

"No buts. If you ain't figured it out yet, he's dominant."

Chassie's eyebrows drew together. "You mean he's a top?"

"No. Trev and I switch off."

"I'm confused."

"I know, so that's why I'm about to define dominant with a hands-on demonstration—using your hands." Edgard cupped Chassie's chin and forced her to look at him. "Undo Trevor's jeans, then undo mine. You're gonna give us both handjobs. At the same time." His thumb swept across her bottom lip when her mouth opened. "That ain't a request."

She attempted to turn her head toward Trevor, probably hoping he'd dispute Edgard's command, but Trevor merely grabbed her left hand and placed it on his crotch. "Been lookin' forward to this since breakfast, baby."

"You guys planned this?"

"This and more."

She choked, "More?"

"Yep." Edgard angled sideways and put his mouth on her ear. "Show me whatcha can do. Make us fly apart at your touch. May seem like I'm the one in charge, but you're the one with all the power."

A little breathy moan burst from her lungs.

Chassie unhooked buckles, unzipped and peeled their jeans open, making sure the zipper teeth weren't anywhere near the delicate skin. When she had a cock in each hand she stroked steadily, from base to head.

"Get us wet with your mouth first."

Chassie buried her face in Trevor's lap.

"Oh. Yes, that's it," Trevor said.

"Now me."

Chassie swiveled and sucked Edgard's cock, letting her saliva coat the length.

"Enough," he said gruffly. "Both of us."

Again those strong fingers palmed his dick. Her thumb brushed the wetness on the crown with every pass and she used the pearly drops seeping from the tip for additional lubrication.

The sounds of her hands moving, skin slapping on skin, echoed in the cab. Tendrils of hair stirred around Chassie's head as the heater vent blew directly on her face. Her eyes were closed, cheeks rosy, lips parted and thighs clamped together tight as she worked them over.

Edgard glanced over to see Trevor white knuckling the steering wheel. It was sexy as hell watching Chassie's hand jacking Trevor off in the same rhythm Edgard felt on his own cock. "Did you teach her how to do this, Trev? Or is she just a goddamn natural?"

"Taught her," Trevor panted. "But Chassie picked up some tricks on her own."

"Damn you're good at that, *querida.*"

Chassie made an affirmative noise, never faltering in her stroking motion.

"How close are you?" Edgard asked, starting to bump his

hips, wanting, needing that explosive rush.

"Real close. Goddamn close. You?"

"Same." Edgard lifted his hand to Chassie's mouth, tracing her lips. "Suck my finger. Suck it like it's my cock."

Trevor did the same. "That's it, baby. Suck 'em both together. Gives me an idea. Wouldn't that be something, Ed? Having both our dicks in her mouth at the same time?"

Edgard growled at the visual and how amazing that would feel.

The feel of Chassie's warm, moist mouth, her rough tongue and Trevor's thick finger rubbing alongside his inside that wet heat had Edgard's balls drawing up.

He and Trevor said, "Faster," at the same time. Her pace increased. Trevor groaned. That sweet familiar sound of Trevor's release and Edgard started coming, fucking Chassie's tight fist, watching as his come coated her fingers. His free hand gripped her thigh and he held his breath until he damn near passed out.

The truck swerved and he looked over at Trevor. "Jesus. Please tell me that you didn't close your eyes."

A sheepish grin appeared. "Just for a second."

Chassie gave both their dicks one last squeeze to twin groans. "Perfect timing. We're almost home."

"Yeah, but we ain't close to done."

After they put away the groceries, Trevor snagged Chassie by the hips and pulled her into his embrace for a long, steamy kiss.

"What was that for?" she asked when they finally broke apart.

"Because I love you. I love you like crazy."

She nuzzled his neck, breathing his scent into her lungs.

"So, you're game to try something...new?"

"Haven't we tried just about everything? Twice?"

Trevor leaned back and looked at her. "Not everything."

Chassie's heart skipped a beat at his challenging expression. "Like what?"

Edgard pressed his front to her back, stringing hot openmouthed kisses down her neck, making her shiver. "Like spanking."

Her heart threatened to beat right out of her chest.

"You've got a great ass," Trevor said, scraping his teeth up the other side of her throat. "I wanna see it nice and pink while Edgard fucks it."

"Oh. Um. Well. I-I—"

"We wouldn't really hurt you," Edgard murmured behind her. "We just wanna play with you a little rough."

She peeked over her shoulder at Edgard.

"You've been bad today. Sassing us with that mouth will just cause us to find more inventive uses for it."

"Damn straight." Trevor asked, "You find what you were lookin' for, Ed?"

"Mmm-hmm."

The exquisite attention to both sides of her neck sent delicious vibrations straight to her pussy. "I take it you've done this sort of thing before?"

"Oh yeah." Trevor chuckled, then sank his teeth into her earlobe. "Been awhile so I'm anxious for you to get them britches off."

"Me too. Where we doing this, Trev?"

"Right here in the living room. Drop them drawers, baby."

She moved back and began to undress.

"Shirt comes off too," Edgard piped in. "And watch us while you're getting ready for us." He stepped into the space she'd vacated and kissed Trevor. Not with his usual ravenous appetite, but pure seduction. Edgard nibbled and licked Trevor's lips, never quite delving inside his mouth. Trevor's low growls didn't spur Edgard to give in. If anything it primed him to back off.

Chassie had no problem doffing her jeans, but her fingers fumbled with the buttons on her shirt as she watched Edgard tormenting her husband.

"Touch me, dammit," Trevor said, arching closer, angling his head for a more complete kiss.

Edgard latched onto Trevor's ass and rolled their hips together. Side to side. Up and down. Tiny circles. Every time he retreated, Trevor's body sought more contact. Edgard teased with his mouth and his body, controlled every movement and countermovement, literally making Trevor sweat.

It was erotic as hell.

Then Edgard backed off and faced Chassie, giving her an appreciative once-over. "Brace your hands on the wall."

She swallowed the small bit of fear and did as Edgard instructed, keeping her body at a right angle as her palms pressed against the paneled wall. She heard clothing being removed, the jingle of belt buckles and coins. The *pop pop pop* of snaps coming undone. She'd focused so completely on sound, she jumped when rough hands caressed the globes of her ass. Over and over. Whisper soft. Her stomach muscles quivered with anticipation and clenched when that first sharp blow finally landed. She gasped, "Oh God."

"Look at me."

Chassie cranked her head and met her husband's glittering eyes as his hand swatted her ass cheeks again. This time it wasn't her stomach that clenched, but her pussy. "Oh."

Edgard stepped into her peripheral view and tipped her chin up. "Not another sound. Take your licks like a good girl, understand?"

She nodded.

"Good. Eyes forward. Keep goin', Trev."

Her husband peppered her ass until every inch of it stung. Every inch of it burned with erotic fire. About halfway through it'd stopped being punishment and became...pleasure. The heart-pounding wait for the connection of his hand. The stinging slap. The excruciating delay, then the delicious payout as the sound of flesh meeting flesh reverberated around her, up her spine, hardening her nipples as her skin burned.

Trevor said, "I can smell those sweet, sweet pussy juices." His fingers slid down the crack of her ass, stopping when they encountered wetness. "You're absolutely drippin' wet, Chass. You like this." He pumped two fingers inside her.

She arched and bumped her hips back for more. Oh God. She was so close.

"Stop," Edgard demanded. "She doesn't get to come yet."

Chassie whimpered.

Four hard spanks, harder than before, landed low, down by her thighs. Then Edgard's voice, dark and dangerous, was in her ear. "Thought I told you no sounds."

She bit her lip.

"Do you think I'm being cruel for not letting you come?"

Chassie nodded.

"But, *querida*," he crooned in that impossibly sexy accent, "the build-up is the best part. When we're done you're gonna come so hard you'll be begging for us to spank you again." Edgard licked the shell of her ear. "And again."

Everything—her burning ass, her wet pussy, the tingles racing down her spine from Edgard's seductive whispers—felt so good Chassie was on sensory overload. She'd chomped her bottom lip with such force she tasted blood.

"Three more. Each side. Down low," Edgard instructed. "Then get what we need."

Trevor hummed his approval and she heard the wet sucking sounds of them kissing.

The blows came fast and hard. Her legs and arms shook. Fingers traced her crack again, delved inside her cunt again. Three fingers this time, pushing deep. In. Out. In. Out. *Almost there, please. Don't stop.*

A slower withdrawal as her own juices were painted up to her tailbone.

"Look at me."

Not Trevor's voice. Edgard's.

Again Chassie twisted to look over her shoulder.

Edgard lowered into a crouch, his tongue licked a line from her clit, through her swollen pussy lips, stopping to swirl around the entrance to her sex, then lapping at her hole and following the split between her butt cheeks up to her tailbone. He stood and smacked his lips.

Chassie couldn't help but groan as her head dropped helplessly between her arms. She couldn't stop the scream when her burning backside was doused with ice.

"That's it. Now let us hear you, baby."

Hot. Cold. Wet. Hands on her. Fingers in her. Too much sensation. She started to collapse from the effort to keep herself upright.

Trevor scooped her up and perched her on the couch. "Spread 'em wide."

Somehow her brain processed the command as the scratchy couch material abraded her bare back. Two mouths kissed up the inside of her thighs and met in the middle of her twitching sex. She screamed when those two tongues began their assault. One hot. One cold. Licking her clit, then stopping to tangle as Edgard and Trevor shared an intimate kiss at the intimate heart of her. She grabbed two handfuls of hair, canting her pelvis, whimpering, wanting, needing.

A finger speared her ass; another speared her pussy. When Trevor sucked her clitoris, Chassie came unglued.

Every muscle in her body contracted and she sobbed through every pulsing, gyrating, wet, throbbing second of the most intensive orgasm of her life.

Soft, sweet kisses on her belly roused her and she shivered, opening her eyes.

Both men wore mighty pleased expressions, but the hunger in their eyes meant one thing: that was the appetizer.

Lord. She'd never survive the main course.

Chapter Twenty-four

Trevor pursed his lips around Chassie's right nipple and suckled softly, releasing the strawberry-colored tip with a loud pop. Jesus, she was sexy. Willing. Giving. Adventurous. Accepting of his and Edgard's harsher edges. Her skin was flushed so prettily, the inside of her thighs were soaked from excitement. His hair actually hurt, she'd pulled it so hard during her climax. "Chass? You okay?"

"Mmm. I think so."

He grinned. "We're switchin' places, darlin'."

"Why?"

"'Cause we ain't done. On your hands and knees on the floor facin' me."

"I gotta warn you, my brain ain't firing on all cylinders yet."

Edgard tweaked her left nipple, then suckled the sting. "We want you so bad we'll take you with the dazed look. You blow my mind." He kissed circles around her breast, nuzzling her in the sweet, comforting way she preferred. "You are hotter than the sun, and if I don't have you right now, I might actually burn up." She snorted her disbelief and he helped her to the floor, still muttering nonsensical phrases.

Trevor slid into position on the couch, his cock at the level of Chassie's mouth as Edgard spun her into place.

Then Edgard stood and rolled on a condom. Keeping his eyes on Trevor's, he greased up his cock and grabbed the mini-vibrator.

Just like that, every bit of urgency returned.

He looked at his wife and stroked her face. "I wanna be like that sweet-talkin' Brazilian and spend hours tellin' you how fantastic you are, but Jesus, I wanna be buried balls deep in this mouth. I wanna see Ed's cock reamin' your ass. I wanna do it now, no waitin'.'"

Chassie whispered, "I want that too."

"Widen your stance and hold still," Edgard said.

As soon as she'd moved, Edgard turned on the compact vibrator and pushed it in her cunt. She gasped, fully opening her mouth, and Trevor shoved his cock in to the root.

"Breathe. 'Cause once we get goin', darlin', this is gonna be a wild ride."

Edgard squirted lube on two fingers. Trevor began to rock in and out of Chassie's mouth, curling his hands around her ears, letting her know he was in control.

She sucked greedily, moaning as Edgard's fingers breached her ass.

"Chassie, you're so damn hot and tight around my fingers, I wanna feel that same heat surrounding my cock." Edgard aligned his cock to the pinkish pucker, pulling Chassie's cheeks apart and canting her hips.

"Go slow at first," Trevor gritted out. "I wanna see every fuckin' inch of your cock disappearin' into her ass."

"Then look now 'cause I ain't waiting." The fat purple head popped in past the ring of muscle.

Chassie tensed.

"Don't clench. There's a good girl."

Trevor watched that length of uncut meat pushing deeper until Edgard's hips were snugged against Chassie's ass. "Wish we had a mirror, so you could see how sexy you look book-ended between us with your ass nice and pink." As Trevor said it, Edgard smoothed a hand over from the curve of Chassie's hip to her thigh and back up, teasing her hot skin with just the tips of his cool fingers.

She shuddered and used her teeth down his shaft and tongued the tip before releasing it. "Please, I'm on the verge of another—"

"It's okay, baby, we'll take care of you."

They pulled back simultaneously, thrust simultaneously.

Trevor concentrated on the perfect wet seal Chassie had created with her mouth as he fucked it hard and fast. Almost there. Almost...

Edgard's pelvis pistoned a half-dozen times and he stopped, throwing back his head as he came.

Chassie bucked and groaned, the vibrating sound just the push Trevor needed to send him over the edge.

Light, sound, air, nothing existed but the series of hot pulses and rhythmic sucking.

When his spent cock popped from her mouth, he opened his eyes. Edgard had already pulled out and was kissing up Chassie's spine, murmuring in Portuguese as he removed the vibrator. He stood and went to take care of the condom.

Trevor lifted his wife into his arms. "You okay?"

"Feelin' all used up—in a good way." Chassie yawned. "I'm toast. You guys wore me out."

"You wanna go upstairs and lay down?"

"Huh-uh. Wanna be with you and Ed down here, 'cause I know neither of you are tired."

"But, baby, you can't keep your eyes open."

Edgard returned. "What's up?"

"She's exhausted. Help me pull out the foldout bed." Trevor set Chassie in the recliner and he and Edgard made up the bed.

"Why didn't you take her to your room?"

"She wants to stay down here for some reason." Trevor swept her up amidst her sleepy protests and deposited her between the sheets.

"This bed is bigger than ours. Plus, I like it when we're all snuggled close together in a big messy pile of naked bodies." Chassie purred, curling up next to Edgard after he slid in beside her. "You're so warm."

"You sure are a cuddly little kitten, Miz Chassie."

"It doesn't bother you I'm a friendly sleeper?"

"No. I like it." Edgard playfully tugged on her braid. "You haven't heard me complaining the last couple nights, have you?"

"Nope, and I'm glad, 'cause macho Trevor doesn't wanna snuggle up nearly as much as I like to. He needs his space."

"I'm well aware of that," Edgard said dryly.

Trevor rolled his eyes. "You two done insultin' me?"

Chassie said, "It's not an insult if it's true."

Edgard laughed.

"Go to sleep, woman. And you"—he pointed at Edgard—"quit encouragin' her." Trevor grabbed the remote and tossed a couple of pillows on the bed, adding another blanket before he crawled in on Chassie's other side. He turned on the TV.

"Comfy?" Edgard asked.

"Yeah. Glad we did chores early 'cause I sure as hell don't feel like gettin' dressed and goin' back outside."

"Me neither. I forgot how damn breath-stealing the cold can be up here."

"You'll get used to it. Next winter you won't even notice."

Edgard turned and looked at him. "You askin' me if I'll be around next year?"

That assumption just slipped out and Trevor had no way to backtrack.

You don't want to take it back. You want him here. Man up and tell him the truth.

"If that's what you want."

"It's all I ever wanted."

The warmth filling Trevor's body owed nothing to the blankets.

Chassie was already asleep, one hand resting on Edgard's bare chest; the other on Trevor's abdomen. Trevor and Edgard were propped up against the back of the couch.

"She's whupped." Trevor brushed a hank of hair from her cheek.

"We were pretty demanding."

Trevor grinned. "And she loved every minute of it."

"True. So did I. You tired?"

"Nah. You?"

Edgard shook his head. "I'm wired."

"Wanna see what's on ESPN2?"

"Sure. Haven't seen a good football game in a while."

"Football season is over. The Superbowl was last month."

"You Americans. Everyone else in the world calls it football and yet you insist on calling it soccer."

"Don't matter 'cause I ain't watchin' soccer," Trevor scoffed. He flipped channels until he landed on one that interested him. "See? Now this is a real sport."

Edgard snorted. "I ain't watchin' a mixed martial arts marathon. Guys beating the shit out of each other? Just like Saturday night in a damn cowboy bar except they ain't yelling insults about the other guys' mama."

"But this guy fightin' is a master of Brazilian jujitsu."

"Don't care. Just 'cause Brazil is in the name of something don't mean shit. And for the record, I don't like Brazil nuts either."

"I like 'em just fine," Trevor said slyly.

"Smartass. Why is it you never let me have the goddamn remote?" Edgard snapped, "Give it to me."

"Here." Trevor passed it over and threaded his fingers through Edgard's, setting their joined hands on the pillow above Chassie's head. "Happy now?"

"Yeah."

Trevor knew it didn't have a damn thing to do with Edgard finally getting control of the remote.

A few hours later, they were still lounging in bed, eating popcorn and watching *Cops* reruns, when Chassie said, "Why are so many people on this show always naked? No one wanders around naked in real life."

"Spoken by a woman who is totally buck-ass nekkid between not one, but two buck-ass nekkid men," Trevor pointed out.

The phone rang, cutting off her response.

Trevor snagged the receiver off the coffee table and answered, "Hello?" He frowned. "Ma? Why're you...No." Pause. "What?" He sprang up. "When?" Pause. "And you're just callin' me *now*?" Pause. "That's a lousy fuckin' excuse and you know it." Trevor inhaled and exhaled slowly, trying to stay calm. "Sorry. No. That's fine." Longer pause as he paced. "I can't imagine what the hell he wants but, yeah, I'll leave first thing in the mornin'. Yeah. Noon, probably. See ya then." He clicked the off button.

"Trevor? Honey, what's wrong?"

Trevor looked at Chassie. "My father had a heart attack."

"Oh no. When?"

"A fuckin' week ago."

Chassie's eyes widened. "And they're just calling you now?"

"Apparently. Jesus. I can't believe it. He's out of the hospital and recovering at home."

Edgard said, "How serious is it?"

"Serious enough that the old man's requested my presence right away." A bitter laugh escaped. "Or what he considers right away."

"What does he want to see you about?"

"No clue. I hafta go tomorrow. Don't know how long I'll be gone." He looked from Chassie to Edgard. "I'm glad you're here to help her. Be just our luck if calves started droppin'."

"But...don't you want me to come with you?" Chassie asked.

Trevor sat next to her and took her hand. "Without soundin' like a dick, you don't wanna meet my family under these circumstances. Hell, I really don't want you to meet them under *any* circumstances." He squeezed his eyes shut. "Chass, baby, they're not nice people."

"How can that be? You're nice."

He grunted.

"You are." Her warm fingers brushed his face. "I don't want you to have to deal with them alone."

"I'll be fine. I just...dammit, I don't wanna have to deal with them *at all.*"

"It's okay. Come back to bed and let me and Ed love you up tonight. We'll give you a happy memory to take with you."

Trevor crawled between them, unprepared for the blitz on his emotions and his body. Edgard and Chassie worked in tandem. Kissing him until he couldn't discern Edgard's taste from Chassie's. Touching him, driving him to the breaking point with dual sensations of rough and soft hands caressing his slick skin. Two mouths sucking and licking. One big hand firmly jacking his cock while tiny fingers delicately rolled his balls.

Chassie and Edgard switched things up as if they'd choreographed this erotic dance a hundred times. She tongued his nipples while Edgard fucked his mouth. Ed came quickly in a molten rush down Trevor's throat. Even as he was still swallowing, Edgard scooted Trevor's ass off the end of the bed. Chassie straddled his head, grinding her sweet, wet pussy against his face as she slipped into sixty-nine position. Edgard was on his knees on the floor, scraping his fingers up and down Trevor's trembling legs and toyed with his balls and prepped his hole as Chassie's tongue continued to keep him on the ragged edge.

Trevor arched when Edgard impaled him. Fast and hard disappeared as he fucked Trevor thoroughly, but with absolute leisure. Chassie bumped her hips and her clit throbbed beneath his flickering tongue; she lifted her mouth off his dick and gasped as he sucked every last pulse from that swollen pearl.

After she'd caught her sanity, Edgard said, "Use your hand on him so I can fuck him harder and not worry about your teeth."

"You want him to see what we're doin'?" she asked as she lay alongside Trevor's body.

"Yeah, we both know how much he likes to watch." Edgard's thrusts were hard and deep and hit Trevor's gland on every stroke. Trevor pumped into Chassie's tight fist, feeling the pace Edgard set in his head, his heart, his cock and his ass. For one breathtaking second he dangled on the precipice of bliss, then he soared over. He watched as milky white spurts arced out of his cockhead onto Chassie's chest and his anal muscles flexed around Edgard's prick, immediately sending Edgard into a shuddering climax.

"Holy hell," Trevor panted. His gaze focused on Edgard and Chassie, who hadn't moved at all. Who weren't paying attention to him at all.

With a sound resembling a growl, Edgard brought Chassie close to him, bent his head and licked the opaque droplets from Chassie's chest with long sweeps of his tongue.

Chassie's head fell back and she moaned seductively as Edgard cleaned up every rivulet, save for a thick spot on the tip of Chassie's nipple. That one he wiped off with the pad of his thumb, bringing it to her mouth so she could suck it clean.

The pure joy displayed between these two people he loved had tears springing to his eyes. He finally had exactly what he wanted and he couldn't bear to let either one go, not for a single night, let alone a lifetime.

But didn't he owe his family a second chance? Part of him screamed no; part of him looked over at Edgard and was thankful for second chances.

No surprise his sleep was troubled as he wrestled with the unknown.

Chapter Twenty-five

The second Trevor pulled up to the place he used to call home, he damn near slammed his old truck in reverse and peeled rubber in an effort to escape.

Nothing had changed outside the house; he suspected nothing had changed inside either.

Trevor parked and took off his University of Wyoming ball cap, running his hands through his hair, unconsciously mimicking Edgard's nervous gesture. He stared at the barns—seven in all—and the gigantic corral surrounded by brand new white metal fencing. Four horse trailers were lined in symmetrical rows along the far left side of the chutes.

Two tractors were parked next to the towering stacks of hay. Must've been a good year if that much remained this late in the season. Then again, his dad could've bought the damn piles of hay. Money had never been an issue for Tater Glanzer. It was both a carrot and a stick—not just for members of his family.

He knocked back a long drink from the bottle of water, wishing it were whiskey. After placing the plastic bottle back in the cup holder, Trevor jammed his hands through his hair again.

You're stalling.

No shit. And how fucking stupid was it that he was cowering in his truck, scared of a sixty-year-old man? He grabbed his duffel bag and ambled up the sidewalk.

Before Trevor decided whether to knock or to walk in, the door opened. His younger brother Brent sneered at him. "Don't be hopin' Pa's heart attack has softened him up. He's still a mean SOB and you're still on his shit list."

"Nice to see you too, Brent." Trevor sidestepped him and paused in the entryway beside the ostentatious curved staircase that would've had a southern plantation owner weeping with envy.

"Hello, Trevor."

He focused on his mother sprawled on the long chaise, a cigarette dangling between her lips. The explosion of flowers on the couch clashed with the floral robe she wore. At noon. On a weekday.

Nothing new there either.

Starla Glanzer still played the part of a rodeo queen, despite the passing of three and a half decades. Her hair was dyed a shiny blonde and teased into an unnatural cloud around her pudgy face. Her eyes were bloodshot from the booze she sucked down like milk, not from bawling over her husband's current health crisis, Trevor thought cynically.

No loving embrace from his mother. Starla loved one thing: money. Her five children ranked below expensive things and her husband ranked even lower.

She exhaled a blue cloud. Her botoxed face remained a mask of boredom as if it'd been two hours since she'd seen her oldest son, not two years. "So you did show up. I didn't think you'd bother."

"Then why'd you call me and ask me to come?"

"Tater told me to. Wouldn't want it to get out that I denied a dyin' man his last wish."

"He ain't close to dead, Ma," Brent said. "Might as well go back to whatever hole you crawled out of, Trevor. It was a wasted trip."

Trevor grinned carelessly, rather than fighting back, knowing it pissed his brother off. "I'm here. Might as well pay my respects to the old man."

His mother snorted and choked on a lungful of smoke.

"Ma? You okay?" A very pregnant woman waddled in from the kitchen. She stopped suddenly and her eyes darted from Trevor to Brent to Starla. "What is he doin' here?"

"Lianna," Trevor drawled, "you're lookin' as lovely as ever."

"Cut the shit, Trevor. What do you want?"

"What do you think he wants?" Brent snapped.

Lianna whirled on Brent, the brother who stood between

them in distance and age. "When I want your opinion, I'll ask Ma or your wife for it."

Jesus. Less than five fucking minutes and he was in the midst of the same old pointless bickering and bullshit. Trevor addressed his mother. "Which room am I stayin' in? I wanna dump my stuff before I see Pa."

Brent and Lianna said simultaneously, "He's *stayin'* here?"

"Of course he is." His mother flashed a smile at him, ignoring his siblings. "Trevor is family. Where else would he stay?"

"In the bunkhouse."

"I'm sorry. Did I hear you say you wanted him to stay at your house, Lianna, darlin'?" Starla cooed in a saccharine tone. "Because I could arrange that."

"No!"

"I didn't think so. Besides, we're havin' a family dinner tonight. You three, Molly, and Tanner."

"Tanner is here?"

"He quit the competition the minute he heard about your father being in the hospital. He drove straight through the night to be at his father's side."

Her meaning—Tanner did his duty and you didn't—was crystal clear. It'd be futile to point out that no one had told him until a week after the incident happened.

"Where is Tanner now?"

"Sleepin' off a drunk in the new horse trailer with some skanky bar maid," Lianna said.

Starla glared at Lianna. "Anyway, everyone will be here."

"Everyone except your wife, Trevor. Why didn't she come with you?"

Because I'm keeping that sweet woman away from this nest of vipers as long as possible. He forced a curt, "She's busy. She sends her regrets." Trevor's hand tensed on the duffel bag strap and he glanced at his mother, perched like a Marlboro rodeo queen among her admiring peasants. "Which room?"

"Same as last time."

"I'll go get settled in. Is Pa up in his bedroom?" His parents hadn't shared a bed for years—a fact they were both mighty proud of—a fact he couldn't fathom since he shared his bed with both Chassie and Edgard in recent days.

"He can't climb stairs yet so he's set up in the den," Lianna said. "And he's sleepin' right now. I ain't about to let you just bull your way in there and wake him up. The man had a heart attack. He needs his rest."

Just then a cowbell clanked from the vicinity of the den.

Everyone froze.

"Can't anyone hear this goddamn bell?" the old man yelled and proceeded to ring the cowbell as if the den had morphed into his own personal bell tower.

"Jesus. I hate that cowbell and it's your fault for givin' it to him, Lianna," his mother snapped and stalked toward the mad ringing.

Trevor didn't jab Lianna for her lie. Instead, he started up the stairs.

In the bedroom at the end of the hall, he tossed his bag on the floor next to the old wooden rocking horse his grandfather had hand carved. Stuck in the trophy room again. A shrine to his father, the great Tater Glanzer, and the man's impact on the sport of rodeo.

Saddles, spurs, belt buckles, trophies, framed newspaper articles, framed magazine covers, more trophies. Trevor knew his mother picked this room in an effort to make Trevor feel inferior in the face of all his father's accomplishments. It didn't work. Not anymore. All it did was remind him how much of his life he'd wasted trying to live up to expectations that weren't his own.

If only he'd been working, not rodeoing, not chasing someone else's dream, then he'd have the money he and Chassie needed to buy Gus's land.

"Stop beating yourself up." Chassie's gentle voice drifted into Trevor's mind like a refreshing breeze, washing away his frustration, if only temporarily. She had that calming effect.

So did Edgard.

He wondered how the two of them were faring without him.

"What do you know about goat births?"

Edgard had joined Chassie and they were draped across the top of Greta's stall in the barn.

His gaze narrowed. "Can't be much different than foals or

calves, can it?"

"I reckon they're the same. That's why I think Greta is in labor." Chassie squinted at the nanny goat chomping on a pile of hay.

"Hate to break it to you, but Greta looks too bored to be in labor. She hasn't lost her appetite a bit, which is a damn shame 'cause she's gonna eat us out of house and home. No wonder he was so anxious to get rid of her."

"Not all females of the species bleat and moan and flop on the ground when their time comes, Ed. Some give birth with quiet dignity."

Edgard's mouth twitched. "My mistake."

"So that's why I think Greta's behavior is mighty suspect. She hasn't shown her hiney in the last half hour."

"Thank God," Edgard muttered.

"It's probably swollen." Chassie gave Edgard an arch look. "I know how that goes."

"No sympathy from me. Maybe next time you'll heed our warnings and save your poor hiney."

She snorted. "I don't remember signing on for gettin' my ass smacked."

"Comes with the territory—and two territorial males." Edgard offered her a sunny smile. "No extra charge."

"Maybe next time I'll spank you."

"Mmm. I'd consider it if you'll kiss it and make it better afterward."

Her face burned when she remembered how erotic it'd been having two mouths and two sets of rough male hands caressing her flaming skin. She hopped down from the fence. "I'm gonna check her."

"Maybe that's not such a good idea."

"You sound like Trevor."

"If you mean I'm concerned about your well-being, *querida*, then I'll take that as a compliment."

"I think I can handle one little goat."

Greta lifted her head and *baaed* a greeting when Chassie entered the stall. Then she returned to mowing hay, allowing Chassie an opportunity to run her hand down the side of Greta's rotund belly. Didn't feel like it was pulling and heaving with labor pains.

"Well?" Edgard asked.

"I can't tell. Need a better look back here." Chassie kept stroking Greta's rear right flank as she dropped to her knees.

"Chass, that's not such a good idea."

"Stop bein' such a worry wart. Look how full her udders are." Greta stilled when Chassie's fingers brushed the closest teat. "You're ready to be a mama, aren't you, pretty girl?"

Greta *baaed* loudly.

"Lemme see how close we are. Okay?" Chassie inched sideways. The second she placed her hand on Greta's rump, Greta panicked.

Her back end flew up, her legs flying high, and her hoof connected with Chassie's forehead.

Chassie literally saw stars as she hit the dirt.

A thud sounded as Edgard jumped the fence, sending hay dust swirling around Chassie's head. "Chassie?"

She forced her eyes open and Edgard's face swam into view.

"Oh damn, baby, your forehead is really bleeding."

"Shit." Her vision was blurry and she had a vicious headache.

"Jesus. Hold still." He stripped off his glove with his teeth and pressed it to where her pulse pounded up by her hairline.

"Jesus fucking Christ would you stop, that hurts!" So much for acting tough.

"Sorry, but you hafta keep pressure on it."

"I'm okay."

"No, you're not. Hang on." Edgard slipped one arm under her knees and the other under her neck as he lifted her.

"I can walk."

"Like hell." Edgard kicked the stall door shut and carried her into the house. When Chassie tried to sit up on the couch, he pushed her back down. "Don't move and let me look at it."

"It's probably just a scratch."

"Let me be the judge of that, okay?" He sucked in a harsh breath when he gently pulled the glove away. "I think it needs stitches. She sliced you open good."

That's when Chassie started to cry. "I don't want stitches. I'll have horrible scars and I'm already not rodeo queen material and I'll end up lookin' worse than I do right now, probably like

Frankenstein."

"Chassie—"

"And we can't afford a trip to the doctor's office," she practically wailed. "Maybe you should just take me to the veterinarian's—"

"Ssh." Edgard wiped her tears and dabbed at the blood. "Calm down. I'm taking you to a real doctor. We'll get you fixed up. And there's no way you could ever look like Frankenstein."

Pain throbbed in her head. "I hate doctors. Hospitals. All that medical shit."

After a minute or so of silence, he asked, "Because of your mother?"

Images of claustrophobic rooms and the stench of antiseptics caused her stomach to pitch. "How'd you know?"

"You never talk about her. You said she was sick. You sort of seemed embarrassed about it."

Chassie nodded. "She was sick for a long time before she died. Most my life, actually. Because she was Native we ended up at the Indian Health Services hospital. No one cared whether she got better, except me. It was like we were both invisible and unwanted. I hated roaming the hospital corridors wondering if I'd return to her room and find her...gone. The worst part was I figured no one would notice when she passed on, and that's exactly what happened the day she finally died. She was dead for an hour before I could get anyone to come into her room."

"I'm sorry."

More tears leaked out even when Edgard's touch soothed her. "You're really gonna make me do this, aren't you? Go to the doctor?"

"Yes, sweetheart, I am. But I'll hold your hand the entire time. I won't leave your side. I promise."

"Thank you. You're so sweet, you probably think I'm such a crybaby—"

"Ssh. I don't think any such thing. It's okay to lean on me." He smoothed the hair from her cheek. "I want you to be able to count on me, Chassie, for whatever you need."

"I'd like that." In a rush, Chassie said, "But you can't tell Trevor what happened when he calls."

Frown lines appeared on Edgard's forehead. "That's not—"

"Please. He'll freak out and there's nothin' he can do. He

needs to stay and sort things out with his family. We both know he'll come racing home if we give him a reason to."

Edgard studied her. He bent down to kiss her cheek. "I disagree, but we've got more important things to do than argue. Stay put. I'll pull the truck up and then we'll go."

Chapter Twenty-six

Trevor killed an hour in his room, alternating between staring out the window and scowling at the rodeo trophies. When he deemed his temper able to handle not only his father, but the rest of his family, he ventured downstairs.

They'd moved out of the doublewide trailer in Crook County and into this testament to Tater Glanzer's ego the year Trevor turned thirteen. Hadn't mattered to his father, uprooting his oldest son at the start of Trevor's high school rodeo career, with one of the most respected high school rodeo teams in the state. Hadn't mattered to his father that Trevor left behind his best friend and the family he'd wished he'd been born into.

Between Tater's rodeo earnings, the untimely death of Starla's father—who'd left every penny of his Wyoming oil money to his only daughter—they set to building the most flamboyant, gaudy house this side of the Big Horn mountains.

Tater demanded their new home be decorated country cabin style, with exotic and domestic animal heads from his various hunting expeditions mounted on the walls and the space littered with his collection of mostly tacky Western art.

Starla ignored Tater's demands and decorated the house in the style of an English country manor, with chintz-covered chairs, plaid and floral couches, lace doilies, ruffles and bows.

The result was pretty hideous, an interior decorator's worst nightmare—Laura Ashley meets Conan the Barbarian. The horse scenes painted on velvet clashed with the velvet draperies. The rusted barbed wire folk art sculptures did not complement the classic Greek marble figurines. The grizzly bear skin rug clashed with the Oriental carpets. Trevor and Chassie were on the same page for how they wanted their home to look.

Hard to be picky when money was an issue. After they'd first gotten married, she'd jokingly suggested they decorate in the theme of cowboy versus Indian to keep with their heritages.

What Brazilian pieces would Edgard add to their eclectic mix? Had he even brought any of his personal stuff over from Brazil?

While he was lost in thought, pondering the changes he wanted to make in his life even as he wondered if he had the guts to follow through with it, his mother had somehow snuck up behind him. "You always were a damn daydreamer."

"Only way to escape from the shitty reality in this family. Besides, I always got my chores done on time. Can't say the same for anyone else." Trevor turned around. "I'm ready to see Pa."

"You sure? He ain't his old piss and vinegar self."

"Like that's a bad thing." An emotion close to worry briefly appeared in Starla's eyes. "How serious is this?"

"Serious enough for him to call *you* home." She sniffed with disdain. "I'll let you judge for yourself." Cigarette in hand, she pushed open the door to the den without knocking. "Get up, you old bastard, Trevor is here."

"Jesus, Ma." Trevor brushed past her. The room was dark except for a lamp in the corner and the glow of the big screen TV mounted on the far wall.

Tater Glanzer was in bed. Trevor didn't remember ever seeing his dad in bed past eight in the morning. Tater wore plaid pajamas, his face was pale and his yellowed hair stuck up like sections of straw.

At one time everyone commented on the resemblance between Trevor and Tater. As years passed and his father packed on weight, the likeness was less pronounced. But for Trevor, the only differences that mattered were those on the inside.

"Trevor."

"Pa."

"Come in, boy. Starla, shut the goddamn door behind you."

"If I leave I ain't comin' back in here to wait on you."

"After thirty-six years you think that's a big surprise to me? Send Lianna in here after a bit. Make sure she knocks first."

The door shut hard enough to rattle the DVDs on the end

table. His parents' sniping and the door slamming barely registered. Trevor pulled up a folding chair, spun it around and straddled it, propping his arms across the back. "So I'm here. What do you want? Now that I can plainly see you ain't gonna die."

"Ain't got much sympathy for me, do ya?"

"Should I?"

"Hell yes. I'm your father."

"Yeah, well, that's something you said embarrassed you on a daily basis, so try again."

Tater looked away. "We've all said and done things we ain't proud of, son."

That admission was the closest he'd ever get to an apology, but it didn't soften Trevor toward the ornery SOB one iota.

"Speaking of...why didn't your wife come with you? Ain't none of us met her yet. Makes me wonder if you're ashamed of her."

Rage erupted inside him, precisely the reaction his father goaded him into, so Trevor refused to grant it to him. "Leave Chassie out of this. You spewed a buncha racist bullshit about her once and you ain't ever doin' it again. So if you can't be civil when you speak of *my wife*, I'll walk out the fuckin' door right now, old man, understand?"

The outburst appeared to have pleased Tater. "See? That's why you'n me didn't get along. You don't have no problem speakin' your mind."

Trevor laughed bitterly. "Don't you mean I ain't never had a problem talkin' back to you? And if I recall, my face met the back of your hand every goddamn time I was stupid enough to speak my mind."

"Didn't do no good. You've still got that same smart mouth."

"I piss you off, you piss me off, old news. If you called me here because you needed someone new to fight with, I'll be hittin' the road. I've got lots of stuff goin' on at home that I'd rather be doin'."

His father considered him in silence.

"Good luck." Trevor stood.

"Sit your ass back down. Now."

Trevor sat.

"Fine. You're right. I ain't ready to lay down and die. But this little spell has shown that I've been short-sighted in decidin' the future for the Glanzer Ranch."

"Again, I ain't a lawyer. What does this have to do with me?"

"Simple. I'm askin' you to move back here and take over. For real. No bullshit. No head games. I'd put you in charge one hundred percent."

"In writin'?"

His dad squirmed, but he nodded. "In writing."

"Why me?"

"Because you're the only one with guts. Brent has no initiative. He's no better'n a trained monkey; he'll do whatever your mother or I tell him to do. Same with Lianna, though she'd like to tell us off, she don't have the balls. And Molly and her husband are both dumb as damn posts so they ain't any help."

"What about Tanner? I thought he raced back here to prove his loyalty, abidin' love and concern for you." Trevor couldn't stop the sarcasm.

"That's what he'd like everyone—includin' me—to think. Truth is, he sucks in the arena, he's pissed away any chance to compete in nationals yet *again*, and he thinks I'm so damn dumb I don't know it."

"Which tells me why you didn't pick Tanner, but it don't tell me why after I've been considered a fuck-up my whole life, that all of a sudden you're offerin' this to me."

"Because you grew up, boy. No more whorin', drinkin', chasin' the rodeo dream. You've shown you can be responsible. By makin' your own way you've shown I can trust you."

"So by me leavin' here...now you're offerin' me everything I ever wanted?" Why did that scenario seem familiar? Because his situation with Edgard had gone along those same lines?

"Yep."

"What's the catch?"

"No catch. I'm serious. As a heart attack."

Trevor didn't know whether to laugh or cry. He stood and paced. "Who else knows about your change of heart attack?"

His dad's rusty chuckle pieced the air. "I ain't told no one, not even your ma. But I'm sure Lianna and Brent suspect. Tanner thinks by suckin' up, I'll be swayed by his so-called charms." Tater harrumphed. "Goddamn idiot. He knocked up another chick in Oklahoma right before Thanksgiving."

"Another?" Trevor scowled. "How many is that now?"

"Four. Three bastard grandbabies spread from California to Florida. Tanner ain't got a pot to piss in after he gets done payin' child support every month. And he could give a shit about any of them kids. The mothers don't want nothin' to do with him so the closest me'n Starla come to seein' them is in pictures."

And yet Trevor didn't feel sorry for Tater. He'd paid no attention to his own kids unless he was whipping them, so Trevor didn't know how Tanner was supposed to have turned out any differently as a father with Tater as a role model.

"So I'm also hopin' when you and Cassie start havin' babies you'll be close by so we can get to know 'em."

"My wife's name is *Chassie*, not Cassie, Pa," Trevor said tersely.

Tater waved him off. "Don't matter just as long as them kids have the Glanzer last name."

His father started to cough. He kept coughing. Trevor handed him a glass of water and his dad choked on it. Just as he was starting to panic, the door flew open and Lianna raced in. She yelled, "Move," and Trevor did.

Lianna rolled their dad to his side and slipped an oxygen mask over his face. Immediately, Tater calmed down and closed his eyes. "Slow and deep, Daddy. I'll be right back." She jerked her head toward the door as a sign for Trevor to leave.

His sister stormed to the dining room and spun around so fast she clipped him with her big belly. "Do you see now? How he pretends to be fine but he's not?"

"Yeah, I see. What's the coughing from?"

Lianna rested her hands on her protruding stomach. "Emphysema."

Trevor lifted both brows. "And yet Ma is still smokin' around him?"

"Like that oughta surprise you. She'll damn well smoke in her own goddamn house if she wants to." Lianna looked over his shoulder. "Ma's words not mine."

"She puffs away while she's takin' care of him?"

"She don't take care of him. Guess who gets stuck takin'

care of him? Me. Tanner's gone most the time. Molly is a coupla bricks short of a load and Brent wouldn't rock the boat for nothin'. I'm not supposed to be doin' half this shit anyway."

Lianna practically invented martyrdom, but it was her own damn fault. "Then why *are* you doin' it?"

"You see any other able-bodied family members lining up?"

"No. But it ain't like Ma and Pa don't have the cash to hire a full-time nurse." Trevor looked Lianna straight in the eyes. "You know why you're stuck doin' this? Because you don't have the balls to stand up to them both and flat-out refuse."

Lianna's mouth opened. Snapped shut.

"I know I ain't been around, so feel free to tell me to blow it out my ass, but if you don't take a stand, your only function will be takin' care of him while Ma smokes in the living room and does word searches all damn day. Is that the contribution you wanna have to the ranch? Think about it." Trevor snagged his coat and wandered outside. Damn cold. He stamped his boots and had no idea why he'd left the warm comfort of the house.

Comfort. Right. Not a word he'd ever associate with the Glanzer abode.

He noticed Tanner's horse trailer and ambled over, beating his fist on the door to the living quarters until a thump sounded inside and the door swung open.

A shirtless Tanner squinted at him. "What the fuck, Trevor? I was sleepin'."

"It's four in the afternoon. Why ain't you helpin' Brent with evenin' chores?"

Tanner laughed. "Right." Then he yawned in Trevor's face and scratched his ass. "I'm up. You might as well come in."

"Gee, thanks." Trevor set an empty cardboard thirty-pack of Keystone Light on the floor so he could squeeze into the bench seat of the dinette table.

"Wanna beer?" Tanner asked, cracking open the mini-fridge.

"Nah. I'm good."

"Little wifey gotcha on a tight leash these days?"

"Yep."

Tanner popped a top. Then a shit-eating grin broke out across his face. "Yeah right. The day you let anyone control you—least of all a woman—is the day I eat my hat."

Trevor studied his brother. Tanner's dark hair stuck up every which way. Dark stubble covered his jaw. Hickeys dotted his neck. Tanner's body frame was slight, and Trevor, at four inches taller, had always outweighed his brother. Not these days. Tanner packed on some serious poundage. His beer gut hung over the unbuttoned waistband of his jeans.

"So the old man called you back here." Tanner plopped on the other end of the bench seat.

"Woulda been nice to know about Pa's heart attack right after it'd happened, not a week later."

Tanner shrugged his thin shoulders. "Maybe if you called to check in once in a while you'd've known."

His brother's attitude was another reminder on why Trevor had chosen to stay away.

"Anyway, we all know why you're here." Tanner chugged the beer. "Pa's offerin' you full control of the place, ain't he?"

Trevor didn't answer.

"You've always been his favorite."

"What the fuck are you babblin' about? Favorite. Right." Trevor snorted. "That's why I ain't been home in years. Because I'm his favorite."

"He ain't puttin' Brent in charge, or neither of the girls. So it leaves you and me as front runners." Tanner twisted the metal tab off the beer can and flicked it at the garbage, yelling, "Score!" and pumping his arms in the air when it pinged into the can. "So I propose a compromise. We tell Pa we're a package deal and we'll both run it."

"What about your rodeo career?"

"I'm havin' a bad go of it. Truth is, if it wasn't for all the free pussy I probably wouldn't be doin' it."

"Don't seem like the pussy is so free if you're knockin' up women all across the country and payin' child support," Trevor said slyly.

Tanner's eyes narrowed. "That ornery fucker told you?"

"Yeah. Four women? You think you'd know what caused that condition by now, Tanner."

"I was drunk. What can you do? Besides, I'm tired of livin' on the pittance Pa gives me every month."

Trevor froze, even as his heart rate spiked. "Pa is payin'

your way on the circuit?"

"Well, yeah. Didn't he pay yours?"

Some favorite son. All the years he'd scraped by, living on next to nothing, and his father had basically given Brent a blank check? That went beyond unfair to plain damn sadistic. "Hell no. If I didn't have enough money to pay the entry fees I didn't compete. Which made it important for me to win."

"But you didn't win." Meanness glinted in Tanner's bloodshot eyes. "You never brought home that all important World Championship belt buckle, didja?"

"I made it a lot further than you ever did."

Tanner shrugged again. "Almost don't cut it. Might as well be at the bottom of the heap rather than stuck in second place."

Trevor stared at his brother. Surprised...yet not.

"That don't have nothin' to do with us runnin' the ranch."

It had everything to do with runnin' the ranch.

The whole scenario unfolded in Trevor's mind like a nightmare. He and Chassie would sell her family home and move here. He'd do all the work. Tanner would continue to be lazy, continue to lie, continue to think his charm made up for his lack of a work ethic. Brent would resent the hell out of him so he wouldn't do shit either. Neither his mother nor his sisters would welcome his wife into their inner circle so Chassie would be alone. After a few kids their marriage would end up like his parents' marriage and her parents' marriage.

Chassie wouldn't stick around if she was miserable. All these cheery scenarios were before Trevor considered Edgard couldn't be part of his life and the thought of losing either of them made him ill.

"...told him I wouldn't do it."

Trevor refocused on his younger brother, chattering away, oblivious to Trevor's silent ruminations. He slid out of the bench seat and stood. "I gotta call Chassie before supper."

"Feelin' the weight of that old ball and chain?"

"Something like that." Trevor felt the weight of her absence like an iron ball in his heart and he bailed before Tanner subjected him to more of his so-called Wyoming charm.

Trevor tried Chassie's cell phone. No answer. He tried the house phone. No answer. He paced in his room. Forcing himself

217

to wait five minutes before he dialed again. Finally after thirty minutes of beating a path in the carpet, Chassie picked up the house phone on the twelfth ring.

"Hello?" she said breathlessly.

"Chassie? Baby, you all right?"

"Uh. Yeah."

"Where you been? I've been tryin' to call and you didn't answer your cell."

"Oh. Umm. Edgard and I were in the barn and I must've forgot it. We just walked in the house."

A rustling noise, like a hand clapped over the receiver.

"Chass?"

"What? Shit. Hang on a second." Mumbled voices. Chassie snapping, "It's fine. Don't even think about it. No!" The receiver crashed and she shouted, "Give it back!"

"Hey, Trev, what's up?" Edgard asked.

"What in the hell is goin' on there?"

"Nothin'. How are things going with your family?"

"Shitty." Trevor heard angry whispering.

Edgard said, "That's good."

Trevor stared at the phone in his hand. "Good that things are goin' shitty?"

"Ah. No. Sorry, Chassie was yammering at me and I didn't hear what you said."

"Let me talk to her."

"She's washing her hands."

"Give her the goddamn phone. Now."

"Fine." Trevor heard them arguing although he couldn't make out the actual words, just the tone.

"So when you comin' home?" In the background he heard Edgard say, "Tell him."

Trevor frowned. "Tell me what?"

"Um. Tell you how much we miss you."

Edgard snorted so loudly Trevor heard him.

"What's happenin' with your family?" Chassie asked.

"My dad offered me full responsibility for runnin' the ranch. Permanently. He'll put it in writin' and everything."

"But..." Chassie sputtered, "B-but you aren't actually considering it?"

"Of course I am. It could be a great opportunity for us." He was such a fucking liar. One lousy day around his family and he gave into the urge to be mean to the people he loved just because he could. Just because he was confused and pissed off they weren't telling him something, and dammit he missed them. Missed being a part of them. Missed who he was when he was with them.

Silence. Then fierce whispers. Then a sniffle.

Jesus. Chassie wasn't crying? "Chass? Baby, you okay?"

Edgard snatched the phone. "No, she's not okay. Don't do this, Trev. Please. Not to her. Not to me, and not to yourself. I'm asking you to wait before making a rash decision."

The phone crashed again. Sounded like they were wrestling for it. In a rush, Chassie said, "I love you, Trevor. I know you think you have to figure this out on your own, but you don't. You have us—both me and Edgard—to help you. Come home to us and we'll talk about it."

Two raps echoed on his door. "Trevor?" Lianna said. "We're takin' Dad into the hospital."

"Chassie. I hafta go. I'll call you later." He hung up.

The rest of the evening was a cluster-fuck of epic proportions. By the time Trevor returned to his room, it was past midnight. Too late to call. Or was he too much of a chickenshit to call because he owed them both an apology?

Either way, he'd make that request for forgiveness in person. He'd grovel if he had to...without qualifications.

Chapter Twenty-seven

Chassie sat in the same place at the kitchen table an hour later when Edgard returned to the house. He snagged a beer from the fridge and straddled the chair opposite hers.

Finally she looked up. "You didn't kill Greta, did you?"

"No. Her reprieve might be short-lived though when Trevor catches wind of it." Edgard took a long, slow drink and eyed the bandage on her forehead. "You should've told him."

"Leave it be, Edgard."

Edgard sighed. Not that he blamed her, but Chassie'd been extremely grouchy all day. Hadn't helped matters hearing Trevor snap off the news he was considering his father's offer to run the Glanzer Ranch on a permanent basis. Not that Edgard believed Trevor would follow through. It reminded Edgard that sometimes Trevor could be thoughtless and a little mean to those he loved just because he didn't know better.

"Sorry. It's just..." Chassie sipped her warm milk, scowling when she realized it'd gone cold. "Trev didn't seem the same."

"Trevor is different when he's around them. Breaking free from his family was the best thing he ever did. I can't imagine why he'd jump back in that cesspool when he's created utopia here with you."

Chassie offered a wan smile. "You're so sweet."

"I try." He scrutinized her face and glanced at the clock. "You take your meds?"

"Yep."

"You hungry? Want me to fix you some supper?"

"No. I'm tired. I really just wanna lay down."

"Let me help you upstairs."

"No. Stop fussin' at me, Ed. I'll just crash on the couch."

"I like fussin' at you, so tough up." Edgard stood. "Will you at least let me tuck you in?"

"I'd like that." Chassie pushed to her feet and grabbed the cordless receiver. "And if it'll make you happy, I'll tell Trevor about the rodeo tattoo Greta's hoof left on my forehead if he calls back."

"Good girl." He kissed the area around the bandage and herded her into the living room. After covering her with a blanket, he headed upstairs to shower.

Twenty minutes later, the receiver nearly dropped from Chassie's nerveless fingers. Her whole body had gone numb and she blinked with disbelief, all thoughts of sleep forgotten.

"Chass? Who was that on the phone? Trevor?"

"No. It was Keely McKay."

"What's wrong?"

The words stuck in her throat.

"Sweetheart, you're scaring me, what's goin' on?"

"My cousin Cameron McKay is missing."

"What?"

Chassie swallowed. Her mouth still felt dry as dust. "The army sent notification to the family that Cam and two other guys were left behind on patrol in Iraq."

"Shit."

"Yeah. Remember when Kade mentioned it was as if that whole family had gone on vacation together? That's why."

"Jesus. How long ago?"

"A week."

"*A week*? What happened?"

"They're not sure. A bomb exploded, knocking out the first two vehicles in a caravan. Cam and his guys got out of their vehicle to help the injured when two more IEDs were detonated. People scattered and took cover. In the mass confusion of smoke, casualties and gunfire, the vehicles remaining in the caravan were ordered to retreat. The brass didn't realize they'd left Cam and the other guys behind until they'd returned to camp."

Edgard didn't say a word.

"The army sent search parties out. Found nothin' so far."

She squeezed her eyes shut, but it didn't block out the horrors filling her brain. "They may never find him or a trace of him. Or the others. How do you deal with that? At least with Dag..."

"Hey, now. Take a deep breath. I'm not gonna tell you everything is gonna be sunshiny rainbows, but sometimes no news is good news."

Chassie folded her arms over her chest. "Know what I hate?"

"That your aunt and uncle and cousins kept this information to themselves?"

"How did you know?"

"Because it's damn near impossible in a close-knit family to know where to draw the line. Carolyn and Carson elected to keep their immediate offspring in the loop. It is their right. I can't imagine that was a painless decision with the way the McKays seem to live in each other's back pockets."

"You're defending them?"

"No, *querida*, I'm trying to give you a different perspective on how different people deal with a difficult family situation."

"What do you know about difficult family issues, Ed? Trevor told me your family was all *sunshiny rainbows*"—she tossed his words back at him—"about you bein' gay. That you had complete acceptance and their support of your lifestyle. How can you possibly understand—"

Without a word, Edgard stormed from the room.

Chassie was flabbergasted he'd taken off mid-sentence, so she followed him to give him a piece of her mind. "I'd appreciate it if you didn't walk away as I'm talkin' to you, Edgard. It's rude."

"Know what else is rude? To make assumptions when you don't know what the hell you're talking about. Only hearing what you wanna hear and tuning everything else out. My life ain't ever been sunshiny rainbows, so don't tell me..." Edgard rattled off a long phrase in Portuguese. "Fuck this. Forget it."

A bad feeling persisted that had nothing to do with Cam. "What kind of assumptions have I made?"

He flapped his hand in the air, waving her off.

"What is it you're not telling me?" She racked her brain, backtracking on conversations that might've held clues she missed. His deflection of answering questions about his ranch.

He'd talked of his last relationship and how he'd taken the man to meet his mother. His mother. Whoa. Then she remembered. "What happened after your mother died, Edgard?"

Edgard whirled around and his face was as cold and hard as an icicle. "My family disowned me."

Chassie automatically stepped back in the face of his rage. "How can they—"

"Evidently my mother was the only one who didn't have an issue with my so-called *perversion*. Evidently she'd kept my stepfather and my brothers and sister in line. So I'd lived years with the lie of complete acceptance about my sexuality. The only reason my *family*"—he spit the word as if it tasted bad—"tolerated me was because of my mother's threats."

"What kind of threats?"

"Financial threats. See, my grandparents—my mother's parents—were rich. She became their only child after my uncle Ramon was murdered when I was eighteen."

"Oh, Ed, I'm so sorry."

"Yeah, well, it gets worse. Turned into a big ugly political deal, no one knew if my uncle's murder was a botched kidnapping and extortion attempt. My mother sent me to the U.S. to live with my real father's parents for the summer in some misguided attempt at protection."

"You knew them?"

"They'd kept in contact with me. Luckily my English was excellent. After I passed the Wyoming test as a real cowboy adept at ridin' and ropin', they took me to a rodeo. I was hooked. Especially after I began to win." A ghostly smile appeared. "I stuck around for three months."

"Did they know you were gay?"

"No."

"When did you...you know...figure it out?"

"First time with a girl was at sixteen. First time with a boy was at eighteen. When I turned nineteen I told my mother which I preferred. She saw no reason to keep it a dirty secret and blabbed to my entire family. Everyone acted supportive. Or so I thought," he added bitterly.

Her thoughts drifted momentarily to Dag. No one in their family would've granted him that false sense of security, even temporarily.

"I returned to the States when I was twenty-two to make a name for myself in U.S. rodeo. Figured out PDQ how 'real' cowboys feel about gays so I stayed in the closet. Had a few random encounters in bigger cities. Was lonely as hell but making enough money to buy my own place in Brazil. I stuck it out for two years before I thought about going home.

"Then I met Trevor. Instantly fell hard, but somehow managed to keep that from him. I was just goddamn happy to be around him all the time. We traveled together as partners, relied on each other for everything until one day he began to look at me differently. And I knew he'd picked up on how I felt about him. I also knew it fucked him up. By the end of the first year of our partnership we were lovers.

"And yeah, I harbored romantic delusions about him pulling up stakes and moving with me to Brazil. After another two years passed of us being together, but not really being together, I left him because I wanted his public acknowledgement of our relationship. Having it in private wasn't good enough for me."

Chassie bit her lip to keep from crying at the unfiltered anguish in his voice.

"Goddamn, I was so childish and needy about proving to everyone that he belonged to me. So stupidly self-righteous and so very, very wrong that I threw it away on a lie."

"A lie?"

"A total fucking lie." Edgard punched the couch cushion, shocking Chassie and himself with his angry gesture. "Sorry. It's just... About a year and a half after I returned home, my mother died in a car accident. In addition to losing the only person who'd understood me, my father—*stepfather*—told me his true feelings; he didn't accept me as a gay man, never had, never would. I was perverted, an embarrassment to his name, his family, to God and the church. He expected me to leave and never return. Problem was, as the oldest male child I was set to inherit everything of my mother's, which meant cutting out his children."

"Your brothers and sister?"

"Yep. He bribed a government official and the verdict handed down decreed we had to sell the homestead that'd been in my family for seven generations." He closed his eyes. "I never once thought about cheating my siblings out of any money and they made me feel so...dirty for everything I was. Everything I thought they'd accepted about me. I lost my mother, my ancestral home, my family, and my...dignity."

"Edgard—"

"The final cut was when my stepfather told everyone in my hometown selling had been my idea because I wanted to live in Sao Paulo with my male lover. I became a pariah. The church forbade me from even visiting my mother's grave."

She couldn't speak.

"So see. I know about difficult family issues. I've lost everything that ever mattered to me."

Except Trevor.

Edgard didn't say it; he didn't have to.

Her heart seemed to shatter into a billion pieces. That's why Edgard had come back. Not to steal Trevor away, but to remind himself of something that'd been good in his life.

Or maybe he'd come back to cement his disillusionment that his time with Trevor hadn't been the sunshiny rainbows he'd remembered?

Poor Edgard. Still grasping at straws, even when he knew them to be hollow. God. It wasn't fair. Why did everything have to be so damn hard? Chassie placed her hands over her face and sobbed.

Strong arms wrapped around her. It took a while for the warmth and heat to offer any solace and she felt guilty for taking from Edgard when she should've been giving to him.

"It's not fair. It's so not fair. Why does bad shit always seem to happen to good people?"

Breathy kisses dotted the crown of her head. "I'm sorry about Cam, sweetheart."

She lifted her face from his wet shirtfront and blinked at him. "You think that's why I'm cryin'?"

Leeriness entered his eyes. "Yes."

"I'm not cryin' about Cam, you big dummy. I'm cryin' about you."

"Me?" he repeated.

"My heart is busted clean apart after hearin' what you've been through. Alone. You're hurtin' so bad and I just wanna fix it. Goddammit, I'd hoped we'd gotten past these secrets and you've been keepin' a big one from me and I'll bet Trevor too, huh?

He nodded warily.

"I wanna punch you and I wanna hug you, you big stupid jerk." Chassie mashed her face into Edgard's chest as more tears poured out in hiccupping stutters.

She tried to squirm away after she'd calmed down. "Sorry about blubbering all over you and swearin' at you."

Edgard tipped her chin up. His eyes were wet and shone pure gold. "Do you realize you're the first person who's cried for me? It is very humbling. Very sweet, and so very...you, Chassie. You've a soft heart and an iron will. It is a potent combination."

A funny tickle started low in her belly. "Ah. Thanks."

Edgard's eyes zeroed in on her mouth. Their bodies were still locked together. "Can you smile for me? So I can taste the happiness on your lips when I kiss you?"

"You're finally gonna kiss me?"

He frowned. "What do you mean?"

"With all the sexual gymnastics we've tried, the one thing you haven't done is give me a real kiss."

"Why do you think that is, *querida*?"

"Maybe because you prefer a mustache on the upper lip of the person you're smooching?"

Edgard laughed softly. "Trevor doesn't have a mustache."

"Maybe you just prefer Trevor?"

"Could be. But how will I know I don't prefer your kisses if I don't give you a fair shot, hmm?"

"Sounds logical." Chassie moistened her lips in expectation.

He bent his head, his gaze solely focused on her lips. Then a soft press of his mouth to hers. He retreated a fraction of an inch, letting his breath fan over hers, letting her anticipation build.

And build.

Her nervous habit of biting her lower lip had him growling. He nibbled the fleshy inside rim. His tongue dipped in, delicately tracing the seam, back and forth. Each wet stroke delved a little deeper. But never all the way.

A whimper escaped.

Then Edgard's hands were on her head and he kissed her voraciously. Thrusting his tongue past her teeth, tasting every inch of her mouth as thoroughly as he pleased.

The change from exploratory to conquering made her wet and weak-kneed. She clung to him, lost, craving every single sensation this complex man could offer her.

He backed off to whisper across her lips, "No need to grow a mustache, darlin'. You kiss just fine. Much better than fine."

She smiled against his mouth.

"Would you like to—"

"Yes."

He chuckled. "You don't know what I was gonna ask."

"You were gonna ask if you can pin me against the wall and fuck me, 'cause you're feelin' all close to me and stuff now that you've spilled your guts, and stopped bein' the strong silent type of tough guy."

"Smartass." Edgard dropped another kiss on her jaw. "But yes, that was it. I want you, Chassie." He dragged his mouth down her throat. "I wanna bury myself in your sweet heat. Lose myself in the softness that is you inside and out."

Chassie rolled her hips into his, getting a heady sense of satisfaction that Edgard was already hard. For her.

"Pants off," he growled.

"Race you." She stepped out of her jeans and panties.

He ditched his jeans, snagged a condom from his pocket and rolled it on. Before Chassie doffed her remaining clothes, Edgard picked her up and pinned her upper body to the wall with his muscular torso. He spread her knees wide and slipped inside her.

"Oh. Wow. That's..." Chassie braced herself for a hard, fast fuck, knowing his preference for rough, dominant sex.

But Edgard stilled. He caressed the tops of her thighs and rotated his hands to cup her ass. Then he rocked his pelvis, pulling out of her wet cunt completely, pausing, and easing back inside on a slow glide until he couldn't go any deeper. "You like that?"

"Uh-huh."

"Me too." Edgard's kisses were as unhurried as his thrusts and she was totally undone at his gentleness.

Her body coiled with eagerness, yet was loose limbed with pleasure. When she realized she'd been wallowing in sexual gratification and not reciprocating, she slid her hands from his wide shoulders, across his collarbones and stopped at the hollow of his throat.

Chassie unbuttoned his shirt, seeking contact with his skin. She loved touching every ridge of his pectorals as her fingers sought the tight male nipples hidden in the hair on his chest.

Edgard groaned. "Pinch them harder."

As she alternated pinching and rasping her thumbs over the hardened nubs, she playfully used her teeth on the strong line of his jaw. That bristly section of his beard scraped her lips and tongue. The valley between his ear and his jawbone seemed to be the source for his intoxicating male scent. She rubbed her mouth, her cheek, her nose in that secret spot, steeping her senses in him, in Edgard, this man who'd gone from her friend to her rival to her lover.

"Arch your neck so I can taste you," he murmured.

His mouth connected unerringly with sensitive spots to send her flesh tingling and her head buzzing. She moaned with complete abandon.

His focus on every nuance of her pleasure was absolute. Wasn't long before her climax swirled through her, not in a sudden burst, but drawn-out twinges that sated her body and filled her soul with an impression of rightness.

Edgard's rhythm accelerated. He plunged deep and his cock jerked, bathing her clenching channel with heat she felt through the latex.

When he whispered, "Chassie," in her hair, her world tilted, her emotions shifted, becoming clearer. She cared about him, not because of Trevor, but because he brought something different to her, something just for her. Edgard was as much a part of Trevor as she was and Edgard was rapidly becoming part of her too.

Chassie let the silence linger while they each caught their breath, leery of ruining the moment.

Edgard sighed and nuzzled her cheek. "You okay?"

"I'm great. You?"

"Pretty stunned, actually."

"Stunned that you enjoyed it?"

"No. How many times do I have to tell you I've loved every second of touching you and being with you?"

"But I'm a woman. Isn't that like against the gay guys'

creed?"

He squeezed her ass. "Dammit, that reminds me, I forgot to check the gay man's handbook. And nailing a real chick—not a man in drag—against the wall, probably will get me permanently kicked out of the club. Then again, a smart cookie like you knows I wouldn't have considered fucking you at all if it hadn't been for our separate relationships with Trevor."

"Yet, this isn't the first time we've done this, Ed."

"It is the first time we've made love alone without Trevor."

"True. Is that why it is so stunning?"

"No. I'm stunned by the way you make me feel, Chass." He pressed his mouth to hers. "Worthy." A soft brush of his lips. "Safe." Another kiss. "That I have value to you beyond what we both feel for Trevor."

Oh God. Don't cry.

Her head thunked back and tears trickled down.

"No, *querida*, don't. Please." Edgard kissed away her tears, murmuring Portuguese sweet-nothings until her cheeks were dry.

"Why are you so goddamned gentlemanly and sweet to me all the time?" Chassie asked half-gruffly, secretly basking in the tender way he soothed her.

Edgard leaned back to gaze in her eyes. "Because you let me. Because I can be softer with you and you don't think any less of me, don't consider me less of a man. You bring out a side in me I'd nearly forgotten and your acceptance of it is one of my favorite things about you."

"I'm glad something is appealing, since I don't have the appendage you prefer."

He smiled gently. "Joke all you want. But I understand now, maybe more than I ever did, Trevor's confusion when he started having feelings for me. I have those same confusing moments with you, Chass. You're not my type, yet I realize for the first time that you really don't fall for a person's gender or appendage so much as you fall for the person. And I'll be damned if I'm not falling for you, Chassie West Glanzer."

In that instant everything between them changed.

"I love him," Chassie said softly.

"I know. I love him too."

"What do we do if he really wants to make a go of it with his family?"

"I don't have any idea."

Silence descended as they stared at each other helplessly.

Edgard withdrew and set her back on her feet. He kept his back to her as he pulled on his jeans and buttoned his shirt. "What are your plans for the rest of the night?"

"Nothin'." She snatched her jeans but didn't bother putting them on. "Pretend I'm not worryin' about Trevor walkin' away from both of us for a bigger piece of goddamn dirt. Pretend I'm not worryin' about what my McKay relatives are dealin' with." *Pretend you didn't just turn me inside out.*

"Maybe you oughta hit the hay early since it's been a rough day. How's your head?"

Chassie kissed his Adam's apple. "You're right, it's sore, and I probably should lay down. But if you tell Trevor I like that you fuss at me I'll punch you in the stomach."

"My lips are sealed."

"Smart man. I will take your advice and change into my pajamas."

"You don't have to wear them on my account, darlin'."

She swatted him on the arm. "Just for that Trevor-ism, I'll be head to toe in granny flannel tonight."

"Still won't deter me." He stole another kiss as he dodged another swat. "I'll do the last check and be up in a bit."

Trevor woke up cranky and lonely. No one was up in the house yet, so he headed outside to help Brent with morning chores, only to learn Brent relied entirely on the three hired men to do everything.

Problem was the hired men did everything wrong and didn't seem to give a shit.

When Brent finally showed up around ten o'clock, Trevor didn't hold back his anger. "Glad you could grace me with your presence. Those hired men are worthless."

"Least I have hired men." Brent permitted a mean smile. "Jealous?"

"Of you still actin' all Lord of the Manor?" Trevor spit tobacco on the ground by Brent's polished and pristine Lucchese boots. "Hell no."

"Right. I'm sure you don't understand what it takes to run an operation this size. Bein's that your 'ranch'"—Brent made exaggerated quotes marks in the air—"is the size of a postage stamp."

Don't take the bait.

"What's your acreage?" Brent taunted. "You even have a thousand acres?"

Don't take the bait.

"My wife has a *garden* that size."

Somehow Trevor stopped himself from snapping off, "Your wife needs that much room to move her fat ass around." Instead he started stacking feed buckets, keeping his back to his brother.

A sarcastic laugh sounded behind him. "Well, well. You're not fightin' back. That must mean you are embarrassed and there is truth to the rumor. How far the mighty have fallen."

Clunk. Thud. Trevor focused on aligning the buckets biggest to smallest and not how much he wanted to pummel his brother's face into the ground.

"Pa ain't foolin' anyone. He just brought you here as a threat to keep me and Tanner in line. He'll never give you control, Trevor."

Tell him. Rub it in his face that it wasn't a threat but a reality. That Pa promised to put it in writing.

"You have no idea how much I'm enjoyin' seein' you crawlin' back here," Brent hissed. "Knowin' you got nothin'. You might act like you don't give a shit, but if that's the case, why'd you bother to show up at all, huh?"

That observation gave Trevor pause. Why *had* he shown up? When he had everything he'd ever wanted waiting for him at home? How long did have to pretend to show a sense of familial duty? How long did he have to suffer for his unfortunate birthright? And why in the hell was he listening to another family member berate and belittle him? When he hated the person he became every time he was around these people?

"You're no different than the rest of us. Stuck, a suck-up, just like us."

"I'm nothin' like you. *Any* of you."

It clicked. Once and for all. How true that statement was. How true it'd always been. After Trevor said it aloud, he finally believed it.

All he had to do was act on it. Not here, but at home, his real home, where he mattered. Where his heart was. Where he was the man he'd always wanted to be. Where his declaration of intent, of love, of change wouldn't be sneered at, but embraced.

He practically burned the rubber off the soles of his boots getting to the house. He bounded up to his room to grab his duffel bag. He didn't stop to chat with his brothers, sisters, and mother gathered in the kitchen; he headed straight for the front door.

"Trevor!" his mother shouted. "Wait. Tater wants to talk to you."

Trevor half-turned, keeping one hand on the doorknob. "I'll pass. You tell him that."

"What? You can't just leave."

"Yeah, I can. I'm goin' home."

"This is your home!"

"No, it's not." He shut the heavy door behind him and didn't look back, and knew he never would again.

Chapter Twenty-eight

After she and Edgard finished chores, Chassie couldn't justify staying away from her McKay relatives. She couldn't stand the idea of them hurting alone so she whipped up a batch of sugar cookies and left Edgard in charge.

She parked her rattletrap pickup alongside Keely's sporty car at the McKay house and tamped down envy. Although the McKays weren't wealthy, they exceeded their local rancher counterparts of being "land rich and cash poor". During a drunken rant, her father had let it slip the McKays' spread was bigger than a couple European countries. Since sections of their land sat on coal and methane gas beds, they might be as ungodly rich as royalty someday.

The McKays' access to funds didn't bode well for her and Trevor. They'd never scrape up the money to buy Gus's land and another part and parcel would be added to the McKays' vast holdings. Still, she wouldn't allow her jealousy of their success drive another wedge between them. Dag's funeral had ended the seven-decade-long feud involving the West and McKay families, and she intended to do her part to keep it that way.

Despite the years of infighting between her father and Carson McKay, Aunt Carolyn had always welcomed her into the McKay stronghold with open arms. Since Chassie, Keely and their cousin Ramona West were the only girls, Aunt C made doubly sure they spent time alone away from their wild boy cousins.

Chassie's thoughts flew to Cam. She couldn't comprehend not ever seeing his teasing smile again. Or being a victim of his practical jokes. Or watching him lace up his battered running shoes before he took off on his daily ten-mile run. Cam's life obsessions were working out and guns. No one had been particularly surprised when he'd enlisted in the armed forces. But his family was shocked when he'd made the military—not the McKay Ranch—his career.

She balanced the tin of cookies. She'd barely climbed the steps when her cousin Colt stepped on the porch.

No smile adorned his lean face and the lines around his eyes were drawn with worry.

"Chassie."

"Colt."

His gaze zoomed to the bandage on her face. "Girl, what happened to your head?"

"Run in with a goat."

"Looks like she bested ya, darlin'." He pointed at the tin. "Whatcha got in there?"

"Sugar cookies for Aunt Carolyn."

"Aw, it was real sweet of you to drive all the way over here. I'm sure Ma will appreciate the goodies once she's feelin' better." Colt attempted to snatch the tin from her hands even as he blocked the door.

Chassie kept the cookies out of reach. "I'd rather give them to her in person."

"And she'd love to see you too, Chass," he inserted with his usual charm, "but it'd be better if you let her heal up first—"

"Cut the shit, Colt. Keely called me and told me about Cam." Colt started to deny it but Chassie held up her hand. "Aunt C was a lifeline to normalcy after Dag and my dad died and I just wanna see if there's anything I can do for her, okay?"

That comment stopped him cold.

Colt studied her, then led them into the house. The stone cold quiet house. The McKay household existed in a perpetual state of chaos and Chassie shivered at the eerie stillness.

She hung her winter jacket on the antique coat tree and dropped the cookies in the messy kitchen—whoa, Carolyn's domain was never in disarray—and hung a right into her aunt's sitting room.

The space, a merry mix of yellow and red, didn't offer the usual cheer. Chassie's heart hurt seeing her normally vibrant aunt subdued. Carolyn McKay always looked put together, whether she wore faded, dusty Wranglers and a Western shirt or a cocktail dress. Today was no exception.

But there was an edge Chassie hadn't seen before. A sense that one wrong word, one wrong move, one wrong look, and she'd unravel like the skein of yarn in her lap.

Chassie watched Carolyn knitting feverishly. The result of her rapidly moving fingers was a pale blue lump piled beside her. Carolyn didn't glance up when she said, "Keely shouldn't have told you."

"I'm glad she did, Aunt C."

No answer.

Chassie crossed the room, her sock feet silent on the wooden floor. She sat on Carolyn's left side. *Click click click* as the metal needles whipped the yarn into shape.

Neither one spoke for the longest time, which was fine by Chassie. She honestly didn't know what to say.

Aunt Carolyn babbled, "I've been putting off finishing this baby blanket for Carter and Macie's newest addition. You know she's due any day, right?"

"Right."

"The baby is a boy. Always a boy in this family, so I have every color of blue yarn you could imagine. I wanted something different for each of my grandchildren. Thane's baby blanket is navy blue and Kyler's blanket is turquoise. It's so sweet Ky still needs that blanket every night before he can sleep even when he claims to be a big boy. Gib's blanket is robin's egg blue. Channing won't let him have it in his crib anymore because she's afraid he'll tie it around the slats and use it to climb out."

Chassie smiled. That sounded like the little wild man.

"I say what goes around comes around because Colby was my climber. Cord always stayed put, patiently waiting for me to lift him out. Colt persuaded Cord and Colby to break him out of his playpen soon as he could talk. Such a charmer at an early age and that hasn't changed. And Cam. Cam rattled the bars on his baby jail until I feared he'd rip them out. When Carter was born I thought Cam would accidentally hurt him because Cam was such a big kid. But Cam was gentle with both Carter and Keely. And patient. Lord, his size scared a lot of folks. Cam is strong and smart and he can't be...there's no way. No way. They're wrong. They're wrong."

The clicking stopped. So did Chassie's heart.

"Oh God. I can't do this...I can't...he's not...not Cam...not one of mine. Not mine."

Chassie gently set the knitting aside and circled her arm around Carolyn's shoulder as she sobbed. Chassie cried silently right along with her, her emotions ripped into shreds.

A cracking noise sounded, followed by a grunt as Carson crouched in front of Carolyn.

Her uncle's face wasn't the usual blank mask, but pinched and pale. Haggard. He paid no attention to Chassie; his sole focus was on his wife. Picking up Carolyn's hands from her lap, he kissed her fingertips. "Sugar?"

Carolyn met his gaze. "What?"

"Are you—"

"Don't you ask me if I'm all right or I swear to God I'll scream."

"O-o-okay," Carson said evenly. "Maybe you oughta—"

"Don't you dare suggest I go lay down either, Carson McKay, or so help me God I'll—" A great gasping sob erupted.

"Hey, now, hush." Carson tenderly kissed Carolyn's palms and the tips of her fingers, then rubbed her knuckles over his razor-stubbled cheeks like her skin was the finest silk. His actions seemed to calm them both a little.

"Sorry," she said. "What were you gonna say?"

"I thought you might wanna give your poor fingers a break for a bit."

"I'm fine. I've gotta get this done."

"I'm sure. But grandbaby number four ain't gonna appreciate you bleedin' all over his blanket any more than I would."

Chassie should've excused herself. But this sweet, solicitous side of her brusque uncle staggered her. She'd never seen Carson McKay as an affectionate man, least of all with his wife. She hadn't thought him capable, given what Chassie's father said about Carson being the coldest, most calculating SOB he'd ever known.

But how much of her father's perceptions were borne out of jealousy? Uncle Carson, while unfailingly polite to her, always made himself scarce when she'd visited his home. In truth, he may've been all touchy-feely and she wouldn't have seen it.

"My fingers aren't bleeding, Carson."

"Not yet. Caro, please give 'em a rest."

"I need something to do with my hands. I'm goin' crazy—"

"I know, sugar, me too." Carson closed his eyes as Carolyn touched his face. The harshest, tightest lines around his mouth relaxed and he sighed as she rubbed his neck.

"You're strung just as tight as me, McKay. Should I give AJ a call and see if she'd swing by and give you a massage?"

"Maybe." His steely blue eyes opened and held a hint of challenge. "If you do something for me first."

When Carolyn arched an eyebrow, Carson grinned. A flat-out bad boy grin, just like the one he'd passed onto his sons. "Not that."

"That'd be a first," Carolyn murmured. "What do you want me to do?"

"Eat something."

"I'm not hungry."

Carson kissed Carolyn's knuckles. "I thought you might say that. But Chassie brought cookies. It'd be rude not to try 'em after she went to all that trouble to bake 'em fresh and bring 'em over here first thing this mornin'."

Chassie bit back a smile. Carson McKay was a sneaky man. Using Aunt Carolyn's innate politeness against her. It had the desired affect because Carolyn caved.

"Maybe just one or two."

"That's my girl." Carson helped Carolyn to her feet. "And some milk."

"Coffee."

"Huh-uh. You're too wired as it is. No coffee."

"Fine, bossy man. Juice."

"Fair enough."

All at once Carolyn seemed to remember Chassie. "Keely's up in her room."

"Thanks."

Carson curled his weathered hands over Carolyn's shoulders, keeping their bodies close as he directed her toward the kitchen.

The McKay house was large enough to have two sets of stairs—a formal set in the front and a narrow set leading upstairs and into the cellar. Chassie took the front set and ambled down the long hallway, pausing to look at the pictures adorning the walls. Everything from Carter's stunning paintings, to family photos dating back to the turn of the century, to Kyler's preschool handprints. She'd always loved Aunt Carolyn's mixed-up, stylish yet personal, decorating style.

She passed several closed oak doors, knocking at one in the middle.

Keely flung open the door with spit in her eye. Her rigid posture relaxed when she realized it was Chassie. After a quick hug, she motioned Chassie into the room. "Thank God it's you."

"I hope that nasty look wasn't meant for your mom or dad."

"No. It was for Colt." Keely frowned at her desk. "Sorry there's no other chairs in here. You're gonna hafta sit on the bed."

"It'll be like old times." Chassie's gaze swept the girlish room. Ruffled white eyelet canopy above the bed. Bright pink Priscilla curtains hung at both windows. A vanity with a lighted mirror panel was shoved along one wall and piled with clothes, shoes and makeup. An overflowing bookcase opposite it crammed with romance novels. Posters of bull riders, bullfighters, PRCA bronc riders were plastered on the lavender walls. Official printouts for the Dodge pro rodeo final standings for the years Colby competed were tacked here and there. Chassie resisted the urge to search for Trevor's name, instead focusing on her cousin. "Really like old times. Wow. This room is exactly the same."

Keely plopped in a wheeled office chair. "Not exactly." She pointed to a bottle of Malibu rum on the dresser. "Back then Daddy would've confiscated that immediately. But now that I'm of age…" She sighed. "Maybe *you* should confiscate it. Been drinking way more than I should in the last few days."

Chassie hopped on the bed and let her legs dangle over the side. "Dare I ask if there's any more news on Cam?"

"None. Every time a goddamn car comes up the driveway, we panic, afraid it's an official army rep here to tell us…" Tears spilled down Keely's cheeks. "I can't say it. And some really superstitious part of me thinks if I don't say it, it won't happen. Stupid, huh?"

"Not stupid. Hopeful."

"Thanks." Keely wiped her nose. "I'm sorry that I brought you into this, Chass. Last night I had a fight with Colt, then I got into the rum and called you. I just needed to vent to someone who wasn't in this house."

"I'm glad you called me. I'll also admit I'm a little pissed off that you guys have been dealin' with this for over a week without tellin' anyone else in the family."

"My thoughts exactly. I don't get why we have to keep it a secret."

Chassie plucked at a thread on the quilt. "Maybe Aunt C is superstitious like you are. If she doesn't tell people he's missin', it can't be true."

"My God. I never considered that." Keely drifted off for a minute.

"So what are you and Colt fightin' about?"

"He's bored. He wants to go home, but he can't because he'll tell Buck what's going on. Dad insists since Colt and I are the only unmarried kids we're here as support for Mom."

"How long are you here for?" Chassie pointed at the open laptop on the desk. "Aren't you supposed to be in school?"

"I am in school. My instructors are letting me keep up online for now, but I'm set to start clinicals in two weeks and that's something I can't miss." Keely twisted a section of her dark hair around her finger—a rare nervous gesture. "So in between studying, I'm trying to talk to Mom, but all she does is knit and drink coffee. Dad barks orders at Cord and Colby over the phone and paces when he's not obsessing over seeing my mother falling to pieces. Colt deals with all the chores around here and anyone who calls or stops by. He has the worst of it, but that doesn't give him the right to nag at me."

"Nag at you about what?"

Keely shrugged. "My plans after I get out of school. My love life."

"Speaking of your love life...how is Justin?"

"I wouldn't know," she said coolly. "He broke up with me."

"What happened?"

"That's what Colt is nagging me about. I won't tell him, even when he offered to cut off that 'little bastard's prick and feed it to him'." Keely's lips turned up, but it was a pale imitation of her usual bad girl grin. "Much as I love Colt's threatening swagger, I need to deal with this fallout on my own. I've tried to talk to AJ, but..."

"But what?"

"She's a great listener, but she doesn't have a frame of reference for that sort of stuff. The only relationship she's ever been in is with Cord." She sighed. "Macie and Channing are cool and I love them to death, but they're pregnant, hormonal, and I don't want them blabbing to my brothers because they'd round up a damn posse."

"I ain't got tons of experience when it comes to relationships, but you wanna tell me what went down?" Chassie offered.

Keely stood and ducked into the extra closet her father converted into a half-bathroom during Keely's teen years. She returned with two Dixie cups and poured a generous slug of rum in each. She handed a cup to Chassie. "I've always had a couple three guys on a string at any given time. Never made any promises, I just wanna have a good time while I'm still young and can."

That attitude sounded exactly like Keely's brothers'.

"After I met Justin, I thought I'd try an actual relationship. We clicked on so many levels and the sex was spectacular. By Christmas I was convinced he was the one."

"Did he feel the same way?"

"I thought so. Remember I went home with him for a couple days during Christmas break?" Chassie nodded. "His mother is awesome. So's his dad. However, Justin's brother Jack is the biggest fuckhead I've ever met. Jesus. I can't believe Carter is such good friends with him.

"Anyway, New Year's Eve we planned to go out with Justin's best friend Logan and Logan's girlfriend, Tiffany. We'd rented a suite in downtown Denver, the whole shebang. Long story short: Tiffany threw a hissy fit and ditched us. Justin didn't want Logan to spend New Year's alone so we headed back to the hotel."

"You, Justin and Logan."

"Yep." Keely drained the contents of her glass and refilled it. "We're having a good time, drinking, bullshitting, listening to music, the usual. Logan tossed off some comment about how he and Justin both would be kissing me at midnight. I said something like 'why wait' and the next thing I knew, Logan and I were kissing. Full body, with him-on-top-of-me type of kissing."

"Justin didn't mind?"

"No. In fact he was really into seeing me get it on with his best friend."

Chassie swallowed hard at the conversational direction. "Were you into it?"

"With two hot, horny cowboys eatin' me up like I was fulfilling their ultimate fantasy? Hell yes. It was a raunchy, wild night of pure sexual debauchery. The next morning we laughed and teased each other like normal. I thought everything was fine."

"It wasn't?"

"At first it was. The next day Justin went skiing with Jack-off. Then he went back on the road and didn't return to Colorado until the Denver Stock Show. When I saw him in person I knew something was up. He admitted he'd had fun in the threesome with his buddy, but afterward he realized I was not the type of girl guys like him married. I was too free, too easy, great for wild sex but nothin' more. It stunned me because I'd never pegged Justin as that type of judgmental guy.

"I suspected he'd told Jack-off the down and dirty details about our private New Year's bash. And Jack-off, being the self-serving, self-righteous prick, convinced him to break up with me. Initially I was so livid I thought about tracking Jack-off down in Chicago to rip him a new one. But as a couple days passed, I put the blame back where it belonged."

Please don't say on yourself, Keely. Please don't say it.

"Justin is to blame. His hang-ups aren't my issue. I'm comfortable with who I am."

Chassie exhaled with relief.

"Maybe his repressed brother filled his head with bullshit, but Justin entertained enough doubts about me to let his opinion be swayed. Hard as it was to swallow, I realized I don't wanna be involved with a man who doesn't know his own mind."

"Smart." She studied Keely's face. "So have you been mopin' around over Justin like a lovesick calf?"

Keely grinned. "Hell no. I've been dating Logan."

Chassie laughed, then clapped her hand over her mouth. "Sorry. For a minute there, I forgot why I'm here."

"It's okay." Keely poured more rum in Chassie's cup. "Enough about me. I wanna hear all about you and that hot-assin husband of yours. How are things going after a year of wedded bliss?"

Chassie tipped the cup, watching the thick liquid stick to the waxy sides as she pondered her answer. "Honestly? It's kind of...confusing right now."

"That's cryptic, Chass. What gives?"

Where should she start? When Edgard sauntered up the driveway? When she caught her husband kissing another man? After she watched them having sex? After all three of them started fucking on a regular basis? "Trevor's dad had a heart attack."

"Shit. I had no idea."

"Yeah, well, neither did he. No one in his family told him until a week after it happened."

Keely whistled. "Double shit. Must seem like everyone is keeping family stuff from you guys. Is Trevor's dad okay?"

"I guess," she hedged. "Trevor's checked in a couple of times, but he's really distracted when he calls. I don't want to press him. He'll tell me when he comes home."

"You're doing everything at the ranch by yourself?"

"No. I have help. Good help, as it turns out."

"Who?"

"Trevor's former ropin' partner. Edgard Mancuso. Know him?"

Chassie heard the expression "bug-eyed" but she'd never seen it on a person until Keely.

"Holy shit. Know him? I've lusted after him almost as long as I have Trevor. Edgard Mancuso. The hot Brazilian? Dark hair and golden eyes? With the ripped body, luminous smile and slow, sexy accent? Knows how to rope and ride like nobody's business? That Edgard Mancuso?"

"Yep."

"How'd you manage that?"

"It gets better." Chassie knocked back the booze in her cup. "I'm sleepin' with him."

"What!"

Two goggle-eyed expressions from the usually unflappable Keely in one day. Not bad. "You heard me. I'm sleepin' with him. And Trevor."

"Omigod. Every detail. Right now."

"This stays between us, right?"

"Absolutely."

"Edgard showed up out of the blue. He and Trev hadn't seen each other since Colby's accident in Cheyenne. Since they'd been partners for years things just clicked back into place easily"—*liar liar*—"and Ed started helpin' out. Found out some bad things happened to him in Brazil and he's not sure if he's ever goin' back. So he's stayin' with us indefinitely. Which is cool, 'cause I really like him and he and I hit it off like gangbusters."

Keely said slyly, "Maybe you mean, you hit it off during a gang *bang*."

Chassie stuck her tongue out at her cousin. "Funny, anyway, one night they're talkin' about all the crazy sex stuff they did on the road and it was the perfect opportunity to experience the raunchy threesome stuff I'd been curious about. So I propositioned them."

"Chassie West Glanzer...I'm impressed!"

She allowed a small smirk. "Trevor is way into it, Edgard is way into it and I'm in heaven, to put it mildly. I've indulged in some of the hottest sex of my life and that's sayin' something with sex-god Trevor Glanzer as my husband."

Keely frowned. "I sense a 'but' coming."

"But I don't want it to be temporary, K. It might seem bizarre, but I want Trevor and Edgard in my bed and in my life for the long haul."

"Is that what they want too?"

"Yeah. But it's not that simple."

"Why not?" Keely countered. "How you live your life is your business, Chass."

"Did you forget we're livin' that life in Wyoming?"

"You worried what people will say down at the feed store?"

"Maybe a little. It's definitely not the norm." Chassie couldn't tell Keely how much out of the norm the situation really was.

A thoughtful expression crossed Keely's face. "Remember old man Jacobs? He and his wife owned a place up by the reservation? Sold veggies and dried herbs?"

Chassie nodded.

"Apparently Jacobs' brother's wife moved in with them after the brother died in some war and they'd lived together for forty years."

"So?"

"So, did it ever cross your mind something hinky might've been going on with three people living together?"

"No." A strange feeling—hope? began to take root.

"That's what I'm saying. No one thought anything of it. Maybe the old man screwed his sister-in-law and his wife every night and twice on Sundays. Maybe the two women were rug munchers and he was a cover. Maybe they didn't have sex ever and preferred to play pinochle."

"Eww. Nice visual, K."

"The point is, no one around here cared. They were good neighbors. Good people. If the three of them held hands and skipped down Main Street naked, screaming about free love, or made out in church, or bragged about their kinky threesomes at the VFW, things would've been different."

"You really think so?"

"I know so. I'll bet you dollars to donuts once it's common knowledge that Edgard's moved in with you guys, everyone will think it's great Trevor's good buddy is there as a live-in ranch hand. The three of you will become entrenched in the minds of the community as a package deal. Honestly, Chass, no one will ever be the wiser that you are the middle of a Trevor and Edgard sandwich every night."

"Except I sorta hinted to that bratty Brandy Martinson we were havin' threesomes before any of this came to pass. She's probably blabbed to the whole county."

"Then the damage is done. Enjoy your notoriety. Be nice not to be a McKay for a change." Keely squeezed Chassie's hand. "There is no such thing as 'normal' even in Wyoming. You create your own family. Do what makes you, Trevor and Edgard happy in your own home. Besides, my mother always says the most meaningful relationships are those that don't have a public face."

"Wise woman, your mother."

"And if Cam was here he'd command you to follow your bliss, say 'fuck you' to the world, and let the chips fall where they may." Keely smiled wistfully. "Grab happiness whenever and wherever you can, Chass, 'cause you know how fleeting it is. It can be gone before you know it or ever get a chance to enjoy it."

The cordless receiver on Keely's desk rang and she grabbed it, spinning it around to check the caller ID. The blood drained from her face.

Chassie's stomach dropped as if she'd swallowed a stone. "Keely. What's wrong? Who is it?"

"U.S. Government. Unlisted. Oh sweet Jesus." She raced out of the room and banged on Colt's door, yelling, "Colt, now," and Keely's footsteps thumped down the stairs, followed by her brother's.

Fifteen minutes passed. Didn't bode well that Keely hadn't burst back with the good news everything was all right. Chassie forced herself to go downstairs.

In the living room Colt stared out the window, his hands jammed in his back pockets. Carolyn sagged into the couch, crying silently as she stroked Keely's hair. Keely sat on the floor with her head in her mother's lap, arms wrapped around her mother's calves. Her eyes were closed through the tears falling to the floor.

Carson's voice drifted from the dining room. Chassie leaned against the wall, waiting for the right moment to ask what'd happened. Her heart ached. God. She wished Trevor and Edgard were with her.

Colt swore and turned around. When he noticed Chassie, he shot a questioning look at his mother, and she slowly nodded at him. "They found Cam."

"Oh thank God. Is he okay?"

"No. He's...fu—screwed up. Bad. Seriously bad. Cam had surgery two days ago, right after they found him, barely alive. Somehow the army misplaced our number and were just now able to let us know what's goin' on."

"Surgery? For what?"

Colt swore again and balled his hands into fists at his sides. His jaw was clenched so tightly Chassie didn't know whether he'd be able to speak.

"Surgery to amputate his mangled left leg. They cut it off below the knee. Evidently he lost the pinky finger on his left hand. He suffered from shrapnel wounds over the lower half of his body, burns to his chest and something...with his face, I didn't catch all of that part. Far as the doctors could tell, he'd sustained no brain damage in the week he was MIA. Luckily none of his internal organs were hit."

She was as dismayed as she was relieved. At least he was alive. "Are they sendin' him home?"

Colt nodded. "As soon as he's stable they're transporting him to Walter Reed. He'll be there for some time before he's discharged. They don't know when."

Carson slipped back into the room and dropped next to Carolyn on the sofa. He put his big hand on Keely's head and stroked her hair. "Carter sends his love. He can't come home with Macie set to go any time..."

Carolyn patted his thigh. "Did you tell him it's all right to stay there and focus on his wife? And Thane?"

"Yeah. Cord and AJ are on their way over. Same for Colby and Channing. And the kids."

"Good."

"Listen, sugar—"

"Did you call Cal and Kimi?" Carolyn interrupted. "Or your other brothers? What about Kade? Kane?"

Chassie wondered if they'd remember to call the West side of the family, but chose not to point it out.

"No."

Colt said, "I'll do it. It'll give me something to do besides think about gettin' drunk."

As much as Chassie wanted to go home to hear what'd happened with Trevor and his family, she knew she'd stay with the McKays. Someone needed to fix meals, wash dishes and watch Gib and Ky so the adults could talk without distractions or interruptions.

Chassie said, "I'll see about fixin' some lunch," and disappeared into the kitchen to call home so Edgard knew not to expect her.

Chapter Twenty-nine

Trevor was halfway home when Chassie called and told him about Cam McKay. Her subdued tone and distraction was a sign for him not to tell her what'd gone down with his family. He owed her a full explanation, face-to-face, not another half-assed deflection of intent. Not another bald-faced lie.

It'd been a shitty test to see how she'd react to moving to the Glanzer ranch. Making her think he was considering it, even when he hadn't been. Because Trevor had passed his own test, and finally understood how perfect his life was. He'd married a wonderful woman he loved with his whole heart. He was able to spend his daytime hours outside working land he owned and loved. He finally acknowledged that he could fill the empty part he'd resigned to remaining empty. The part of him that'd belonged to Edgard; the part of him that'd always loved Edgard.

Even as the words repeated in his head he felt foolish. Loving another man. But he did. What Trevor felt for Edgard went beyond simple lust and sexual experimentation. Friendship, companionship, shared interests, rockin' sex— exactly what he and Chassie shared, which near as he could figure, was love.

Could Edgard live with Trevor's affection only in private? Could Chassie deal with sharing Trevor with Edgard? Could Trevor handle both Chassie and Edgard's demands? Could he let a relationship develop between them without jealousy?

Most importantly, could he convince Edgard that it didn't matter if people outside their household knew they loved each other, just as long as they knew? It wasn't hiding the truth. It wasn't giving into outdated societal morals. What passed between the three of them was private. Not boasting near and far about their sexual preferences and dynamics wasn't unusual, it was normal.

Let it go. Your brain is fixin' to explode.

Soon as Chassie came home they'd address the questions and concerns reasonably, like rational adults, because he'd be damned if he'd let Edgard walk out of his life again.

Edgard's pickup was parked by the barn. The woodpile had been split and stacked. The driveway cleared after a day's worth of snow. A light shone in the kitchen. Smoke curled against the purplish twilight sky, making the little farmhouse tucked among the trees postcard worthy.

He grabbed his duffel and headed inside, wondering what Edgard was doing after the last cattle check, wishing Chassie was here to meet him. Trevor hung up his coat and shed his boots, and noticed Edgard in the kitchen waiting for him instead. Automatically his heart lightened a bit.

"Hey. How were the roads?" Edgard asked.

"No problems except outside of Lusk. But even that wasn't bad." Trevor rubbed his cold hands together. "Hear anything else from Chassie?"

Edgard shook his head. "Nothin' new. Damn shame about that McKay brother. Gonna be rough on the whole family. I'd say he's lucky to be alive, but that sounds a little hollow."

"I know what you mean." Trevor tamped down his nerves and moved in front of Edgard, setting his hands on Edgard's shoulders.

Before the wariness in Edgard's eyes scared him off completely, Trevor jerked the man into a full body hug. "I missed you."

Edgard read Trevor's underlying meaning. Trevor hadn't meant missing him for the last day, but for the last three and a half years. Edgard returned the embrace with a murmured, "Same here."

They were content to hold each other for a good long while, just because they could.

Trevor pulled back and cupped Edgard's face—that beautiful, familiar, smiling face. He gloried in the pleasure shining in those topaz eyes. "Ah hell, Ed"—he cleared his throat—"I love you. I ain't ever said it to you, but that don't mean I didn't feel it then or now."

Edgard's long pause seemed to steal every bit of wind from Trevor's sails. Until that magnificent smile appeared. "I could be a total dick and say it's about fuckin' time, but I won't. I've changed too. I realize we're both in a different place than we were years ago. I'll confess I like hearing it now, *meu amor.*"

"I figured you would." Trevor bent his head, letting their breath mingle but never breaking eye contact. "I ain't ever gonna be ashamed of admittin' it to you. I don't care what anyone else thinks. I care what you think. Can you live with that?"

"Yeah, especially after living without it."

Trevor let his mouth deliver on the promise with an extensive, lazy, wet kiss. A full-body kiss, pelvis grinding on pelvis, cocks perfectly aligned. They were breathing hard when they broke apart.

Edgard tasted Trevor's bottom lip with a measured sweep of his tongue. "I want you. Now. I don't care where, but it needs to be now."

"Goddamn right." Trevor's hands flew to Edgard's belt. Buckle undone, button undone, zipper undone, Trevor was damn near undone wanting to get his hands and mouth all over this man's tempting body. He sank to his knees as he tugged Edgard's jeans down his corded thighs and off, on to the floor. "Least you ain't wearin' boots," he said, rubbing his cheek against the hot, hard length and inhaling Edgard's unique scent.

"Trevor, this isn't what I—"

He eased back. "You got a problem with me suckin' you off?"

"Ah. No."

"Then shut the fuck up." Trevor wrapped his hand around the base of Edgard's cock and stroked as his mouth went to work on the wet tip. He sucked, saturating his tongue with Ed's flavor, bathing that throbbing organ with his saliva. On every downstroke, his mouth went a little further.

Hands grasped his hair, forcing him deeper.

With the plump cockhead resting on his lips, Trevor warned, "Your hands better be grippin' the counter. Don't make me tell you twice."

"Jesus. All right."

He watched as Edgard's palms clamped around the counter's edge. "Move your legs apart." Trevor's dick pressed painfully against his fly and he shifted his stance. His lips parted to take every hot inch of that rigid cock. Greedily. Hungrily. Using his teeth to tease. Flicking his tongue over the sweet spot below the purplish crown.

Edgard groaned. "I love that, but oh man, I love it when you suck my balls."

Keeping Edgard's prick buried in his mouth, Trevor reached between Edgard's widespread thighs to fondle the tight sac. He rolled the balls over his fingertips, letting the saliva run down his chin to coat those tight, furry globes.

"Sweet mother of God."

Trevor released the shaft and held it aside, still jacking Edgard off, opening wide to suck both balls into his mouth.

Another enthusiastic moan rumbled from Edgard's chest.

He sucked on the taut globes, loving the pearls of pre-come sliding down Edgard's cock and dripping on his face. The wet balls slipped free from his mouth and he used his tongue to trace the thick, pulsing root back to that tempting pucker.

"Fuck. More. Please. *Please.*"

Tickling the velvety hole proved difficult given the position of his head. Trevor licked as far back as he could, knowing the teasing sweep of wetness over the sensitive knot of nerves drove Edgard insane. "Can't reach. My tongue ain't long enough at this angle."

"Chassie's is," Edgard murmured. "That's something new we'll have to teach her."

Trevor purred his agreement, half-surprised how natural it was talking about teaching his wife new sex tricks while satisfying his male lover. He lapped and licked, sweeping his tongue over the drops leaking from the slit in the head.

"Finish me," Edgard half-pleaded. His hands plowed through Trevor's hair and he plunged into Trevor's mouth with a growl. Back out. In. Out. In. Out. Without pause, an animalistic rhythm.

Trevor loved to make the man lose control. Absolutely fucking loved it.

"Suck harder. Christ, like that."

He dug his fingers into the tops of Edgard's solid thighs as those lean hips hammered into his face with absolute abandon.

Edgard rammed his dick to the hilt. Each stroke stretched Trevor's mouth wider, each stroke became harder, harsher, taking Ed to the point of detonation. Edgard slapped his hands on Trevor's cheeks, holding his face as he came with a hoarse shout.

Satisfaction surged as Edgard poured his salty, bitter heat down the back of Trevor's throat. When Edgard neared the end of his orgasm, Trevor let the shaft slip from his mouth until his teeth circled the flared rim of the crown. He focused on the cockhead, feeling the thick vein running on the underside of Edgard's dick still twitching beneath Trevor's lips.

"Goddamn." Edgard grunted and kept coming.

He kept right on tonguing him until he had nothing left.

Spent, Edgard released his grip on Trevor's hair. Acting somewhat weak-kneed, he braced one hand behind him on the counter ledge and lovingly caressed the contours of Trevor's cheek and jaw with his other hand. "Trev. I—don't...damn."

One last suckle of that still half-hard cock, one last nuzzle of the damp hair coated with Edgard's musk and Trevor eased off. He scrambled to his feet. "Good. Because my dick is about to explode and I want it buried balls deep in your ass when it happens."

Without waiting Trevor grabbed Edgard's hand and led him upstairs to the bedroom he shared with Chassie. The sheets were rumpled. The quilt dangled off the end of the bed and a twinge of guilt surfaced.

Edgard sensed it. Wrapping his arms around Trevor's waist, he nestled his chin in the curve of Trevor's shoulder. "I didn't make up the bed after Chassie left this morning." He nipped Trevor's earlobe.

Electric tingles shot down Trevor's arm and distorted his already ragged breathing.

"If it'll make you feel less guilty about you and me bein' together, Chassie and I made love in that bed last night."

"How was it?"

"Sweet and hot, but we missed you."

Trevor was actually turned on by the idea of watching

Lorelei James

Edgard and Chassie fucking alone—with him jacking off and then joining in for round two.

"I'm sure Chassie will be hungry for details of our hot monkey sex when she comes home."

"Then we'd better not disappoint her."

Shirts were stripped away. Same for T-shirts. Trevor's jeans, underwear and socks.

They faced each other. Reached for each other. Matched chest-to-chest, cock-to-cock, mouth-to-mouth. Even as Edgard tried to seduce him with teasing kisses, Trevor was strung tight, crazy for release.

Again, Edgard was tuned in to his signals. "Get on the bed. Let me take care of you."

"I don't wanna blowjob. I wanna fuck you."

"Don't argue. Do it."

Trevor crawled on the bed on his hands and knees. Just as he was about to roll over, Edgard's hands were on his ass, spreading his butt cheeks apart. Then a hot, wet tongue traced his crack.

"Jesus." He stretched his arms above his head and pressed the side of his face to the mattress. The sheets smelled like Chassie. Like Edgard. Like them. Trevor breathed the enthralling scent deep into his lungs.

Light tongue flicks tantalized his hole, followed by hard-lipped nibbles and soft sucking.

Edgard was an expert at anal play and held nothing back. "I am such a slut for that. Been so long."

"I know. That's why I love to do it." Another wet flicker of his tongue over the pucker. "This whips you into that wheezing-whimpering-impatient-to-fuck state." Edgard pierced his ass with one deep jab. He lapped at Trevor's hole, teasing, and then plunging that wicked tongue deep again.

Trevor clutched handfuls of the sheet, bumping his hips back to meet every searching thrust. Pressure built in his balls and he desperately wanted to come. And not to come.

Edgard knew when to back off. He rubbed his jaw over Trevor's cheeks and scattered kisses up the line of Trevor's spine. A gentle scrape of teeth on his shoulder blades set Trevor's body quaking. Hot breath in his ear. "Next time I'm gonna make you come like that. Right now, get the lube."

"Damn you look good all stretched out on my bed," Trevor said.

"You ain't such a hardship yourself." Trevor's muscle-bound body always fascinated Edgard. The pale blond hair on Trevor's brawny forearms was softer than the coarse hair covering his long legs. Yet, his upper torso was nearly hairless, with the exception of the golden trail leading to his crotch. Abs of steel, a result of Trevor's insistence on three hundred core-strengthening crunches every morning—evidently a habit he'd maintained after he'd left the circuit. Old white scars stood out on his bronze skin like badges of honor or of shame. Freckles ranging in color from cinnamon to gold were scattered across his broad shoulders and down his broad back as testament to the sheer amount of hours Trevor spent in the sun.

The click of the cap of lubricant drew Edgard's attention to Trevor's face. He squirted gel on his palm and fisted his cock. Then he ran a line of gel down the seam of his index and middle fingers as he moved between Edgard's legs.

Edgard pulled his knees back, exposing his entrance for Trevor's pleasure. His cock had gone rigid with arousal again and slapped against his belly.

"No foreplay. I want you so bad it hurts." Trevor rubbed the cool gel on Edgard's hole and pushed one finger in, and pumped it in and out a few times before wiggling the second one in beside it.

As much as Edgard craved Trevor's tongue licking his nipples, it was a serious turn on witnessing the vein below Trevor's jawbone pop as his fingers repeatedly breached Edgard's body. His sharp cheekbones were flushed with arousal. His lips—oh man, those pouty lips he'd dreamed about—were plumped and red from sucking Edgar's cock. He was beautiful. Trevor was everything. Not a passing fancy, not an unattainable dream, but the man Edgard wanted to spend his life with.

"I'm ready, wanna feel you in me." Edgard reached for Trevor, looping his arms around Trevor's neck.

Trevor nailed Edgard's gland a couple times and grinned when Edgard moaned, arching into his intimate touch. "Jesus you're tight. Think you can take me hard?"

"I'll take you any way I can get you."

Then the fingers disappeared and Trevor levered his body over Edgard's. The thick head of Trevor's cock brushed Edgard's hole once before Trevor plowed in to the hilt.

Edgard hissed.

"Ah fuck." Trevor lowered his face against Edgard's neck. "I ain't gonna last. Blowin' you and then the way you used that talented tongue has done me in, Ed." He withdrew fully and plunged in, setting a rhythm that made it impossible to maintain a kiss.

Instead, Edgard settled for sucking the tendons in Trevor's neck while pinching his pebbled nipples. Trevor grunted his approval and slammed into Edgard harder.

"Next time I'm gonna take my time touchin' you and lovin' on you." He gritted his teeth, looking down to watch his thick cock tunneling in and out of Edgard's ass.

Feeling the slickness on his stomach from his own cock, tasting the sweat running down Trevor's straining throat made Edgard's blood pump hotter. Witnessing the ecstasy on Trevor's face had Edgard clamping down with his anal muscles every time Trevor's pistoning cock filled his ass. "Come on, Trev. Don't hold back."

"Never. Not ever again."

"You ain't gonna break me."

Trevor growled. "Christ, I love fucking you." His palms landed on Edgard's kneecaps and he pushed Edgard flat as he let loose with all the raw power his body could offer. "Fucking." *Thrust.* "Love." *Thrust.* "You." *Thrust.* Trevor tipped his head back; a moan burst from his mouth and his lips went slack. His eyes squeezed shut as his orgasm hit and he grunted and pounded harder, coating Edgard's channel with jets of his hot come.

It was too much. Edgard took himself in hand, beating off until he shot his load all over his belly, biting his lip to keep from crying out his pleasure as Trevor took his.

Broken breaths filled the humid, sex-scented air.

Soon as Trevor opened his pretty eyes, Edgard urged him forward. His mouth teased across Trevor's until his moist lips parted. Edgard swallowed his sweet breath, and his sweet words, indulging them both in a drawn-out, tongue-tangling kiss.

"I missed that."

"Just the sex?"

"No. Just everything about you. Goddamn, my memories don't come close to the reality of bein' with you. Not even fuckin' close." Trevor nuzzled Edgard's jaw, pressing wet kisses down the slope to his chin.

"Same goes. I could get used to this sweet talkin'."

"Yeah? You always wanted them sappy kind of love words."

"Maybe they have more impact now, Trev, because you actually mean them."

"That I do. So, what we doin' for our next monkey sex trick? I'm thinkin' of a repeat of the one we did in Tulsa after we won first place, where you're layin' on your back, kinda spread-eagled. And I'm sittin' on top of you, reverse cowgirl style as I'm bouncin' on your pole."

Edgard's cock twitched between them and Trevor laughed.

"Or a little sixty-nine action?" The very tip of Trevor's tongue outlined the rim of Edgard's ear. "Or maybe just with my head hangin' off the end of the bed so you can redefine deep throatin'...'course, you'd be suckin' on me too."

Edgard squirmed at the goose bumps racing down his arms.

"Or—"

"Or we could talk."

Trevor lifted his head. "Why?"

"Because I have a confession to make."

Those pale blue eyes narrowed.

Just say it. Straight up. "I love you, man. I've always loved you. But it appears I'm also falling for your wife."

"Run that by me again."

"I'm crazy about that woman who's crazy enough to love you."

"You are?"

"Yeah. From the second I met her I knew she was different—not the same shallow type of pretty, cheap, easy bimbos you preferred to bed in the past."

Trevor grunted.

"Don't get me wrong, Chassie is pretty. She's sweet as pie. She's unassuming, yet there's no doubt she is borne of grit and a whole lotta try. Not to mention she's funny. And I swear, she's as raunchy as any man I've ever known."

"Preachin' to the choir here, Ed," he said testily.

He closed his eyes and bucked his hips. "Fine. Forget it. Get off me."

"Oh hell no." Trevor made his weight feel heavier. "I'm gonna be in you and on you when you tell me you ain't pullin' my leg when you confess you've got the hots for Chassie, *meu amigo*."

"I wouldn't joke, especially not about this."

A pause filled the air. "Hey," Trevor intoned softly, but with a gruff edge. "Look at me."

Edgard blinked his eyes open with surprise.

"Sorry." Trevor smooched Edgard's nose. "It just caught me off guard, okay? Ain't every day your best friend tells you he's got a thing for your wife. Go ahead and finish. I'll keep my trap shut for a change."

Edgard inhaled and exhaled slowly, amazed by how much Trevor had changed. How glad he was the changes didn't come at the expense of everything else he'd liked about Trevor. "Chassie and I hung out and worked side-by-side after I first arrived here, since you didn't want anything to do with me. I got to know her. I genuinely liked her as a person before I figured out she really did make you happy. After I kissed you and Chassie left, I felt bad, but not bad enough that I'd've given you up if she didn't come back."

"Did you tell her that?"

"No. When she returned and worked so hard at understanding our relationship, then wanted to be a part of it, I thought if I could have you occasionally, I'd put up with being in bed with Chassie too."

Trevor just stared at him.

"But see, there is no *put up with*. And I've been as freaked out about my attraction to her as I imagine you were when you figured out you were attracted to me."

"Is it just sex?"

"I thought so at first. Strictly on a sexual level I love touching her. Having her touch me. Watching you two together. Having her watching you and me. And the three of us in bed is beyond explosive."

A smile tilted the corners of Trevor's mouth. "But?"

"On a personal level...it might sound lame, but Chassie lets me soothe her and she soothes me in a way no one else ever has."

"Not even me?"

Edgard shook his head. "Not even my mother."

"Whoa. That's some serious shit, Ed."

"Yeah. There's a softness about her that doesn't have anything to do with her female parts. The other night, when I told her everything that'd gone on in my life, things I never told anyone, not even you, she broke down and cried for me. Cried. For me. No one's ever cried for me before."

"I did. After you went back to Brazil." Trevor scowled. "But I was really cryin' for myself, wasn't I?"

"A tough cowboy like you really shed a tear? For me?" When Trevor ducked his head, Edgard forced it back up. "I'm glad you told me. There was a time when you wouldn't have."

"Times change."

"Thank God. Anyway, the morning after the first night we were all together? She showed honest-to-God genuine sorrow that I'd slept alone. The next night and every night after that she welcomed me. Not only into your bed, but...into her heart."

"That woman has a mighty big, mighty soft heart. I kid her that her breasts are so small because her heart is so dang big," Trevor added with a chuckle. "Long as we're spillin' our guts... Lemme ask you something."

Threading his fingers through the damp hair at Trevor's temple, Edgard let his thumb caress the hollow of Trevor's cheek and the man practically purred. "Anything."

"Do you think Chassie would be so acceptin' about us if it wasn't for Dag?"

"No."

Trevor's eyes were serious. "Me neither. Why is that?"

"She watched her brother, the first man she loved, wither up inside and die because he couldn't be who he wanted to be or live his life on his own terms. She doesn't want that to happen to her or to you, or now, even to me. Not when she has the power to change it. Not in a crusading way, trying to right old wrongs, but in accepting things change."

"It goes deeper than rollin' with the punches, don't it?"

"Yeah. I'm amazed that Chassie loves unconditionally, which is why she's at her aunt and uncle's place helping out even when she's mad as hell at the whole lot of 'em. Even when she'd rather be here with you, hearing what happened with your family."

"Doesn't seem like there's enough of her sweet goodness to go around, does there?" Trevor said.

"No. She just..." Edgard stared at Trevor helplessly, hoping he'd fill in the blanks.

"I know, buddy. Chassie is like...*it*, ain't she? I discovered that the very first time we spent time together. Made me goddamn glad no other bozos around these parts figured it out before I snapped her up as mine."

"You're not mad?"

"No. That pint-sized woman brings out the best in everyone, even degenerates like us. Bein' with her has made me a better man. I think that's why I'm able to accept how I feel about you because she accepts it. Encourages it." Trevor kissed his forehead. "Besides, I knew you were a goner for Miz Sassy Chassie when you bought her that goddamn goat."

"Chass was kinda putty in my hands after that, wasn't she?" Edgard mused.

Trevor laughed. Hard. His whole body shook atop Edgard's. "Putty. Right. She's steel, not putty. My advice? She's a helluva shot too, so don't piss her off."

The dead coyote flashed in his mind and Edgard shuddered.

Trevor pulled his softened cock out and took his time melting Edgard with his sweet and hot brand of kisses.

Edgard sighed with absolute contentment as Trevor hopped off the bed, gifting him with another glimpse of the hottest ass he'd ever had.

"You wanna shower?

"Now?"

"Yep." Trevor grinned and pointed at the interest stirring in Edgard's cock. "After we have another round of monkey sex, we'll talk more about all this. In detail. I wanna make it work this time, Ed. Don't know how we're gonna go about it, but I figure we can come up with something."

"But you always bolted when I attempted to talk about anything serious before."

"I think us both bein' here together like this is proof

contrary to that statement, doncha think?"

"Yeah. I do. Know what else I think?"

"Mmm."

Edgard wanted to tell him of the conversation he'd had with Gus, but something made him hold off. He smiled cockily. "I think you'd better plan on checkin' cattle with the four-wheelers in the morning and grab the lube 'cause it's gonna be one long damn night."

Chapter Thirty

After Colby and Cord's families left, Carson convinced Carolyn to go to bed. Chassie couldn't sleep. She paced in the guest bedroom, wondering what Trevor and Edgard were up to even when she knew exactly what they were doing: each other. Odd, she didn't feel so much jealous as curious.

Keely locked herself in her bedroom on the pretext of studying, but Chassie suspected Keely wouldn't crack a single textbook. Keely freely shared graphic details about her sex life, but when it came to talking about her feelings she was as closed-mouthed as her brothers, maybe worse.

Chassie meandered downstairs into the dark kitchen. She poured a mug of milk and heated it up in the microwave. When she noticed the small lamp glowing from Aunt Carolyn's sitting room, she went to turn it off and saw Colt standing in front of the big windows, staring out into the darkness.

He said, "Couldn't sleep either, huh?"

"Nope."

Colt glanced over his shoulder at her and the mug in her hand. He smiled slightly. "You still drinkin' warm milk at night?"

Chassie froze. "How did you know?"

"Dag. He told me he never understood how you preferred milk to whiskey, even when you were older and had the choice. Said he used to get up with you sometimes. That way if Uncle Harland heard noise he'd put the smackdown on Dag, not you."

A lump lodged in Chassie's throat, remembering those nights she couldn't sleep and she'd tiptoe downstairs. Usually Dag would follow, grumbling she'd made enough noise to wake the dead. They'd sit in the sun porch—winter or summer—

talking until she finished her "good girl toddy" or until Dag admonished her for being chatty as a magpie. "I'm surprised Dag told you."

"Dag told me a lot of things. Might sound sappy as shit, Chass, but he loved you. Probably had a piss-poor way of showin' it, but he thought you were the greatest. He always wanted more for you than he wanted for himself. That's what made him such a great guy, in my mind anyway." Colt faced the windows again.

Tears filled her eyes and splashed into her cup. "I didn't know if he cared about me, especially the last couple years. He was always so angry and bitter."

"Yeah, well, there's quite a bit you didn't know about him."

"There's lots I did know about him that he wouldn't admit. Or more importantly, he didn't have the guts to face up to. With me or anyone else."

That comment caught Colt off-guard and he whirled around, his eyes narrowed. "Like what?"

"Are we really gonna tiptoe around the subject, Colt? Dag's dead and we can't even talk about this?"

Colt didn't utter a sound.

"I knew Dag was gay. Or bi. Or whatever. Did you?"

After a healthy pause, he nodded. "Not because he told me, because I stumbled across him and another guy at the Boars Nest. Not my thing but I didn't give a rat's ass if it was his. I told him that."

"Did he believe you?"

"Nah."

"I would've told him the same thing if given the chance."

"Dag thought it was the booze talkin' when I tried to convince him no one would care who he fucked behind closed doors. Hell, that philosophy holds true for everyone."

"Everyone except my dad."

"Except for him. And without soundin' like a prick I hope those fool-headed ideas died right along with him." Colt cocked his head with a quizzical look. "Uncle Harland would've freaked about Dag. Disowned him and all that shit, right?"

Talking about her dad always made Chassie uncomfortable. "Pretty much."

"Then the shitstorm would've come down on you. Dag knew

how much you already did around your place. Plus you were stuck takin' care of your old man, barely scrapin' by. He felt guilty he couldn't contribute more."

"It would've been worse if Dag hadn't sent us cash from his rodeo earnin's when he was on the circuit. It woulda pissed Daddy off if he knew, so I hid it in a separate account and he didn't find out." She shook her head. "'Course, there's none left now. Trevor and I used it to bulk up the herd last spring when the cattle prices were low. Doubled the size of the herd for about half of what it'd normally cost."

"Smart. You've always had a sharp eye when it comes to livestock."

Chassie appreciated the compliment. "Thanks."

"So where'd you end up grazin' all them extras?"

"It's been a challenge," she admitted. "We had grazin' rights to Forest Service land that we hadn't used for a couple of years because the amount of cattle we were runnin' decreased dramatically. Then we moved the bulls in with Junior Anderson's for the summer. No doubt we need more space or we're gonna hafta cut back and sell some off."

"You heard the rumors that Gus Dutton is lookin' to sell his place?" Colt asked.

Chassie thought about lying but in the scheme of things the McKays would end up with the land anyway. "Yeah."

"Any truth to 'em?"

Chassie measured him. Coolly. Honestly. Since Colt sobered up, he'd shed twenty pounds. His handsome face was sharp angles again. No beer gut or flab distorted his sturdy frame. If anything he'd bulked up, adding more muscle to his arms and chest. His eyes weren't bloodshot, but they held a wary edge. Not only was Colt the most resourceful of her McKay cousins, he'd always been the best looking—and that was saying something. Colt's cowboy charm also knew no bounds, so Colt's bad attitude had been the worst part of his slide into alcoholism. He'd turned mean, cynical, nasty to his family. Just like Dag. But unlike Dag, he'd overcome his demons.

"You gonna keep gawkin' at me, or you gonna answer the question?"

"Sorry. I...just noticed sobriety agrees with you, Colt. You look great."

Colt frowned. "Uh. Thanks."

"Anyway, Gus is sellin'. He approached us first since he knew Trevor and I were lookin' to expand."

"That chunk of land borders ours on our southwest end."

Chassie twisted her index finger around the cup handle. "I know. Which is why he'll be contacting the McKays to see if you all are interested in addin' to your spread."

"Why?" Colt's frown deepened. "Don't you want it? That place'd be perfect to expand into."

"Yeah. Well. I-I—"

"Stop stuttering and shut your mouth. Our family business ain't none of the McKays' business."

Lousy time for her dad's voice to interject an opinion. Chassie tried for nonchalance. "Because we can't afford it. Hardly enough cash on hand for operating expenses, say nothin' of layin' out a chunk of change for more. We talked to the banker and he agreed to a loan if we came up with cash collateral."

"Who you dealin' with at the bank?"

"Slim Jim Beal. He's been more than fair, but we can't come up with the ten percent down payment."

"What dollar amount did you agree on with Gus?"

"Quarter of a million." It hurt her stomach to even say a number that big.

Colt's eyes became accusatory. "You say anything about this to my dad?"

Chassie shook her head.

"Cord? Colby?"

"No. I probably should've tonight when I had the chance. Right now, the twenty-five grand we need is as hard to come by as the two hundred thousand. We're just sick about it, but ain't nothin' we can do." Mortified by her admission, Chassie drained her milk. "Thanks for keepin' me company. I'm goin' to bed."

Colt merely stared at her and crossed his arms over his chest. The sleeve of his T-shirt lifted, revealing a brightly colored tattoo on his biceps.

"When'd you get that?" She pointed at the tat.

He glanced down. "Last year."

"What is it?"

"One of the four horseman of the apocalypse."

"Can I see it?"

"Sure." Colt rolled his sleeve to the top of his shoulder.

"Whoa. That's gorgeous. India did that?"

"Yeah. She's good, ain't she?"

Chassie squinted at the flames that swirled around the horse's hooves. "Yep, although it don't seem like something you'd pick, cuz."

"It ain't." Colt grimaced. "This is what you get when you leave the choice in the hands of a smartass tattoo artist. Indy thought it'd be hilarious tattooin' a horse on me when my name is Colt. That woman is seriously warped from havin' so many holes pierced in her head." His gruff attitude belied his oddly affectionate tone.

"I'd love to have her design one for me one day when I can afford it. But you can be damn sure I ain't gonna let her tattoo a car chassis on me."

Colt rolled his sleeve back down. "She ain't that expensive."

"Money's relative when you don't have any." She sighed. "Look, I'd appreciate it if you didn't say nothin' about me'n Trevor havin' to pass on Gus's place. It's hard enough to know we're losin' out, and havin' the whole county gossiping about our financial troubles would just make it worse."

"Don't worry, Chass, I can keep my mouth shut and I'd suggest you do the same."

"Meanin' what?"

"Keepin' things to yourself is a damn fine way to get to keep the things you want to yourself, know what I mean?"

No. She had no clue. Chassie half-wondered if he'd overheard her conversation with Keely earlier this morning about having both Trevor and Edgard in her bed and in her life.

Colt did a curious thing. He leaned down and kissed the top of her head. "Sweet dreams, sweet little cuz. See you in the morning." Then Colt re-crossed his arms over his chest and turned back to the window, gazing into the night.

Feeling dismissed, Chassie crept back to her room, wondering how she could get to sleep without at least one warm body beside her.

Chapter Thirty-one

Chassie left the McKays around nine the next morning. She'd run a few errands for Aunt Carolyn, including driving to Moorcroft to talk to Kade and Skylar in person about Cam. Her cell phone died, which meant she hadn't spoken to Trevor for twenty-four hours. She missed her husband. She missed home. She missed Edgard. She missed her damn goat.

Her head throbbed, her heart hurt, her jaw was sore from clenching her teeth to keep from bawling. She was an emotional wreck when she considered the jumbled messes in her life: Trevor's status with his family, the situation with Edgard, losing out on Gus's land, and dealing with family tragedies. All Chassie wanted was to climb in bed for three solid days. She damn near wept when the old farmhouse came into view.

And tears did leak out when both her men ambled up to the truck right after she'd parked.

"Missed you, baby." Trevor pulled her into his arms and laid a big, wet kiss on her. He frowned at her forehead. "What the hell happened to your face?"

"I knew I forgot to tell him something." Edgard gave Trevor the abbreviated version of the run-in with Greta, which didn't appease Trevor at all.

"That goddamn goat was a bad idea. We shoulda talked about buyin' it first."

"You're the one who's always bitchin' about me talkin' stuff to death, Trev."

"That is true," Edgard added.

"Shut up, Ed." Trevor traced the area around the bandage that looked a little worse for the wear. "Does it hurt?"

"Actually, yeah. I forgot my painkillers and antibiotics here because I didn't expect to be at the McKays' that long." Chassie nestled her face into Trevor's chest. "I wanna shower and then I wanna crawl in bed."

Edgard grabbed her hand and rubbed his mouth over the inside of her wrist. "Missed you. I'm glad you're home and I won't let Trevor kill Greta. I'll make certain he treats her with kid gloves while you're resting up."

Trevor snorted.

Tires crunched and a big white Dodge Dually crept up the driveway. It wasn't a vehicle Chassie recognized until she saw the big winch sticking out of the front. She muttered, "Shit," under her breath.

"Who is it?" Edgard asked.

"Colt McKay," Trevor answered. "What the hell is he doin' here?"

"I hope it's not more bad news about Cam."

The truck bounced as Colt stepped off the chrome running board. He'd taken to wearing ball caps rather than cowboy hats during the workday. Chassie thought Colt seemed more accessible, not a larger than life drop-dead gorgeous cowboy in his prime who hid his eyes and emotions under the brim of a big black hat.

Colt thrust out his hand to Edgard. "If it ain't the Brazilian. I heard you were around these parts. Nice seein' you again."

"You too, Colt."

Edgard knew Colt? Then Chassie realized Edgard must've met Colby's family members at various rodeo events in the years they traveled together.

After Colt shook Trevor's hand, he faced Ed again and asked, "How long you stayin', Edgard?"

The moment of truth. A collective pause hung in the air as Chassie waited for someone—anyone—to answer.

Trevor clapped Edgard on the back. "Ed's decided to move here with us. Ain't that great?"

Relief so profound swept through Chassie she almost crumpled to the ground and wept.

"Sure is." Colt smiled. "I'll look forward to seein' you around. I suppose with you partnerin' up with Trevor again there ain't a chance in hell that Kade and I will ever win the team ropin' championship at the Devil's Tower Rodeo, eh?"

Edgard grinned back. "You can try."

"That you can bank on." Colt turned to Chassie. "Thanks for comin' over yesterday. I didn't get a chance to say thank you this mornin' with all the hullabaloo that's goin' on."

"No problem. What's up? Something new with Cam?"

"No. My folks are already workin' on gettin' Cam transferred to the VA hospital in Cheyenne."

"How's he doin'? Have you talked to him?"

Colt frowned. "No. He ain't talkin' to nobody. Anyway, the good news is Macie had the baby about an hour ago. A boy named Parker. They're both fine."

"And you drove all the way out here to tell me that?"

"Yeah. No. Hell." He paused. "The other reason I'm here is 'cause you left before I got to talk to you about something else." Alone was heavily implied.

Dammit, she didn't want to talk to Colt. She wanted to talk to Trevor and Edgard.

Trevor frowned. "Will this take long? 'Cause Chassie's exhausted."

"Not to mention she's injured and she needs to get some rest," Edgard said.

"Won't take long at all."

"We'll be back in about ten minutes, baby." The men headed to the machine shed.

"Trevor's real protective of you, ain't he?" Colt said.

"Yeah."

"So's Edgard."

She squirmed, not sure how much she should reveal.

"That's good, Chass. Real good. You're lucky you've got two good men watchin' out for you. You deserve it. Don't ever let nobody tell you otherwise."

Chassie's stomach pitched in a mixture of fear, exhaustion and emotional turmoil. "Colt, why are you here? What's really goin' on?"

Colt took off his hat, crumpled it in his hands and looked over Chassie's left shoulder. "Last night when we were talkin' in Ma's sittin' room, something you said started to bug me." Colt ran his fingers through his hair before he settled his cap back on his head.

"It's been eatin' me up all damn day, that's why I followed

you out here. The only excuse I can give you for forgettin' is that...well, I was a drunk. There's a whole helluva lot I don't remember." Colt reached in his inside jacket pocket and shoved an envelope at her. "Here."

"What is this?"

"Open it and I'll explain." Colt jammed his hands in his front pockets and rocked back on his heels.

Chassie loosened the flap, reaching inside the envelope for a piece of paper. She pulled it out, gaping at it before she glanced up at her cousin in complete shock. "What the hell? This is a check for twenty-five thousand dollars!"

"I know. It's ah...yours."

"Mine? What? It can't be."

"It is. The money belonged to Dag. Over the years he, ah, sent me some of his rodeo winnings too."

Skeptical, Chassie said, "Oh really?"

"Uh-huh." Colt focused on the upper bedroom window above the porch—anywhere besides her face. "See, Dag and I were gonna...start a bar when he retired from the circuit. He knew if he kept the money with him or in his bank account where he could access it, it'd be gone in a New York minute. So he mailed it to me and I deposited it for him."

"And you *just* remembered this?"

"Only when you mentioned the bank account Uncle Harland didn't know nothin' about, I realized I probably was supposed to've been puttin' the money in there. Instead I deposited it in my own account." Restless, Colt shifted his stance and studied the tips of his boots. "An honest oversight and one I'm sincerely sorry about. So since Dag is dead, I figure the money is yours now."

"Bullshit."

Colt finally looked at her. "Excuse me?"

Chassie whapped him in the chest with the envelope. "Is it a coincidence this just happens to be the *exact* amount of money we need to guarantee a bank loan for Gus's land? And isn't it another *coincidence* you just happened to remember my brother—who never had two nickels to rub together—gave you *exactly* the same amount of money to squirrel away for him?"

At least Colt had the decency to look sheepish.

Pride caused Chassie to snap, "I don't want charity.

Especially not from the McKays." She stuffed the check in his outside coat pocket and spun on her heel, humiliation vibrating in every fiber of her body.

Lightning fast, Colt stepped in front of her. "Hey, now, wait a darn minute and listen to me."

"No way. I am so pissed off at you right now, Colt McKay, it isn't even funny."

"Hear me out. Please."

Chassie glanced up at him. The last time she'd seen him so distressed was after he'd heard Dag died. Pain and regret and...tears? shimmered in Colt's bright blue eyes.

Dammit. She was such a sucker. "Fine. After you answer a question for me."

"Anything."

"Did you honestly believe I'd be that gullible? Just take the check and skip to the bank not questioning my sudden good fortune?"

"Ah, actually, yeah, I had hoped that'd be the case."

A growl-like snarl escaped and she sidestepped him.

"But I expected you'd at least hear me out and not be as stubborn as your daddy."

Chassie whirled, tired, angry, frustrated and ready to pop him one square in the mouth.

Colt grinned at her. "Knew that one'd get your back up, Sassy Chassie."

Her old nickname brought a smile. "Funny, Colt the Dolt."

"Now that that's out of the way, will you at least listen to me?"

She sighed. "I suppose."

"First off. What I said wasn't a complete lie. At one time Dag did send me money. I don't recall how much. Coupla hundred bucks probably. Anyway, when I heard how badly you wanted Gus's place, but couldn't swing the down payment, I thought this was the least I could do to help you out."

"Why do you want to help me?"

"I could give you a bullshit answer and say because you're family. But the truth is, Dag and Uncle Harland died leavin' you holdin' an empty bag with no means to refill it and that don't seem fair."

"Your family's always had more money than us, Colt," she

said tactfully. "I don't begrudge you for it like my dad did."

"You should. At least my ma squirreled away the money Granddad West left us."

"What money?"

Colt's face was troubled. "Granddad West left each grandkid ten thousand bucks."

Chassie's mouth dropped open. "You're joking."

"No. Ma deposited ours in the bank and wouldn't let us have it until we turned twenty-one. I told Dag when I got mine. So Dag asked Uncle Harland about his, and…"

Ugly, thick pause.

"Dad spent it all, didn't he?"

Colt nodded. "I'm sorry. Dag found out Uncle Harland blew every bit. My understandin' was that was the last straw between them. Dag didn't so much care about his inheritance, but yours was a different story."

She felt ill.

"See you were doomed to fail before you got outta the gate, Chass. It ain't your fault," Colt said hotly. "I don't want you to fail, 'cause I know all about failure."

"Colt—"

"I've felt like a failure most my adult life. Cord is the oldest and a natural born rancher. Colby is the rodeo star. Cam is the hero." Colt squeezed his eyes shut briefly. "Cam is even more a hero now. Carter is the smart college boy. And Keely is the long-awaited girl. Which leaves me as the fuck-up, the ne'er do well middle child, the charmer, the womanizer, the drunken fool. I lived up to that bad reputation because it was all I had. All I ever saw myself as.

"My brothers've done noble things while I've done nothin' worth mentionin' and done plenty of things I'm ashamed of. Here's a chance to make things right for someone besides myself." His vivid blue eyes were beseeching. "This is something I wanna do, something that'll let me feel as if I'm lookin' after you like Dag might've wanted me to. I'm payin' off my debt to the past by helpin' you to secure the future you've always deserved, Chass, is that so wrong?"

"By givin' me your hard earned money?"

"How else are you gonna buy Gus's land and increase the size of your operation?"

Chassie frowned. "But I thought your family wanted that section?"

"Fuck my family. Maybe it's time they realized they can't always get what they want just 'cause their last name is McKay."

His vehemence surprised her.

Colt paced. "Do you really think we need another coupla thousand acres? No. But McKay Ranches would snap it up just because they could. That acreage won't take a nickel away from our livelihood, but it sure as hell will make a huge difference in yours and Trevor's. And honestly, I've done enough shitty things to people I care about to last me a lifetime. Jesus, Chassie, you're one of the few that's not on the list of folks I've wronged and I'd like to keep it that way. Takin' this land out from under you feels wrong."

Chassie placed her hand on his arm, stopping his nervous activity. When Colt looked at her, Chassie finally understood this offer was about more than money. It wasn't about charity. It wasn't really about guilt. It was about Colt proving he'd changed, probably when no one in his family believed he could. Proving that same streak of decency running through his brothers ran through him too, even if he and Chassie were the only ones who were aware he'd acted on it.

Colt's problems with his family were not her issues, but a niggling voice pointed out by Colt coming to her, he'd taken on the responsibility of helping her overcome *her* family issues—chiefly financial, by bucking his own family's best interests.

"If I take the money, what will you want in return?"

Colt blanched. "Nothin'. I swear."

"No unlimited grazin' rights? Water rights? Mineral rights? Huntin' rights?"

He shook his head.

Seemed too good to be true. "I'll have to clear it with Trevor."

"I'd expect nothin' less. I wanted to talk to you first."

Chassie yelled, "Hey, guys, come here."

"Guys? But—"

She locked her gaze to Colt's. "Edgard is a permanent part of the operation and of our life now."

After a second, Colt nodded.

That wasn't so hard. She expected it'd get even easier in time.

When Trevor and Edgard ambled over, Chassie and Colt explained the situation.

No surprise Trevor was adamantly opposed. "Absolutely not. Like you said, Chass, if we can't come up with the cash ourselves then ownin' that place wasn't meant to be."

"You'd've had no problem borrowin' the money from your dad," Chassie pointed out.

"That's different," Trevor said.

"How so?" Colt demanded. "A loan from family is a loan from family. I'm Chassie's family, which makes you family too."

"So you're lendin' us the money?" Trevor asked.

"I sure as hell ain't *givin'* it to you."

A sharp bark of laughter. "That's a big relief."

Colt relaxed slightly. "Think of it as a long-term investment."

Trevor studied him distrustfully, not because Colt was dishonest, but because in Trevor's mind, all dealings with family were suspect. "If you ain't gettin' interest on the loan, then what's in it for you short term?"

"I dunno." Colt scratched his cheek thoughtfully. "I'm lookin' to diversify my part of the herd. How about you gimme first pick of your male calves durin' brandin'? They're worth about a thousand bucks at that age."

"You want all twenty-five this spring?"

"Nope. One or two a year'll be just fine."

Chassie gawked at her cousin in disbelief. "But that'll take years!"

"Like I told you, I'm lookin' at long-term." That flash of shame appeared in his eyes again, but he soldiered on. "Ask me where the money I'm lendin' you came from, Chassie."

"Where?"

"It's what I would've spent on booze and women in just the last year. It's sittin' there starin' me in the face like guilt and blood money. I wanna invest it in something I believe in, which is a family ranchin' operation." Colt looked across the field, but Chassie knew he was looking far beyond what she could see. "So many of my friends are gone to greener pastures. I couldn't stand it if you were another one of 'em to leave, and not out of choice."

Chassie was one of the few who knew Colt's life hadn't been as carefree as people assumed and he'd had fewer choices than any of his siblings.

"Anyway, when I build a house on the frontage between the creek and the bluff, we'll be even closer neighbors, so it makes sense we look out for each other's best interests."

"Got a flesh and blood woman all picked out to settle down with in this phantom house you're describin'?" Trevor prompted with a wicked grin.

"Possibly." Colt shrugged. "Mostly I'm tired of livin' at the Boars Nest. I want my own place. Chet and Remy drew up specs and we're just waitin' on the county to clear the permits."

That surprised her. Chassie wondered if his family was privy to his plans to move away from the McKay stronghold.

"So do we have a deal?" Colt asked.

"Yes!" Chassie launched herself at Colt, hugging him tightly. "Thank you. You have no idea what this means to us."

"Yeah, little cuz, I believe I do."

"Contrary to what you think, you are a good guy," she whispered. "A credit to the McKay name. Dag would be proud of you and I'll try like hell to live up to your faith in me."

"The fact you were one of the few who never lost faith in me is worth every damn penny." He hugged her and climbed in his truck without another word.

"That bastard stole my thunder," Edgard groused.

"What?"

"I'd planned on talkin' to you and Chass about me making the down payment for Gus's place with the money from selling my ranch in Brazil."

Trevor caught Edgard's golden gaze. "You serious?"

"Serious enough I spoke to Gus yesterday and guaranteed you and Chassie had the cash and asked him not to contact the McKays."

Trevor didn't—couldn't speak.

"Hell, you ain't mad, are you?" Edgard twisted the toe of his boot into a pile of snow.

"Not mad. Just wonderin' why you did it." Wondering why Ed hasn't said anything when they'd talked last night.

"Time was running out. You were both preoccupied with family shit and I couldn't stand it if we lost out on something important to all of us because of pride or fear or mixed signals. I waited until Chassie got home to discuss it because it's her future too."

Trevor's heart damn near danced out of his chest. Everything he'd ever wanted was within reach; he just had to grab it with both hands. He circled one arm around Chassie's shoulder and the other around Ed's. "Come on inside. Too damn cold out here."

In the kitchen, Chassie said, "Trev, what happened with your dad?"

Trevor poured milk in Chassie's favorite cup and put it in the microwave. "Pa's fine." He relayed the trip, detailing events even when he'd rather avoid discussing them. "Hope you didn't have your heart set on cozyin' up to my family."

"You're my family. You deserve better than the way they've treated you and I'm damn glad you didn't knuckle under."

"Amen." Edgard gently swept a piece of Chassie's hair away from the bandage on her forehead. She smiled, showing her acceptance of Ed's easy affection. It also showed Trevor how badly Edgard needed to share that side of himself with someone who not only welcomed it, but appreciated it and reciprocated.

It brought a lump to Trevor's throat and a balm to his soul to think Chassie was the bridge that allowed him to connect to Edgard. Without her, he'd be lost on so many levels. She'd taught him he was worthy of love. She'd showed him how to love without conditions. She'd proven understanding and acceptance were not parts of love that could be parceled out, but real, honest love needed all those components to be successful, fulfilling and long lasting.

Without Chassie, Trevor never would've reached the point that he could accept how he felt about Edgard, say nothing of flying in the face of conventionality and proposing what he was about to propose.

"As long as we're spilling family secrets, Ed, did you tell Trevor everything that happened the last year you lived in Brazil?"

He nodded. "I shoulda told you both right away, but I didn't want you to feel sorry for me and realize I didn't have anywhere else to go."

"Which brings us back to what we've been talkin' about." Trevor focused on his wife. "How would you feel about all three of us livin' together like we've been? On a permanent basis?"

Chassie's fingers relaxed around her cup and her gaze zipped between his and Edgard's faces. "I thought that was a given."

"You did?"

"Didn't you? Both of you? I mean, come on. After all we've done, not just sexually, but emotionally? We've already begun to form a weird sort of three amigos thing. I hated it when Trevor was gone and I imagine you two missed me. And I can't fathom Trevor and me standin' on the porch waving at Ed as he drives away for good."

The mental image of Edgard leaving brought back the acute ache Trevor never recovered from that day in Cheyenne—until now.

Chassie set down her cup and covered his hand with hers. "Trevor, as much as I loved our life before, havin' Edgard here makes it better because you're happier."

"With this many people involved, the three amigos—as you've called us—decisions can't be based on just one person's happiness when that decision affects all of us. Does Edgard bein' here make *you* happier, darlin'?"

"Yes."

Not a bit of hesitation in her answer, which boggled Trevor's mind. "Why? I mean you'll be sharin' me on a permanent basis."

"I don't mind sharing you, especially since he's brought to life the part of you that's always been missing, a part I never had in the first place. Edgard's given me a gift by letting me see all of you, not just the part you wanted me to see because you were ashamed of the rest." She winked at Edgard. "Plus, Ed can cook."

"I love you so damn much." Trevor lifted her hand and kissed her knuckles. "I'm so goddamn lucky to have you."

"Amen," Edgard said and kissed her other hand.

"I never want either of you to be ashamed of what you feel for each other, or feel like you have to hold back in front of me or in our home," Chassie said. "What you had was private, but now it belongs to all three of us. Can you guys handle that?"

"I can," Trevor said.

"I'm good with it."

"So, I'm thinkin' this three-way relationship will work as long as we talk to each other, just like this. No secrets. No half-truths. Tackle issues head on. Take it one step at a time to ensure we get it right for everyone." Chassie bit her lip and looked at Edgard. "I know we ended up together because of how we feel about Trev, but Lord, it's crazy scary what I'm startin' to feel for you."

"I know." Edgard touched her face. "I feel the same, *querida*."

The confession didn't bother Trevor, but it seemed too easy. "Right now we're all pumped up and cocky with 'screw what the rest of the world thinks of us', but can you live with the *don't ask, don't tell* reality for the long term?" Trevor watched the play of emotions on Edgard's face. "We've talked about this on and off, Ed, so now's the time to speak up if it's gonna be a problem for you."

"I lost you once due to that line of black and white thinking, so I'm past it. I could give a rat's ass about anyone who ain't in this room right now."

A sneaky smile curled Chassie's lips. "Well said. Just as it won't bother me for the local busybodies to believe I'm so crazy for cock I've gotta have two of 'em to keep me satisfied."

Edgard choked, "Jesus, Chassie."

"Oh please. My whole life I've listened to the outrageous sexual exploits and preferences of my male McKay cousins. It'll be a hoot to set tongues a-waggin' in Crook County that the Wests can be just as wild. As long as you're not double-teaming me on the bar top at the Rusty Spur, I don't think anyone will muster the guts to ask how good our hired man is with his hands or who he prefers to put them on."

Trevor said, "My God, woman, you're actually enjoyin' this, ain't ya?"

"Yep." She batted her lashes at Edgard. "And to sweeten the pot of revenge, I'll make it clear to Brandy or any other woman the Brazilian meat market is *not* open for monkey business and you both belong to me because our relationship goes beyond business. That oughta keep all the single women in town from angling for a piece of you."

Edgard smiled. "Which brings me to my other point. In the eyes of the law you two are married, but I ain't gonna be considered just a hired hand. I'm not looking to prove anything to the community beyond we're in a committed partnership. Let them make of it what they will. I just want to prove to both of you I'm as financially invested in the life we're building as I am physically and emotionally."

"Buddy, if that'll make you happy and convince you we ain't kickin' you to the curb, then that's what we'll do. We'll draw up the bank paperwork as a three-way partnership."

"Sounds good." He squeezed Trevor's hand. "I'm beyond happy, *meu amor*."

"Me too. Jesus. I never thought..."

"Oh, stop makin' goo goo eyes at each other at least until we've discussed this thoroughly," Chassie gently scolded. "I've already come up with a way we can demonstrate the permanence of this relationship to ourselves."

"How?"

"By gettin' matching tattoos."

Trevor's mouth dropped open. "Hell, woman, how much time *have* you spent with India and Colt?"

"Enough. For design, I'm leanin' toward searin' our cattle brand on our butts."

Edgard mock-whispered, "Is she serious? Or has she been drinkin'?"

Chassie slapped his arm. "As far as us havin' babies? I want them. Bad. We've all survived shitty family stuff, and there is potential for problems with any child we raise in an unorthodox household. Can you imagine how much that'll change the dynamic between the three of us? How hard it'll be if I have one blond-haired one and one dark-haired one, and what last name we'll give 'em—"

"We'll cross the baby bridge when we come to it."

"Oh yeah? Ed brought up finances and you brushed him aside—"

"You weren't just a woofin' about her talkin' something to death, were you, Trev?"

"Nope. Maybe we oughta gag her. There's a bandana in the dining room."

"Rope too," Edgard said. "Let's tie her hands so they're not flailing around makin' random tattoo designs."

She huffed out a breath. "I'm serious. This is serious stuff, guys."

"It is serious stuff. Life altering stuff." Trevor's strong fingers circled her wrist. "But there comes a point where you are beatin' a dead horse, and, darlin', you've reached it."

Chassie looked to Edgard for support.

He shrugged. "I'm of the 'less talk, more action' school of thought."

Nice sidestep, Ed. "How about we take the action upstairs to the bedroom and *hammer* out the rest of the details there?"

"Damn fine idea, Trev. I think you *nailed* it."

They grinned at each other and Trevor thought it felt damn right and damn fine and was about damned time.

"You guys always gonna reroute every conversation around to sex?"

"Yep," they said in unison.

Chassie sighed. "Neither of you have asked what'll make *me* happy."

"What's that, baby?" Trevor murmured.

"A much bigger bed."

"That's it?" Edgard asked.

"Yep."

Trevor realized not every request would be so simple and easy to handle. There'd be problems and adjustments. But as he looked at the two people who were his entire world, who owned his heart, who soothed his soul, and who'd stand beside him no matter what, he knew he was finally ready for whatever rough challenges life threw at them.

"I'd say a bigger bed is a damn fine place to start."

About the Author

To learn more about Lorelei James, please visit www.loreleijames.com or send an email to lorelei@loreleijames.com or join her Yahoo! group to join in the fun with other readers as well as Lorelei. http://groups.yahoo.com/group/LoreleiJamesGang

GREAT cheap fun

Discover eBooks!

THE FASTEST WAY TO GET THE HOTTEST NAMES

Get your favorite authors on your favorite reader, long before they're out in print! Ebooks from Samhain go wherever you go, and work with whatever you carry—Palm, PDF, Mobi, and more.

Samhain Publishing ltd